THE
INHERITANCE

THE INHERITANCE

Ally Bunbury

POOLBEG

This novel is entirely a work of fiction. The names,
characters and incidents portrayed in it are the work of the
author's imagination. Any resemblance to actual persons,
living or dead, events or localities is entirely coincidental.

Published 2017
by Poolbeg Press Ltd
123 Grange Hill, Baldoyle
Dublin 13, Ireland
E-mail: poolbeg@poolbeg.com
www.poolbeg.com

A catalogue record for this book is available from the British Library.

ISBN 978-1-78199-871-7

Typeset by Poolbeg in Sabon
Printed and bound by CPI Group (UK) Ltd, Croydon, CR0 4YY

www.poolbeg.com

About the Author

Ally Bunbury was brought up with her three sisters and a menagerie of animals in County Monaghan. Following a serendipitous encounter at a dinner party, Ally landed a dream internship with a PR agency on New York's Fifth Avenue, which, in turn, led to a flourishing career in London and Dublin. Ally now runs her own PR company and continues to create dynamic media campaigns for her clients. She lives in County Carlow with her husband, Turtle Bunbury, and their daughters, Jemima and Bay.

The Inheritance is Ally's debut novel.

www.allybunbury.com

Acknowledgements

"If you are going to be unhappy, be unhappy in Paris," is amongst the best pieces of advice I have ever been given and, for this, I would like to thank Lucy Madden. Her wisdom came at a time when I was feeling deeply lost and in need of change. Then, due to the immense kindness of Nicola and Daisy Jacquier, and Renuad Semerdjian, I moved to the prettiest apartment on rue Saint Dominique, with the Eiffel Tower but a breath away. It was there, in 2003, at a wooden table in the bright yellow kitchen, that I began writing this book. Happiness slowly returned, replacing my sadness. Lucy's advice proved so true; positive, uplifting surroundings do increase your chance of rediscovering genuine contentment and exploring the brighter possibilities.

And so, *The Inheritance* was born in Paris, although it had plenty of mileage to go before coming to fruition. Upon the arrival of my two sweet daughters, I put the manuscript to one side for at least a decade, though the story kept nudging me onwards until I was prompted to begin writing again.

I have received such extraordinary support while writing this book, and there are some people I would like to particularly thank.

Thanks to Sarah Beth Casey, who urged me on from the very beginning and made me believe that I could really write this novel. Thank you for *Absolutely Fabulous* days and for your beautifully crafted *Riders II*, reminding me that Jilly Cooper truly is my idol.

Thanks to my brilliant sisters, who cheered me on all the way across the finish line: huge thanks to Gilly Fogg, for the immense amount of time she gave in helping me to solve a multitude of conundrums, way beyond the call of Aquarian duty, Faenia Moore Extraordinaire, for playing audience to my plot lines, and lovely Liz Cairns, for reading through so many chapters.

Thank you to my godmother, Helen Price, for teaching me the value of family history. Conlan Abú!

Thank you, Alice Forde and Nicola Coveney, two bright and constant shining stars, for all those uplifting chats when I needed them most.

Thank you, Tom and Sasha Sykes, for all of your amazing encouragement.

Thank you, Clare Durdin Robertson, for keeping me tuned into *Tatler* and glamorous urban adventure, which especially helped on the days when I had to subconsciously transport myself into the luxurious lives of my characters. Thank you also for your artistic guidance (long live the VIP ICA!).

My thanks to Rachael Comiskey, a natural-born photographer who always makes me smile, for so splendidly taking my picture.

Thank you to Roly Ramsden for sage advice and memorable scaffolding adventures.

Thanks to the supreme radio broadcaster, Mary Claire Rogers, for introducing me to Rupert Campbell Black all those years ago.

Mille fois merci to Susy de Serra for the best ever lollipop analogies, and to the Charleston Avenue beauties, Lucy Kelly, Iona Hoare and Tiffany Black, for inspiring party themes – who could forget *Glitz, Glimmer, Shine and Shimmer* ...

Thanks to Dominique Patton, for *Valser Mathilde* and long walks. No matter what the distance, it never feels like you are far away.

For your serenity, thank you, Charlotte Capel Cure and Joan Boyle, and thanks to Matthew and Gráinne Dennison, for your incredibly understanding and insightful ways (Clones Pink).

My special thanks to Sheana Forrest, Sofia Couchman and Bex Shelford, for spurring me on to stop worrying and get writing.

Thanks to the finely named Annabel Butler and Coibhe Butler, for introducing me to ever-stylish London abodes, and to Louise Knatchbull, for her perpetual bounteousness. Massive thanks also to Nicola Hamilton, for her dazzling dinner-party placement skills.

My thanks to Ben Rathdonnell, my father-in-law, and to Andy Verney for advising me so eloquently on estate matters, and to my mother-in-law Jessica Rathdonnell for reading over chapters with such good humour.

Duže diakuju to Daria Blackwell, who transformed my life by introducing me to the world of PR on Fifth Avenue. Many thanks also to Marianne Gunn O'Connor for her exceptionally generous counsel. Thanks to Valery Mahoney, style personified, for your excellent judgment.

For helping me take my characters to task, thank you, Peter Bland. And my thanks also to Hugo Jellett for listening to my ramblings.

For making me feel like I could actually write, I am enormously indebted to Herbie & Jacquie Brennan, and to Sebastian & Ali Barry. Thank you all, so much, for the time you have each taken to encourage me with my writing, when at times I felt so unsure. You made a real difference.

Thank you, Ahmed Salman, for your incredible kindness – my father is smiling down on you, always.

Remembering my wonderful aunt, Sue Craigie, for her astonishing enthusiasm, deep love and extraordinary courage that made her so very special, and my cousins Matthew and Patrick Gallagher, and how we sang around the kitchen table to lighten our souls – *One Time*.

My thanks to Susan Rossney for so kindly introducing me to my publisher, Paula Campbell of Poolbeg. Paula's bountiful sense of fun and 'can do' attitude has been particularly special, and I am extremely grateful for her professionalism and all-round goodness. And to my very patient and hardworking editor, Gaye Shortland, who must think I'm fairly bats, as I added ever more bathtubs and butlers to the plot … thank you enormously. Thank you also to David Prendergast for his great expertise and skill.

All my love and thanks to (Aunt) Meike Blackwell for several decades of inspirational Easters at Ross House and for reading this book in its infancy.

Thanks to Rosebud, for your true eloquence and I will do my best to remember *Solvitur Ambulando*.

Thank you, Ross O'Driscoll, for all those fireside chats, discussing the characters in the book, and for the brilliance of your Latin.

Thank you to my late father, Archie Moore, for helping me realise that if you put your mind to something you really can make it happen.

And thanks to the living, breathing buildings that so often swept me away into another world. I bow to Bishopscourt, Rosturk Castle, Hilton Park, Ross House, Hôtel de Crillon and Lisnavagh House.

Where would we be without the Craigie Spirit? Huge thanks to my sparkling aunt, Virginia Hartley, for all your help with this novel. Paris loves you.

For immeasurable guidance, my thanks to Johnny Madden, who so graciously walked me down the aisle on that lucky day when I married Turtle Bunbury.

And to Turtle, for all the time and space you have given me to write and muse and dream, and for all the plot discussions from dawn 'til dusk to dawn, thank you to the moon and back, my darling. And to our little daughters, Jemima and Bay, thank you, my sweethearts, for all your love.

And finally thank you to my awe-inspiring mother, Miriam Moore. I have so much to thank you for, especially your very great ability to shine with positivity. No matter how hopeless the situation, you always manage to lead the way and march us all back into the sunlight. And along with the *eleven-hour* phone call, for all those days I took refuge to write in the dining room, whilst you so brilliantly entertained Jemima and Bay, thank you gigantically. Your goodness and ability to take things in your stride is a truly wonderful thing. *Inula magnifica*.

My tremendous gratitude also goes to:

Alex Blackwell, Jago Butler, Emily Bunbury, Aisling Killoran, Jamie and Lola Cahalane, Kate Campbell, Hugh Casey, Michael Colgan, Esme Colley, Megan Comiskey, Ann Craigie, Cully & Sully, W.J.P. Curley, Cathy Curran, Bernard de Croix, Edward Denniston, Jacqui Doyle, Ciara Doorley, Bernard Dunne, Taylor Swift, Alexander Durdin Robertson, Freddie Durdin Robertson, George and Eve Fasenfeld, Larry Fogg, Lucy Forbes, Celeste Forde, Mathew Forde, Deborah Gaynor, Bo Guirey, Mandy Hartley, Barbara Herring, The Hidden Ireland Group, Francis Hoar, Karmendra Jaisi, Ned Kelly, Jay Krehbiel, Marina Lawlor, Laetitia Lefroy, Gabrielle Luthy, Cilla Patton, Fred & Joanna Madden, John McDermot, Kathy McGuinness, Father Rupert McHardy, Mary McManus, Roderick and Helena Perceval, Tee McNeill, Wendy Mae Millar, Conti Moll, Susan Morley, Deirdre Nolan, Jonathan W. O'Grady, Heidi Rice, Timothy Rearden, Stan Ridgeway, Eleanor Ronaghan, Suzanne Ronaghan, John Schwatchke, Tish Simonnet and Betty Scott.

In memory of Franz

Preface

Ayrshire

January 30th, 1989

Against the brightening morning sky, Robert Wyndham's tall figure gazed towards the riverbank as he bent forward and loaded two fresh cartridges into his shotgun. Smoke billowed into the icy air from a cigarette clamped in the corner of his mouth as he tried to fend off a hangover, his temples throbbing beneath his raven-black hair. Robert was the sixteenth generation of the Wyndham family to live at Rousey, a ten-bedroom Tudor mansion, and he was feeling profoundly out of control. Like many ancestors before him, he had married for money – an injection of 'heiress cash' as he called it – but his bride, Gussy Campbell, had turned out to be an unexpectedly dominant character. She made it clear that infidelities would not be tolerated, and that if Robert did cheat on her, she would very quickly leave with both her enormous fortune and their son George.

A bird came into view as Teal, Robert's spaniel, barked and fussed at a bramble thicket. Robert's eyes were straight on it, his strong arms holding the gun completely true, as he traced the woodcock's flight against the clear sky. He fleetingly noted a red Limousin bull tossing his head and impatiently pawing the ground on the far side of the bracken bank. With the early-morning sun shining on the bull's enormous rump, he looked like he was straight

1

out of a Constable painting. Such bovine concerns didn't bother Robert as he closed one eye and prepared to pull the trigger. At that exact moment a high-pitched voice screamed out, causing the woodcock to veer sharply and dart into the bracken.

"Goddamn it," cursed Robert, lowering the gun.

Looking up, he saw the bull crashing over the bracken bank and thundering towards a young woman running for her life. Instinctively raising the gun again, Robert pulled the trigger and in a split second the bull reeled as the lead entered his skull. As the bull staggered and slumped to the ground, the woman fell to her knees and began shrieking into her hands. Deeply relieved that his shot had been on the mark, Robert broke his gun and laid it on the bank before calmly walking towards the woman whose head of long dark hair was shaking into her knees. Feeling chivalrous, he took off his jacket and placed it around her shoulders.

Unscrewing the lid of his silver hipflask, he held it out to her. "Ginger and honey poitín," he said.

"Thank you," she said, staring upwards, her blue eyes framed by long black lashes. "He came out of nowhere." She had a broad Ayrshire accent. Shivering and inappropriately dressed in a cotton dress, she ran her hands up and down her arms.

"You're all right, thank God," said Robert, taking in the fullness of her bosom. "What on earth are you walking around here dressed like that in this weather?"

"I had a row with my father – I needed to cool down," she said and, trying to stand, her shaky legs appeared to buckle.

"You can't possibly walk in this state," said Robert. "Look, the bothy is just beyond that turn. There'll be coffee waiting for me and the fire will be lit. Come on, let's get you warmed up and then I can run you home."

Accepting Robert's arm for support, she walked with him towards a small timber-fronted bothy tucked into a wide laurel hedge just up from the River Garvin. Finlay MacLeod, the estate manager, had lit a fire an hour earlier and the turf was still burning steadily in the fireplace. A thermos flask of coffee, a bottle of whiskey and a plate of heavily buttered brown bread were laid out on an oak table.

"People have been taking shelter here for years," said Robert,

2

twisting open the flask as she sat down. "I've even met a few who have slept out here," he nodded towards the bothy's wooden sleeping platform, "just so as not to miss the first rise of a trout."

He poured two mugs of coffee, adding a generous drop of whiskey to each.

"The weather can turn so quickly here. Sunshine on your face one moment and then next thing you know it's driving rain or snow. It's always the same once you get inside. Relief. Immense relief. And strangely warm too, with or without a fire."

He stirred the mugs while the woman looked at him, trying to work out if he was for real, noting the mugs festooned with dancing pheasants. She hadn't been around someone from the Big House before and, though she had no idea what to say to him, she sensed that this was a moment of great opportunity.

Putting down the mugs, Robert suddenly reached out his hand.

"So sorry, I've only just realised that I haven't introduced myself, even though my bull almost murdered you." He smiled. "Robert Wyndham, the owner of that murderous bull."

"It's okay," she said, feeling the back of her neck with one hand and shaking his hand with the other. "I'm Blaire."

"Hello, Blaire. Are you from the village?"

"Yes. My name is Davies. Blaire Davies. My father sometimes works for your keeper. A bit of beating during the season."

The expression on Robert's face told Blaire he had made the connection. Her father, known as Jim 'Poacher' Davies, had been banned from the estate the previous year for leaving a young doe half dead, courtesy of a rusty gun and insufficient cartridges. Blaire knew she would have to play this carefully if Robert was to accept her as a different type to her father.

"I'm the youngest of seven – the only girl and I'm the one left at home," she said, as he passed her a mug and sat down. "The others got away. My brothers – every one of them – left Ayrshire. Never looked back. Like good soldiers, Mam used to say, they never looked back."

Blaire felt conscious of the roughness of her hands and her nails, which were bitten to the quick. She hated her life. During the shooting season, her father put her in charge of mucking out sheds filled with the sticky feathers and hideous innards of the birds he had caught, gutted and bagged up for sale. This encounter with Robert Wyndham might very well be lucky – her chance to escape from her rough, repetitive world, to step up from being a mere 'local' girl.

"What about you?" she asked, easing a little with the help of the whiskey.

"Me? Ah, well," he said, trying to laugh it off, "my life was mapped out a long time ago. Soon after I inherited this place, I married." He blew out his cheeks. "Not much of a choice, and here I am – a rather empty existence, I suppose."

"But you have a son."

"Yes – he's ten years old now," he said.

Blaire noticed how he clenched his jaw as he spoke.

"Born almost nine months after our wedding day." Robert lifted the whiskey bottle and poured another generous splash into his mug.

Blaire felt the silk inner lining and weight of the tweed of Robert's jacket around her shoulders. Those were textures she had always longed for: expensive and traditional. She was sure her face would look just fine in a family portrait on the wall of Rousey. "Life can change in an instant, can't it? And chance can bring change," she said, shrugging off the jacket as if it were a fur coat, letting it slide from her back onto the chair. "Thanks for coming to the rescue."

Finishing her drink and standing up, she smiled coyly and stretched up her arms so that Robert could admire her slender figure.

"Must you go already?" he asked.

Blaire was satisfied that she had given him a hint of the pleasure she could offer him.

"Aye. And next time keep your livestock on the right side of the fence."

Robert stood up, awkwardly putting his hands in his pockets and then pulling them out again.

"I should see you again," he said, his lust utterly transparent.

As Blaire sauntered towards the door, Teal pounced from under the table, wagging his tail and snuffling into her ankles. She pushed him away and positioned herself in her most provocative pose by the doorway, her thin dress showing the shape of her breasts.

Tilting her head to one side, she watched as Robert's breathing began to speed up, until, with a flushed face, he strode across the room and urgently pulled her towards him, running his hands over her bottom as he kissed her. Blaire responded immediately by reaching for the buckle of his belt, but Robert pulled away.

"Wait a moment, please," he said. "I'd like to make things more comfortable."

Flipping open a wicker basket by the door, he found a red tartan blanket and flicked it out in one deft manoeuvre across the sleeping platform, as Blaire moved towards him, untying the ribbon at the neck of her dress.

Teal just then began to whine.

"You're not used to this sort of thing, are you, boy?" Robert said, rubbing Teal's head. "I'd better put you out."

"Little beggar," muttered Blaire under her breath, disliking dogs. As soon as Robert left the room, she whisked off her dress, kicked off her boots, pulled off her underwear and lay naked on the rug.

Robert returned to see her long legs and slim body awaiting him, and surrendered entirely to his desires. When he left the house that morning he had felt overwhelmingly depressed by the make-up of his life, and all the more because it was a life he had chosen. With Blaire, for the first time in years, he felt wanted, lusted for, desired.

The affair began then and there, and in the months that followed Robert invented shooting-syndicate and estate-business meetings as excuses to his wife for his frequent absences. The bothy had become a sanctuary for Robert, where he and Blaire would spend long afternoons making their way through *The Joy of Sex*. Following adventurous passion, as they smoked cigarettes Blaire would speak of the travels she and Robert would make together, of the big hotels and exciting cities they would visit. In time, she would live in the Big House and she would sit for a portrait, which would grace the drawing room.

Robert, so completely besotted during the early months, simply listened, smiled and dreamt with her.

One afternoon the following summer Blaire was lying on the riverbank, her head cushioned on Robert's Barbour jacket.

"This September, Robert," she said, sweetly.

"What's that?" he asked, picking a pink dog rose from the hedge and putting it behind her ear.

"You'll leave Gussy, as promised. Your wife, you'll leave her, won't you?"

Robert was silent and, throwing a pebble into the water, he stood up and tightened his trouser belt. He had known this was coming, but he hadn't thought she would ask so soon.

"Robert?"

He looked down at her, so beautiful, and thought of how she had brought him back to life.

"Blaire, I ..."

"Yes?"

"I've thought much about plans for the future, the idea that we could run away together ... but you do know that the moment I leave Gussy will pull the rug."

"The rug?"

"My cash flow would come to an immediate halt. We'd have nothing to live on. Your talk of hotels and first-class travel, it's just not realistic." Not to mention having to leave his life of fine shooting and excellent claret, he thought to himself. "And I do feel dreadful about it, really I do, and I feel strongly for you, my dear, you must believe me, but what it comes down to is –"

"What do you mean your cash flow? You've got a huge estate, all those people working for you!"

"Yes, and all paid for by Gussy."

"You're joking," said Blaire.

"I'm afraid I'm not. I can't survive without my wife's money, that's the bottom line."

"And what about me? Leading me on all this time!" she said, pulling the blouse over her head as Robert caught a final glance of her breasts, pert and smooth as river stones.

"Surely it's been obvious all along that I'm tied to the place? It just isn't practical for us to run off like a pair of innocents – we'd have nothing to live on."

"You're all the same, you lot with your posh accents and your traditions!"

"But Blaire, darling, why can't we just continue as we are? We have a good time, don't we?"

"Aye, we do, and you get to walk back up to a house with hot water in the pipes to fill a hot bath, and sleep in a big bed with your white sheets." Blaire picked up a large stone with two hands and hurled it into the river. "But I go back to Aunt Mary's, to a cold bed with a thin blanket."

"Look, Blaire, why don't we go back to the bothy and discuss this over a drink ..."

"And end up back in bed as if we'd never had this conversation?" said Blaire quietly, staring out over the river before turning to him with eyes like slits. "Not this time, Robert Wyndham."

"I understand, my darling, truly I do."

"Don't give me that," she hissed, "and don't think my father will take me back under his roof. He might as well have spat at me when I told him I wanted to stop working in the yard for him."

"Then what will you do?" asked Robert, his eyes to the ground, feeling desperately guilty for letting his reliance on his wife's income dictate the decisions of his lust.

"I'm going to follow my Aunty Mary's advice and go where I'm wanted, where there's someone to look after me, the way I deserve to be looked after." Blaire's cold expression didn't waver.

Picking up her cardigan, she shot him a look that would haunt him. It was a look that made it absolutely clear that she was the most desirable woman he was ever going to meet in his life and that he had just blown it.

And, in the years that followed, Blaire Davies would become ever more desirable in the increasingly addled mind of Robert Wyndham.

Chapter 1

London

January 30th, 2016

A security guard, dressed in a white linen suit despite the freezing night, nodded approvingly at affluent guests as they glided through the front door of Sofia Tamper's town house. Anna Rose stood shivering on the footpath beneath him, feeling the strap of her yellow bikini top rising up her back. Why on earth had she agreed to go to this party and where was Tilly Fairfax? Just as Anna was about to send another text, a red hackney cab pulled up to the curb and Tilly emerged from the back seat, sporting a high ponytail of chestnut hair and an apologetic smile.

"Oh God, I'm so sorry," said Tilly, throwing her arms around Anna. "I had to race into Tinto Libby's for something to wear. What do you think? Goldilicious?"

Anna turned to the security man whose dark glasses made it impossible to tell whether or not his eyeballs had dilated when Tilly slipped off her coat to reveal a sensational gold boob tube, skimming her slim tanned waist and generous cleavage.

"You look amazing," said Anna.

"And you, Anna, look divine. The glitter around your eyes makes them look even more enormous and heavenly, and I'm glad you wore your hair loose – your long blonde curls are so gorgeous. Now, come on, let's roll up our sleeves and get busy with the fizzy

– the invitation promised exotic cocktails."

Bounding up the steps, Tilly and Anna passed the security guard and stepped into the hallway where their heels promptly sank into a thick carpet of sand. Anna had been to theme parties before but this one was on a whole different scale – the sound of crashing waves blending into dance tracks, exotic maritime flower arrangements, huge ornate shell mobiles dangling from the ceilings and waiters dressed in nothing but tight black shorts and liberty-print bow ties.

Appearing from behind a large rail of decadent furs and wraps, a cloakroom attendant dressed in a grass skirt with a headdress of flowers attempted to take Anna's coat from around her shoulders. Following a mini tug-of-war, Anna finally gave in and tried not to look down at her yellow bikini-top and pink-velvet hot pants.

"Guess what?" said Tilly, scooping up a couple of Mojitos from a waiter and passing one to Anna. "Not even one minute through the door and I've spotted Jamie Lord. You know, the dishy barrister? And he is even more gorgeous in the flesh."

"Oh yes?" said Anna, not particularly interested. Taking a large gulp from her drink and nearly choking on a mint leaf, she looked around to see if there was any sign of Sofia Tamper. Anna's boss had emphatically instructed her to make sure she introduced herself and mentioned the PR company name in case there was any chance of new business.

"Anna, you have got to come with me – I want to introduce myself to Jamie Lord – I can't possibly pass up this opportunity."

"Okay, for a moment, but then I need to seek out Sofia."

Draining the remainder of her Mojito, Anna followed Tilly through an array of model-like creatures sporting tans and oversized watches, to find a handsome blond man beneath a palm tree.

"Any coconuts up there?" asked Tilly, peering up the trunk of the tree and then smiling at Jamie.

"Not as yet, though anything seems to be possible around here," he said. "I'm Jamie, by the way."

"I know," said Tilly. "I read about you in that amazing case – you know, with the listed building in Piccadilly." Swaying to the music, she added, "And this is Anna, my long-time flatmate."

"Good to meet you, Jamie," said Anna. "It's all very glamorous, isn't it?"

"Oh, I don't know about that," said Jamie, who held a lifebuoy in one hand and a tall empty glass in the other. "It's really just a great big posing session and it's so bloody hot in here there's a strong chance we shall all perish from heatstroke."

The arrival of a waitress carrying fresh drinks distracted them momentarily and Tilly soon had Jamie sidelined into close conversation.

Anna turned around and her eyes were immediately drawn to the unmistakable face of Sofia Tamper, surveying her guests from halfway up a staircase with her smoky eyes beneath a thick black fringe, as she posed in a zebra-print bikini top with denim hot pants. As the daughter of one of Hollywood's richest producers, Sofia had graduated from being a child who starred in commercials for soap powder and ice pops to a twenty-five-year-old IT girl and insatiable party animal, constantly sending the gossip feeds on Twitter into a spin with inappropriate tangles outside nightclubs and three-day blowouts in Vegas. Next to Sofia stood a beautiful girl, wearing a luminous yellow dress complementing her rich brown skin and eyes. They could have graced the cover of *Vogue* there and then.

"Do you know Sofia well?" asked Tilly, gazing at Jamie.

"No, not really – we've met a few times at some art exhibitions that my friend George is a patron of. I hope he pops in later," he looked straight at Tilly, "as it is already a very memorable party."

"Who's that with Sofia?" asked Anna.

"Ruby Beecham, a hotshot set designer from LA," said Jamie. "I used to know her cousin – but look sharp, people, because Miss Beecham and our hostess are headed this way."

Anna watched Sofia saunter towards them like a leopardess in a deer enclosure.

"Hey, Jamie," said Sofia, in her Anglo-Los-Angeles accent, air-kissing either side of his cheek.

"Great party, Sofia," said Jamie. "Life's a beach, hey? And you know Tilly and Anna?"

Sofia raised her eyebrows uncertainly.

"We met at a charity ball in the Savoy last year," said Tilly enthusiastically.

"Oh, okay. Good to see you. I go to so many events, it's hard to keep track, you know," said Sofia, lazily, "but obviously we must have spoken if my agent put you on the guest list."

Anna thought she was kidding, but there was no smile forthcoming.

"Sofia, these girls should be on every guest list in London," said Jamie, putting his arms around Tilly and Anna.

"Hey, guys," said Ruby, pushing into the conversation with an e-cigarette between her fingers. With tightly cropped dark hair, high cheekbones and diamond earrings setting off her caramel eyes, Ruby was a knockout. "Hello, Jamie, nice to see you again. It's been a long time."

"It sure has," said Jamie, scratching his head awkwardly.

"When you and my cousin Kerina were hanging out, I can't have been more than ten, but I still remember you guys."

"A long time ago," said Jamie, looking keen to change the subject.

"Wild party days," said Ruby, smiling knowingly at him.

"Yes," said Jamie.

Tilly, sensing the awkwardness, jumped into the conversation. "I adore your haircut, Ruby – very cool – and those earrings."

"Oh these?" said Ruby. "They were my grandmother's – she gave them to me when I was eighteen to go with a dress I was wearing to my very first party at the Will Rogers Polo Club. I felt like *Pretty Woman*." Ruby had fallen into the childhood accent of her native Barbados as she sometimes did, particularly when she'd had a drink. She generally spoke with the diction of a girl transported to Los Angeles at thirteen when her mother co-founded an e-commerce company which brought the family's already considerable wealth, made through textile importation, to an all-new high. "And I love those sequins on your top – Stella McCartney, right?"

"Oh my God, what is this?" snapped Sofia, not liking the attention to be drawn away from her. "Mutual Appreciation Night? Don't let the gorgeous face and perfect bone structure fool you – Ruby is not a model but a businesswoman, chip off the old block."

"I'm a set designer, Sofia, not a techie," said Ruby, snapping back.

"They say the same about me when I approach the bar, as in 'He's a barrister, not a model'," said Jamie, with a cheeky grin. "Though I'm considering ditching my wig – not sure just how attractive it looks."

Sofia ignored him and glared at Anna.

"And you are?" said Sofia.

"Anna, Anna Rose. I'm here in place of my boss, Gilda."

"Who?"

"Gilda Winterbottom?"

"You've lost me," said Sofia.

"Winterbottom PR?" said Anna, surprised by Sofia's reaction considering Gilda had received a handwritten note from Sofia's agent, urging her to come along in case she could spot any publicity opportunities.

"Oh, yes," said Sofia vaguely.

"Gilda's sorry she couldn't make it this evening, and so she asked me to come in her place," said Anna, wishing she had worn her highest pair of wedges to at least be a few inches closer to seeing Sofia eye to eye.

Reaching for a Martini from a waiter, who had been directed to keep a tray of booze close to his hostess at all times, Sofia looked Anna up and down.

"That's a fun bikini-top." Sofia's tone made it difficult to work out whether or not she meant it as a compliment. "And what exactly do you do, Hannah?"

"It's Anna," she said, disliking Sofia more every second.

"You do know that Anna is Gilda Winterbottom's number two?" said Tilly, putting her arm around her flatmate, "and she's going to be London's next PR Queen."

Clearly disinterested, Sofia waved at another bunch of guests arriving. "Listen, enjoy the party, I gotta dash. Post up here if you want but the best bar is on the terrace. Go get yourselves another drink – you all look like you could do with loosening up."

"Later, guys," said Ruby, following Sofia.

"Christ, she's an absolute shark tonight," said Jamie.

"Only tonight?" asked Anna. "She's incredibly unfriendly."

"Don't worry," said Jamie. "Take it as a compliment that she can even be bothered to speak to you. I don't know how much she paid the party planners for turning this place into such a hideous pineapple, but let's hope for her sake they can turn it back into some semblance of a house afterwards."

"It's certainly opulent," said Anna.

"Have you seen the bathroom downstairs?" said Jamie. "Talk about an igloo, I actually thought I was going to come out with snow blindness. Even the soap is white."

"Anyway, it's Friday night," said Tilly. "God, I adore Friday nights. Who's on for another cocktail?"

"Or, better still, how about a dance?" said Jamie, taking Tilly's hand as if it were the most natural thing in the world. "That's if we're not totally abandoning you, Anna?"

"No, no, go on," said Anna, fiddling with the back of her bikini. "I think I'll go to the bar and have one more drink – then I'll make a run for it."

"Are you sure?" asked Tilly.

"Very sure. At least I can tell Gilda that I met Sofia and 'rubbed shoulders' as instructed. Have fun, you two."

But, making her way through a melée of beautiful people, Anna couldn't help but feel a tiny bit fabulous herself.

George Wyndham, oblivious to the admiring stares, scanned the crowd in search of Jamie and was in no mood for meaningless chitchat. Deciding to stay for a quick drink, which would at least fend off the freezing cold on his way home, he walked onto the terrace and noticed a girl with white-blonde hair tied back, looking out over the garden beneath a large mushroom heater. Admiring her pink shorts, George was about to walk towards the bar when the girl suddenly yelped and crouched down to her knees.

"Oh bugger, I cannot believe this is happening," he heard her say.

"Hello," said George, walking towards her and trying to work out what the problem was.

"Oh no, I mean, oh bugger it! No, don't worry," said Anna, feeling tiny beads of sweat bubbling on her forehead. "I'm sure I can manage."

"Are you sure? Anything I can do to help?"

Turning her head, Anna almost froze when she saw George's

face, instantly recognising him from a feature *Harper's Bazaar* had run on him the previous month, entitled 'Bachelor of Arts'. She knew without any doubt that she had turned bright red. "Well, could you pass me that bag, please?"

"This one?" George picked up a green velvet bag from the nearby table.

"Yes, thanks." Not making eye contact with him, Anna kept one arm over her naked breasts while the other pulled out a gold-and-white silk caftan. Shaking it out, she slipped it over her head as George stepped back, trying not to encroach on her space.

Anna had never felt such relief as she stood up and smoothed out the fabric of the caftan.

"Thank you," she said, smiling at George and putting out her hand.

He shook it. "I'm George," he said, then signalled to a stubbly barman that he'd like to order drinks.

His voice was lovely, deep and very slightly Scottish, she thought.

George looked over at a sofa, book-ended by large heaters, edged with large plastic orange roses and quilted in purple silk.

"Dare to sit down? First time I've seen a sofa that's been modelled on a great-aunt's shower cap," he said dryly.

Feeling so much better, now that she was covered up, Anna sat on the sofa and picked a temaki roll from a huge platter offered by a waiter who was wearing a luminous snorkel on his head.

"I'm Anna, by the way," she said as George sat next to her and, putting the entire temaki roll into her mouth, she only just managed to swallow it without choking.

"Water?" asked George, smiling at her.

She noticed his eyes, so dark and intense.

"No, I'm okay. God, as if I wasn't ridiculous enough, I had to choke!" said Anna, wishing she could check her face in the mirror.

"What can I get you? A glass of white? A cocktail? Something stronger? I'm not at all sure about the colour of some of those cocktails. Hangover in a glass?"

"I'd love a glass of white wine, thank you," she said. "My father always says 'when in doubt, favour the grape'. He swears by red wine for warming up on freezing nights at home in Ireland – better than whiskey, he says."

15

"You're Irish?" asked George, having ordered two glasses of Chablis from a passing waiter.

"Yes – born and raised there but I went to school in England. My mum's from Hampshire – you know, 'where hurricanes hardly happen'."

"You liked it? The school, I mean," asked George, not taking his eyes off her.

"Well, yes, when I wasn't feeling homesick."

"Brothers or sisters?" he asked.

"No, one child was enough for Mum. She had a nightmare delivering me. I came out with the cord wrapped around my neck, which was more than a little alarming for her. How about you – brothers or sisters?"

"Just me," said George, as a waiter arrived and presented two glasses of wine. "And your father?"

"He's an artist," she said, taking one of the glasses. "Mostly landscapes, sometimes portraits. He's never happier than when he's splashing paint on canvas and, when he's on a painting spree, he'll vanish for weeks on end. Of course he loves nudes." Anna was wishing she would stop babbling.

"Who doesn't love a nude?" replied George.

Anna grinned and took a large sip of wine. "Mum always says that whenever she asks Dad to do something he goes off to paint another one – a nude, I mean."

George laughed and they both leant back into the sofa.

"And are you enjoying London?"

"I think so, though I work pretty long hours and my boss is quite, well, let's say, needy."

Anna noticed how George watched her mouth as she spoke.

"You know, I was planning to go straight home?" he said. "I only popped in for a quick drink."

"So why are you still here?"

"Well, that's easy," he said, sipping his wine and gazing at Anna as Coldplay sang 'Magic' from the sound system. "How about a dance?"

"I'd love to," said Anna.

As they stood up George took her hand and, sidestepping a smooching couple by the terrace door, he led her into the dining room where large candles flickered on the sideboard.

Weaving their way across the floor, with each song that played Anna felt that she and George were moving increasingly in sync. Sofia had transported them all to a make-believe Tropicana and Anna felt hazy, like anything was possible. George was signalling it would be a good time to have another drink, after several dance tracks, when Tilly skipped onto the dance floor.

"There you are," she said, looking up at George in fascination.

Smiling down at her, he pointed to himself, mouthing his name as the music blared.

"Yes, I know!" yelled Tilly. "Would you mind if I steal Anna for a sec?"

"Not at all." Turning to Anna, he said, "You will come back though? I'll wait for you over there." He pointed at the fireplace in a small alcove next to the dining room.

Not wanting to go anywhere, Anna reluctantly followed Tilly off the dance floor, almost pinching herself. But she did need to check her face, so she led Tilly back to where she had left her bag.

"Oh my God," said Tilly, "I have just spent an incredible time with Jamie Lord."

"Where is he?" asked Anna.

"He's got a big case on, so he had to get an early night … I wish I could join him."

"I can tell," said Anna, smiling.

"But he did ask for my number before he left."

"That's so cool," said Anna, loving Tilly's unbeatable enthusiasm but longing to get back to George.

"And, you know, he and George were at school together since they were small boys. They are seriously good friends. And now, can you believe you're dancing with George? There's serendipity afoot, I'm telling you."

Half of Anna wanted to go to the bathroom to check her face and the other half wanted to get back on the dance-floor. "Tilly, I've literally only just met George but if I am to know him any longer, I had better get back in there."

"Lovebirds already, Anna! I have such a good feeling about this. Come on, let's have a drink – you don't want to seem too keen." Tilly wanted to talk about Jamie.

"All right, just a quick one," said Anna, quite used to being led astray by her best friend.

Walking into the dining room, Sofia watched her guests, so elite, so expensive, dancing, knocking back drinks her father would pay for, even though she hardly knew any of them. The wall beside her was bedecked in photos of herself, posing with Hollywood stars. Life on camera looked so amazing but the truth was that her career was going nowhere. By now she should have had a hat trick of movies under her belt, but the combination of her father's generous allowance and her love of partying had long taken over.

Across the room her eyes lit upon George Wyndham, London's most sought-after bachelor, standing by the fireplace in the alcove off the dining room. Ripe for the picking at the age of thirty-eight, he was beautifully tall, with a Greek nose softened by dark brown hair spilling over slate-grey eyes. Ambitious mothers, swooning daughters, they all wanted him. Sofia knew the press would be more likely to go easy on her if a rumour got out that she had steady people like George in her social circle. She had long been envious of his public profile and the press showed him such respect, even though he never gave interviews unless it was to promote a charity event or to speak out on a cause he felt strongly about.

Walking across the room, Sofia winked at the photographer briefed to capture good PR material from the evening for her social-media pages.

She walked up behind George, reached up and slid her hands over his eyes. "Guess who?" she said loudly, above the music.

"Hello, Sofia," said George, slipping his hands over her wrists and gently pulling them down. He turned around. "I told you I'd be here," he said.

"As good as your word as always," said Sofia, her lips shining with red Dior gloss. "I thought it would be fun to meet you at a party for a change, rather than those dreary art exhibitions or charity things."

George picked up a tightly rolled piece of sushi from a banana-leaf tray and wolfed it down. Lunch felt like too long ago.

"How on earth did you get the palm trees in here?" he asked. "You've thought of everything."

"Oh, you know me. I'm a one-hundred-and-one-per-cent kind of girl," she said, almost eye-to-eye with George thanks to her heels. "I figured if I wasn't going to have time to relax in the sun this winter, I'd better bring a little island paradise to London." Pushing her hips towards George, she moulded her hand into his lower back. "I'm so glad you came though. I was thinking maybe we could hang out more … now that you know where I live?"

"Sorry, Sofia," said George, taking his phone out of his pocket to check a text message. "I'm waiting for a shipment of paintings to come through customs. There's some kind of delay."

"Christ, George," said Sofia, disliking not having his full attention, "what is with you? On the rare occasions that I see you, there you are, still banging on about your work. I mean, really," she fiddled with her tassel earrings, "just look at that old tat over there."

George followed her eyes to three Dutch Masters, gaudily framed reproductions, hung far too close together and much too low.

"Daddy loves traditional art, of course. Your sort of art, I mean. But why he has to inflict those sour-faced trolls on my place is beyond me. Give me Damien Hirst or Jeff Koons. You know, con-tem-po-rary. I just don't get this whole passion for the old stuff. I'm more of a modern girl, you know?"

George thought of all the paperwork he needed to get through before his trip to Scotland.

"Tate Modern is certainly one to watch – I'm sure you enjoy your visits there," said George, politely engaging with Sofia and hoping she wouldn't get deeper into her rant.

Following a swift cocktail, Anna returned to the dining room to find bodies swooning and sashaying around each other on the dance floor. There was no doubt that Sofia's party was a success. The DJ, with one leg propped up on a chair, grooved his entire body as he lined up the next track.

Then Anna's heart sank as she spotted Sofia leading George by the hand onto the dance floor. As Sofia stepped into his arms and they began to dance to Rihanna singing about diamonds, Anna felt a sharp breeze cut across the room and the music stopped abruptly.

Double doors leading from the garden had opened, and a very tall police officer began walking across the floor towards Sofia. It looked like George didn't know what was happening, as he squinted his eyes and then realised that he needed to step back. The policeman stood in front of Sofia, put one hand on his hat and reached for a mobile phone from his shirt pocket with the other. And then he held the device in front of Sofia and a flash of light emitted from the camera. At Ruby's signal, 'Single Ladies' by Beyoncé started up on the sound system and the officer began to sway his hips. Pulling a truncheon out of his belt, he expertly twirled it through his fingers.

Balancing on a chair, Ruby clapped her hands above her head and shrieked with laughter.

"Here's to you, Sofia, sweetie!" she yelled, as a crowd gathered around Sofia and her admiring officer until he had stripped right down to leopard-print Y-fronts. Instinctively knowing how to make the most of a situation, Sofia playfully danced around her enthusiastic stripogram, before breaking back in George's direction. Guests clapped as she and George began to dance again. Anna saw George turn his head to the doorway – maybe looking for her? Taking the lead, he twirled Sofia and pulled her towards him before resting her body on his arm and lowering her backwards as the music slowed.

Hope faded for Anna as she watched Sofia nestling into George. Turning away, she felt deflated at having lost what she thought might have been a chance with him. Then, seeing crystal photograph frames on a sideboard, documenting Sofia's life, sun-kissed on a super-yacht, looking divine in a slinky dress at some sort of debutante ball, she had a reality check. Sofia was famous for being an IT girl who partied around the world; Anna couldn't even begin to compete.

Sloping off to the bathroom, she felt she needed sunglasses as she walked into an unbelievably bright room – she understood what Jamie meant about it being an igloo. The room was huge and completely white.

Standing in front of the full-length mirror, Anna decided she looked rather like some kind of arthouse character in her mother's caftan, and the only saving grace was that her face hadn't turned red. She wondered whether she should fly home next weekend if her boss didn't plan to monopolise her.

Squinting from the bright lights in the loo, she made her way to the hall in search of Tilly. Instead she found George, sitting on the edge of a chair, holding his scarf and coat.

"Anna," he said, standing up and sweeping back his hair. "I was looking for you but figured you had left."

"Really?" she said, trying to rein back her enthusiasm. "I'm actually just leaving, as soon as I can find Tilly."

"I'm sorry I had to abandon you," he said, smiling. "No option, I'm afraid."

Anna couldn't help but smile back.

"I was about to leave but, now that I've found you, how about one more dance?" he asked.

"Okay, one more dance," she replied.

And, leaving her bag beneath George's coat and scarf on the chair, she walked with him back into the dining room. There was almost a hush from the speakers as a slow dance mellowed the room, whispering beats as George and Anna slipped into each other's arms.

Chapter 2

Monday, February 1st

Bicycling along Buckingham Palace Road, up Pall Mall and around Trafalgar Square, Anna narrowly missed a courier racing around the corner as she wondered if George would call. At least she and Tilly had managed to get home at a reasonable hour the night before, having polished off enormous helpings of roast chicken in the Duke of Wellington, along with several Bloody Marys.

Anna parked her bike in the long row of stands before collecting her usual takeaway of a skinny chai tea and a toasted bagel with butter and Marmite from her favourite Israeli-run café. The same large lady dressed in a white apron would without fail elbow her much smaller husband when she saw Anna. As the large lady made the tea while her husband toasted the bagel, they would sing in unison to the radio pop music as if they were competing for the Eurovision Song Contest or maybe because they suspected Anna to be a talent scout.

Winterbottom PR headquarters was abuzz with adrenalin as account executives and managers crafted slogans and dreamt up publicity campaigns for continuously needy clients. Fortunately, high ceilings, tall windows and open workspaces created enough light to warrant wearing designer sunglasses indoors if the night before had been late enough, and Anna frequently took full advantage.

Entering the open-plan office on the ground floor, Anna was met by a full-bosomed woman dressed in floral dungarees with long beads around her neck.

"Yellow symbolises the sunshine and blue reflects the feeling of hope," said the Feng Shui expert in a very high-pitched and exaggerated tone. She had been engaged by Gilda Winterbottom to re-energise the walls and all items within.

Along one such wall, an intern wrestled with a new delivery of cat-food samples destined for The Master Cat Food Challenge for which the public could enter their cats into a feline version of a pie-eating contest. Beneath a gigantic window looking out over St. Martin's Lane, a Healthcare PR manager sucked on Vitamin C tablets to keep her mind off cigarettes and doled out headache tablets to those too hung over to make it to the pharmacy. There were clients to schmooze and professors to get on side for endorsements, along with journalists to lure into stories – but not before the week's media packs of cosmetics arrived. Girls flocked like vultures on the morning's arrival of jiffy bags filled with palettes of shimmering eye shadow, fruity scented lip gloss, face polish, mud packs to exfoliate and sublime self-tanning bronzer.

Making a beeline for her desk, Anna passed a pile of the day's newspapers and spotted Sofia swooning on the cover of the *Red Carpet* supplement in the *Daily Mail*, wearing a long pink satin dress at a charity fundraiser. Taking the lid off her paper coffee cup, Anna sipped on her chai tea as she took in Sofia's long slender figure and high cheekbones accentuated by her hair being pulled tightly back. Just twenty-four hours earlier Anna had been dancing with George Wyndham in Sofia's dining room and Sofia had called her Hannah. It was a wonder that Sofia even spoke with her at all. Anna tore open the paper bag, pulled out the bagel and took a huge bite of buttery Marmite deliciousness. Then her phone bellowed out the sound of a hunting horn. It had been her father's idea to remind her of the hunt galloping across the fields around her family home in Ireland.

Not being one to ever refuse a phone call, Anna chewed quickly on her mouthful of bagel and answered.

"Hello," she said, her mouth still half full.

"Anna, hi. I'm sorry it's so early. It's just that I'm flying to Paris this afternoon and I'm getting my diary straight for the weekend."

"George?" asked Anna, licking Marmite away from the corner of her mouth.

He had called, and it was only Monday.

"Sorry again, I know it's early," he said.

"What? No. It's lovely to hear from you. I mean, great you called."

"How are you?" they both asked at the same time.

"Sorry, you first," said George.

"Really great, thanks." Anna's heart thumped as butterflies catapulted from one side of her stomach to another. Dusting bagel crumbs from her desk, she nervously fidgeted with a pen then pulled the zip of her brown-suede ankle-boot up and down.

"Are you around on Thursday evening?" he asked.

"Thursday, afraid not – I help out at a soup kitchen on the first Thursday of every month – it's in Knightsbridge. You know, we make sandwiches and things. It's for the homeless." Getting up from her chair to take the call outside, Anna promptly sat down again as a deliveryman arrived with a large cardboard box packed with mini-sweaters emblazoned with a *I'm the Cat's Pyjamas* logo for the Master Cat contestants.

"How about I join you? I can help," said George.

"You want to?" asked Anna.

"Yes, I want to."

Then all chances of a conversation were obliterated as Gilda Winterbottom came crashing into the office, hurling her car keys into a large Perspex bowl, which had been filled with seashells by the Feng Shui lady.

"Anna," Gilda squeezed her eyes together impatiently, "come on, sweetie, I need you."

"I'm sorry, George, I've got to go," Anna whispered into the phone, hurling the remains of her bagel into the wastepaper basket. "I'll text you details about Thursday, see you soon."

"Now, darlings," hollered Gilda, doing her jazz-hands impression. "Listen up. Everyone pile into the boardroom pronto – we've got to get this week in order."

As the troops mustered, they ducked and dived past Gilda's secretary, Chrissy Wilton, who toppled towards the nearest desk carrying a high stack of brochures and out-of-date calendars, following orders to clear space in the name of Feng Shui.

"Chrissy, darling!" yelled Gilda, pointing her team in the direction of the boardroom as if she were a flight attendant. "Order me a coffee from Asia de Cuba, will you? And make sure they include those snappy biscuity things. I am starving. Come on, people, we've got clients to please!"

Gilda, in leather jeans and leopard-print flats, was feeling highly motivated. She was high as a kite following her feature in the *Sunday Express*. **Winterbottom PR for All Seasons**, read the headline. *The best publicist since Cadbury Crème Eggs asked how do you eat yours.*

Gilda Winterbottom was one of the most prominent and respected names on the London PR circuit. As the charismatic owner of Winterbottom PR, the combination of Gilda's sharp thinking, ever-present Dior scent and heart-shaped salutes from her behind proved that all the old-fashioned PR moves still carried their weight in gold. She was known for her high-energy persona and ingenuity for crafting bespoke branding and social messaging, which had earned her both the custom and respect of a wide range of star players, from media training CEO's to companies that needed new life to be pumped into existing products. Clients also loved Gilda for her extravagance and party-on attitude, particularly the poor darlings who travelled all the way from Hull to see her. She brought them straight to the Ivy where she had kept a table for the past twenty years.

In the boardroom, a gaggle of account managers were swapping stories of weekend adventures while two interns swung around in huge office chairs looking like Simon Cowell and David Walliams ready to choose a line-up of boy-band contestants. Swishing people like flies from the head of the table, Gilda took her seat and, with fingers poised together, she surveyed the room, homing in on a smiley and fresh-faced account executive.

"Now, Kate, I do not want to see your face until you have got that topaz pashmina around Pippa Middleton's neck and on the cover of *ES Magazine*. You know what you have to do. Pull strings, darling, and tell them the scarves were woven in Kashmir, you know, soft gold. Get to it, sweetheart."

Then, tapping the nib of a neon-yellow pencil on the table with increasing speed, Gilda looked like she was about to explode. Then she threw the pencil over her shoulder and slammed the palms of her hands on the table.

The room was completely silent. Not a sound. All devices dropped and jaws opened as they wondered what Gilda was going to say next.

"Out," she said quietly. "You can all get out. But, Anna, you stay. The rest of you, I'll let you know when we've worked out who is doing what."

There was no tantrum, no finger-pointing of betrayal, just a straight-up instruction resulting in utter relief spreading across the bevy of hung-over faces who longed to tweet and Instagram-gossip about the weekend more than anything else.

As the room cleared, Gilda breathed deeply and began massaging her head. "I get a sense about people, Anna. You know, auras and yin-yang?"

Anna tried to focus on Gilda against the backdrop of newspaper wallpaper sporting iconic products and brand ambassadors from past media campaigns, but she couldn't help thinking about what she was going to wear to the soup kitchen on Thursday evening and if she had been crazy to agree to George coming along. But the expression on Gilda's face made it clear that today was not the day to feel intoxicated by love and, clicking herself into gear, Anna sat poised with a ring-bound notebook and Uni-ball pen at the ready, nodding at Gilda whose mind was reeling with ideas.

"Look, darling," said Gilda, "I make plenty of lolly here, and I work hard to keep my wardrobe up to date. Clients expect it, you know. I am their inspiration. They depend on me to make their products sexy. I am the product." Getting out of her chair, Gilda strutted past Anna to the other end of the room and stood with hands on hips as if she were auditioning for a role as Cat Woman.

Not sure where to look, Anna was relieved to hear a series of knocks on the door, which Gilda promptly opened to find Chrissy arriving with profuse apologies, a large coffee and a pink-striped paper bag of biscuits. Her husband Bryan had been particularly demanding in bed last night, celebrating the news that his once super-hot seventies rock band had agreed to a reunion tour. He had been a lead guitarist but, having got Chrissy pregnant with twins, he had no option but to take a job at his family's storage company. For years he had hankered for life on the road and had continued with delusions of importance, never leaving the house without sunglasses and a fountain pen topped up with ink in case autographs were required. He also refused to give up on his black hair, so the bathroom sink was frequently covered in black powder-dye. But, for Chrissy, the most cringeworthy aspect of Bryan's obsession with his past was the necklace that a certain female rock star had given to him years ago in exchange for a bag of weed at the very first Glastonbury in 1971. He continued to wear the necklace like an Olympic medal, except there was no sign of gold as it contained more tin than the packaging around spaghetti hoops.

"Gilda, I'm afraid I've got something to tell you," said Chrissy, lifting the coffee out of its recycled holder.

"Chrissy, darling, are you still here?" said Gilda, now sitting on the sofa and swiping through a series of Instagram pictures.

"I've just picked up a voicemail from Hans," said Chrissy.

"Oh yes. What news from my Swedish delight?" said Gilda.

"The thing is, Gilda ..." Chrissy fiddled with her sunglasses as Gilda lifted off the plastic coffee lid and tore the edge off a sachet of sugar with pink-painted nails.

"Out with it," said Gilda, closing her eyes as she put two ginger thins at once into her mouth. "I know it's something hideous."

"Okay," said Chrissy, "Hans was taking the children to Waitrose and they sneaked through the door of the security guard's office."

"And," said Gilda, pouring another two sachets of sugar into her coffee.

"They have locked themselves in the security guard's room and they have taken Hans' phone."

"*And*," said Gilda between gritted teeth. "Get to the point, will you?"

"Okay. There's no easy way to say it. Orlando has posted photos of you and Hans on Snapchat. You know, the photos with the cat suit?"

"The little bugger," said Gilda and taking a deep breath she filed the information deep into a place she couldn't reach. Her therapist liked to call it 'Gilda's little black box'.

Appearing to be not even vaguely flushed by the news, Gilda leapt out of her chair again and flipped over the top page of a white chart balancing on an easel. With a thick red-felt pen, she drew three large balloons with question marks.

"I want to fill these balloons with ideas, big juicy ones. So, let's think big picture. Chrissy darling, will you tell Hans I'll be late home, and he needs to take the children to Zoe's Salon this afternoon. You have booked them in for haircuts, haven't you, darling?"

Chrissy looked at Gilda, amazed at her ability to move on from a crisis. "Yes, Gilda. It's for the Aber Crombie magazine shoot?"

"Exactly. It's for my profile, darling, you know, the work-life balance, PR and working mum all at the same time." She signalled for Chrissy to get back to work with a whoosh of hands towards the door. "Smooth over Waitrose, won't you, darling? And do tell security to keep their doors firmly closed in future."

Chrissy gave Anna a supportive smile as she left the room, both aware that this was the unpredictable job they had signed up for. Gilda was unbelievably impatient and completely bonkers and, somehow, inexplicably likeable.

Stretching out her arm with the red-felt pen, Gilda drew an imaginary circle in the air.

"This is my world, Anna, and you're a central figure."

"I am?" asked Anna, wondering where this conversation was leading to.

"Of course. Now stay focused, Anna." Gilda put her hands around her waist and thumbed into her Gucci belt. "I think I need to hula-hoop more. Do you agree with me, darling?" and before Anna could reply Gilda picked up her iPad and swiped through several pages of magazine titles. "Okay, now, I need you to invite these people personally to the launch next week."

"Launch?"

Gilda held up a turquoise glass jar. "This is what I'm so psyched about!"

"The jar?"

"Correct. It's the best truly organic Shea butter available on the mainstream market. Fabulous stuff, it's the next coconut oil, the new black. I'll have skincare competitors quaking at their moisturised knees at the thought of us." Rolling up the sleeves of her red-silk shirt patterned with tiny hummingbirds in flight, she opened the jar and extravagantly rubbed the cream onto her arms. "I've lined up five stunning models, and they are going to rub the Shea butter on their smooth-as-silkworm tummies in front of the journalists, proving how gorgeous this stuff is. It is going to be a massive hit, darling."

Even though each day at Winterbottom PR was like *Fawlty Towers* meets *Mad Men* (or, in this case, Women), Anna felt she was right in the middle of where she wanted to be. Yes, it was vague, rather barking, definitely whacky, but PR was a career with variety, character and eccentricity.

"Before you get cracking, Anna, there's one more thing," said Gilda, reading glasses now resting on the end of her nose. Taking hold of Anna's hands, she was suddenly close to tears, which must have been brought on by a lack of sleep judging by her eyes.

Feeling sure Gilda was about to reveal something deep and personal, Anna nodded her head reassuringly, ready to play the role of confidante.

"Anna, you know this is a crucial job."

"Of course," said Anna.

"It's this new guideline that the Winterbottom Board of Directors has sent in to me. They want me to ease up on corporate entertaining but you have no idea how many client lunches I have to deal with, and I simply can't ply them with sparkling water, darling, Lord only knows how it would affect the business. I must steer my own ship – I mean my clients like to be shown a good time. If they want a glass of Chateau Margaux as we talk over campaign strategies, then I simply must deliver."

And then, her thin lips breaking into a huge smile, Gilda pointed her nose upwards, dabbing her eyes before a teardrop could betray any sign of weakness.

"No time to waste, Anna," she said and, scooping up her iPad, she swung out of the boardroom and breezed into her office, a haven complete with a huge screen for Skyping.

Chapter 3

At the soup kitchen on Thursday evening, Anna was using all her strength to push the knife through a block of rock-hard butter. Dozens of brown-bread slices lay across a long trestle table, which had been scrubbed by Anthea Hicks in preparation for her leading eight volunteers in a foray of sandwich-making for the homeless.

"Anna dear, do you have the catering cling film?" asked Anthea, anxiously checking her Rolex. "Father Christopher is due at any moment and we still have another three containers to fill."

Anthea had been the director of the Brompton Oratory Soup Kitchen for the past fifteen years and she took immense pride in running an efficient and ruthlessly spotless set-up.

Distracted by thoughts of George, Anna continued to butter bread and pass slices to fellow volunteers. She thought of Alfred Hitchcock, who had married Alma Reville just metres away in the Brompton Oratory. The media referred to Alma Reville as the 'Mistress of the Master of Suspense' and during fifty-four years of marriage they reputedly spent only a single night apart. Anna wondered what the media might label her if she too married into the spotlight.

"Hello?" said George, popping his head around the door. He inhaled sharply at the sight of Anna, in black jeans and an olive-green cardigan, even more gorgeous than he had remembered.

Anna pressed a tea towel against her forehead when she saw him and began to blush.

"I hope I'm not too late – the Knightsbridge traffic was a nightmare."

"Ah, greetings," said Anthea, pulling off her blue catering gloves finger by finger before thrusting out an eager hand to welcome their new celebrity member. "Delighted you've come to join us. A new pair of hands is always welcome, isn't that right, Anna?"

Anna was still unsure what to say and simply nodded and continued with buttering the bread.

"Well, George," Anthea continued, "if I may take the liberty of calling you George?"

"Please do," he said, smiling at Anna.

"We are honoured indeed," said Anthea. "Of course, I watched that excellent interview with you and Jeremy Paxman last week. Your knowledge of the Renaissance in particular is quite breathtaking. The Medicis and Da Vinci and Mona Lisa," she babbled, "your expertise in art is so extensive." One of Anthea's eyes began to twitch slightly and so she retreated, almost bowing as she backed away towards a stack of empty sandwich crates.

"For you," said Anna from behind the table, holding a stainless-steel knife and a block of cheese out to George. "Ready to slice?"

"Never been readier," said George, stepping behind the table next to Anna.

Side by side, they assembled sandwiches and wrapped them in cling film as other volunteers elbowed each other, recognising George from recent newspaper coverage about an attempted purchase of a Van Dyck portrait. George had advised the British government to block the sale by placing an export ban on the piece, citing its national importance, but opposing parties accused George of being greedy, declaring that both he and Great Britain had quite enough treasure. However, the majority saw George as a valiant hero standing up for British heritage.

Arriving through the back entrance, Father Christopher raced in the door clutching a blue rain jacket. "Oh Lord, I am so sorry. I had to meet the organ tuner and once we started discussing hymns for the Easter service, well, he hardly drew breath." Catching sight of

Anna and George, he straightened his dog collar. "George Wyndham, well, well! Very good indeed it is to have you here. Dear Anna called earlier to say you'd be joining us." Like Anthea, Father Christopher felt rather star-struck, as last week he had watched a documentary on Sky Arts about George's private collection of miniatures. "Of course, I married Anna's parents, you know?"

"Ah, no, actually, I haven't met Anna's parents yet," said George, looking at Anna while she blushed.

"Oh, I see," said Father Christopher, tying to work out if George and Anna were an item or not. "And I gather you're an Old Harrovian like myself?" Taking a pristine handkerchief from his pocket he pointed to the Harrow school emblem. "So, as my housemaster used to say each morning, *Stet Fortuna Domus – Let the Fortune of the House Stand*!" He struck a pose, one heel kicked back in the air like a sailor embracing a waitress in a war scene. "And fortune has certainly smiled on you this morning, George," he added, looking at Anna.

Unperturbed by Father Christopher's admiring gaze, Anna picked up the pace with the sandwiches as Anthea blew her whistle to motivate the team.

"It's my little way of mustering the troops," Anthea told George proudly. "Actually, George and Anna, a little favour to ask. Any chance you might take a meander to collect sandwiches and cakes from the tea shop around the corner? They very kindly donate any unsold food at the end of the day to our cause."

"Quite so," agreed Father Christopher, keen for any excuse to converse with George. "And perhaps you might like to borrow my umbrella for your fair maiden, George? It's from my golf club in Henley."

The sleety rain pelted down as George held the umbrella over Anna and they set off on their gourmet-sandwich quest. The treasure was bountiful, with smoked salmon and rocket, prawn and spinach, all sealed in plastic wrapping and neatly packed into small brown cardboard boxes. On the way back, reversing roles, Anna held the umbrella as George carried a stack of boxes, leaping over puddles in hoots of laughter and purposely bumping into each other.

By the time Anthea's team had loaded all the crates of sandwiches, large vats of soup and blankets into the Brompton

Oratory's white minibus, it was pitch dark. Eight volunteers had squeezed into three rows of seats and George was very aware that his thigh was pressing against Anna's leg, They all sat quietly as the minibus made its way, holding onto the crates, making sure the soup containers stayed upright.

A queue of about forty people had formed in the floodlit alleyway in Croydon, mostly young men, looking lonely and frightened. Quietly they stood, hands in their pockets, chins tucked into the collars of their jackets, trying to fend off the wind.

George watched as Anna confidently handed out sandwiches and ladled the soup into tall polystyrene cups. He felt instinctively protective of her. He began to feel both awkward and guilty about his situation in life but then pulled himself together, realising he wasn't there to have a crisis of conscience but to help those standing in front of him.

The supplies of food and blankets were soon distributed and people disappeared into the night. It was almost ghostly as the team folded up the trestle tables and lifted the empty crates and containers into the van.

On the way back into town, the volunteers were dropped off on street corners and bus stops. George and Anna jumped out on King's Road and stood either side of a large, icy puddle.

"That puts life in perspective, doesn't it?" said George. "I'm not sure how much help I was."

"No, you were great," said Anna, pulling her woolly hat down over her ears and feeling her toes beginning to freeze through her ankle boots. "You saw how pleased the team were to have you there, particularly Anthea."

George flashed that smile that made Anna melt inside and then he looked at her, his face more serious. "I guess it's been a long evening," he said.

"I guess," said Anna.

George looked up at the sky. "I've got this amazing new astronomy app that can tell what star or planet you are looking at when you point the screen at it, even if you can't actually see the stars from the city."

Standing behind Anna, he pulled out his phone and directed it towards the sky.

"See, we are standing beneath Venus," he said. "Just over there. Though not a star, it's a planet, named for the goddess of love and beauty."

Anna looked at an array of tiny bright lights on the screen of George's phone but could only think of how she must reek of vegetable soup.

"Anna, if you aren't too tired, can I take you for a drink?" he asked. "I know a lovely cosy pub just a few minutes' walk from here."

"I'd love to." Anna felt instantly better.

Walking into a small pub on Mossop Street, George saluted the barman who was polishing a tumbler.

"How about red wine, Anna?"

"Sounds wonderful," she said, as she took off her dark green Barbour. She settled into a booth close to a fireplace, which was throwing out welcome heat.

"A bottle of Cherubino's cabernet shiraz, please," said George to the barman. Taking off his coat, he pointed to a print above the fireplace. "You see that, Anna?"

"The woman and goat?"

"Well, you'd think it was a goat," he said, throwing his coat over a bar stool before sitting down next to Anna in the booth, "but it's actually a unicorn – it's hard to tell when it's a black-and-white print. Can you see what I mean?"

Anna squinted. "Actually, yes. It's pretty odd though, isn't it?"

"It's from the fifteenth century," said George. "The unicorn was meant to represent a sort of pseudo-masculine force that could only be tamed by a good or pure woman."

"A good or pure woman?" laughed Anna. "Do you say that to all the girls?"

"Only the really pretty ones," said George. "Oh look, here comes our wine – you've been rescued from having to listen to my art rant."

"Would you like to taste, sir?" asked the waitress, her eyes fluttering at George like a butterfly seeking a mate.

"I'm sure it's fine, thank you – pour away. I know this wine well." Turning to Anna, he said, "I often meet clients here for lunch."

Anna noticed how the waitress glanced back to look at George as she walked away from the table. She clearly fancied him, but George seemed to take no notice.

As he passed a glass of wine to Anna, their fingers touched, very slightly.

"I can't believe Sofia's party was only last weekend – it seems ages ago," said Anna. "I actually saw pictures of Sofia in the press during the week …" Then, worried that she might seem like a sort of fan, she quickly qualified, "You know, as part of my job we have to follow the headlines, checking out the stories that are trending, making sure our clients are in the news for the right reasons. All that sort of stuff."

"I really only come across Sofia a couple of times a year, a party here or there," said George. "Jamie is always trying to drag me out. I'm afraid I can turn into a bit of a hermit if I have my way."

"I'm the same. Tilly's much more social than me. But then, when we get together, well, you know, we can sort of slip back to our university days and I find myself waking up with a dreadful hangover compliments of dearest Tills."

"Like Jamie and me?"

"Yes." Anna didn't want to bring up the rumour about Jamie's seriously wild past, but George beat her to it.

"Jamie was a bit of a lady's man and, as you've probably heard, he struggled with drugs for a time."

"I did read something about it," said Anna, discreetly. "But you know what the media's like, blowing things out of proportion."

"Not always though. Jamie deserved a lot of the little-rich-kid accusations. He got in with a very fast crowd during his gap year. They raced around the world like they were taking the Tube, hopping from yachts to parties on private islands then onto private planes, and at the roll of a dice it was a night of clubbing. Jamie became infatuated with an Austrian girl. She was white as snow, and by that I mean her cocaine habit, and Jamie got badly involved."

"And you?"

"Well, I was Mister Sensible and spent a year at Christie's to get some experience in the art world. But by the time Jamie arrived back to England in time for Cambridge, he was a real mess, unbelievably run down, his bounce and enthusiasm completely gone. Having wanted to go to the Bar for as long I can remember, he just wanted to pack in any chance of a law degree."

"Rehab?" asked Anna, who had actually read online, when she and Tilly were researching their potential love interests, that George had checked Jamie into rehab and covered the bill – something crazy like $10,000 per week.

"Well, after much persuasion from his parents and me, we managed to convince him to defer the degree for one year and checked him into the Beau Monde on California's Laguna Beach. Jamie became known as the 'Duke of Beau Monde' as he was the closest thing to Prince William the Beau Monde residents had ever met."

"You're a good friend to him, by the sounds of it," said Anna.

"He's great guy, and managed to kick drugs completely and these days will only very occasionally have a glass or two of wine. So, you have nothing to worry about in terms of Tilly."

"Did I look worried?" asked Anna, finding herself seriously liking this guy.

"Maybe a little," he said, taking the wineglass out of her hand and putting it on the table. "However, as for me, I'm afraid you've got a slight problem on your hands."

"I do?"

"Yes," he said, slowly leaning towards her, "because I am utterly besotted with you."

She turned her face towards him and as they kissed the barman rang an old-fashioned bell mounted on the wall, signalling closing time. Looking at each other, George and Anna both knew they couldn't go home alone.

George held up Anna's Barbour so that she could slip it on with ease and they took a short walk to his house on Cheyne Walk, which faced the River Thames. Pulling out a key, George opened a tall black gate. They walked through. Anna saw a beautiful Georgian doorway lit up, with a small topiary garden either side of the path.

"This place used to belong to my grandmother," he said. "She called it her urban bolt-hole."

Opening the front door, he guided Anna into the darkness.

"Quite a bolt-hole," said Anna, feeling long velvet curtains brushing over her as she entered the doorway. "And you live here by yourself?"

"I do," said George, running his fingers gently across her forehead, feeling the contours of her face and breathing in her scent. He gently held her lower back and kissed her behind each ear. "Anna," he whispered, taking her hand, "I think there's something watching us ..."

Anna started and then giggled when he turned on the lights of the hallway and pointed to a pair of marble lions standing guard at the foot of a staircase.

"Ah, so you don't live alone after all," she said. Taking in the large paintings and tapestries, she wasn't quite sure if she felt like she was in an art gallery or a museum, but either way there she was, standing opposite George Wyndham. "It's lovely. Really gorgeous."

George smiled at Anna and, taking her coat from her, he draped it over the head of one of the lions.

"Just to give us a little privacy," he said, "and we may even need to cover the other lion's head, do you think?"

Slowly, George unravelled the pashmina from around Anna's neck until it fell to the floor. Kissing as they side-stepped into the study, almost knocking over a freestanding lamp, they lay down on a long, green sofa. George pulled off his jumper as Anna lay back, her long curls spreading out around her head like a flower that had come into bloom and, unbuttoning her blouse, George kissed her nakedness as each button opened.

Anna saw a crescent moon peering through the sash window, while George took off her bra and swirled his tongue over her nipples, his hands continuously attentive, and as their eyes met she knew they had found each other at the right time.

"Anna," he said, burying his head into the small of her neck, "let's go upstairs."

As they climbed the stairs, George and Anna's fingers intertwined. They walked into the bedroom and a lamp turned on, lighting a majestic landscape hanging above a double bed with mahogany bedside tables either side.

"In case you get chilly?" teased Anna as she looked at a large fireplace.

"No danger of that happening while you're around," said George, unbuttoning his shirt.

Climbing onto the bed, Anna could feel her heart racing as

George eased his hands over her hips and, as she tried to kick off her skinny jeans, one foot got caught in the ankle, making her crack up.

"Sorry, I'm out of practice," she said, as George gently freed her ankle from the jeans.

"I'm pleased to hear it," he chuckled. "Now, let's make the most of tonight, as I'm afraid I have to fly out tomorrow."

"For how long?"

"Just a few days," he whispered, kissing her neck. "Some matters to sort out in Scotland."

"Hard work?" asked Anna, with her head lying back on the softest of pillows, trying not to squirm as George ran his hand along the inside of her leg.

"The hardest thing about it will be leaving you, having just found you. Now, how about we slip beneath the blankets?"

Anna did just that and closed her eyes, feeling her heart pounding as he whispered her name.

Chapter 4

The next morning, Anna arrived back at her flat with only just enough time to shower and change – Gilda was on her way to collect her, to drive to Bristol for a midday client meeting. Each time Anna had so much as hinted to George that she needed to get out of bed, he would lure her back into their harmonious tangle, making her wish that she could jack in her job. When she finally left his house, looking up at the four-storey redbrick building with four shining windows on each floor, she pulled the heavy iron gate shut behind her just as a photographer leapt out from behind a car and, following a clicking sound, asked for her name. Fortunately, Anna had been wearing sunglasses and feeling just a little bit fabulous, so once she got over the initial shock of being landed upon she quickly walked along the river towards Pimlico, wondering if she might appear in some kind of tabloid headline as George's mysterious new lover.

As Anna emerged from her flat with wet hair and her face feeling flushed, Gilda arrived. She belted out a succession of whopping beeps as she skidded the Volvo onto Elizabeth Street and parked, seemingly oblivious to multiple triangular County Council signs stating that ground works were in progress.

Revving the engine as Anna made her way towards the car with a handful of Ryvita and an armful of printouts, Gilda put down the passenger window.

"Anna, my love," she shouted, showing a rare moment of maternal instinct, "there are enough crumbs in this car without you adding to them with that rabbit food. What you need is a good bacon sarnie – a late night by the looks of it!"

As Gilda's navigator for the journey, Anna tried to put her mind into efficient business mode as Gilda whizzed onto the M50. Having pinpointed Thermidor International Headquarters on Google maps, she began texting Tilly to tell her about the amazing night with George, while Gilda had her children's nanny on loudspeaker, lecturing her about cutting out sweets at breakfast time for her little daughter Cresta. Then, to Anna's absolute horror, when she checked Google maps again she realised they had missed Exit 19 to Bristol. Gilda might blow a complete fuse at such a boo-boo and Anna braced herself – but, unpredictable as ever, this time she merely shrugged her shoulders.

"Okay, darling, no need to panic," she said, checking the rearview mirror. "You do get yourself into a flap." And, putting her foot down, she weaved between cars before reaching the inside lane while Anna closed her eyes and held her breath. Taking a sharp right turn, Gilda bumped the Volvo up onto the concrete border, crossing the wide grass verge, which divided the six-lane motorway, before shooting like a bullet to join a fast lane of cars in the other direction. "*Oh yes!*" she shrieked with delight, punching her fist through the open sunroof as Anna crouched down to her knees. "Thank Christ I chose fuel injection when buying this car!" She turned to Anna who was deathly pale and shaking her head. "Light me a ciggy, would you, Anna, sweetie?" She began to apply mascara, whilst driving well over the speed limit. Gilda was one of those women who could put on a full face of make-up without a mirror and nine out of ten times it was immaculate. "And check my emails, would you? The *Express* is threatening to run an article on Knicker Glories, terribly rude, and they have asked for my comment on the quality of the garments but they don't seem to believe that the design really is inspired by J. Lo's behind."

"No sign, as yet," said Anna, checking Gilda's phone. "Have you given them a quote?"

"Yes, I have, but not a terribly polite one."

"Really?" asked Anna, knowing that Gilda could possibly have put her foot majorly in it.

"Oh don't worry about it, sweetie, it's all part of the business."

Anna was still recovering from the shocking drive when they arrived at the entrance to Thermidor International and paused beside a red-and-white-striped barrier. A security guard smiled down at Gilda as she raised her red Dior sunglasses to give him a wink.

The building was a typical suburban glass-box office except for the windows, which were tinted blood-red, and a gigantic lobster perched on the roof with claws reaching for the stars. Forbes had listed Thermidor International as best newcomer for 2016 in the kitchen-utensils market and pressure to keep the success-rate up was at a premium.

Parking at a right angle across two parking spaces, Gilda yanked up the handbrake and leapt out of the car. "Tell me I don't have a VPL, Anna, darling?"

Anna stood back from Gilda, who was wiggling her bottom and applying a fresh coat of lipstick.

"All smooth, Gilda," said Anna, finding her sense of humour. She walked quickly to keep up with Gilda, who could cut a serious pace in her Jimmy Choo stilettos.

"Let's hope Thermidor's PR budget for the coming year is as meaty as that well-fed-looking chap," said Gilda, pointing to a silicon lobster, holding a knife and fork, mounted on a plinth by the revolving door to the building.

Pushing through the rotating glass doors, Gilda and Anna were met by a recently hired and highly enthusiastic receptionist dressed in a tightly fitting navy suit, complete with a Thermidor lobster logo perched neatly on the lapel of her jacket.

"The name's Winterbottom," said Gilda, flatly. "Winterbottom PR."

The receptionist raised her eyebrows and wisely chose not to laugh out loud. "And I'm Mandy."

"How lovely for you," said Gilda, utterly disinterested. "Any sign of Martin?"

"Mr Horne asked me to escort you to the Lime Room. He is on a call at the moment."

They followed Mandy along a bright-red corridor lined with glass cabinets, each one showcasing Thermidor International products from lobster scissors and lobster crackers to a multitude of thin metal seafood picks in faded packaging along with plastic lobster toys losing their colour.

"Here you are, ladies," said Mandy, grandly opening the door of the meeting room.

"That water looks rather stagnant, wouldn't you say?" said Gilda, putting on her red spectacles to inspect a mural of a pair of lobsters lying side by side in a pond.

"Oh, I don't know about that," said Mandy defensively. "Mr Horne says the pair of lobsters signify harmony and a good working relationship."

"Surely a big fat cooking pot is a more apt domestic setting for those poor crustaceans," said Gilda, finding Mandy's presence utterly painful, "with a large dollop of butter sauce to boot."

"Being an outsider of Thermidor International I wouldn't expect you to truly understand," said Mandy, as she strutted out of the room.

"Cheeky mare," hissed Gilda, "and I'm sure she's having it off with Martin. Right, we had better get this bloody proposal in the bag, darling, and scoot as quickly as possible."

"*Shhh*, Gilda," said Anna, as a flushed Martin Horne arrived into the room.

"Sorry to keep you, ladies – my meeting ran over," he said in a broad West Country accent, patting his forehead with his red polka-dot tie.

Anna watched as Gilda, beaming her finest smile, turned from a squinting weapon into a submissive and cooing creature.

"Darling Martin, how are you? You look a tad harassed?"

Hitching up his trousers, he let out a long and heartfelt sigh and sat down. "I feel like being CEO of this company is giving me an ulcer. Just one of those weeks where there are endless decisions to be made."

"Ah yes, you poor thing," purred Gilda soothingly. "I completely understand. You always work so hard." Pulling out a grey chair from the table, she placed her hand on Martin's shoulder and, as she sat down beside him, he gave her a grateful look. "Now that we are sitting down, Martin, let Anna and me do the work for a while."

Anna passed an agenda and PR proposal to Martin and walked around to sit on the other side of the table, opposite Gilda.

"We feel strongly passionate about Thermidor, don't we, Anna?" said Gilda, giving her a nod.

"Oh yes, Gilda, we do. We absolutely do," agreed Anna, straightening up the pile of papers in front of her.

Gilda planted her eyes firmly on Martin, drawing him in. "And to show you just how loyal Winterbottom's is going to be to your wonderful brand, we propose going beyond the known boundaries, seeking out ideas that are as fresh as sea water in order to bring your luxurious range of must-have kitchen utensils to the fore."

Shrugging off her cardigan and discreetly wiggling her bosom in Martin's direction, Gilda was in her comfort zone.

"And as part of our key strategy," she continued, "we are putting forward the suggestion to have –"

She broke off as Mandy came through the door, carefully balancing a tray of coffees and plate of custard creams.

"Mandy," said Martin, perking up at the sight of his secretarial totty.

"Don't mind me," said Mandy, sliding the tray onto the table. "I know you like to have your favourite biscuits at midday, Mr Horne."

Martin gave her a wink and grinned up at her.

"As I was saying," said Gilda, trying not to get rattled by Mandy's syrupy sweetness.

"Actually, Gilda, hold that thought," said Martin. "I'd like to bring in Laurence before we go any further."

Turning to Mandy, Martin gave her another wink and she teetered over to the conference telephone to dial in Laurence Philips, Head of Marketing.

"Do you read me – Roger?" asked Mandy, pressing a long, manicured nail on the loudspeaker button.

"No, it's Laurence," crackled a voice on the loudspeaker.

"Yes, Laurence, I know it's you," said Mandy, as if she were a game-show host. "I'm testing the line. You are now linked to the Thermidor Conference room."

"I know," said Laurence.

With a flick of her hair, Mandy left the room.

"Greetings, Laurence darling, it's Gilda and Anna here from Winterbottom PR," said Gilda.

"Lovely," said Laurence.

"Are you well?" asked Gilda, covering the niceties.

"Well? You could say that. I'm in Monaco, checking out the yachting demand for Thermidor's products, and I can safely say that the muscles of those boat boys are really quite something!"

Unsure as to where Laurence's conversation was leading, Gilda cut straight to her proposal.

"As I was just about to explain to Martin, we are plotting an extravagant product giveaway through high-end magazines and travel companies and what not. We are talking serious prizes including a three-week private rental of a Colorado spa resort, along with luxurious hampers filled with all the Thermidor delights."

"And what does one have to do to win these prizes?" asked Martin, tapping his fingers on the boardroom table.

Holding her nerve, Gilda stood up and struck a pose. "Well, Martin, it's about to get super-hot in the Thermidor kitchen."

"Oh yes," said Martin, his imagination captured for a moment at least.

"We, at Winterbottom PR, are going to search for Europe's hottest chef. Oh, and they have to be creative too. We want someone who will complement one's Lobster Thermidor in more ways than one."

"I like the sound of this," raved Laurence. "Perhaps we could have a Thermidor Men's Calendar while we're at it? I can see him now, perhaps wearing bathing trunks with the Thermidor logo on the waistband?"

"Or picture this instead," said Gilda firmly, keeping the proposal on course. "We are going to team up with the fabulous Rocco Vegal, Hollywood stuntman and a dear friend to Winterbottom PR."

Anna tried not to giggle as Martin's eyes blatantly followed Gilda's breasts rising up and then disappointingly down into her DVF jungle wrap-dress.

Laurence bellowed "*Oh goody!*" into the telephone. "Rocco

was terribly good in the film where he had to fend off the octopus!"

"Exactly, Laurence," said Gilda. "The man is a genius both in and out of the water. He is like an underwater James Bond of the Sea. Sexy as hell and if you think he looks good in a wet suit, well, darlings, you should see him in the flesh."

"And Rocco is going to head up the judging panel," said Anna, taking the baton from Gilda, "and while he and his handpicked team dine on creamy and delicious Lobster Thermidor with organic egg yolks and cognac, naturally using Thermidor utensils, they will view a line of hot chef contestants decked out in puffy white hats and little aprons."

"How little?" said Laurence.

"Martin, you don't look particularly excited by our suggestions?" said Gilda, sitting down again. "You must understand that via the winning chef we can communicate the key messages of the Thermidor brand, driving home the thinking that these kitchen utensils should be in every household utensil drawer, not just on yachts and villas. You want mass-market sales and so we need to reach the public, and by having the voice of the people is how we shall prevail."

Martin looked confused. "Like *Big Brother*, you mean? Getting to know a random punter, what they eat for breakfast and so on?"

"Well, more that we communicate that Thermidor products can make people glamorous. The very use of the word ... *Thermidor* ..." said Gilda theatrically, "will make people feel more Hollywood than Merseyside."

"I think I follow," said Martin, checking his watch.

"And to top it all, like Hollandaise on your Lobster Eggs Benedict, shall I tell you what happens next?"

"Oh do, Gilda, do go on," panted Laurence, with the sound of splashing water in the background.

"Eh, what's going on there, Laurence lad – you're never on the beach, are you?" said Martin, clearly not very interested.

"Oh no, Martin, no, no, no. I'm by the pool, going through my contact list. Thought I'd have a little paddle as I make calls."

"Fair enough," said Martin. "I'd do the same, lad, if I were you. And if it weren't for that wife of mine I'd be over there in your place right now."

Gilda glared at Anna, who realised the last thing they needed was for Martin to start talking about his domestic situation, which could involve chat about his wife Norma, about whom they knew far too much already, including her habit of cutting her toenails in bed without gathering the cuttings up after herself.

"Yes, as I say, we are obsessed with Thermidor, utterly obsessed," said Gilda. "Thank you, Laurence. Leave it in our hands. Goodbye now."

She spoke with such authority that Martin hastily ended the conference call.

Clearly geared up by the prospect of an enormous fee, Gilda insisted on lunch at the acclaimed restaurant, The Single Vault, well known for having different themes of cuisine each month.

Martin seemed equally thrilled by the PR proposal and the prospect of lunch.

"I'll get Mandy to bring my driver out front. Norma's only gone and put me on a diet, just because I split my trousers on the golf course last month."

Chapter 5

Following the short drive into Bristol, Martin's driver rolled the Mercedes right up to the entrance to The Single Vault, which had Italian flags flying above the doorway as part of the restaurant's theme of the week.

"Lord, it's freezing," said Gilda, taking Martin's arm as she stepped onto the icy pavement. "Let's go straight inside and warm ourselves up, shall we?"

Anna felt almost sick with relief when her phone bleeped with a text from George.

Landed in Preswick. Miss you so much, darling xxx

Breathing into her pashmina, she could still smell a faint aroma of his aftershave. God, she missed him.

Looking forward to a lunchtime glass of wine to take the edge off, Anna walked into the restaurant to find Martin and Gilda sitting at a corner table, listening to a waiter reciting a mouthwatering menu.

"And to complement the lunch, we have a delicious range of wine from the foothills of the Veneto."

"Right-oh," said Gilda, slipping on a pair of Iris Apfel tinted glasses, which she saved specifically for dining in public spaces. Turning to the waiter, she smiled. "Sentina Pinot Rosé, darling, and quick as you can."

Taking her seat, Anna could tell Martin wasn't thrilled with Gilda's choice, but his nose was soon sniffing in the direction of a plate of pork pit ribs being served at the neighbouring table and he forgot to complain.

"Pork ribs to start with and then a fillet steak. That'll do the trick nicely. And lots of gravy," said Martin, rubbing his hands together. "What about you, Anna, love?"

"Mackerel paté for me, please, followed by … the duck," said Anna, choosing the first things to catch her eye on the menu. "How about you, Gilda?"

"I'll stick with the rosé for now," she said, "though perhaps a quick voddy and ton to quench my thirst?"

Anna ordered a glass of Chablis, sensing the pressure wasn't off yet. The question of budgets and strategy often arose over these working lunches, and it was her job to make sure she had all necessary answers to hand.

"Just checking a few emails, darlings," said Gilda. "You won't mind if I take out my iPad, will you, Martin?"

"You go ahead, Gilda, as long as it's to the benefit of Thermidor. As CEO, I like to keep my brand present at all times."

"All the time, Martin?" asked Gilda, with a naughty look in her eye.

"Well, Norma, granted, isn't fond of shellfish, so we don't have much need for the lobster scissors in our house sadly. Mandy on the other hand, well, she's a different cuttle of fish altogether," he said with a grin.

Anna and Gilda looked at each other, then Gilda's eyes brightened at the sight of her first drink of the day before gravitating her nose in the direction of her emails while Anna had to make small talk.

"Have you been here before, Anna?" said Martin, his eyes following a waitress as she passed by.

"No," said Anna. "The menu looks pretty delicious, though."

"Aye, and the waitresses ain't half bad either," said Martin, relaxing into his chair. "Seriously though," he said, seeing Anna's expression waver at his joke, "they seem right fond of sherry in this place. Reminds me of my dear old mother, God rest her soul, making Sunday lunch. She always assured us the bottle of kitchen sherry was for the gravy but I suspect a great deal of it went directly down the hatch."

Having checked her emails, Gilda was not impressed to find a pernickety fashion journalist from *The Mail on Sunday* questioning the integrity of Winterbottom PR's new client Knicker Glories, suggesting the designs were reminiscent of an 'old granny's knicker drawer'. She showed Anna. "Honestly, hasn't that woman ever heard of body-shape wear?" she snorted, finishing her drink. "Martin, what was that about your mother and gravy?"

Just as Martin was about to answer, the sommelier arrived with the bottle of rosé for Gilda and a glass of Chablis for Anna. He poured a splash into Gilda's glass, who took a sip, turning her head from one side to the other.

Suddenly she lurched across the table and shot her hand out for a napkin. "Are you trying to poison me? This tastes like putrid chicken-piddle – utter muck!" she spluttered.

With flushed cheeks, the sommelier cleared his throat. "I can assure you, madam, the Pinot Rosé is of the highest quality."

Martin shifted awkwardly in his chair as Anna sat back, knowing Gilda's short fuse only too well. She had witnessed such scenes before and knew there was little chance of putting a lid on Gilda once the steam was rising.

"Gilda, my lovely," said Martin, trying his best to smooth things over as he spied his pork-ribs starter arriving with a waiter, "let's just order another bottle. It doesn't matter, does it?"

Gilda would not be tamed. "It bloody well does. I will not be taken for a fool. I know my Italian wines and that wine stinks."

Martin, losing his patience, reached out for Gilda's glass. Taking a noisy glug, he swirled the rosé around his mouth and shook his head. "Now, I'm not much of a wine buff, but this isn't half bad. Not a thing wrong with it."

"Oh, what would you know, you bald baby!" spat Gilda.

"Jesus, Gilda," whispered Anna and could just about bring herself to look at Martin's face with one eye closed.

"I beg your pardon?" said Martin, his face turning purple while the sommelier's mouth fell open and took a couple of moments to close.

Not even the arrival of the pork pit ribs was enough to keep Martin at the table. Hurling a starched white napkin on his chair, he glared from Gilda to Anna and shook his head.

As he about-turned, Gilda indiscreetly kicked Anna's ankle.

"Well, go on then!" she hissed. "Do something."

"Martin," said Anna, calmly standing up. "Just a moment. Please, at least allow me to walk you to the reception and we'll call your driver."

"Sod off," said Martin, shooting an icy scowl at Gilda, who had nonchalantly plucked a nail file from her handbag and was now blowing on her fingers as if she had just had an imaginary shootout. "I know when I'm not wanted."

He stormed out of the restaurant with Anna in hot pursuit, dialling his driver as she walked. On the footpath, Martin pulled off his tie and undid the top button of his shirt, which was much too tight.

"I am so sorry about this, Martin,' said Anna. "Gilda forgets herself sometimes. Is there any way back from this?"

"Anna, you're a good girl," said Martin, as his car arrived, hazard lights flashing. "That Gilda, she just goes too far.'

"The Thermidor Hottest Chef competition will be a hit, we're sure of it." Anna was almost surprised at the words coming out of her mouth. "And we'll get you all the coverage you could possibly want."

He paused, his car door open, and turned to her, the thunder having left his face.

"*Desert Island Discs*."

"Sorry?"

"You get me on *Desert Island Discs* and I'll consider it."

"But Martin, that's rather a tall order," said Anna, and then thinking quickly she went for it. "I mean, you're much too young, aren't you? Surely you'd prefer to wait until you have climbed the steps all the way to the, um, crème de la crème job at Thermidor International?"

Martin considered things. "Well, I have noticed some hints coming from head office in Miami. They do seem fond of me all right."

"There we are then," said Anna, feeling slight relief. "Let's aim for the weekend supplements and take it from there, shall we?"

"I tell you what, knock ten per cent off the PR bill and get a handwritten apology from Gilda on my desk by Monday morning and I'll keep Winterbottom on, but tell that Gilda that she's as erratic as a Peking Duck."

"Um, all right, will do," said Anna, not understanding the Peking reference at all, and as Martin climbed into the car like a ravenous MP, Anna heard him instruct his driver to go straight to KFC on the high street for a bucket of chicken wings and a tub of hot curry sauce. It must have been his only solution to suffering another night of his wife's unendurable diet.

Relieved to have sent Martin off on a slightly better footing, Anna returned to the table to find Gilda merrily eating a bowl of tiramisu.

"Oh hello, darling," said Gilda, waving a silver spoon as Anna sat down. "This is utterly delectable. I'll order you one, shall I? And this bottle is quite fabulous. It's a Shiraz. Honestly, that sommelier really is pants. The dishy waiter over there brought me into the cellar. I rather hoped he might chain me up and keep me there."

"Gilda? What on earth is going on?"

"I just told you. We went into the cellar. I pulled out the first bottle I laid eyes on and I think I got lucky all in all."

"Gilda, hold on. What was that all about with Martin? He was furious. You can't call a client a bald baby!'

"Well, he is bald."

"Yes, I know that," said Anna, "but you can't actually point it out."

"And he stormed off like a baby. How furious was he?"

"Very, but I think he'll come round, hopefully."

"Darling, how did you manage that?" Gilda sat up, less interested now in the tiramisu and quite fascinated to see Anna taking charge.

"We need Thermidor on our client list," said Anna. "If we lose the contract it will be a major hole."

Gilda's eyes darted from left to right as Anna spoke. Taking a large drink of wine, she propped up a menu to shield her face from the nearby table. "Anna," she whispered urgently, "keep it down. I don't want them overhearing."

"What?" said Anna.

"That brunette. Look, over there. She's from the *Daily Mail*. I'm sure of it."

"Was she here when Martin left?"

"I don't know. I've only just seen her."

"Bugger."

"Yes, bugger indeed."

Signalling to the waiter for the bill, Anna poured the remainder of the Shiraz into a wineglass, realising that Gilda had drunk almost a whole bottle, on top of her glass of Chablis and the vodka, and seriously hoping the journalist hadn't brought a photographer pal along to capture Martin's steaming exit.

"Ladies," said a waitress, arriving with the bill and a tray of dangerous looking liquors, "as you hardly touched your plates, we naturally will reduce the bill accordingly. However, Chef is concerned that you are not pleased with the menu."

"We've been a little distracted," said Anna, wondering how best to handle Gilda.

"And so," continued the waitress, "we'd like to offer you two complimentary glasses of sherry."

"I'm not sure it's a great idea," said Anna, trying to make eye contact with the girl, far from keen to put more alcohol in front of Gilda.

"I am going to light a match and rest the flame against this orange peel," said the waitress, not clocking Anna's signal. "I then rub the orange peel around the edge of the glass, which will enhance the sherry's vintage –"

"Such tosh!" said Gilda, sinking a little further into her chair. "Honestly, are you trying to turn this place into an aromatherapy centre?"

Hiking up her oversized Mulberry handbag onto her lap, Gilda pulled out her Visa card and waved it at the waitress who tried several times to release it from her grasp until Anna pulled the card free and handed it over.

"Now, Anna, tell me exactly what the status is with Martin," said Gilda in a hushed tone, swirling her glass of sherry under her nose before pressing numbers into the waitress's card machine. "Actually no, that man is such a diva that from now on I think we shall refer to him as Martina."

Anna explained Martin's terms and conditions but Gilda remained unrepentant, burying her Visa card down her bra when the waitress returned it to her.

"Darling, he can't possibly expect me to kowtow. The man knows I am the best in the business. If he wants that shiny head of his massaged and his lobster scissors and seafood what-nots to reach the big time, then he is going to have to find a sense of humour. I mean, really, you'd have thought that Martin … sorry, I mean Martina … you'd think he's fresh out of marketing school. How Thermidor International employs a man with such poor taste in wine in beyond me."

Gilda broke off as her eyes latched onto a curvaceous blonde leading a considerably younger man by the tie to meet their driver outside.

"Christ, look at those breasts!" said Gilda, failing to whisper. "Quite magnificent, tanned as coconuts." Her hands were now cupping her own bosom. "I am totally fed up with these poached eggs. The life has been sucked out of them," and slamming her fist on the table, she sent her glass of sherry flying.

Anna grimaced as she saw the brunette from the *Daily Mail* look over and smile in a scary way. Meanwhile, the handsome waiter rushed over and began blotting the table with a cloth.

Gilda nodded her head extravagantly. "No, no, my darling," she said, wagging a finger at him and attempting to get on her feet. "Don't even think of picking me up. If you so much as try, I think I might spill."

Anna signalled a T for taxi to the waiter who bolted immediately to the phone. She then linked one arm through Gilda's, and grabbed both their handbags with her spare hand.

"I wouldn't mind him driving me home," murmured Gilda, as the maître d' arrived to open the door to the taxi. In his hand he held a long cream envelope with a claret-coloured ribbon tied around it.

"An envelope for you, madam," he said, beautifully trained, perfectly controlled.

"Is there any money in it?" asked Gilda, fanning herself with the envelope.

"Ah, no, madam, it's simply an invoice for your records."

Pressing her hand against the coolness of his navy suit, Gilda pulled out the polka-dot handkerchief from his pocket. "Well, I can't possibly read an invoice without my lipstick. How about you come home with me?"

Just as Gilda's knees gave way, Anna and the maître d' tipped her headfirst into the back seat of the taxi.

Sitting next to the driver as they traversed up the M25 from Bristol towards London, Anna called Hans to prepare him to receive a drop-off of Gilda, who was snoring sprawled across the back seat.

"I'm afraid it's been a rather long day, Hans. You might want to run a cold shower and make a very large pot of coffee."

"This is becoming boring," said Hans, his Swedish accent somehow sounding much less romantic than when Anna first met him. She remembered how crazy he was about Gilda, how he loved her wild side and spontaneity.

But there wasn't much Anna could say to smooth the runway for Gilda.

"Oh bugger off," was Gilda's response to Hans when she woke up and he asked why she had to go over the top, again.

Anna got out of the front of the taxi and into the back seat. She needed to let her hair down, literally, and shaking out her long blonde curls she called George.

"Crikey, you won't believe the day I've had. I've just dropped Gilda home and it was not a pretty sight. I had to warn Hans that he might need a stretcher, or better still, a wheelbarrow for her."

"Oh dear. Let's talk about it tomorrow evening, on our Saint Valentine's date? I should be back at Cheyne Walk by six. I was thinking of a bubble theme."

"I like bubbles," said Anna.

"How about we begin with bubbles in a glass and then move on to bubbles in a hot bath?"

"You read my mind," said Anna, longing for tomorrow already.

Chapter 6

Standing in her agent's London office, Sofia continued to feel put out following her beach-themed party last weekend. She had expected multitudes of photographs and glowing comments to be posted online by her guests, showing her looking beautiful in her lavishly decorated town house but instead there was nothing but a watery trickle of feedback, homing in on the hot waiters rather than the hostess. As she watched a silvery blue fish eyeball her from an aquarium, with a cloud of minnows swooshing below it, Sofia was feeling that fame and respect from once-enthusiastic followers was as hard to get hold of as a slippery eel.

"A blue gourami," observed Victoria Wakefield, arriving into the room with a bowl filled with ice cubes. "It seems to be getting bigger by the day ... and more aggressive."

Sofia withdrew the finger she was about to dip into the water.

"And someday it'll taste pretty good with a splash of chilli sauce," chuckled Victoria. A fast-talking Californian blonde, she frequently had her mobile phone pressed to her ear, putting a lid on bad rumours and making sure anything untoward was swept beneath the red carpet over which her clients liked to glide.

"That time already?" said Sofia, eyeing the ice and flicking her middle finger at the blue fish. "Make mine a vodka, neat as a pin."

"This ice is for my orchid," said Victoria, walking towards the windowsill.

Sofia watched as her image guru carefully placed a handful of cubes beneath thick leaves growing out of a small pot.

"You're wasting your time trying to keep that thing alive," said Sofia, as if she knew about plants. "They always wither after the first bloom."

Victoria picked up the white flowering orchid and carried it over to her desk. She was pleased with the hour she had spent in the gym that morning, toning not only her abs but also her temper so that she could handle Sofia professionally. Victoria was also concerned about her bank balance. On top of renting a small flat in Marylebone, she had recently bought a farm in Connecticut, one she planned to retire to, and her accountant was getting antsy about Victoria's nest egg being swallowed up by barn renovations along with post and rails to keep in her newly acquired mare. She needed things with Sofia to go without a hitch so that she could take both their careers to the next level.

"Okay, Sofia, we need to talk," she said, sitting on the sofa.

"How come you have no cushions on the sofa?"

Victoria glared at Sofia. "Um, excuse me? Are we here to discuss interior design, or your somewhat uncertain leap into an acting career?"

"Just saying," pouted Sofia. "No need to go all guard dog on me."

"If you must know," said Victoria, flipping open her iPad on her lap, "I think cushions make people lazy. They make people slouch, and in my office there will be no slouching."

Sofia straightened her back.

"See that orchid?" continued Victoria, not looking up. "I want you to think of it along the same lines as your career."

"I don't follow," said Sofia, pulling out a chair from behind Victoria's desk and sitting down.

"Well, it needs to be nurtured. It likes plenty of water but it doesn't like getting its leaves wet. It also likes to dry out but it doesn't like to be overexposed. It's the same for you, Sofia. You like plenty to drink too, but sometimes you get your leaves wet."

Sofia shot her a seething look but said nothing.

"I'm concerned about the exposure side of things," said Victoria. "See, with orchids, a whole lot of patience is required but get it right and you will you be rewarded with a bloom, and in your case, a contract. But get it wrong …"

"So you're calling me a goddamn orchid? I don't pay you to compare me to plants with a limited shelf life."

"No, Sofia, I am not calling you an orchid," said Victoria, holding up the iPad. On the screen was a snapshot of Sofia yelling at a photographer outside a club in New York, mascara running and hair tangled. "I'm calling you irresponsible. I've been following your raggedy-doll media trail of destruction while you've been trotting the globe in your little princess heels."

"That photographer was a complete bastard."

"No need to explain. I know what you were doing in the club."

"What?"

"Sofia, have you never heard of social media? You seem to think you're invisible to the gossips."

"So what? Why does it matter who I'm dancing with in a goddamn nightclub?"

"It was the way you were dancing, Sofia. Hollywood socialites can't get that intimate without a lot of talk coming out afterwards. I've been flat out sweeping up the crumbs after you, paying the bouncers to keep their CCTV footage away from the media hounds clustered outside just waiting for you to fall out of yet another club, with cocaine and heaven knows what else stuffed up your nostrils."

Victoria's freshly blow-dried hair gave her an appearance of calm, but she was evidently seething beneath her scalp.

"I can only keep going for so long, Sofia. I've got my own reputation to think of. So, do I really want to represent an actress who seems to think she's some sort of new-age Elizabeth Taylor born again?"

"And?" said Sofia, not even vaguely bothered by Victoria's rant. She'd heard it all before.

"And," said Victoria, keeping a cool head, "I've had your mom on the phone."

"So?"

"Well, I'd be grateful if I were you, because your mother – following some serious wooing of EXR producers and, make no mistake, several substantial bank transfers – has got you a part in a new series."

"Go on?" Sofia was now taking notice.

"Filming starts in three months, and between now and then we are under instruction to give your reputation a serious spring clean."

"Well, at least we've got the timing right for a spring clean, it being February and all."

"Sofia, this is serious. This is a proper opportunity for you to graduate from having a frivolous party-girl image to being taken seriously as a woman with talent."

"Okay, who am I starring next to?"

"Honey, this is not a starring role. Not yet anyway."

"What? So I'm playing some second-rate stand-in? I'm not a downtown soap star."

"You can't expect to just walk into a part any more. Your reputation has suffered and that means you need to rebuild. Anyway, they've got a big male star playing the lead role but ... they won't release the name yet."

"But you know, right? Who is it? Come on! Ryan? Zac? They're bound to go for a pretty boy, aren't they? Isn't that what they always do?"

"Don't judge, Sofia. Just suck it up, take the role, and remember to say thank you to our dear new friend at EXR, Larry Keinsberg, the deputy chairman, who you will be meeting. You'll need to charm him, okay?"

"Yes, all right, I get it. So, what's the series about? And can you get me a coffee?"

"It's about a tiger," said Victoria, seeing her little-rich-girl client taking it all for granted, yet again.

"What do you mean 'a tiger'? I hate tigers."

"Well, you're about to start loving one. You'll play the role of a young mother in Ohio. She befriends a runaway tiger, which has been cast off as a 'just for Christmas' pet. You nurture the tiger back to trusting humans all over again. Simple as."

"And what about Zac?"

"Zac?"

"Or Ryan? The big star?"

"Oh, well, he kind of also befriends the tiger, but he falls for an older woman."

"How much older?"

"Don't get caught up in the detail, Sofia – you won't be in the same shot as the leading man, okay, you're more subtle to the plot," said Victoria, springing off the sofa and pulling two Diet Cokes from the fridge. She handed one to Sophia. "But don't worry, you do what you're told and we'll make you the star. You'll be like the Tiger Whisperer in waiting. Consider this series as a warm up."

"But I can't stand cats of any kind," said Sofia, feeling peculiarly feline.

"Hey, that tabby your parents had in LA was just grumpy, that's all."

"They make me sneeze."

"The tiger won't exist. Not as such. It will all be CGI so you won't have to be within a fifty-mile radius of his whiskers."

Sofia stood up, walked over to Victoria's sofa, lay down and sighed. Victoria pinged open the Coke can and drank for a while, watching her wayward protégé digest the news.

"So, we need you in mint condition, young lady. Starting now. Lay off the booze and turn that body of yours into a temple. Come on, up you get!"

Sofia stood up and, putting her hands on her hips, legs slender in black skinny jeans, arms toned in a sleeveless turtleneck sweater, she walked across the room like she was on the catwalk.

"I think you'll find I'm in fine condition, thank you."

"It's your mind I'm more concerned about. Your brain is a muscle too and you need to exercise it, okay?"

Sofia's education at a boarding school in England had been carefully thought out by her parents. A transatlantic accent would give her a broad scope for acting roles and, with gold-star connections and prudent choices, she had the potential to make it. Continually bankrolled by her father, she had never had to work and the incentive wasn't there. She already had a secure place in the media as a society girl; keeping up with party invitations was as good as a full-time career. Travel, presents, what to wear, maintaining her silky locks, facials, pedicures, Pilates with her personal trainer. Time was at a premium and she could see no reason to stress over work. She once had a small role in a pilot for a mini-series in the US but, within hours of arriving at the studio to watch the trailer, she screamed at the director so loudly that she was sacked.

"I just like things to be done properly. I am a professional," she reasoned in an interview that later went viral. "Where were my lilies? It was a simple question and he couldn't answer. There should have been white lilies in my trailer. The guy took his eye off the ball. I mean, if he can't get that sort of detail right, what kind of series is he gonna damn well make?"

The thought of going back on set was a nightmare. She couldn't bear feeling trapped in a trailer, awakening early for make-up, having to run through the lines with half-rate actors, substitutes waiting for the call. If it wasn't for her mother's obsession with turning her into an actress, she figured she'd run a business somewhere. She envisioned a huge, fifty-storey building with her name sprawled across the top of it: TAMPER. But Sofia was her mother's trophy and, as her only child, expectations were high. For now she was to live a life of high achievement and then, in due course, she could produce a string of grandchildren and so ensure a long line of Tamper heirs to keep the new empire going. Her mother had been micromanaging her to within an inch of her sanity and Sofia wanted out. But she continued to draw from her father's bank account and, until she had a proper salary on board to maintain her lavish lifestyle, she would have to answer to the beat of her parental drum.

Victoria opened the window. Down on the King's Road, shoppers wrapped up in long coats and woolly hats whooshed this way and that.

"Once you finish your Diet Coke, I want you to go straight to Rita Striker's on the King's Road. She's going to open the store exclusively to you. Choose an appropriate dress for the *Violet Tiger* party next week."

"The what party?"

"*Violet Tiger*, the name of your new series. Your mom has also talked EXR into hosting a party for you. This is the one where we will announce your new role to the press. The invitations are already in motion and the theme is 'Call to the Wild'. I ran though the guest list for that beach party you had last week and at least you had some steady eddies there. Like that lawyer guy, Jamie Lord, and his art dealer friend. Like a sort of Prince William of Scotland, right? These are the kind of guys we need to get you around, Sofia. Don't look at me like that."

"Like what?"

"Like I'm your nanny. This is what I am paid to do."

"And what am I wearing? Cinderella's ball gown?"

Sofia jumped when she heard a splash from the aquarium. Victoria walked over and looked inside the tank.

"Oh dear, the gourami's had a tantrum and swallowed one of those poor sweet minnows."

Sofia squeezed her eyes together.

"You see, Sofia, if you don't keep an eye on your game, you'll get gobbled up like a minnow. This is a big pond you're in. Keep swimming. And remember, the EXR execs have cast you on the condition that you keep your public persona nice and tidy. It has taken much extensive persuasion on your mother's behalf so please ensure that you are no longer going to make a fool of yourself. EXR is a conservative production company, backed by Mormon money, okay? So nothing messy, keep it cute and PC. If you're going to party, from now on you show the press you're a girl who knows how to party with dignity. Okay?"

"Yes, I hear you. Christ, this is starting to sound like some kind of etiquette purgatory. I need to let loose now and again."

"I know you do, and as long as it's behind closed doors and free from any recording devices, you do your thing. But let those doors open for a second and your career, as you know it, is over and out. I will be gone and your mother won't be coming to me any more – she'll be straight on to you."

Chapter 7

At Winterbottom headquarters, Desmond Spicer pulled out a cigar and leant back into a chair next to Anna's desk.

"Mind if I smoke?" he asked.

"Sorry, Desmond, no can do here, our insurance policy won't allow it," said Chrissy, stacking cups by the coffee machine. "Particularly on a Monday. Don't most of us try to curb our bad habits at least at the beginning of the week?"

"Oh, come on, Chrissy," said Gilda, hand on waist with red-rimmed glasses balanced on the end of her nose, poised to take over the helm of the Spicer Tweed media ship, "I'm sure Desmond only smokes the finest Havanas. A little Cuban, is it, darling?"

"Only the best, as you know, Gilda," said Desmond, lighting up, and swirling the smoke around his mouth he blew out his cheeks like a pufferfish.

As a fourth-generation tweed-maker from Edinburgh, at sixty years of age Desmond was known for being both a shrewd and charming operator in the textile business. Through the power of his herringbone suit, he commanded a loyal harem of "ladies at the loom" as he called them, and with an elegant moustache and chiselled good looks he was undeniably appealing to women of all ages. His twenty-five-year-old wife, Jenny, was testament to such a fact. As the owner, and, as he saw it, custodian of Spicer Tweed, Desmond knew his brand had a quality and design that would work beautifully around tender waistlines and well-postured shoulders across Europe.

"When I met my first wife," he went on, admiring Anna's little ankles, "I concurred with Sybil Connolly's line that a woman cannot be elegant until she is over forty. The same mantra, of course, could be applied to my second wife. But then," he said, holding his cigar above his head, "I met my Jenny, my third and present wife who, at the age of twenty-five, is elegance personified, though she does have a penchant for poodles. It's the only area in which we disagree. Much too yappy for my liking – I'd prefer a sturdier dog, myself."

"Yes, yes, Desmond," said Gilda, who didn't want the office to be monopolised by Spicer memoirs. "Youth and energy, something a little bit edgy, that's what Spicer Tweed needs, I'm sure of it." She paced the floor with a pink battery-operated fan. "Now, that Sofia Tamper girl – you know, the American socialite, her father's a huge fish in Hollywood. I read somewhere that Sofia's on the cards for a new EXR drama and if we can get in early and sign her as ambassador to Spicer Tweed before her rates go up, that would be just the ticket."

"Quite," agreed Desmond. "We want a bit of leg all right. However, it is also key that our ambassador, whoever she is, will be true to our ethos. Tweed to me is a living and breathing creation, and our ambassador must be prepared to wrap each thread of Spicer's heritage around her fingers. And I am very keen on launching in Paris this summer – we have a new line of silk-lined mini-kilts coming out, perfect for autumn."

Desmond exuded a certain confidence that came from good living and hard work. His life success was undeniably attractive and even Kate, usually oblivious to charm, hurled her media call list to one side and pulled up a chair to listen to the dulcet tones of Desmond.

"I am extraordinarily lucky," he said. "I was born in a family of strong moral values, and in my life I was able to do what I liked best: to make women look beautiful and to make them feel desired."

Chrissy and Kate couldn't help but sigh; Anna, meanwhile, was swooning at a message from George.

"My father taught me two things in life, how to mix a drink and how to mix fabric, and that is why my wool and alpaca-blend bouclé-tweed dress for example, is such a success."

Irked by Desmond's ongoing attempts at a soliloquy, Gilda scrambled on with her ideas on Sofia. "Her mother is originally Scottish, you know? Lord, I wonder if *Who Do You Think You Are?* has approached her yet?" Pausing for a moment, she checked her watch. "Desmond, are you with me?"

"Quite," he said, having moved on to asking Kate if she had a boyfriend.

Gilda glared at him and then, remembering that she had not as yet won the business, she changed her tack. "I was saying how we want to nourish your brand – we want to feed it *fillet de boeuf* and *pommes frites* – we are talking haute cuisine for your Spicer Tweed. And I think Sofia Tamper's beauty and jet-set appeal could bring a sense of Hollywood Royalty, don't you agree?" Then, feeling her tummy gurgle, she snapped at Chrissy. "Where are those biscuits? What does a woman have to do to get a biscuit around here?"

"Sofia is royal all right," muttered Anna to Kate. "A bloody great royal cow who I suspect wants to jump my boyfriend."

As Desmond was trying to decipher Gilda's steak-and-chips analogy to his tweed, Gilda grabbed Anna by the wrist and led her into her office while Kate and Chrissy began looking through samples Desmond had brought from the factory.

"Now look, Anna, Desmond Spicer is on the verge of putting his precious family business reputation into our mittens and we need to show him just what we're made of. That man is so traditional he makes the Queen's tea party at Buckingham Palace look like a common cake-fest. You can't make snide comments like that – it makes us look, you know, scatty."

"Scatty? Gilda, you are kidding?" said Anna. "What about your performance in front of Martin yesterday? You called him a bald baby to his face! I mean really, Gilda."

"And why not? The man has no backbone."

"You also called him a stinker, when we got into the taxi, and then a cad ... before you fell asleep."

"Well, I was exhausted. Dealing with those sorts of men takes a lot of energy. Besides, I do think Martin Horne is a cod, but he is Winterbottom's cod, my client. And if I want to call him a codfish I will."

"You called him a cad, Gilda, not a cod."

Anna and Gilda were now smiling at each other.

"Come on, Anna, enough dissection of yesterday's minor blip. I think we should all go out for lunch, don't you, darling? I had Orlando crying down the phone from prep school last night. Adrian seems sure it's the right place for him but you know, that English public-school business, I'm just not sure about it. And it is quiet at home without him."

"You are actually missing Orlando? The child you refer to as Demolition Dan?"

"I am a mother, Anna. Maybe not around the clock, but I can have my moments," said Gilda, lying back on her sofa and putting on her sunglasses. "A glass of fizz if you would, Anna."

"Gilda, it's barely ten thirty."

"Fizzy water, darling, really, what on earth do you think I am? Mind you, how about a drop of sauvignon blanc to go with the fizz, a spritzer if you will. Just to ease myself into the day. Honestly, Anna, no one understands the pressure I'm under."

Anna had been landed with the role of therapist again.

"By the time Cresta turned two, and Orlando was six, I had founded Winterbottom PR and it all happened so fast – in a blur."

Clinking bottles in the fridge, Anna tried to make Gilda the weakest drink possible.

"Hans in his pink shirt and city-boy suit along with that accent, it sent me flying. And before I knew it I moved the children and our nanny to Battersea and left Adrian crying into his spinach soup." Gilda stared at her ring finger. "I could never stand it."

"Spinach?" asked Anna, longing to lighten the conversation.

"No, crying. It's just not in me. It was a version of being left-handed when I was growing up. If my mother found me crying she as good as shoved handkerchiefs into my mouth, as she just couldn't bear it. And so I learnt not to, literally. When I felt like crying I would climb a tree or tear pages from a book, something that gave me a rush. I was never going to be a pipe-and-slippers wife. Adrian must have been delusional when he thought I could fit into his tidy box."

"And then?" asked Anna as she handed Gilda the spritzer, wondering if she and George had the full measure of each other.

"Thank you, darling. Well, I let him down. I know I did," she sniffed, and shook her head. "And the way he looks at me, a cross between pity and disdain, well, I deserve it, don't I?"

"No. Look, I don't know. I have no experience of it." Anna could hear Desmond's laughter bellowing from the centre office. "But it does sound difficult for you, Gilda. I mean my parents frequently alternate between riding a merry-go-round and a roller coaster with their marriage, but somehow they stagger along."

"When I left Adrian, I turned to kale smoothies and I got my trademark red hair and tiny waistline back onto the A-list – working rooms and plotting PR campaigns. Adrian only served the papers to me when things got serious with Sara. I mean, she is the wettest creature you could ever come across. Her humour is as thin as those old airmail envelopes we used to send."

"Like tracing paper."

"Even thinner. But look, that's beside the point. There's something about the divorce papers that makes my hands feel somehow empty. I can't explain."

Gilda had always been flighty and, as the youngest in her family, she had been lavished with oceans of attention and was told she was the special one as she inherited Granny Winterbottom's fiery red hair. When she and her husband Adrian met at Oxford, Gilda's hair was a flowing mane of red silk and she wore her academic gown like a magic cloak, giving her the confidence to sail from person to person, soaking up ideas and influences. Gilda knew Adrian had fallen for her like a lead weight through a cloud and, having been told over and over by her mother that she needed a good steady reliable man to balance her tendency to enthuse in multiple directions at once, she walked up the aisle with Adrian while the ink of the provost's signature on their degrees was still drying. Gilda defiantly held onto her maiden name. On their honeymoon, when they weren't drinking cocktails and making love, Gilda was like a waterfall of energy, pouring ideas and strategy on anyone willing to listen, scribbling ideas on the back of paper napkins and chatting up potential clients. She looked at the country house Adrian had bought in Hampshire as being merely a launch pad for Winterbottom PR. Gilda was thirty before she had their first child, Orlando, and two years later Cresta was born. Neither child inherited the red mop.

"And I know I'm not the best mother, my clothes are expensive and I just can't handle ketchup or bubblegum-flavoured toothpaste. But I do love the little monsters." Pulling her phone from beneath a copy of *ES Magazine*, Gilda's eyes lit up when she showed Anna pictures of Cresta standing proudly on the podium, coming third in the sack race, and another with Orlando sporting a broken arm in a luminous green plaster following an attempt to backflip on the high-jump mat but misjudging the landing space. "And we do have fun, with spontaneous trips to Hamley's, Legoland and entrée to premières of every child's movie that's landed in the West End."

"It's hard to know what to say," said Anna, picking up a newspaper and then noticing the headline: **Tamper Tantrum**, "Oh, um, Gilda, before we go back in to Desmond – I promise I had no idea this page was open, but look at the headline. I just don't think Sofia quite fits in with that whole country-living tweed look we are after."

"Yes, alright, never mind that now, we'll do the nitty-gritty later. The main thing is we've got to nail this Spicer business, and then we've got Thermidor to think about and that Martin Horne is getting right up my nose, and not in a good way."

"How can there ever be a good way to get up someone's nose?" asked Anna, who was longing for the evening to come so she could melt into George's arms.

And then she caught her breath when she saw a photograph of herself, pulling her beanie over her head, with sunglasses, in the top right corner of the week's diary in the *Express*. "**George's Girl, but Who is She?**" And that was it, with small print about George Wyndham, sought-after bachelor who lived on Cheyne Walk, the street of royalty, romance, rock 'n' roll and politics. Usually she was the one reading about other people in the papers. This was a strange feeling, but not a bad one.

"Cocaine, darling. It was crucial to my early years in PR – you wouldn't believe the amount of work we got done in an evening."

"Oh, I think we have a fair idea," said Chrissy, popping her head around the door. "Gilda," she went on, lowering her tone, "Desmond wants to introduce Kate to his nephew, who is next in line to inherit Spicer Tweed apparently, but I don't think she's terribly keen."

"Desmond is terribly thoughtful, you must admit," said Gilda, with a wiggle. "Anna, are you listening?"

"Sorry, yes, Gilda," said Anna, frisbeeing the newspaper onto a pile of press in a corner of the room.

"Surely we can at least discuss the idea. We must make Desmond feel part of the Winterbottom family, and what better way than for us to be open to all sorts of introductions," and, running her fingers through her hair, Gilda turned to Anna. "Just one more thing, darling. I want to talk about Paris again. You are the only member of my team who speaks French."

"Well, loosely, Gilda."

"Yes, but you can basically speak it, *oui*?"

"*Oui*," said Anna. "Gilda, you aren't going to bribe me with an irresistible offer, are you?"

"Even six months, sweetie. Just to get Winterbottom *à Paris* started?"

"It's just, I'm really beginning to get stuck into the London life. It's become quite exciting lately." Anna felt the back of her neck and thought of George tenderly kissing her, smoothing his hands around her waist, his strength.

"What could be more exciting than your own pad in Paris and the city of lights at your fingertips? *Mais non!* Do not say a word, just consider, okay?"

"All right," said Anna, wondering if George might even move over with her. But what was she thinking? They had only known each other for a couple of weeks. No harm in dreaming though, was there? George had already bought her an electric toothbrush, which he had left in his bathroom with a red ribbon tied around it. They seemed to have so quickly landed into a rhythm of spending nights together and their lovemaking was becoming ever better, exploring each other, knowing the places that made each other squirm with pleasure. She couldn't possibly leave George, not at this tender stage.

Chapter 8

"Yes! Double sixes," said Tilly, as she lay on the rug in the sitting room of the flat. "Aha, down to your boxers now!"

"Tilly Fairfax, you are such a minx," said Jamie, crawling over to her. "Who knew you were a poker fiend? Now this pretty little top is just going to have to come off, dice or no dice."

He slipped his hands around her waist and as they kissed he pushed the tray of cards in front of the fireplace to one side, so they could tumble across the floor. Jamie felt wild about her. They made each other laugh and she even got his terrible jokes. She made him feel strong and capable and, even though he had managed to take silk in his twenties and his prospects of becoming a high-ranking barrister were looking good, in his private life he sometimes felt concerned that he might return to where he had been, years ago now – that a slight chance might make him slip. Right now Jamie had everything he wanted, and above all else he wanted to please Tilly, loving the sounds of her breath rising as he touched her, knowing exactly what made her feel the pleasure he wanted to give. It was the ultimate natural high.

"You know," he said, pulling a blanket from the sofa and wrapping it around them, "I hadn't expected to meet you so soon."

"What do you mean?"

"You know, to meet someone like you."

"Oh come on, Jamie, you are such a kidder," said Tilly, sounding like she was trying to laugh it off.

But he knew she wasn't. He could tell she felt the same way, nervous and elated and knowing they were right together.

"Okay, how about our first night?" he said. "I woke up the next morning feeling like I had won an Olympic Gold."

"My, you're very confident, aren't you? Mind you, it was quite a performance."

"No," said Jamie, running his fingers through her long hair, "I meant about you, silly. That I had been lucky enough to lure you into my clutches!"

Turning her over, he began to tickle her and she went into stitches, shrieking with laughter. Pressing her body against Jamie's bare chest, she whispered into his ear.

"I'm the lucky one."

"Do we have time?"

"Oh, I think so," said Tilly, just as they heard a jangle of keys, followed by the push of the front door and Anna's voice calling "Hello!" as she came straight into the sitting room.

"Oh my God, oh no, guys, I'm so sorry, I had no idea," said Anna, backing out the door.

"No, Anna, come in, honestly, just in the nick of time actually," said Jamie, grabbing a very large cushion to hold in front of his legs and jumping up, as Tilly lay back on the floor, languishing in her cashmere blanket. "I'm afraid our game of cards got a little out of hand," he said, beaming at Tilly. "I had no idea your friend was so competitive, Anna – she's a vixen with the dice."

"You're one to talk," giggled Tilly. "Really sorry, Anna – we both got off work early and thought a little strip poker was in order."

"Oh no, I'm the sorry one, really sorry, guys. It has been a very long week and this is one Friday night when I'm just going to chill for the evening – so carry on as if I'm not here."

"Hold on," said Jamie, moving behind the sofa. Finding his jeans, he pulled them on at speed. "I'm afraid dear Tilly has lined you up as my pseudo-sidekick for the evening."

"No, sorry. Tonight is my night off. I've got it all planned: a long bath, scrambled eggs on toast, a demi-bottle of *vin* and a long overdue box set I haven't touched since I first met George."

"Speaking of," said Tilly. "Where is Prince Charming?"

"Scotland," said Anna. "Counting stags or something, all part of keeping the deer sanctuary in order apparently. Arriving back tomorrow, sometime in the early hours."

"Why can't he just count sheep like the rest of us?" asked Tilly.

"George isn't like the rest of us though, is he?" said Jamie. "If he isn't hunting down a painting for a client, you'll find him checking the salmon log book at Rousey or pulling ivy from a bunch of trees. He never stops, but that's why we love the chap, isn't that right, Anna?"

"Exactly right," said Tilly, "and George would never forgive us if we left you home alone – what if you choked on your scrambled eggs or something?"

"It's a Safari-themed party for Sofia Tamper," said Jamie. "Super smart and lots of my mates are going."

"But I can't stand Sofia! I'd feel like a real hypocrite being there," said Anna.

"It's not about her, Anna," said Jamie. "The party is celebrating *Violet Tiger*. We won't even have to stand within three feet of Sofia, believe me. She'll be too busy schmoozing the press to notice the guests. I've been geared up for the party all day and then Tilly had to back out."

"My boss," said Tilly. "It's a last-minute pull-together of the team, a massive pitch to get involved with designing a huge shopping centre in Birmingham."

"Well ..." said Anna.

"Purr-lease, I've got a costume all ready for you," said Tilly. "In fact, I'm very disappointed not to be wearing it."

"Oh all right, but first I have got to have a bath. Gilda insisted on testing out the Master Cat Food Challenge in the office today – we had five cat finalists, not one of them wearing a collar, and even worse their owners. God, it was hideous, cat food all over our desks and cats throwing up in corners of the room. Utter disaster."

"Well, don't be put off cats too much, will you?" said Tilly, grinning. "I picked up some gorgeous tiger masks and leopard-print leggings for the party and they'll look *purrfect* on you!"

Wearing faux-fur tied around his waist over very small Speedos and a zebra-striped tie around his forehead, Jamie ushered Anna through an archway made of vines with exotic animal noises shrieking from surround-sound speakers.

Lion tamers with long leather canes pretended to whip him as he sauntered past and a girl dressed in green fishnet tights and khaki-green shorts lassoed a rope around him, then quickly released him as Anna raised her tiger mask and said: "I don't think his girlfriend would like that – you might want to release him?"

"You can be feisty when you want to be, can't you, Anna?"

"Well, when my best friend dresses me up as a tiger, the least I can do is defend her prey, don't you think?"

"I think this debut outing sans our other halves calls for a proper drink?" said Jamie. Swiping up a pair of Wild Berry cocktails from a bar lined with enthusiastic-looking barmen poised to mix and shake, he put a glass into Anna's hand and called out, "To Integrity, Excellence and Justice!" before downing his drink in one. "Rather tasty! Let's have another."

As the band played African bush music amidst neon trees with enormous gold and orange balloons floating overhead, Victoria, in long boots and a metallic blue dress, pounded the club floor like a media-circus ringmaster, monitoring the arrival of scheduled journalists. She had made sure to place Sofia in pole position on a leopard-print sofa, sipping angelically on soda and lime, despite the mirrored table next to her crammed with expensive-looking bottles of booze. This must have been earning brownie points from Larry Keinsberg of EXR who was nodding favourably at Sofia from a distance. Beautiful and composed was how Victoria wanted Larry to see Sofia. Her hair slicked back into a tight knot, wearing silver cat ears and eyes darkly pencilled, she was a real beauty.

With one more interview to go, an EXR representative presented a journalist, wearing Doc Marten boots and a much too short denim skirt, to Sofia.

"What about rumours about the nightclub in Miami last month, Sofia?" she asked, pouring herself a glass of water. "It sounds like there might have been rather a lot of weed involved?"

"Nope. The only greenery I touch is spinach for my juicer in the morning. Don't you juice? I mean, who doesn't juice? You should try it," said Sofia coolly.

That's my girl, thought Victoria, nodding at a bouncer to swiftly boot out the journalist who was going off piste. Sofia couldn't afford for any tricky questions or answers to get into the press.

"Okay, Sofia, that's the last journalist out of your hair now, and the good news is that Larry's off the premises too and he looked rather happy, I thought. Your driver's waiting for you outside, when you're ready."

"To go where?" asked Sofia, getting up from the sofa and stretching out her arms like she had just stepped off long-haul in economy.

"Back to your hotel, my dear Sofia. Mother's orders."

"Oh screw *mother's orders*! I'm letting loose," Sofia said and as Katy Perry's 'Roar' blasted from the speakers, she ran onto the dance floor and sang out, *"I've got the eye of the tiger!"* waving her hands in the air as she inched her body against well-turned-out safari-party animals. She was feeling like a star again, the magic of sensing those dancing around her wanted to be around her, to look like her, maybe even to *be* her. Maybe she really could make it as an actress? Then seeing Ruby, who had been on the dance floor for most of the evening, shining in the lights with such confidence and beauty, Sofia wondered about the future.

An hour later, Anna and Jamie were still propping up the bar having found themselves surrounded by a cameramen crew from EXR, who had spent the day filming a jaw-achingly dull politician doing the rounds of his constituents in Fulham. Delighted to score a freebie night on the house, they had persuaded Jamie and Anna to do shots. Feeling rather drunk by now, Anna was struggling with her conscience, knowing that she should have called Tilly earlier to let her know that Jamie was taking it all a step too far but somehow she had got caught up in the moment and didn't want to ruin the fun. She knew George wouldn't be impressed either.

"Jamie!" she shouted over the din of music. "How about we dance, you know, get away from the bar for a bit?"

"I think one more," he shouted. "Christ, there's a lot more people in here now, don't you think? It's like a cattle mart."

"Or a buffalo crush? Considering the Safari theme?" yelled Anna back to him.

"Well, I might settle by the bar for a moment or two, and see if this herd might pad off somewhere. I've never been keen on a crowded dance floor."

Unsure whether or not to leave him, Anna checked her phone to find a text from Tilly, to say that her boss had released her from the meeting.

"All right, one more drink then I'm dancing, okay?"

"Cheers to that," said Jamie.

"So tell me, Jamie," slurred Anna. "One thing I've been wondering. How is that George can be so good-looking and yet not be a complete asshole?"

"He's a good guy, and we good guys like to stick together, don't you know," said Jamie, bowing to Anna. "But watch out, because if you get on his bad side he is seething, bubbling away beneath like molasses on a hot pan. A dark cloud doesn't come close."

"Really?" said Anna.

"But that's a rare sight and I think he reserves it for his father, or an annoying photographer who forgets his p's and q's and lands on George when he's minding his own business buying something as nonchalant as a wooden spoon in a Conran shop or something."

"I guess he just wants to live an ordinary life."

"Well, not that ordinary. It's hard work trying to be like everyone else when you plainly aren't. He was eleven when his mother died but somehow she managed to instill in him the importance of discretion, not to be ashamed of wealth but just to be careful as to what people you open yourself up to. And don't get me started on his girlfriends in the past."

"Why?" asked Anna, unashamedly longing to hear how awful they were and how she was a right fit.

"Nothing you need to worry about, Anna. Let's just say they had their eye on the prize."

"Well, I think he's the prize. And I miss him. Uh oh." Anna, raised her hand to her mouth as she found Tilly staring at her from the other side of the bar. "I think I'm in trouble."

"Why is that?" asked Jamie, wiggling his finger over their shot glasses for a refill. "Do you suppose we may be ossified?" and both doubled over in hoots of laughter.

They looked up to find Tilly before them, unimpressed and stone cold sober.

"You've been busy," said Tilly, glaring at Jamie, and then at Anna.

"Tills baby, where have you been?" he yelled, attempting to throw his arms around Tilly, who moved out of the way so that he fell against the wall by the bar. "Whoops! I think I may have overdone it?" and as Tom Petty's 'Free Fallin'' began to play, Jamie wasn't about repent either, as his slid onto his knees and began to play air guitar.

"You're *free falling* all right," said Tilly. "Forget it, Jamie, I'm leaving."

"Not without me you're not," said Anna, who had started hiccupping. "Come on, Tills."

"The taxi's waiting outside, Anna, but don't expect me to utter a word on the way home. You should have bloody well called to tell me what a state he was getting into, and you're not much better."

"Night, Jamie," said Anna, feeling very guilty.

"Oh come on, Tilly!" Jamie yelled after her. "I'm just getting going!" And getting to his feet, rather than chasing after Tilly he waved at Sofia on the dance floor and went in her direction.

Chapter 9

Heaping spoonfuls of Columbian coffee into a cafetière, hearing the buzzer of the gate, George checked his watch and hoped it wasn't an art delivery. The thought of having to inspect a painting, confirming it had arrived in one piece with a courier hovering for a signature, was on the bottom of his agenda.

"Hello there," said Jamie into the speaker on the gate. "You're home, then? Oh, international man of mystery. Where have you been? Visiting the Queen?"

"Not unless she recently shacked up with my father," said George. "I'll buzz you in."

Opening the front door, George found Jamie dressed in a pair of green overalls.

"Cup of tea might be a good idea," said Jamie.

"So I see," said George, "and I'm not going to ask about the overalls."

"Kind of you but, to settle your curiosity, I had to swipe them from a room of cleaning equipment next to where I slept last night."

"I think I'll need a coffee before I hear this," said George. "I didn't get in until far too late last night, must have been midnight."

"That was just around the time that I was really letting my hair down on the dance floor."

"I see," said George, flicking on the kettle switch. "Go on then, spill the beans."

"Well, I think it's more a can of worms than beans actually."

"Oh Christ, you haven't upset Tilly, have you? The first decent girlfriend you've had in years."

"I think I might have given Tilly a slight insight into what I might have been like in the past."

"Might have been like?"

"Let's say, about one drink too many," said Jamie, trying not to sound defensive but not really succeeding.

"Just one?"

"Well, I lost count early on," said Jamie, trying to smile, "but it's not as if it was a line of Charlie."

"Nothing else?"

"Nothing else. It's just I've been feeling so well and happy having Tilly around I just thought I'd push the boat out."

"Sounds like you capsized," said George, filling the cafetière far too full so that coffee clung to the outside of the lid.

"Tilly arrived, told me off."

"And?"

"And then she left with Anna."

"Anna?"

"She came to the party with me."

"Whose party?"

"Well, that's just what I was getting to," said Jamie, taking the lid off the biscuit jar. "It was EXR, pushing the boat out about the new series that Sofia Tamper is involved in. *Violet Tiger*. And as Tilly couldn't come with me, Anna came instead. George, she looked adorable as a tiger kitten, can't you imagine?"

"All too easily," said George, plunging the coffee and annoyed to find himself feeling jealous that Anna had gone to the party with Jamie.

"But to get to the point ..."

"Which is?"

"Sofia."

"What about her?"

"Well . . ." said Jamie.

"You *didn't*, Jamie ... I can't –"

"No, I didn't, at least, I don't think so. Let's just say she and Ruby took me under their wing. The club where the party was, well, it had bedrooms upstairs and so they brought me up, pulled off my shoes ..."

George just looked at Jamie and wondered what the hell he was playing at. If Tilly found out about this there would be no chance in hell she'd ever look at him again. "Go on, what happened?"

"I passed out, I guess, and woke up about three hours ago."

"It's 10am, so you've been walking the streets trying to find yourself like some classic lost soul?"

"That's the one. And here I am."

George sat down and let out a sigh. "I can't believe you'd risk Tilly for a night on the batter."

"Take it gently, George, will you? My head is pounding and I haven't even brushed my teeth yet. I came here for guidance, not a royal whipping."

"So you're sure that nothing happened with Sofia and Ruby – and if that is the case ..."

"Which it is."

"Then Tilly doesn't need to know."

"Correct," said Jamie, relief in his voice that George was taking control of his mess-up, and he pushed his mug out in front of him. "Please sir, can I have some coffee?"

"And so Tilly has no idea about what happened after she left?" asked George, filling Jamie's mug.

"No."

"Well, then, the best thing to do now is get on the phone pronto to the finest florist and chocolatier in London and load her with 'grovelling, please forgive me, I've utterly screwed up and will never do it again' style gifts."

"George, just to say, and I know I've said it before, but I am truly sorry to be such a pain. And I'm fine, really I am. I just felt that I needed sound advice after last night's fiasco."

"That's what I'm here for, and it's no more than what you have done for me. If it hadn't been for you, I don't know how I would have coped with my mother's death."

"The older we get, the younger your mother was when she died. And you, only eleven, it's still too awful, George, even after all these years."

"Okay," said George, keen to move things onto a more uplifting note. "I'm going to give you some totally privileged information."

"I'm guessing it's good news, as I was just thinking you are in remarkably good form considering you've just been hanging out with your old man in freezing Scotland. And don't hog all the biscuits, I haven't even had breakfast."

"So" said George, his face lighting up, "I've had a hunch about a painting at Rousey for a while, but somehow until now I didn't feel ready to look into it."

"Go on."

"I'm not sure if you remember it? It's in the music room – quite small and quite marked from years of neglect, so it's dark."

"And? I'm very intrigued despite the feeling that I am going to throw my guts up at any moment. I am never, and I mean *never* drinking shots again," said Jamie.

"Delighted to hear it. As I was saying," said George, wanting complete attention from Jamie, "it's been there since I was a child. My mother adored it and I guess because she spent a lot of time playing the piano there, keeping out of my father's way no doubt, she kept it there."

"And?"

"And my father still never goes in there – I think maybe because it was where my mother used to be. Anyway, since I've met Anna, I've just been feeling so energised I've been dealing with matters that have been bothering me."

"Are you going to tell me what I think you're going to tell me?"

"I happened to meet an amazing guy from Milan, likes to sail on Lake Garda at the weekend."

"And does he want to float your painting?"

"Well, as it turns out my hunch was correct. He brought over a friend of his to Rousey, and it only took them thirty minutes to hand on heart verify that the painting is ..."

"How special?"

George closed one eye and raised his mug of tea. "It's a Titian."

"Crickey!"

"It's only one of a handful of his compositions remaining in private hands."

"And worth a small fortune?"

"Hmmm …"

"And?"

"My mother adored it – so much so she wanted to keep it out of my father and others' line of vision."

"So not a word to your old man?"

"Nope. Just in case. Although I think we're on a better footing now these days."

"But will you sell? I mean, what are we talking?"

"Silly money, and no, I don't want to sell. It was a favourite of my mother's and I just feel it should stay put, and I can see it whenever I want."

"And what did your father think about the Italians – were they undercover?"

"No, my father is used to me bringing clients to Rousey, not that many but certainly five or six over the past few years, introducing them to Scotland, letting them get a sense of the river, of nature."

"So, your Italians were just clients?"

"Exactly. And Claudio was very discreet. Besides, I paid a small fortune for him to fly over with his colleague. They won't breathe a word. The Titian is going to be a beautiful secret between my mother and me."

"Well, and me."

"Yes, Jamie, and you," and pulling the biscuits far out of Jamie's grasp, George laughed. "Some things change, don't they?"

"And other things stay the same, like your dreadful taste in biscuits. Anyway, here's to dear old Titian!" said Jamie, lifting his mug of coffee.

The Queen's Gate Club's low lighting and dark wood gave a library-like atmosphere except for the expertly choreographed bar staff who weaved delicately around their affluent clientele with extensive drinks lists, including a large set of cocktails.

Anna scouted the room and her heart sank when the only person she recognised was Sofia, dressed immaculately in a fitted jacket, exactly the same colour as Anna's, with jeans and cowboy boots. Standing to her full height, Anna spied an empty sofa in a far corner and tried to catch George's attention, but Sofia got there first.

"Over here!" waved Sofia. "George, darling, your timing is

perfect as ever. We are just plotting our entry into Maggie's. It's VIP night on a Sunday, so tickets won't be a problem."

George reached out for Anna's hand and stepped back when Sofia attempted her standard air-kiss.

"And Anne, you're here too," said Sofia, swirling ice cubes around the base of a tall glass. "This is becoming quite a ritual, isn't it? Seeing you two together."

"Her name is Anna. Ann-a," said George.

"Isn't that Prince Harry over there?" said a model-like creature standing next to Sofia.

"Cut it out," said Sofia sharply. "Just go with it – we don't make a fuss about Royals in here. Live and let live. Why else do you think I've based myself here? The attention I received in the States was almost unbearable."

"Sofia," said George. "We haven't come over to socialise."

"Oh?" she said.

"I just want to let you know that if you ever so much as sneeze in Jamie Lord's direction again, so help he, I'll make your life hell."

Anna looked up at George and could see a muscle tense and ripple in his cheek.

"And what's bought this on, George?" asked Sofia.

"As if you don't know," he said quietly. "You're trouble, Sofia."

"I am?" she said, smiling.

"Don't think I'm joking. You remember what I said."

"You do look even more attractive when you come over all manly, don't you, George?"

Anna didn't know where to look as Sofia, clearly put out, was trying to bring George around by flashing seductive eyes at him but it wasn't working.

"Come on, Anna," he said and, as he put his arm around her shoulders, she tried to ignore the feeling of Sofia's eyes burning into her.

Feeling like a fish swimming in contaminated waters, Anna decided to take a breather while George ordered drinks. In the basement, she found the wooden door to the ladies' and pushed the door, but it didn't budge. Then she tried pulling it, but still no movement. Then a small woman, dressed in a cleaner's apron, walked up to the door and tapped a tiny ruby in the centre of it – it hissed into the side of the wall. Anna waited for the cleaning woman to tick the checklist on the wall, and then approached the mirror, lined with small white bulbs like a theatrical dressing room, stretching over three sinks. Beneath the lights, glaring and unflattering, Anna dabbed away a spec of mascara from the corner of her eye. Her face was flushed, and she could see a spot breaking out on her chin. Rotten timing. Before she left the flat she had felt so sleek and confident. And then she found herself looking at Sofia's face in the mirror.

"Hi, Anne. Oh whoops, I've done it again, haven't I? You are fond of the 'a', aren't you?"

Sofia looked wonderful – Chanel red lipstick expertly applied, hair tied back showing off her long slender neck.

Anna stepped back, picking up her pashmina like a matador using his cape as a form of defence. Then she put it down again with her bag and washed her hands for the second time.

Sofia intimidated her, and they both knew it.

"You move quickly for such a small person, don't you?" said Sofia, lifting up her top to admire her own smooth, flat midriff in the mirror.

Anna turned away, feeling like a piglet beside a lioness.

"George is on rather edgy form, don't you think?"

Feeling pinheads of sweat dotting around her forehead, Anna dried her hands finger by finger. "I really don't, Sofia," she said flatly. "I'm going to go back upstairs."

"Oh, okay," said Sofia, attempting to sound surprised. "But before you do, tell me one thing."

Anna could smell a sickening aroma of smoked trout wafting from Sofia's breath.

"How well do you know George?" asked Sofia. "Do you see what I'm getting at?" She didn't take her eyes off Anna as she spoke. "I suggest that you save your shovel for digging gold in Ireland," and turning her face to the mirror, she pouted at her own reflection.

"Sofia, you are kidding," said Anna.

"Believe me, I've seen girls come and go around George. All PLU's."

"What?" Anna didn't have a clue what Sofia meant. "I don't know what you mean."

"People Like Us. The fact you have to ask should confirm what you can't seem to grasp."

"Why," said Anna, feeling the heat rising in her face, "are you being such a bitch?"

But leaving the question unanswered, Sofia flicked her hair and whisked out the door. Anna shot out the door after her. "Sofia, you are insane!" she yelled and the only saving grace for her dignity was that Sofia had, at least, five sheets of loo paper stuck to the spike of one of her heels.

With Sofia's overly articulated voice still lingering in her head, she was climbing the narrow stairs lined with *New Yorker* cartoons, when a barman came racing down the stairs and nearly sent her flying.

"Oh my God, what is it with this place? You nearly floored me!" she yelled out. Clutching onto the banisters, feeling flushed, she could hear Sofia's voice bellowing from the bar and, peeking her head around the corner, saw Sofia with a tight group around her.

"You should have seen them," said Sofia. "The dolphins surfed on waves that were, at least, twenty feet higher than our yacht."

Her designer friends looked enthralled by her stories of fabulous holidays.

There was no sign of George and, feeling like a spy undercover, Anna pulled out her phone, considered calling him but then found a text from Tilly to say that she was going to spend the night with Jamie, who had clearly earned her forgiveness. Anna and Tilly had both been blown away by the flowers he had sent to the flat by way of an apology, but it was the poet, who recited a cleverly written apology by Jamie, that got him over the line and back into Tilly's good books. Relationships are never a smooth run, Anna thought to herself.

Making a run for it, she darted to the side entrance of the bar and pulled open the door to find Gilda gliding into the club wearing a full-length mink coat.

"Anna, darling!" squealed Gilda. "Such a pleasure. Hans, sweetie, you remember Anna?"

"Good evening," said Hans, clearly unimpressed to have been dragged out.

"We are popping in for a stiffener, darling," said Gilda. "Honestly, we've just been to the heaviest performance at the Royal

Albert. I mean eye-watering, emotional and painful all at the same time."

Hans stood beside Gilda, beautifully turned out in his Jermyn Street suit. Gilda often told Anna how her spontaneity bamboozled Hans on a regular basis and, usually, he found it exciting, but he didn't look like he was enjoying the Gilda Experience tonight, looking more like a dog on Cruella de Vil's leash.

Dismissing Hans with a wave of her hand, Gilda slipped her arm into Anna's and began walking towards the bar. "Darling Anna, your skin is looking a tad blotchy, isn't it? Are you all right?"

Anna closed her eyes and just wanted to disappear. The icing on the Crisis Cake would be for George to arrive, resulting in Gilda having palpitations over the fact that Anna and George knew each other.

"I've got to go, Gilda. I'm sorry."

"But, darling, have you read through the drinks menu here? It's extensive, my love. I'm sure I can persuade Hans to stay for a glass of Cristal before bed, don't you think, my sweet?"

"I'll see you in the office first thing, Gilda," said Anna.

Running out the door, to Anna's utter relief she spotted a taxi pulling up across the street with a bright orange light shining brightly. Home, James!

Chapter 10

Anna woke up with the taste of burnt chocolate in her mouth and, grappling for her phone on the bedside table, she knocked over a cracked mug with gloopy remains of hot chocolate, which slowly trickled over the edge and onto the carpet.

"*Oh hell!*" yelled Anna and in response she could hear Tilly's upbeat and jaunty walk in the direction of her bedroom.

"Anna? You're here?" said Tilly. "I only just got back from Jamie's."

"Oh God," groaned Anna, putting a pillow over her head. "Well, I think I'm fifty per cent alive, and I think I've lost my phone."

Tilly kicked into gear immediately, racing to the kitchen to get a cloth and dish of water, and wiping up the hot chocolate. Then she called Anna's phone and they both jumped when vibrations came from the mantelpiece underneath a painting of Tilly's grandmother.

"Aha, there it is. I thought Granny was trying to communicate with us for a moment there," said Tilly, picking up the phone. "You're popular," she said, looking at the screen to find six missed calls from George and a screen full of text messages.

Anna sat up and pulled a pillow feather from the corner of her mouth. "Oh God, it's eight already. I drank most of a bottle of white wine last night. I can't believe it's Monday. Why does it have to be Monday?" She pressed the voice mail on her phone.

"Can you call in sick?"

"Gilda would go crazy," said Anna, smiling as she heard George's gorgeous voice, so worried about her. He had left three voice messages. "She's all over the place at the moment."

"What about George then? What happened last night?"

"Sort of long story. Anyway, when I was getting changed last night, I was thinking about how beautiful and wise and dignified your grandmother looks in the painting, and so I sort of paid homage to the portrait of her before I went to bed ... and took a selfie with her picture."

"Okay, rather nuts?"

"I think I was a little drunk."

"Granny would totally support a little drunken behaviour, don't worry. I remember how she used to belt her walking stick against the bedhead when she wanted another evening gin and tonic. It was her favourite, you know." Tilly blew a kiss to the portrait in Anna's room. "I hope you don't mind having Granny's portrait in here?"

"Not at all, she's amazing," said Anna.

"It's just, this was her favourite room, even though it's smaller than mine."

"Tilly, it's your amazing flat and you don't have to explain. Just give me a sec, I need to listen to some messages from George."

"Trouble in paradise?"

"Let's just say we came across Sofia and things very quickly became weird. Not with George, but with Sofia. She cornered me in the bathroom."

"She what?"

"It's stupid," said Anna.

"What did she say?"

"It was just so weird. I mean she really has it in for me. George was like ice with her when we first met by the bar – he told her to stay away from Jamie."

"Jamie?"

"Weird, right? And then I met her in the bathroom and I literally thought she was going to pull a gun out of her clutch. She had an insane look in her eye and wait for it . . ."

"Go on."

"She called me a gold-digger."

"No."

"Yes, can you believe it?"

"Okay, so it makes sense. George blanks her, well, as good as, and then she takes it out on you."

"I guess so."

"Okay, well, that's a good explanation. But how does Jamie come into it?"

Anna could only think that it had something to do with the *Violet Tiger* party, but she did not want to mention that to Tilly, given that she had only just forgiven Jamie for going on a bender.

On her way to work, Anna couldn't face her usual chai tea and instead opted for an Americano in the hope the caffeine hit would improve matters. Walking up St. Martin's Lane and trying not to think about George, she was taking a sip of coffee and nearly spilt the contents all over herself as Gilda pulled up beside her in an Audi convertible wearing a fur hat and dark glasses. Gilda smoking a cigarette in the morning was never a good sign.

"Jump in, Anna darling," she said, as a line of cars began to beep behind her. Climbing into the sports car, Anna could smell an aroma coming from the very new and very clean cream-leather seats as *The Spy Who Loved Me* theme tune wafted gently from the speakers.

"Now, look," said Gilda, inhaling deeply on her cigarette, "there has been activity over the weekend."

"Gilda, what's happening?" said Anna, with her hand on the door-handle, ready to jump out as a loud succession of beeps came from the dashboard.

"No need for panic, darling – I think we could both use some extra air, don't you?" said Gilda as the canvas roof opened and folded neatly behind the backseat. "This should open the airwaves, darling! Breathe deeply now!"

Anna was glad to take a few deep relaxing breaths.

As Gilda drove along Shaftesbury Avenue and cut across a rubbish truck, she turned to Anna. "I've left Hans," she said, pressing her palm against her forehead.

"Oh Gilda, I'm so sorry," said Anna, immediately shuffling George aside in her head.

"Or at least, Hans left me. I don't know." Gilda reached out for Anna's coffee. "And to top it all, Mummy has arrived, and the bloody woman has sacked the nanny, can you believe it?"

"Oh dear," said Anna. "And what does Cresta think?"

"Cresta adored the nanny and so she is naturally heartbroken, especially as Mother laid on a breakfast of kippers and porridge. I mean Cresta was weaned on Krispie Whatsits." Gilda beeped at a cyclist, who swiftly gave her the finger. "Cheeky sod! Granted, Nanny wasn't the best influence in the world, and there was her questionable habit of taking the children to her burlesque dancing classes but how am I to cope without her?" Genuinely vulnerable for a moment, Gilda let her head hang and closed her eyes when she stopped at the traffic lights.

"Gilda, the lights!" said Anna.

"Yes, all right," said Gilda, revving the engine. "Look, it's just one of those bloody challenges life seems to throw at me from time to time." Pulling up the car by Green Park, she turned to Anna. "This has got me thinking, though, it's time to take things to the next level."

"The next level?" asked Anna, feeling desperately in need of Alka-Seltzer.

"Yes, and I need you to help me." Gilda turned off the radio.

"How can I help?"

"Okay, firstly not a word to the others, except for Kate and Chrissy, we'll need their input. We need to plan our strategic moves carefully. I'm thinking New York, Paris, and Hong Kong," said Gilda, restarting the engine while applying lip gloss. "Oh look," she went on, pointing to Buckingham Palace. "She must be out."

Anna looked sideways at Gilda. "Who must be out?"

"Her Majesty, of course. When the sovereign is not present, the Union Jack flies instead of the Royal Standard," she said grandly.

"Okay ..."

"Anyway," said Gilda, "the point is that Adrian has just been given an enormous bonus from Credit Suisse, and so it is about time he spoilt me, starting with this little motor. What is the point of having an ex-husband otherwise? Well, almost ex-husband – I still have to deal with the paperwork."

"What about the children? You can't ferry them about in a sports car surely?"

"Lord, no. Mother has the Volvo. This little mover is all part of my new image." Gilda was getting brighter by the second. "What's more, I'm sure I can persuade Adrian to inject some cash into the business, considering he has just paid for his girlfriend to have a *lift*."

"A lift?"

"I'm talking about a bum lift, darling. Sara's could rival Mount Everest at this point!"

Anna giggled and Gilda grinned at her.

"Now," she said, lighting another ciggy, "what would you say to a little retail?"

The beauty department at Tinto Libby's was like a sweet shop to a child. Surrounded by heavenly murals and cherubs, with chandeliers overhead and assistants looking like angels themselves, it was a cocoon of every possible indulgence a body could want. As Gilda darted from one counter to another, brushes swept indulgent powders around her contours and designer tubes squeezed out luscious creamy swirls. Pampering was just what was needed to ease the stress of domestic complications. Sipping from a glass of champagne, Gilda sat down on a chair next to the threading bar.

"I've just booked myself in for a consultation with a lash stylist," she yelled over to Anna, who was in the middle of having primer applied to her forehead by a wispy model-like beauty specialist.

"What's a lash stylist?" asked Anna, feeling increasingly relaxed.

"They are going to assess my lashes and create bespoke mascara especially for me. Fabulous, don't you think? It's the lynchpin of all make-up, darling."

Anna moved on to her favourite make-up counter. Julius was there as usual with thick, black and immaculately shaped eyebrows. He was Anna's favourite cosmetics consultant and they squeezed each other's elbows with excitement over creamy blush and translucent foundations.

"So when are you moving to the new store on Sloane Street?" asked Anna, much too loudly.

"Shush," snapped Julius. "Ai 'ave not told my boss yet. Eet ees a secret."

"Oh bugger, sorry, Julius."

Most put out, Julius passed Anna on to a consultant with poker-straight hair from the neighbouring counter, who advised Anna that she had enlarged pores and only the application of vastly expensive cream could solve the problem. Noting that Anna was not so keen on a morning discussion of pores, a savvy assistant at the eye-sculpting counter fortunately overheard and took over. He dabbed and brushed and by the time translucent powder sparkled on Anna's brow bones she looked stunning.

HA HA

Just as she was just about to rejoin Gilda, who was surrounded by several bags of beauty products wrapped in gold tissue paper, she saw a man apprehensively approaching.

"Gilda?" he said.

"Oh lord, Adrian. What are you doing here?" Gilda said, slipping her glass of bubbly behind a cardboard cutout of a poodle wearing a tiara.

Behold Gilda's ex-husband, with grey tightly clipped hair, flushed cheeks, expensive tortoiseshell glasses and immaculate fingernails.

"I just popped in to pick up some cricket whites," he said, poking his finger into the collar of his shirt as if to let in some air. "Sara is hosting a charity match to raise funds for the local dogs' home."

"Is she now," said Gilda.

"And what about you?" asked Adrian politely, eyeing Gilda's glass of champagne behind the cardboard poodle. "Working hard, I see."

"Actually," said Gilda standing up, "Anna and I are here on official client business. Aren't we, Anna?"

Quickly stepping forward, Anna reached out to shake Adrian's hand as he nodded politely before turning back to Gilda.

"And you thought you'd have a glass of champagne while you shop, or should I say, work?" said Adrian.

"Still doubting me, aren't you, Adrian? We are meeting our client for lunch on the Fifth Floor," and checking her Omega classic, Gilda picked up her handbag. "And just look at the time, midday already."

"I think you'll find it's one o'clock, Gilda,' said Adrian, smiling a little.

"Yes, well," said Gilda, rubbing a blue fox-fur key-ring against her cheek, "I'm sorry, Adrian, but we'll have to catch up another time. Do give my love to Sara, won't you, and I do hope the stitches from the lift are healing."

"You always manage to stick the knife in, don't you, Gilda?" he said quietly. "Anyway, I'll be in touch about taking the children to St. Bart's for Easter, and it's only a matter of time before a string of complaints come in from Orlando's house master, I expect."

"He is spirited, that's all," said Gilda.

And for a few moments, they stood in silence, trying not to look at each other.

"Is Cresta sleeping all right?" asked Adrian.

"She still has Mr Bunny attached to her like a vice grip."

"And the nanny?"

"Oh Adrian, really, it's too early in the day to discuss such things. My mother's staying if you must know."

Adrian missed his children hugely and the fact that Sara didn't hide the fact that she was not keen on matters maternal didn't make having them to stay at weekends all that easy.

He nodded politely in Gilda's direction, "Goodbye, Gilda," he said and then he turned to Anna. "I recommend not ever getting divorced."

He then walked to the lift and pressed the button for the men's lifestyle department. His life had once run like clockwork and he'd had it all mapped out: a lucrative accounting career, a stunning wife, who was exciting and spontaneous, and would give him children. He had loved Gilda with all his heart. She was the yin to his yang. He arrived on time, she arrived late, she dressed in accordance to her moods while he had separate areas in their dressing room for work and leisure, linen suits in summer, tweed in the winter and always a Pringle V-neck at the ready. And now, Sara was making it clear that she wanted to marry him, though how she'd have time to arrange a wedding when she was on every committee possible from water voles to rare wild orchids was another matter. She showed little interest in his children except to dress them in practical outdoor clothes and arrange for them to go to midterm camps. Seeing Gilda again made him long for a little mayhem. He missed his family.

Gilda sat back down and drained her glass.

"What does Adrian do?" asked Anna.

"Adrian? He comes from a long dreary line of accountants." She took the lid off a tube of cream and shot a splodge onto the counter. "Adrian practically counts the peas on his plate, he's so obsessed with numbers. Mind you, he knows how to make lolly, I'll give him that. Now, speaking of making money, Anna, can you get Chrissy on the phone? I want a meeting with that fellow Greg from the *Telegraph*. It's time I made a big media splash and I'll show that ex-husband of mine that I'm better than any cheek-enhanced bimbo who likes cucumber sandwiches and cricket." Gilda stood up and shook her head from side to side, trying to remember what it felt like in the days when she had long, glossy red hair. "As for you, Anna, I need you to spark up. You are like a little rabbit, nibbling away at your projects. I need a cat! I want you to be a scratchy cat and to hiss at the opposition."

But Anna was staring at the screen of her phone, wondering whether to be over the moon or deadly nervous.

This is totally out of the blue and I know you haven't even invited me yet – but can we spend this weekend in Ireland – if you like the idea? XXX

Chapter 11

For Anna, flying out of Heathrow usually involved a long Tube ride from Victoria Station before shuffling down endless corridors to where her low-cost airline awaited. Today George arranged for her to be collected from her flat by a driver in a supremely comfortable Jaguar who took her to Heathrow. She was then guided to a VIP suite, which was a bastion of comfort with leather armchairs, cashmere cushions and marble floors.

Having gone through the pros and cons with Tilly, Anna had decided that accepting George's invitation was the only option. She tried her best to treat it all as casually as possible. Now here she was, slipping off her loafers and lying back on a sofa reading about the interiors of Lauren Bacall's Dakota apartment in *Vogue*.

George arrived just as a flight attendant was bringing her a cup of chamomile tea. He had a small bubble-wrapped painting under one arm and a bundled-up scarf under the other.

"There you are," he said, kissing her. "So wonderful to see you. Is everything okay?"

"All amazing, as you can see. I've been given the royal treatment."

Sitting down beside her, George kissed Anna's neck, running his hands inside her tightknit wool jumper. "You're wearing a lot of layers."

93

"March in Ireland? It's still pretty chilly, especially at our house. Dad always says hot-water bottles should be replaced by warm claret."

They looked at one another and George gently swept his arms around her and they kissed again with a tenderness neither of them had felt before. They were so lost in the moment that the flight assistant's only way of getting their attention was to knock on the door.

"So sorry to disturb you, Mr Wyndham. We're ready for boarding now."

"Thank you, thank you. We won't be a moment."

As he winked at Anna, she loved how natural everything felt. She was in first class. No, better than first class. She was with George, bringing him to visit her home, her world.

Boarding the plane and turning left through a thick navy curtain, she tried not to be too impressed, but she couldn't help but sigh with contentment when a glass of champagne was quickly placed into her hand by a very spruce blond male flight attendant who was much more interested in George than in her. Usually she was an edgy flyer, but with one hand curled into George's arm and the other nursing the champagne, she felt like a proper veteran of private air travel by the time they arrived into Ireland West Airport.

She also felt deeply excited at the thought of a whole weekend with George.

As they journeyed away from the airport in a convertible Golf, Anna gazed out the car window, seeing the hedgerow awakening to spring with hawthorn coming into leaf. George's hand rested on her leg when he wasn't changing gear. Putting down the window, Anna breathed in the damp afternoon air and watched George, so gorgeous with a grey woolly hat pulled right over his ears, his dark eyebrows peeking out, framing his face. They looked at each other and smiled, both knowing it was an exciting step.

"Wow!" she laughed, as George pressed a button on the dashboard that brought down the hatch. "Open air in Ireland!"

"It's my first time in this country and I don't want to miss a thing."

"In five degrees?"

"If I need to warm up, all I have to do is look at you."

"Nice line. Originally yours?"

"But of course. Gosh, these roads are narrow. Did Tilly seem surprised I was coming to Ireland with you?"

"Not really," said Anna, recalling how insistent Tilly was that it was 'totally the right time' to take George home.

Coldplay's 'Magic' began to play on the car radio.

"That song seems to be following us around," said George, turning up the volume. "Sofia's party seems like a long time ago now."

"I know," said Anna, longing to satisfy herself that George wasn't part of Sofia's inner circle. "I don't think she likes me actually." She wondered if she was right to bring up the conversation.

"Why do you say that?"

"Oh, just, you know, the way she looks at me."

"Well, I'd look the other way if I were you, which is what I'll be doing from now on. I was so bloody angry when I saw her at the Queen's Club last weekend."

"I noticed!" said Anna.

"Well, sorry, but I really felt strongly about it. She totally led Jamie astray at the *Violet Tiger* party. And I know it takes two, and all that, but she must have known how drunk he was."

"Hold on, George – but nothing happened between Jamie and Sofia, right?"

"Of course nothing happened, but that was only because Jamie passed out."

"Tilly doesn't know, I'm sure she doesn't."

"And we'll have to keep it that way. I'm sorry, Anna, there's nothing worse than getting caught up in other people's business. Let's just give Sofia a wide berth from now on."

"Agreed," said Anna, feeling relief that George didn't seem to twig that she had been drinking on a par with Jamie at the party and that she hadn't persuaded him to call it a night. "At least Tilly and Jamie are back on track now."

"She's very good for him," said George, "and Jamie's assured me that he's back on top of things."

"Well, speaking of being on top ..."

"Yes ..."

"Do you see the cows on top of the hill over there?" She was following her mother's advice that one should always know when to change the subject. "It's considered a good sign if they're standing up, a sign of warm weather, but if they're lying down then it's going to rain. At least, that's what Bernard says."

"Bernard?"

"Our gardener. He's been at Farley Hall for years."

Pulling the car into a gap in the hedge to let a tractor pass by, George stretched over to kiss Anna.

"Better?" he asked.

"Better," she said, knowing what he meant. They'd had the Sofia chat and George had confirmed that Sofia was not going to be a part of their lives. 'Wide berth' was the buzz phrase.

Shortly after they crossed the River Shannon, they drove into Drummare, a sleepy village with postcard-perfect buildings of whitewashed stone.

"There's Mrs Murray's," said Anna, pointing at one of the cottages. "It's a grocery, a bakery and a pub all rolled into one. Mrs Murray is still serving pints behind the counter at the age of eighty-four. Pretty good going, isn't it?" Nostalgia weaved through every inch of her body. "You can buy bread and milk there, eggs and sausages too – not your average pub."

"It certainly is not."

"We'll pop in there at some point."

"I like the sound of eggs and sausages. I've heard about the full Irish from Jamie. He's been shooting in County Meath a few times and I remember him talking about how the other fellows poured whiskey into their porridge to heat up their toes before taking to the hills. Jamie preferred to get stuck into black pudding and eggs sunny-side up."

"Do you shoot?" asked Anna. Butterflies raced around her tummy as they passed through what was known as the Five Road Cross, before turning onto an unkempt lane with a grass strip down the middle and tiny muddy stones either side.

"It was never my thing. Much to my father's dismay, I never had the killing instinct. I much prefer to see the birds plump and enjoying the countryside. I think it has much to do with my relationship with my father."

"Difficult?"

"Yes, but now is not the time to ponder such dourness."

"Quite right," said Anna. "It's the next turn, on the right, just here."

Turning the car in through the gates to Farley Hall, George could immediately see why Anna was so in love with the place.

"Look at this wonderful house," he said.

His eyes followed a long stretch of avenue ahead of them, with giant snowdrops and daffodils blooming on either side. At the far end was a three-storey Georgian beauty, standing tall and elegant, with chalky mustard walls, surrounded by sweeps of rolling lawns and old trees. He stopped the car by a huge beech tree on the curve of the avenue, and pulled out his camera.

"Don't worry," he said, seeing Anna's face. "I promise not to take photos all weekend. I just can't resist a beautiful shot."

And, pointing the lens at Anna, he took several pictures and was leaning over to kiss her when they were suddenly disrupted by a big, silky black Labrador who propped his paws up on the passenger door, barking in ecstasy.

"Guinness!" said Anna, shooing him away from the door so that she could push it open to let the dog bound onto her lap, big, panting and muddy-pawed.

"Well, hello there, Mr Guinness," said George, loving the sight of Anna being so happy to be home.

"And look, there's Penthouse!" She pointed at a chestnut horse, grazing some distance away. "Do you see him, George? Doesn't he look well?" Anna put the window down further. "Hello, my love!" she called out. "I'll bring you some Polos, won't be long!"

The horse continued to graze regardless.

"He doesn't hear me," said Anna, disappointed.

"Polos? As in Polo mints?" said George, rubbing Guinness's ears.

"Yes, horses love Polos, don't you know? You should hear the crunching sound, it makes me giggle every time – they even have minty breath afterwards."

"Well, just as well I have a good supply in my pocket then, isn't it?"

"Great! I threw a couple of packets in my case too – so Penthouse won't go short! Look – you see the rusty old windmill in the centre of the field? My grandfather had it installed in the seventies to power water into the drinkers for the horses."

"It sounds like he was a modern thinker?"

"Yes, though I think my grandmother would have referred to him as being more of a modern drinker! Something my darling father has inherited, as no doubt you'll find out."

Putting the car into gear, George drove on up the avenue.

"Oh George, I'm afraid you're rather in at the deep end," said Anna, when they saw a woman engaged in a yoga headstand on the front lawn, slowly bending her knees into her chest before lowering her feet to the ground and resting in a child's pose, "and I don't mean the lake, which is over there, you see, just down by the bank of trees?"

"Yes, I do."

"The thing is, when Mum is in headstand mode it usually means that she and Dad are rowing."

Pulling up in front of the house, George popped opened the car door and Guinness leapt off Anna's lap, scrambled over George and careered over to the woman on the lawn.

"Oh Guinness, you great big muddy monster!" said Freddie Rose, getting to her feet and reaching her arms up to the sky to draw a heart shape in the air. She was wearing a navy-blue leotard teamed with stripy legwarmers. Thick blonde hair swirled around her shoulders.

As George advanced to meet her, he remembered an article he had read in *Esquire* magazine, advising one to look at the potential mother-in-law before proposing to a girlfriend. Seeing Anna's mother further underlined his feeling that Anna was the girl for him. He could clearly see where Anna had inherited her large, expressive blue eyes and wonderful hair.

Light and nimble, Freddie crossed the lawn and neatly walked on the gravel in bare feet to give Anna, and then George, an enormous hug.

"*Namaste,*" she said, pressing her hands together with gold bracelets jangling on her wrists. "You are very welcome to Farley Hall, George. Now, let me look at you." Putting her arm around Anna's neck, she nodded approvingly. "Such lovely long legs, just what we need in our family."

"Mum ..." said Anna.

"Lovely to meet you, Mrs Rose," said George. "I've heard a lot about you."

"Oh no, George, you must call me Freddie. Everyone does. I haven't even been called Fredericka since I left London and came to this blissful place. Thirty years ago, can you believe it?"

Standing behind Anna, Freddie gently pulled her daughter's hair back from her face.

"That's how long we've been here, George, working hard to nurture and create but I can tell you this young lady is much the best thing we ever created."

"Mum!" said Anna, cringing.

"Hello, you lot!" said a man, stepping out the front door in yellow cords and a faded red polo-neck and walking towards them at speed. "Good to see you, darling," he said, throwing his arms around Anna. "Don't you look a sight for sore eyes!"

"George," said Anna, linking arms with her father, "as you can guess, this is my dad, Harry."

"Good to meet you," Harry said, giving George a vigorous handshake. "Ouch, that hurt! Sorry, I'm afraid I took my horse out yesterday and I am stiff as a board today." He slapped his thighs abruptly and then continued. "Penthouse likes a good gallop, but I'm afraid I'm just not as fit as I should be."

A little taller than Freddie, with a round bald patch, Harry had a smile that reminded George of Jack Nicholson.

"If you'd just let Dharma teach you some yoga stretches, Harry, you wouldn't have that problem," said Freddie.

"She's trying to turn me into a vegan, you know," said Harry to Anna. "And what do I say? No way, José! So she's drafted in Dharma to fight her battle. Can't see what on earth he's doing here anyway, except distracting everyone with his bizarrely bendy body."

Anna glared at both her parents, desperately hoping they weren't going to have a row in front of George.

"Oh Harry, come on!" said Freddie, hands on her hips. "This is my one chance to build a firm routine for myself, without the distractions of getting caught up with the blinking church fete or running a coffee morning or having the garden society chase me down for a garden tour. It's called 'Me Time', Harry, and Me Time is what I need."

"Sorry, George," said Harry. "How terribly rude we are. We forget ourselves. We are discussing Freddie's yoga guru, Dharma, who has arrived here from Sri Lanka and who, I have recently learned, is apparently staying with us for the entirety of the summer."

"Until July, Harry."

"And he is apparently going to transform my wife's life into one of heavenly equilibrium."

Harry was now holding both of Guinness's paws as he spoke, and pretending to dance with the dog.

"And within minutes of him being here, literally minutes, he introduced the most remarkably energising vibes to Farley. You have to admit that, Harry? You said it yourself."

"Did I? If you say so, my darling," said Harry dismissively. With new guests to entertain, he was much more interested in rustling up an early evening whiskey and soda.

"Remember, Harry, happy wife, happy life?" said Freddie, pulling on a pair of runners.

"Indeed. How could I not? So there we are now, George," said Harry. "A little insight into our curious world. We live in a constant stream of roundabout discussions but we muddle through, don't we, darling?" And with that he planted a large kiss on his wife's cheek.

Freddie shook her head and raised her eyes heavenwards but it was clear the row was now over.

"Now then, Anna," said Harry, "a hamper arrived for you this morning, stuffed with French cheese and champagne from what I could see. A second admirer, I wonder?"

"That sounds like a Gilda delivery," replied Anna, squeezing George's hand. "She's trying to persuade me to open an office in Paris for her."

"Paris? How amazing! And …?" Freddie looked at George.

"Come on now, there'll be plenty of time for all that career discussion later," said Harry, patting George on the back. "Not too early for a little snifter, is it, George? Shame you're not here for St. Patrick's celebrations next weekend – Mrs B lays on a proper old-fashioned feast, and I break out a nice bottle of Irish," and before George could get a word in, he went on, "The Irish are not unlike the French, you see, George, nothing we both like more than an afternoon tipple. You can spare him for an hour, can't you, Anna darling?"

"Of course, Dad."

"Then I'm going to take Anna for a walk, and, Guinness, you can come too," said Freddie defiantly and, turning to George, she said, "Try to keep my husband under control if you can."

"We'll be fine," said Harry, giving Anna a wink. "You take the air, Anna, and I'll give George a blow-by-blow rundown of the locality from the comfort of my armchair."

"All right, Dad, don't strain yourself now," said Anna, smiling, as George reached out to her and slipped a packet of Polo mints into her hand.

"For Penthouse," he said and, blowing her a kiss, headed indoors with Harry.

Feeling so in love, Anna went into the front hall and pulled on a pair of boots that stood next to an array of walking sticks and hats. Going back outside she found Freddie clearing dead leaves around the base of a huge pot of japonicas.

"You will be extra kind to Dharma when you meet him, won't you, Anna?" said Freddie. "It's his first time out of Sri Lanka and I want him to feel as at home as possible. Your father is so quick to pooh-pooh things – any mention of yoga or mindfulness and he switches off."

"Then I won't ask what Mrs B thinks of Dharma," said Anna. "We all know that she's not keen on your bendy yoga moves."

"Actually, Mrs B's being surprisingly good," said Freddie, linking arms with Anna as they walked with Guinness towards a series of steps leading down to a jetty on the lake, "and she seems to be slowly getting used to my morning routine of sun salutations on the landing. Oh, it's so lovely to have you home again, darling. Now tell me all about everything. Don't spare a single detail. In fact, let's start in reverse order. How is the ... you know?"

"Mum," said Anna grinning, "don't ask me that! But do tell me about you and Dad. You seem to arguing a lot these days. Pretty much whenever I see you."

"Which is how often, darling?"

"Well, often enough to know that you aren't getting on. I can tell."

"Just look at that gang of greedy ducks. They come and go as they please." Freddie was the queen of changing the subject. "And the wild garlic – those white flowers so thickly intertwined with the bluebells and marsh marigolds. The garden is going to bloom early this year. Just look at the celandine, and the red campion is practically blushing with embarrassment, like arriving to a party too early. So it's all rather topsy-turvy, isn't it? Which is how I would describe life at the moment, sweetheart. It all seems deliciously in place and out of place at once."

As Anna had returned to Farley feeling utterly happy and fulfilled for the first time in ages, she decided to let her mother lead the conversation.

"Now remember, Anna, you need to have lots of boyfriends. Have you had enough at this stage? That is the question. Even if it seems like George is the one, and he may be, you must keep an open mind."

"Really, Mum, you don't have to –"

"Think of it as shopping for clothes," Freddie said, hurling a stick into the lake for Guinness who splashed in after it. "You need to try things on, Anna, or take them for a test run, you know what I mean?"

"How I have missed your analogies, Mother," laughed Anna, watching the water ripples reaching the bank.

"Your father will soon be swimming again, of course."

"I love his May to September morning swims. He's always so rigorous about it, no matter what the weather."

"Yes, it's one of the few aspects of his life where rigour plays a part. Every year he looks more and more like a huge bear doing the backstroke. No wonder the fish stay hidden from sight most of the time."

Guinness dropped the stick at Freddie's feet and she threw it out into the lake again.

"When I met your father I was a devotee of Monica Dickens and Hendricks's gin, perfect companions for me in my little London flat. But then I gave all that up because your father was such a catch that he required my undivided attention to reel him in. Not that I pandered to him. Quite the opposite, in fact."

"I'm sure," said Anna, who had heard this story so many times before.

"He had this place, of course, but I'd never been to Ireland so it wasn't a huge draw for me. I was a good London girl but, gosh, he was so good-looking and a brilliant dancer. Not to mention the divine Lotus sports car he drove. Just the thought of those warm leather seats …"

"Mum, you've told me all of this before."

"Oh, I know, but I do like to talk about those days when your father and I … well, it was all so thrilling."

"And things now seem flat?" asked Anna, but Freddie didn't answer and Anna didn't press as they walked past the jetty and through the boggy wood in the direction of the windmill field. "Good to hear that Dad is riding again, though?"

"Yes," said Freddie, whimsically, "and you'd think that Penthouse, being a three-quarter bred with racehorse tendencies, would energise his creativity, but he still hasn't picked up a paintbrush. He's become lazy, Anna, and he won't even contemplate listening to Dharma's advice about seeking one's inner mentor."

"Dad was never going to go down that road, Mum, you know that. He still thinks of yoga as being all about carrot sticks and woolly jumpers."

"Well, he needs to modernise then," said Freddie, as they climbed over a fence. "I've spent years supporting him with his art, soothing his ego and encouraging him to keep going. I just feel the least he could do is indulge me in my new era."

"Maybe he's jealous of Dharma?" suggested Anna, as Penthouse whinnied, pricked up his ears and trotted towards them.

"No, that isn't the problem. In fact, I'm not even sure he finds me attractive any more."

Grinding to a halt next to Anna, Penthouse, a chestnut gelding with no markings except for a white blaze and a white sock, nuzzled her pocket.

"Are you searching for something, my sweet Penthouse?" said Anna.

"Oh Anna, think of his teeth!" said Freddie.

"But how can I resist?" said Anna, taking a Polo mint from the packet and giggling as Penthouse carefully hoovered it up from her hand. "Besides, how often am I here to share my mints with him?"

"That's true, and he's so pleased to see you, darling."

"Wait for the crunch ..." said Anna. "Yes, there it is. So, Penthouse, you'll now have lovely fresh minty breath for George when you meet him."

After a walk around the windmill field, with Guinness trailing behind crunching the occasional Polo mint, Anna and Freddie slowly made their way towards the house and, as they approached the kitchen garden, a woman with short greying hair, dressed in a blue apron, came flying out of the house, waving a stripy green tea towel behind a peacock with a raw pink sausage clamped in its beak like an oversized worm.

"Not this time and not in my kitchen!" yelled the woman, her face red and puffed. When she spotted Freddie and Anna, the woman shrieked, threw her hands in the air and crossed herself.

"Well, there she is! Thanks be to God – my sweet girl!"

And she began walking as fast as her short legs would carry her towards Anna.

"Mrs B!" Anna ran towards her.

They hugged and Mrs B held Anna's face in her hands as Guinness went after the peacock. He got just close enough to make it fly up onto the wall by the herbaceous border.

"Serves you right, you cheeky beggar!" said Mrs B, raising her fist at the peacock balancing elegantly on high. "Guinness, you're too polite. Next time I think you should take him by the neck!"

"Mrs B," said Anna, laughing and hoping she was joking, "don't encourage him."

"The peacocks are just extremely sensitive," said Freddie, who had already kicked off her boots and started into a headstand on the lawn. "Just like when they can tell you're plucking pheasants in the larder. What's for supper, Mrs B? Is it a bird from the freezer? I'm sure that's why they keep wandering into the kitchen."

"The larder is where those sassy peacocks should be themselves," said Mrs B, "strung up where the pheasants go during the shooting season, I'll be telling you."

Following Mrs B into the kitchen, Anna watched as she picked half a dozen potatoes out of a basket and, opening the Aga door, hurled them in like she was at a bowling alley.

As Guinness tore into the kitchen from the garden, George arrived in from the corridor with some gifts he had brought – two bottles of Veuve Cliquot, Fortnum & Mason fois gras and a small, smart-looking floral paper bag.

"Nice drink with Dad, George?" said Anna as he placed the items on the table.

"Yes, great, thank you. History of house fully recounted," he said as Guinness rubbed his side against his legs. Then he smiled at Mrs B and waited to be introduced.

"Now, Guinness, don't be a pest," said Mrs B, momentarily disarmed by George's broad smile. "What sort of way is that to treat our guest?"

"Mrs B, this is George," said Anna proudly.

Mrs B had seen it all over the thirty years since she first came to work at Farley Hall: Mr Rose toppling into hedgerows after a night of cards and a row of whiskeys, Mrs Rose getting stuck in the splits position on the landing at 5 am paying homage to her yoga mentor in Sri Lanka – and so on. She often wondered how Anna could be so normal, and now here she was with a good steady young man.

"I've heard all lovely things about you, Mrs B, including your fondness for lavender," George said, presenting her with the pretty paper bag which was tied with ribbon. "It's soap, handmade in Scotland."

"Thank you, George," said Mrs B, smiling shyly, holding the bag in both her hands. "And aren't I just in need of a new bar? Thank you." Placing the bag carefully on a shelf, she picked up a tea towel and turned to the sink, which was where she preferred to be. Standing back from the family but close to them all the same.

"Those beams are stunning," said George, looking up to the ceiling, which had lamps hanging in the centre.

"Yes, as long as they stay in that position," said Anna, remembering the last debate she'd had with her parents as to whether they'd need to put in support columns to keep the ceiling intact.

Then the kitchen door opened, and a man, maybe in his fifties, with breathtaking beauty, shining eyes and a big, wide smile peered around the door.

"Am I disturbing?" he asked.

"You must be Dharma," said Anna, holding out her hand. "I'm Anna."

"Ah, the daughter. Good to meet you."

"And Dharma, this is my friend George."

"*Namaste*," said George, bowing his head, "*Maalai vanakkam*."

"*Nandri*," said Dharma, who looked delighted with the exchange.

"I learnt a little Tamil through a Sri Lankan art dealer I worked with a few years ago," explained George. "Just the basics, you know."

"Well, I think it's very nice indeed," said Freddie, who had just come in from the garden.

"And do I hear that this is the first time you've been to this beautiful country, George?" asked Mrs B, impressed by his good manners.

"Yes, it is," said George, kneeling down to rub Guinness behind the ears. "And, as you say, the beauty is breathtaking." He looked pointedly at Anna as he spoke. She reacted by opening the fridge and putting her head in to cool down. George was making them all melt.

Chapter 12

Before supper, Anna and George sat out in the garden, wrapped up in woolly hats and puffa jackets, sipping on glasses of red wine. The evening was cold, but the air was still, and they watched the darkness creep over the drumlins, each field spilling into the other. Candles flickered on the iron table as George told Anna a funny story about the actor Richard E. Grant, who only realised he was famous when someone approached him in the gents' of a hotel and asked if he would pose for a selfie. Anna thought about the photographer snapping her the other day outside George's house. She hadn't mentioned it to him, in fact she hadn't even told Tilly about it. The photographer had made her feel a little timid. Was this a little taste of what life with George would be like? He certainly didn't encourage media attention. He drove an Audi estate, he came and went to parties without a song and dance, or at least this was how life seemed to be with him. But these were early days. She had read some online statements that he had made about high-profile art auctions. His opinions were occasionally controversial, especially in his denunciation of art sales out of the country despite instructions to the contrary by deceased owners. He was a man true to himself, Anna was sure of it.

When they were called to the kitchen for supper, Harry held

court at the head of the table, making sure to have George to his left for his good ear. Anna, Freddie and Dharma giggled frequently as Harry regaled them with his favourite stories of his time as an art student in London and Paris during the 1970's, while they all tucked into Mrs B's lamb casserole. Anna watched George smiling and laughing at all the appropriate places as he dutifully listened to Harry's ramblings. By the time Harry was halfway down the second bottle of Chianti, he was singing the praises of everything from German supermarkets to BBC Radio 4's *Woman's Hour*.

"Now, George," he said, searching for a cigar in his jacket pocket, "in the late nineties I started to see women dancing in the most incredible shoes. Remember, darling?"

"I do, my sweet," said Freddie, thinking of the nights they had spent in Annabel's on Berkeley Square.

"I read a study on high heels once," continued Harry. "Really quite fascinating how the heel brings out the elegance in a woman. It's all about the illusion of height, which in turn you can link to the perception of power and good breeding. Look at all the women ruling the world today. None of them would have got there without high heels."

"Dad, that's rubbish!" protested Anna.

"Okay, well, let me put it another way. The taller the woman, the higher they can reach."

"Oh dear," said Anna, looking at George, "that doesn't say much for me then."

"I often find the best things come in small packages," said George, with a deliberately cheesy grin.

"Yes, we say this too in Sri Lanka," said Dharma, enjoying the conversation immensely. "*Small in height, huge in wisdom*."

"Perfect," said George. "That is Anna to a tee."

"But seriously," said Harry, "the higher the heel the longer the leg."

Feeling buoyed up by several glasses of wine, Freddie was feeling restless and tired of Harry's garrulousness.

"Who's up for a little hen rescue?" she enquired, her face bright with anticipation.

"Oh Freddie," said Harry, arms outstretched, "come on! We're not ready for that sort of lark now. I was just about to move on to

Dalí. It's not every day that I have a fellow art buff in the house and I want to make the most of it."

George looked at Anna, wondering whose lead he should follow, but Freddie wasn't backing down.

"And I need to make the most of having some strong men in the house to help me catch those poor hens on the loose."

Harry thought about saying something but then changed his mind. He sat back, topped up his glass and put another wedge of Brie on his plate.

"Run free, my pretties – you'd better get to the ruddy birds before Mr Foxy Loxy gobbles them up."

Having wrapped up well, George, Anna and Dharma followed Freddie down a dark corridor that led to the yard. Just inside the door was a wicker basket full of torches.

"Help yourself, everyone," said Freddie, taking a bright yellow torch and switching it on as she walked outside. "Now, I spotted a half bald and dreadfully undernourished hen here earlier," she said, pointing to a battery henhouse built on the other side of the yard. "Believe it or not, George, that land – and that hen factory – does not belong to us. There's a stream running just this side of that shed and that is where the Rose estate now ends. So, you see, I have my hens out in a glorious run full of apple trees and daffodils while less than a hundred metres away our neighbour has umpteen thousand chickens all cooped up in that monstrosity. The contrast, George, is heartbreaking. I've tried to persuade the farmer to give them up but he won't budge. And so, every now and then, a lucky hen makes an escape."

George held Anna's hand and she felt exquisitely in love. She couldn't believe that he was there, at Farley Hall on a hen-rescue mission with her mother.

"The disparity between our hens pottering around their lovely big run and that prison of feathers gives me nightmares quite frankly,' said Freddie, with feeling. "Those poor battery victims."

Dharma was fascinated and walked close to Freddie. He was entirely unfamiliar with what sort of animals might be lurking in Ireland at night.

"Can you see her, George?" whispered Freddie. "Look, she's just over there by the ditch."

Slowly approaching the hen, George cornered her in the bushes and, taking off his jacket, threw it over the startled bird before gently lifting her up. As he held the squawking hen to his chest, Anna ran over to help him steady the bird.

"Don't worry, George," she said, "this lucky lady will soon be running around with our birds. We'll quarantine her for a couple of weeks in case she's contaminated. And once she gets the all-clear from our vet friend, who is a supporter of our hen-rescue missions, she can join the other hens and she'll feel like she's died and arrived into Hen Heaven."

Raising his hands above his head, clearly exhilarated by the rescue, Dharma called out, "*We shine like the full moon!*"

"Dharma, how lovely to hear your voice so strongly," said Freddie.

"The energy is strong tonight," said Dharma, holding the torch to his face so they could all see his infectious smile.

Walking back to the house, the hen-rescue heroes passed a small house with eaves.

The door opened and Mrs B popped her head out.

"Good evening, Mrs B," said Freddie. "Sorry to disturb you. George has just completed his first hen-rescue mission."

"There you are now, young man," said Mrs B, clapping her hands. "You've been well and truly immersed in the ways of Farley Hall now!"

Slipping into bed, George turned off the bedside light and Anna rolled into his arms. The moon, the cold outside, the warmth in bed, the deep and intense kisses as they made love – Anna had to almost inhale her sighs of utter pleasure. George was in her bed, in Ireland, and he wanted to please her in every possible way.

"George, what did I do to deserve you?" she asked.

"Oh, I can think of quite a few things," he said, sweeping a hand over her soft curls. He laughed aloud and then asked, "Are your parents on this floor?"

"No, just me, but I'm not in the habit of having, well, you know, guests, in my bedroom, so I'm just not sure how much they can hear."

"Well," said George, "we'll just have to keep testing ways to reduce the squeakiness of this bed, then, won't we?" And slipping his hand behind her back, he gently pulled her towards him and eased his way inside her.

The next morning George and Anna walked around the fields and then back up towards the garden, George talking about Saint Sulpice and how he longed to persuade the French Arts Council to complete its restoration. Guinness was also present and had taken on the role of chaperone, striding next to Anna every step of the way. He began to bark as he saw a figure emerge from behind a yew tree but quickly stopped. The figure was a man with a potbelly, sporting a check shirt and braces, with greying hair swept beneath a peaked cap. He was carrying a shovel.

"Oh great, there's Bernard," said Anna, waving to him. "He'll love to meet you. He's been working here for years, mostly in the garden but sometimes you'll find him up a tree or on the garden wall."

"Sounds like quite the stunt man," said George.

"Ah, how yeh doing, Anna? It's a pure joy to see you. How's life over there in London?"

"Terrific, thank you, Bernard. You're doing a great job here. I haven't seen the gardens looking so super-organised in a long time."

Bernard leaned upon his shovel and exhaled noisily. "Ah, the grass is running away with me, Anna. I'm trying to catch it with that ride-on machine but it's too wet. We're waiting for a bit of dry weather, then I'll be off and running again. I need that old horse of yours to mow up the avenue. That'd keep the grass down."

"Bernard, I'd like you to meet George. George, this is Bernard, the essential part of Farley, isn't that right? You're the engine that makes this place run."

"Ach, I don't know about that, Anna. And where are you from, George? Are you from the big city?"

"Scotland actually."

"Scotland? That's far from here, so it is. I'd like to go to Scotland someday. And you've no kilt on yeh?"

"It's too early in the day for a kilt," said George.

"I'd love to see you a kilt," said Anna, smiling up at her very own boyfriend. Everyone seemed to instantly adore him. "And here comes the rain, just look at that enormous cloud! We'd better run for it, Bernard – see you later."

"Aye, will do, Anna, will do," said Bernard.

Anna led George across the lawn to a large Weeping Ash and, pulling back the branches like a curtain, she ushered him inside. George felt like he had stepped into Narnia as they found themselves cocooned in this green cavern. He watched as Anna pressed her hand against the bark of the pale trunk.

"This was probably my favourite place when I was little," she said. "I used to stand here and make endless wishes."

"What kind of wishes?"

"Oh, you know, I'd wish for things like a freckly pony and a box of Belgian chocolates."

"Belgian chocolates no less?" asked George, watching her mouth as she spoke.

"They are the most delicious, don't you think?" she said.

George moved closer and pressed his hand over Anna's against the tree trunk.

"Anna."

"Yes?"

"I love you, Anna Rose. Every inch of you."

Anna smiled. "You do?"

"I do."

"So the tree really is magical after all. I always used to think so when I was little. And now I know so."

Brushing blonde curls back from Anna's face, George kissed her.

"*Anna!*" yelled Freddie's voice, at a high pitch from close range. "*Anna?*"

Anna looked at George and giggled.

"Oh God, my mother's timing! I'm so sorry."

"*Anna!*"

"I'm here, Mum," said Anna, parting the branches so that she and George could peer out at her mother like children from a tree house.

"Oh, there you are. Hello, George. Are you drenched? Listen, I need your help. It's got to go. I don't care – this time it has got to go."

Freddie was wearing yellow leggings and a stripy top. Her cheeks were red but her blue eyes looked like they were about to spill with tears.

"What has got to go, Mum?"

"Your father's artistic license. Please, can you come with me?"

Walking into the front hall, they found Harry standing over a large stuffed sea otter in a glass case.

"See what I mean?" said Freddie, her voice high-pitched and stressed. "This is Damien Hirst meets Stephen King's *Pet Cemetery*. Just look at the horrendous expression that dreadful taxidermist has given the poor otter!"

Anna and George looked down at the otter, its face frozen in an angry snarl.

"Really, Freddie, I think you're overreacting," said Harry, already exhausted by the conversation.

"They aren't vicious, you know?" said Freddie, turning to George in search of an ally. "You know, George, don't you? Sea otters are gentle, playful creatures, aren't they? So what on earth was the taxidermist thinking to make the creature look so furious? See how he has exposed the fangs."

"All I wanted to do was to put the otter on the sideboard in the dining room," said Harry.

"The dining room? It'll not be in the dining room of any house where I live. Do you want to put a complete downer on our dinner parties, Harry? Not that we have many of them these days, mind you."

"Ah yes, harping back to the old days again," sighed Harry. "Remember, remember, when we used to have fun?"

Sensing that the argument was moving into a new sphere, Anna needed to act quickly.

"Dad, maybe we could move the otter into your studio for now?" she suggested.

"And that way you won't have to look at it, Freddie?" added George, softly, trying to play the diplomat.

"Exactly, George. And maybe the otter can inspire some very trendy pieces on canvas?" said Harry.

"Oh, all right," said Freddie, "the otter can stay in your studio, but the next time Guinness catches something please can we just bury it in the compost heap and be done with it?"

"It's a deal," said Harry. "Ready to lift, George?"

"Ready," said George as he and Harry lifted the glass-encased otter out of the hall and out to Harry's studio in the yard.

"Well, Mum," said Anna, putting her arm around Freddie, "George is certainly getting an insight into how our family operates."

"Oh Lord, let's hope he doesn't make a run for it," said Freddie. And then she whispered, "But I don't think he will, Anna. I've been watching him closely and it looks like he's yours for keeps. I've a very good feeling about this man, darling."

Anna smiled but said nothing.

"And, by the way," said Freddie, warming up for some indiscretion, "you do realise your father is plotting to sell the wardrobe in the Oak Room to pay for your wedding?"

"Um, one slight hurdle there, Mum. No one has proposed as yet, have they? So maybe we should back up a little?"

"He's roped in Sir Gilbert," said Freddie, ignoring Anna's comment. "You might recall that it was Sir Gilbert who arranged for a replica of the wardrobe to be made for Ted Kennedy and shipped to the USA when you were a tot. So your father rang him out of the blue a couple of weeks ago and, within a second of mentioning the wardrobe, Sir Gilbert agreed to take it on to auction. He says it will make a small fortune."

While Anna digested this news, Freddie stretched one leg behind her, pushing her hand against the architrave around the large hall door. Anna marvelled at how her mother could almost have passed for a teenage dancer.

After lunch, Harry brought the visitors' book out to the front of the house and put it on the bonnet of George's car.

"How about a signature and then one for the road, George?"

"Harry, you are naughty," said Freddie. "Take no notice of my wayward husband, George. And make sure you come back to see us very soon."

"It was wonderful visit, Freddie – thank you so much."

Anna walked out the front door dressed in a long cardigan and

Ugg boots. Looking at George with her parents, she almost didn't want to interrupt.

"Look, there's Anna," said Freddie. "We'll leave you two to say your goodbyes."

She gave George a huge hug and then, taking Harry by the hand, led him into the house and closed the door.

"These are for you, George," said Anna, handing him a small package wrapped in parchment paper. "Roast beef sandwiches. It looks like you have Mrs B's seal of approval."

"I do hope so," he said, tossing the sandwiches onto the passenger seat before taking Anna into his arms.

"I'm sorry that we can't travel back together," said Anna.

"Me too, but look, next time we'll just vanish here for a week"

"Really? Even with my mad parents?"

"Yes, even with your mad parents. Will you be here for Easter?"

"No, Tilly has invited me to her parents' house in Wiltshire, but I'll be home mid-April. Maybe we can fly over together."

Neither of them wanting to say goodbye, they kissed until Guinness arrived and jumped up on them. Laughing, they parted and, as George got into the car and drove slowly down the avenue pursued by Guinness, Anna wondered if this was all a dream and hoped that if it was she'd never awaken.

Chapter 13

Landing in Terminal 5 at Los Angeles International Airport, Sofia walked down the steps of her father's jet to find a Porsche Cayenne hybrid awaiting her on the tarmac. A flight attendant was also on hand to lift her cherry-red Louis Vuitton case into the boot.

"The Linx Club, downtown," said Sofia, barely acknowledging the driver who was holding the door open for her.

LA was a city with a long history of making people believe in themselves and feel utterly fabulous. And yet Sofia was far from such positive feelings. She was certainly not optimistic about the new series, *Violet Tiger*, uncomfortable that she had only been cast because her mother had produced enough bundles of large green notes to put a down-payment on a house in the Hamptons. She was also nervous that the critics would pounce; as a famous *IT girl*, a term she could not bear, she knew they would examine every step of her performance under a microscope, and if they didn't like what they found she was out of the game. That was how it worked. The media were always hot and cold about her public extravagances. Hot, because people loved to know what designer label she was wearing, or whose yacht she was sailing on, or what takeout she got her 3am sushi order from. But then there were the scathing editors, who just couldn't stomach the flash, the bling and the squeaky sound of new money. But then, she had paid her way from the early days by being a success as a cute child face for advertising billboards. Her income at that time supported her parents while her father began to produce films, and she had to endure the make-up, the lights, the endless waiting around in humid waiting rooms for ad casting, while her friends in primary school played in the park, ate ice cream and skipped in their back yards.

Arriving at the Linx Club, the driver popped the Porsche's boot and took out her case. He then pulled up its handle so that all she had to do was hold and pull. She then paced at speed through the Renaissance-style lobby and summoned a lift.

"Good afternoon, Miss Tamper." The head concierge, Nordic-looking and exquisitely groomed, appeared at her side.

"Hello, Benedict," said Sofia, pressing her fingers against the bridge of her dark glasses.

"Is there anything I can help you with this afternoon?"

"No, thank you."

Taking off her glasses, she turned to the concierge who was at least a head shorter than her.

"I know the route. Fourth floor, first on the left."

He nodded as she reinstated her shades and stepped into the lift. Beautifully trained in the art of dealing with high-maintenance guests, he held the door and coughed a little.

"I'm afraid there is a problem, Miss Tamper."

"Problem?"

"I have been asked by the Club's executive secretary to … how can I put this … mention to the Tamper family that there is particular strain on the membership."

"Excuse me?"

"I understand your father has been difficult to get hold of, and so the situation has been brought to my attention, though it must be acknowledged that this is beyond my role as concierge."

Sofia raised her chin and pulled out her phone from her handbag.

"Is this some kind client liaison thing?" she said, flashing a fabulous smile, but he didn't return it. "Well, there is clearly some kind of misunderstanding regarding this so-called *situation*. I'll call Daddy from the suite, okay?"

Sofia delivered her line more as a statement than a question.

"If you're sure it will be sorted today, Miss Tamper?"

"I am," she said, as the doors of the lift closed.

Sofia didn't look in the lift mirror during the short ride to the fourth floor, afraid that she might cry if she saw the fear in her eyes. She didn't want to think about the rumours she had heard about her father during the past few months. Those people were jealous, nothing more.

Pushing the key card into the door, she picked up a *'Do Not Disturb'* sign from a table inside and rammed it on the door handle as she pulled the case in behind her. Flinging her phone and handbag onto the bed, she unzipped the side of her dress, feeling a powerful urge to release. Slipping the straps of her dress over her shoulders, she let it fall to the floor and then took off her push-up bra and panties. Opening the glass doors that led onto the balcony, she could hear jazz filtering down from the bar upstairs. She stood naked on the balcony, feeling the cool April air of LA on her skin. Closing her eyes, she stretched out her arms and wondered what the headlines would say if she were to topple over the balcony edge. She longed to break out, to dance, to get drunk, to let loose, but she had an invisible noose around her neck.

The party to celebrate her role in *Violet Tiger* had been painful. She knew the press were mocking her – she was about to tame a goddamn tiger, like some kind of female Grizzly Adams, when everything she'd ever talked about in her past interviews had been about how she was on the verge of becoming a tigress, securing her place on the casting agent's most-wanted list.

Feeling small raindrops on her face, she peeked her head over the Perspex balcony wall and looked down upon a kaleidoscope of bright yellow-and-blue cabs on the street, stuck in a jam, trying to get their clients to their destinations on time and yet most likely relishing the meter tick-tock-tick-tocking away.

Back in her room, Sofia opened the drinks cabinet and took out a vodka mini. Sipping from the neck of the bottle, she picked her phone up from the bed and pressed a button on speed dial.

"Ruby?" asked Sofia, putting on the loudspeaker.

"Yeah, sweetie?"

"I'm at the Club," said Sofia, standing in front of the long mirror, admiring her lean, bronzed body.

"In your usual suite, with that dangerous drinks cabinet?"

"You bet. Come on over?"

Standing by the lift in the Linx Club lobby, Benedict as head concierge recognised Ruby and approached with a fixed smile.

"Ah, Miss Beecham, may I enquire as to where you are going?"

"Tampers' suite," said Ruby, flatly.

"Indeed. You know the way? Fourth floor, first on the left."

"Indeed I do," replied Ruby, mimicking his voice, and as she stepped into the lift she blew on her nails as the doors closed.

Up on the fourth floor, Ruby knocked on the door of Sofia's suite.

"Hey, sweetie," said Ruby, kissing her on the cheek. "Are you okay?"

"Fine. Why do you ask? You look great by the way."

"Oh thanks, that's what a five-hour workout does for you."

"Five hours? Really?"

"And I can tell you it was worth it. Before I went to the gym I could literally feel the cellulite creeping across my thighs."

"No, I don't think so, Ruby. You're only twenty-six, for Christssake."

"Well," Ruby said, kicking off her suede heels and opening the fridge, "if you ask me, you can't take a moment away from looking after your body." She chose a bottle of sparkling water and poured it into a wineglass.

"Don't you even want a spritzer?" asked Sofia, tipping the remainder of her vodka mini-bottle into her mouth.

"No thanks, I like to keep a clear head. By the way, the concierge guy downstairs was really weird with me just now. He sort of stared at me when I said I was going to your suite."

"It's nothing. Some confusion with my parents' account."

"You're sure?" asked Ruby, who was suspicious by nature. "Also, did you happen to notice that you are totally naked?"

"I did," said Sofia, now lying on the floor next to the window with her hands resting behind her head.

"And?" asked Ruby, unbuttoning her shirtdress and sitting down on the bed above her.

"I've been waiting for you."

119

"I see."

Taking the sunglasses from her head, Ruby knelt on the floor as Sofia's phone rang from the bed.

"Oh man, does the phone have to ring at this moment?" said Ruby, grabbing it. "Want me to pass it to you?"

"No, cut the call."

Ruby pressed a button and the phone stopped ringing.

Sofia wriggled a little and looked up at Ruby with her naughty-girl face.

And then her phone rang again.

"Dammit!" She grabbed the phone from Ruby. "Hello?"

"Sofia!"

"Mom, hi. What's going on?"

"They came to the house this morning. They took all the files, laptops, and even my goddamn iPad. Everything. If it had a plug, they took it."

"Mom, wait, who? Who came to the house?"

"The FBI."

"What the hell? Why? Where's Dad?"

Sofia's heart was thumping.

"He's fine, Sofia. It's you I'm concerned about."

Sofia, on the verge of tears, barely noticed as Ruby slid down on the floor beside her and snuggled into her back.

"Sofia, are you there?"

"I'm here, Mom. What is happening?"

"We are not getting caught up in his mess, Sofia."

"I don't get it."

"Put two and two together, darling. He's been caught out, okay? It's a lot sooner than I expected but it's happened, and we need to distance ourselves."

"Mom, hold on just a second."

Putting her hand over the handset, she shook her head at Ruby and whispered, "I'm sorry, Ruby, you need to leave. I'll call you, okay?"

"Sofia, who's with you?" asked Blaire.

"Nobody, Mom, I'm home alone. Now tell me what to do."

"Let me stay, I can help," mouthed Ruby, but Sofia shook her head and pointed to the door.

"Get yourself on the next flight to London," said her mother. "Victoria is on standby for you. She will contact you, okay? And remember, she is the publicist, not you. Do not, I repeat, do not speak to the press. Word isn't out yet but it's only a matter of time. They'll do all they can to trip you up. You know what they're like."

"Mom, what about money?" asked Sofia, as Ruby looked back at her anxiously before closing the door behind her. "The concierge in the Club said there was some sort of problem with the membership. Is this the knock-on effect?"

"I'm trying to work it out, okay? Your UK account will be okay for now but for God's sake don't go on a spending spree. This is extremely complicated and it could go either way."

"Mom, before you go can I just –"

But Blaire hung up before Sofia got to ask about her father and whether there was any chance that he might be arrested. What now? Her mind was racing. She had flashbacks to strange people arriving to the house late at night, when she was a child. Her ears pressed to the big door of her father's office at home, listening to the sound of corks popping and grizzly laughter. Men making big deals, she thought to herself. That was what her father did and that was why she got to fly where she wanted, when she wanted, in her own plane, dressed as she pleased, with whom she pleased, how she pleased. Was all this about to end? She went to the fridge and pulled out two more mini-vodkas, twisted both lids off and drained the first bottle in a mouthful.

Her phone rang and Victoria's name flashed up.

"Sofia, I've spoken with your mom and I gather you've talked with her also. So, as you know, it's all about to hit the fan. Tough going, sweetheart, but stay chilled, I've got this. I'll ping you an email in a mo with an itinerary. The jet's chartered for London Gatwick tonight and I need you to go straight to Cadogan Square. I'll call you there, okay? It's hot here, Sofia, so have your shades at the ready."

"I always do," said Sofia, buoyed by Victoria's sense of control.

"Good for you. Speak soon. And Sofia?"

"Yeah?"

"Stay away from the carbs and the booze, especially on the

121

flight. We need you looking better than ever before for the next phase."

At home amid the greenery beneath Hollywood's iconic sign, Max Tamper pulled off his tie and carefully placed his empty Hugo Boss briefcase by the staircase. He thought about the irony of the street being named after Henry Gaylord Childer, a man who made and lost fortunes in real estate and goldmining. Now they could add fraud and embezzlement to the list of white-collar crimes associated with the zip code. Walking into his study, Max rubbed his hands over his balding hairline and sat at his desk. With sweaty palms and bulges of flesh uncomfortably spilling over his belt, he opened the document his lawyers had sent detailing the bail terms. The plea was out for him to stand trial in England as he had a British passport, which made him almost chuckle as his mother from London's East End always told him he'd be grateful one day to have an English mother even though he did his best to distance himself from his working-class roots. From the moment he landed on American soil, he felt he belonged there and being the sole heir to his late uncle's house out in the outskirts of LA had been a good start.

He surveyed the long line of photographs of him and Blaire posing with Hollywood stars, documenting his rise as a lucrative producer. Side-tables glittered with awards and crystal trophies with an entire wall made up of a glass-fronted cabinet crammed with key rings, T-shirts, toys and every possible kind of promotional gadget from his movies. There was no Oscar, but then Max knew he didn't deserve one. His career had begun with a chain of video stores before he slowly crept into the movie-production business. When he managed to raise $600 million from private equity firms to found White Bear Pictures 2000, the whole of Hollywood sat up. He was a force of persuasion and, as he said to his investors, "Get big or get nothing," and this was his mantra. And he had gone big. There was the superyacht, the Caribbean island, the Miami apartment, the Porsche and the Amex Black Card, along with lavish three-day parties on private islands to celebrate landmark anniversaries, including his sixtieth birthday in Mustique last year. The Tampers had the best of everything.

Constant holidays, relentless shopping, front-row seats at every première, sneak previews at the latest designer seasons, diamonds, convertibles, perfumes, show horses, private boxes, private planes, the whole damned lot.

Max always had an inkling that his corrupt dealings would eventually lead to trouble but, seeing his wife and daughter thrive upon his spoils, he could never have afforded to play things straight. Now he was about to lose it all. He was going broke. It was just a matter of time before the bank processed the paperwork and all his properties would go under the hammer. The beauty of his Porsche dashboard was about to be transformed into the crammed metallic confines of a prisoner transport van. At best, his future would involve a small rented apartment some place, but no chauffeur and certainly no maid. Maybe he might be able to scrape enough for a car.

He had always used other people's money to get ahead but now the game was up.

In the kitchen, Blaire was cutting red peppers into long thin slices and one by one dropping them into a wide-rimmed salad bowl. She had heard the front door open and the door to Max's study close, but she'd stayed where she was. A stiff drink before they talked could only improve things. She'd known this day was coming and somehow she didn't feel so much a sense of shock as, strangely, relief. She had never really loved Max but he had been her ticket out of England, a place she desperately needed to leave at the time. He had found her trailing around a bar in the East End, accepting occasional drinks from strangers and turning down offers of a bed for the night. Max was different though – he had a proper sense of purpose and a hunger for success that Blaire could identify with – and so it began with a whiskey and ginger by the bar, and within days Blaire had latched onto his shirttails and they were both poised to begin the climb up the Hollywood ladder, using her beauty as collateral and his talent for sharp thinking.

Max was delighted by Blaire's pregnancy, even though they discovered it only weeks into their relationship, and being an old-fashioned guy their first port of call was a wedding in Vegas, funded by his savings. Blaire suggested it might be wise to spend their money on more practical matters including new clothes for when she shook off the baby weight but Max insisted on "doing the right thing".

Over twenty-eight years later, Blaire was about to realise what had been her intention all along, though she hadn't ever intended to be forced into it for financial reasons. She excelled in the role of the perfect wife for a minted producer, chatting up the directors and sponsors, hosting charity functions to increase Max's profile and later raising their daughter to be an independent dynamo. Within a few short years, her private address book read like a Hollywood fairytale: the Governor of California, the directors of Paramount, Disney, Twentieth Century Fox and a dozen other studios, vineyard owners, fashion moguls, members of the British and Italian aristocracy. Her social life was vibrant and potent.

In recent months, things had slowed a little. People were starting to suspect that there was something not quite right about Max's excessive spending and outlandish IOU's. And now someone had finally pulled the trigger. She didn't know who had called the FBI. She didn't particularly care. She had been waiting for a knock on the door for several months and a plan she had always kept in the back of her mind was looking like the only answer. Socially she was now dead weight in LA. Not one person had reached out to help, but she distrusted most of their friends anyway. She was the only person she could rely on.

Chapter 14

It had taken most of the morning for Gilda to shake off the shock of April Fool's Day, her daughter Cresta having dug up two fat slugs in the garden and presented them to her on a buttery piece of brown bread for breakfast.

Lying back on the sofa in her office, with her gold runners bouncing on top of a bright orange Mr Hopper ball, Gilda raised her latte like a glass of champagne at Anna, who walked by the open door.

"This is fabulous, darling!" she shouted out. "It's toning my thighs and requires incredibly little effort."

"Sorry, Gilda, what did you say?" asked Anna, ducking back, distracted by thoughts of George and where she could afford to take him for dinner this evening. So far he had footed the bill for everything, including the flights to Ireland.

"So much easier than the gym, darling, and I can hold my skinny latte and iPad at the same time." Swiping the headlines on her iPad, Gilda squeaked when she read, **Tamper-ing with Hollywood Could Lead to the UK Slammer.**

"Anna! Holy hell!"

Anna closed the door and, stretching her arms up to the ceiling to realign her back after a bedside romp with George, she looked at

Gilda, wondering what was up.

"No need to look so uptight, darling," said Gilda. "I've just found a story about Max Tamper in the newsfeed. He's up for fraud, millions apparently. Been cutting off large percentages from funds raised for movies. All sounds very crooked."

"Sofia's father?"

"Exactly. Right, no doubt about it, we need to rethink our ambassador for Spicer Tweed. We can't possibly risk it."

Anna tried not to look pleased about that, and it wasn't that she was but she couldn't help but feel a tiny bit of relief that Sofia's perfect world was flawed.

"And I know you are not a fan of Sofia's," said Gilda, pushing away the orange ball. "Lord, my thighs – they feel tighter already."

"You were saying, Gilda?" said Anna, who was feeling defensive.

"What I mean is that it's no secret that you are not keen on Sofia Tamper, and so you may have your way after all."

"Gilda, come on, that's not true," said Anna, kicking Mr Hopper to one side.

"Really? Anyway, let's get to the here and now. Get Lavinia de Vere Parker's people on the phone. Sort it out, darling, will you?"

"What do you mean, sort it out? What exactly am I supposed to do?" asked Anna, unusually impatient.

"The role of ambassador, darling. We need dear Lavinia to pull out the rouge and all the stops. There's no way she'll turn down the opportunity to rev up her publicity machine, so make sure her agent realises this is a golden opportunity for Lavinia to score some double-page spread decked out in Spicer Tweed's finest kit."

"Fine," said Anna, still grumpy. "I'll be at my desk."

"*Kate!*" roared Gilda, "*Kate!*"

"Sorry, Gilda," said Kate, running into her office, cheeks pink and excited. "I've just had my cousin on the phone. Christmas this year will be a stonker, a huge family gathering in Val-d'Isère."

"Now look, Kate, if you want to stay on this team you need to think about putting as much effort into your clients as you do into booking your skiing holidays."

"Yes, Gilda," said Kate, trying to give the impression of being like an immaculately trained spaniel.

"And let it be known that I am not keen on the phrase 'stonker'."

"Understood, Gilda," said Kate, standing up super-straight.

"And what's more, if I don't see an improvement in your concentration levels, you'll be thinking about the festive season full-time, as you'll be asking Father Christmas for a new job, are we clear?"

"Loud and clear, Gilda."

"Now, what are you wearing?"

"What? These!" she said, doing a twirl in a pair of Spicer tweed trousers, and a waistcoat lined with lime-green silk. "Desmond sent his assistant to take Chrissy's and my measurements when you and Anna were in Bristol with Thermidor."

"I must say," say Gilda, standing up, "that really is rather fabulous, and makes me think about the Parisian launch for the brand."

Kate could see Gilda's mind whirling with ideas.

"Right," Gilda said. "I need you on the next flight to Paris and I want you to wear that suit. Pop into the Ritz and check out the ballroom and check availability for a launch on a Thursday in August."

"Wow, okay, Gilda, that all sounds smashing. Any Thursday in August?"

"As long as it's a Thursday in August," said Gilda, dismissing Kate with her hand like she was pulling a cobweb out of the air. "And now I've got to deal with Martin. Can you believe he wants to feature in *Time*? Says he's prepared to pose naked for *Esquire* too. What planet, I ask you?"

"Planet Mandy?" said Chrissy, bumping into Kate who was racing over to her desk, full of *ooh-la-la's* with the prospect of her first business trip on behalf of Winterbottom PR.

"Well, it's one I'm keen to sidestep. The only bugger about it is that we need his business." Gilda kicked the Mr Hopper ball into the side of her desk, knocking over a bright pink orchid. "Oh woops! That can't be good – better get the Feng Shui expert on the phone."

As planned, a double-page feature had appeared in the *Daily Telegraph magazine* with an expertly worked-out headline: **Winterbottom at the Top:** *At 53, Gilda Winterbottom is having the* *time of her life – and now she's going global.* She had been expertly styled into a vision of chic, wearing an emerald-green figure-hugging Dior dress that flowed with the contours of her body and a pair of green gemstone earrings, her red hair perfectly coiffed into a side-parting that Gretta Garbo would have been proud of. Gilda looked younger than her age by miles; it was exactly the look she wanted. An immediate result was a call from Martin Horne, thrilled with Gilda for mentioning Thermidor International as being a favourite client and, as a result, Martin signed the contract for another two years of Winterbottom PR guidance.

"*Chrissy!*"

Kate and Anna looked at each other. It was like a mini-convention to answer Gilda's to-do list, and everything was very urgent – Gilda's world would collapse if immediate action was not seen to be taken.

"Chrissy, about time."

"Sorry, Gilda, I was dealing with a delivery of chefs' costumes."

"Oh good. We'll deal with that in a moment. In the meantime, I think we need a repaint – my office is looking terribly old. Can you sort it, sweetie? Oh and Anna, before you dash out, can you deal with Martin?"

"Oh yes," said Chrissy, looking flustered. "I meant to say. He's looking for a pair of tickets for Wimbledon, centre court."

"More than that," said Gilda, "he wants a face-to-face update on what he calls the Chef with the Hottest Tail competition. He has to meet the head honchos of Thermidor and let them know how the marketing plan is going."

"If you don't mind me saying, though, Gilda, he did seem keener on the idea of Wimbledon. But it's April now, and so the chances of snaffling tickets for centre court will be minimal."

"That Martin, I tell you, he just wants to bring floozy Mandy with him, I just know it." Gilda stood up and lifted a mug with '*I'd Rather Be Drinking Champagne*' across the front. "Let's have a coffee, shall we, darlings? And biscuits, Chrissie. We need to energise, we need sustenance, don't you agree? Let's fill the tank and then get motoring."

Chrissy paused. "Chocolate?"

"Chrissy, what is the matter with you?"

"Would you like chocolate biscuits or plain, Gilda?"

"Neither, actually. Macaroons. Yes, let's order some from the pâtisserie just beside the National Gallery. That will help us to focus on Paris, not to mention the launch this evening. Now, Anna and Kate, are we all set?"

Renaissance cherubs sat neatly above the doors into the French Salon of Claridge's as Gilda stood at the podium surrounded by the luxuriant blue shades of the set behind her. She was wearing black drainpipe trousers and a fitted pink jacket, teamed with a silver belt spelling SEX in large letters.

She tapped the microphone.

"*One, two, three, are we ready to par-tee?*" she said loudly.

Anna and Kate put their thumbs up in Gilda's direction, while they smiled at curious journalists, most of whom had come to the launch because it was six o'clock on a Thursday evening and champagne was promised, along with taxi rides home.

"This evening, ladies and gentleman, members of the respected British press, I am beyond thrilled to exclusively announce to you that we are taking luxury toiletries to a whole new level!" Gilda waved to Anna to encourage her onto the stage. "And it is with great pleasure that I welcome you here as we launch the must-have luxury product of the year: *Helloo Roll!*" She eyeballed a reluctant Anna to hurry up and get on stage beside her. "Trust me, this is a two-birds, one-stone scenario. I want to introduce you to a whole new bathroom experience. We are talking loo paper with news, and even better, celebrity gossip! Helloo Roll!"

Anna reluctantly held a length of loo paper over her head like an air-hostess showing the cabin how to fasten a seatbelt as journalists struggled to keep their faces straight and attempted to take notes, knowing the wrath of Gilda if they showed any form of amusement. And, to be fair, they all agreed there was no one in the PR business as good as laying it on as Winterbottom PR. To be on Gilda's contacts list held rewards from reviewing six-star hotels to theatre tickets in the West End and shopping trips to New York.

Having spent the past week persuading journalists to attend the launch, Anna was cringing and knew that securing any coverage was going to be more than difficult. She had spent the previous evening making a list of possible storylines, which she could feed to the press afterwards as they wolfed canapés and guzzled Claridge's house wine. *Whose loo is it anyway? What does your loo say about you? Snobbery in the lavatory. Do you judge people by their loos? Are you loo-sing your mind? You snooze, you loos? Studies show that keeping the latest news reviews and magazines in the loo can increase your IQ level.*

"Each sheet will feature a celebrity profile, informing you of the latest exploits in their personal and professional lives: the Helloo Roll Celebrity Edition! The Galaxy Hotel chain is already signed up to run the special-edition loo paper in their deluxe suites, and all with three-ply aloe-vera-fragranced tissue to soothe the skin, ladies and gentlemen. And as part of the launch of the Helloo Roll Celebrity Edition, we are thrilled to present *Poetry on the Porcelain*, featuring insightful verses from actors, models and key opinion-leaders such as Louise King, who recently spoke out about her desire to improve the nine-to-five week. And each month, on the A-Class Helloo Roll, a soap star will feature."

A man, who looked far too old to be on the journalism trail, approached Anna. "This is all terribly interesting – and you are?"

"Anna – I'm Account Manager at Winterbottom."

"Ah, and have you been working with Helloo Roll for long?"

"Not terribly – since January?"

"What I'm angling at is – perhaps you and I could discuss the branding further over a –"

"I'm so sorry, I didn't catch your name," Anna cut in, terrified of what he was going to suggest.

"Nigel."

"Nigel, I'm sorry but I have to arrange cars for some other journalists."

"I was going to suggest a lemonade – perhaps I could take you out for a lemonade sometime?"

Feeling a creeping sensation down her spine, Anna smiled at the man in the brown corduroy jacket, and hot-stepped it to the lobby, where she found Gilda with her hand on her forehead.

"Gilda, what's happened?"

"It's not working, Anna. It's just not working."

"What isn't working?"

"I had set up a three-way screen call with editor of the *Luxury Times*, but he is ignoring my calls. No one ignores my calls. I'm losing my touch, I know it."

"No, Gilda, just hold on," said Anna, catching the attention of a passing waiter. "A ham sandwich and a glass of wine please, and fast as you can."

"And mustard on the side," said Gilda.

"Yes, mustard on the side, please, fast as you can," said Anna, nodding at the waiter as he moved away from them at speed. "Gilda, I think you just need to eat – you must be exhausted. Honestly, you've been chatting to journalists from the *Pharmacy Times* to *Lavatories Weekly* all afternoon – it was a busy launch. It was a successful launch – all the titles were there."

"The joke's on me, Anna. I should have taken Adrian's name."

"What?"

"Hamilton, if my name was Gilda Hamilton they would have taken me more seriously this evening, but instead I could see them in stitches. I even heard one little wretch say 'Imagine wiping your Winterbottom with Helloo Roll!' The cheek of it, you see? There's just no getting away from it."

Chapter 15

Blaire Tamper felt utter relief to find that she had enough air miles with her travel agent to book a first-class ticket to Glasgow Preswick International. The banks had frozen all of Max and Blaire's bank accounts and it was only a matter of days before Sofia's allowance would come to a grinding halt. Not wanting her daughter to see her in a position of weakness, she needed to get Plan A into action as fast as possible. Taking a taxi from the airport, she wondered what it would feel like to see the River Garvin after so long. She had achieved an almost unbelievable amount since she last put foot on Scottish soil and since then her parents had passed away and so all family ties had gone.

Driving up the avenue to Rousey, Blaire checked the position of her hat in her compact. Dressed in a black stretch-wool dress beneath a fur-lined coat, she knew she was looking her best.

She glared out the window, feeling cheated that she had been away from Scotland since she became pregnant with Sofia. The big house was as imposing as ever, but things were different now. For Blaire, the end goal was at last in sight. Robert had been in love with her, and she could have made him happy. And now it was time for Blaire to have it her way, and she knew just how to go about it.

Raking gravel in front of the house, Finlay MacLeod, with squinting eyes, tried to identify who was in the taxi. He walked to the car and, making brief eye contact, quickly realised who she was. He hadn't thought of Blaire's father, the damned poacher, for years now.

Blaire, determined not to display any emotion at being back in Scotland, looked away. She was remembering the old days too, when she walked along the River Garvin, deeply in love, and hope, with Robert Wyndham.

"Blaire," said Finlay, opening the door of the taxi.

"Hello – Finlay, isn't it?" she replied in her acquired American accent as she got out. "Well, you've certainly been around a long time. Never had the desire for pastures new?"

"No, Grace and I are very much at home on Rousey estate," he said, feeling very sceptical about her.

"Oh yes, Grace. I had forgotten. Still pottering around the kitchen of the Big House, is she?"

"Runs the place smoothly, she does," said Finlay, defending his dedicated wife.

"Well, I mustn't keep you from your chores, Finlay. Good to see you. Oh, don't worry about my luggage, it can stay in the taxi for now."

Walking into the hall, Blaire slowly walked by the oak-panelled boot room and couldn't help but stop and walk into the room, which had an array of old Barbours, walking sticks, riding hats and boots, epitomising the privileged landed country set once entertained at Rousey during its glory days. Blaire thought bitterly how she could have been part of all that and by now she could have been a good shot, the kind of woman who could handle a gun, a horse, maybe even ride to hounds.

Taking off her leather gloves and returning to the hall, Blaire found herself beneath wide-eyed deer with delicate antlers peering down from their trophy heights. She picked up a framed photograph from the sideboard and rubbed the sleeve of her coat gently across the glass. It showed Robert walking up the main stairs in his hunting pinks, while a rather stern-looking young woman, who must have been his wife Gussy, pulled on her long boots sitting on a wooden bench, with a great big blonde Great Dane lying at her feet on a beanbag. They looked almost like a normal happily married couple.

Following the scent of smoke and whiskey, along with the noise of a television, Blaire walked along a dark corridor lined with Lionel Edwards prints and came to a door, half open. With her heart thumping and sweat seeping, she pushed it open to find a room with the shutters half closed and a cloud of swirling, grey cigar smoke rising above the television.

Raven and Arthur, two big black Labradors, leapt up from their baskets and barked enough to make Blaire take several steps back.

"Shut up, you pair," snapped Robert, making no attempt to reach for the remote to lower the volume. "George, is that you?" He was sitting deep in an armchair that was more like a throne with winged sides, blocking his view unless he made an effort to lean forward, which he did not.

Blaire tried to control her breathing and for a moment she thought she was going to be sick. This was not the scene she had been expecting. Straightening her neck and remembering what was riding on this visit, she bit the bullet.

"Robert," she said, with strength in her voice, "it's me."

After a moment or two, Robert reached out for the black remote control, his finger searching for the pause button. A young thoroughbred, foaming at the bit, froze on the television. And, as Robert leant forward, he very slowly turned his head and looked like he had seen a ghost. He had what looked like dried egg in the corner of his mouth, cheekbones pink and dry, his eyes squinting.

Blaire walked forward, the dogs silent now that Robert was involved and, with as much confidence as she could muster, she opened the shutters of the study, making Robert wince at the daylight.

"Don't you have recycling in Scotland?" she asked, as she lifted a tray from on top of the Super Ser and placed it on a sideboard, which was covered in several months of newspapers. Plumping up a cushion on the sofa, she made sure her skirt reached her knees perfectly as she sat down, positioning her ankles like the royal family always do.

She looked at Robert's red-veined cheeks – he was jowly, a little bloated, short of breath, slightly bloodshot eyes. He had gone to seed. He was still wearing a tweed shooting cap.

They sat in silence for at least five minutes and then, breaking the stalemate, Grace arrived in with a tray of tea and shortbread.

"Mrs McCleod," said Blaire, remaining sitting, "I don't think we've met before."

"No, we have not," said Grace with a sniff, placing the tray on the low coffee table. But Grace knew about Blaire all right, for Finlay had been forced to lie to Mrs Wyndham, God rest her, during Blaire's affair with Robert,

"I see housework may not be your forte?" said Blaire, looking pointedly at the piles of newspapers and sticky bottles of tonic water.

"I do what I'm told, and Mr Wyndham doesn't like this room to be touched."

Robert, still mesmerised, stared at the fireplace.

"You'll understand that after such a long journey from the United States I might prefer a glass of vodka and ice," said Blaire.

"Is that right?" asked Grace.

"It is right," said Robert firmly.

"Well, then, I'll go and fetch a glass."

"And a twist of lemon," said Blaire.

"Will that be all?"

"Get on with you, Grace!" barked Robert.

As Grace closed the door behind her, Blaire realigned her skirt. She looked at the worn carpet and the tired walls, which looked as neglected as Robert.

"Remember when you saved me from the bull, Robert?"

"Of course, I do," he said, his voice shaking. Blaire was still as beautiful as the day they first met. Wiping his eyes, he held the palms of his hands together.

"Your hand, Robert, what happened?" asked Blaire, taking in the scarring around the base of his thumb.

"A missed fire," he said, splaying out his fingers. "It's nothing." Feeling emotional for the first time in years, he sat forward, the knees of his cords grey with cigar ash. "You did understand, didn't you? Why I had to stay married to Gussy?"

"You loved her," said Blaire. "I can understand that."

"No. I had a fondness for her in the early days, but you know it didn't last and fondness wasn't what I wanted."

"Wasn't it?" asked Blaire, teasing out the truth.

"It was you, Blaire. You were the one I wanted. You know that."

"And when you pulled the trigger, Robert?" Blaire wasn't going to leave anything to chance. She needed to arouse all the drama and emotion she could if this was to work.

"The bull was only a couple of feet away from you. If I hadn't been out shooting that morning, God only knows what would have happened," said Robert, his eyes wide and staring.

"But, Robert, you were there," said Blaire, leaving the sofa to kneel down beside him. "I remember how I shook when the bull fell. I will never forget how you held me." She reached for his hand. "You saved my life then … and now I need you to do it all over again."

Robert wiped the sweat from his upper lip. Blaire could see that the whiskey had taken its toll. For a man of sixty, he was in bad shape.

"I visited you sometimes," said Robert, "you know, in my dreams. It was the only place I could reach you. When I think back to the days when we lay on the riverbank, feeling free as wild salmon."

She looked at the Peter Curling originals on the walls, curtains in tatters. A room dedicated to racing, to whiskey and more than anything else, to self-pity. It looked like the shutters hadn't been fully opened for months.

Blaire's expression didn't waver. Her eyes were teary as she clutched his shaking hand.

Robert thought back to the afternoon when he had to call off their affair.

And now she had returned. Blaire Davies.

"*Christ!*" Robert shouted out, clenching his fists and grimacing. "Did you love him?"

"Love who?" asked Blaire, trying to keep Robert calm. She needed him to stay calm.

"Tamper," said Robert.

"Of course not. You were the only one. You know that, don't you? You have to listen to me."

"You must have loved him!"

"Listen to me!" she shouted. "I am here. I am here to tell you that she's your daughter, Robert. She's yours." She sank down and put her cheek on his knee. "Sofia," she whispered, "she is your daughter."

Blaire smiled and felt almost god-like, knowing this was what Robert had waited twenty-eight years to hear.

"Sofia is our daughter?" he said, bursting into tears. "I always knew!" Standing up, he put his hands on his head. "Deep down, I knew it. When I read about you and Tamper in those magazines, Christ, all those pictures of you playing happy families. I knew we had created something, you and I."

Blaire jumped as the door opened. It was Grace, returning with a glass of vodka, and a lemon, which sat with a knife in a small bowl.

"She can bloody well add her twist of lemon," Grace had said to Finlay, who was eating a piece of ginger cake in the kitchen. "The cheek of that woman. Twenty years at least younger than me. Who does she think she is, Finlay?"

"She's come back for something," said Finlay, "that's for sure, it is."

When Grace left the room, Blaire walked to the drinks cabinet and found a finger of whiskey left at the bottom of a bottle. Pouring it into a glass, she planted it in Robert's hand.

"And you're telling me now," he said, coarsely downing the whiskey in one. "And shall I tell you why?"

"Robert?"

"What do you take me for? I've seen the news. I know Tamper has lost everything and is heading for prison." He looked at Blaire, his eyes darting around her face. "What? Are you surprised that we get the international news in rural Scotland? I even know he's been extradited to the U.K. for trial. You see, ancestors can come in handy now and again – nothing like having a British passport when times get tough."

"Robert ... I ..."

"You don't need to explain," he said, calming down. "I've been here on my own for years, suffocating in memories, regretting the choices I've made."

"You broke my heart," said Blaire, meaning it. "You pushed me to one side, just like that. What did you expect me to do?" She sat back down on the sofa.

"I don't know," Robert snapped, slamming his hand against the architrave. "But if I had known . . ." Gathering himself together, he toned down his voice. "If I had known you were carrying my firstborn child I would have changed things. I would have gone with you."

"And you would have been penniless."

"Maybe. But we had love. What more could we have needed? And anyway, it would have been no different to how I am now."

"What do you mean?" she snapped.

"As I said, I've made some bad decisions. My wife did leave a chunk of fortune to me, but I was so ... well, no point in excuses . . . I took to the horses."

"Gambling?"

"Yes."

Blaire looked over to a round table filled with framed photographs including Robert posing on the cover of *Country Life* as he graduated from Cirencester.

"I have a small amount all right."

"Enough to keep you in whiskey," said Blaire, who couldn't help but feel disgust at what Robert had done to himself. His good looks were still there, but only just, his face was now so drawn, and his eyes, once so striking, were nothing but watery and tired.

"Yes, the whiskey," he said, smiling as they both looked at his check-shirted elbow pushing out of his navy V-neck jumper.

Blaire tried to muster a smile, hoping he was joking. "This place must be worth a fortune surely? Why don't you downsize?"

"What do you mean?"

"The land," said Blaire, "and the house, why not sell?"

Robert looked at Blaire like she was speaking double Dutch. "Rousey has been in the Wyndham family for twelve generations, and it must go on to the thirteenth."

Blaire knew she couldn't argue with history – Robert was clearly still staunchly traditional.

"Grace does the basics, cooks for me and keeps the place clean enough. No need to use most of the rooms. George comes to stay of course, but he's more bothered about the deer sanctuary and planting to bother with the house. The place is too big, it's not for me any more. I'm an old man now."

"But you're only sixty, right? That's not old, Robert!" Blaire needed to change tack. Trying not to panic, she was trying to find a way to save her future. "But, Robert …"

"Now listen," he said, walking to the window and looking out to the river, "it's patently clear that I need to make amends to my daughter." He puffed out his chest for the first time in years, like an old hawk preparing for battle in the skies. "I'm going to call my lawyer." His voice was gaining strength as he ran his finger down the edge of the sash window, damp with condensation.

"What?" Blaire stood up. It sounded like Robert was reacting as she had hoped, following the revelation of his first-born child. But she hadn't expected it to be quite so easy. Her timing must have been spot on.

"Yes, Sofia must have Rousey. Gussy was hell bent on George getting it all. He isn't a bad boy but he always took after his mother. Only ever interested in nature and bloody art. But in Sofia I can see a Wyndham. Real backbone. Proper spirit."

"God, I felt for you when Augusta died, I really did," Blaire said, and she meant it. "But I knew the best chance for Sofia was in LA. And look at her now."

"She's a beauty."

"But, more than that, she's an independent woman. Something I have never been. I had to stay with Max all that time, for her sake," and, gazing towards Robert, her face softened. "This is our second chance, Robert."

Crossing the room, Robert pulled Blaire into his arms and kissed her. For the first time in years he felt that he had something to live for. All this time he had been fading away behind racing channels and clouds of smoke. But he needed to think carefully and, looking at a framed picture of a five-year-old George sitting on a branch of an oak tree, he knew the first move was to visit Gussy's grave in the family mausoleum. He needed to ease his conscience by baring all.

"I'm going to take care of you from now on, Blaire. Whatever you need, whatever you want, I am going to give it to you."

"I was hoping you might say that," said Blaire, then correcting her enthusiasm added, "I mean, life has been hard in America." She

a bit unlikely

139

looked down at her smooth and manicured hands.

It was like Robert had just received an injection. Once he got over the initial shock, he seemed to stand taller, head up.

"Blaire, I'm going to send you to the Celtic Thistle Hotel in Edinburgh. Stay there until you hear from me. Don't contact anyone. I need to get things in order."

"Robert, are you sure?" Blaire didn't have a Plan B. She needed this to work.

"I'm sure." Robert stared at her intently. "But there will be a condition."

"Such as?"

"It has been many years since you and I have been together and since then there has been no one else."

"No one at all?"

"Well, no one like you," he said, pulling up his belt.

"And?"

"And, my condition, Blaire Davies –"

"It's Tamper," she snapped. "I am no longer a Davies."

"All right, as you wish. My condition is that we make up for lost time. I'd like to have an informal arrangement with you."

Blaire hoped she was wrong in guessing what he seemed to be angling towards.

"Robert, I have given you a daughter. Don't you think that's enough?"

But his expression didn't waver.

"All these years I've been thinking of you, dreaming of you in fact. We had something special, Blaire, and now I'd like it back."

Blaire felt her face freeze and it wasn't due to Botox injections.

"I'll make you happy, Blaire. Whatever you need, I'll get it for you. Starting with a place in Geneva. I've always had my eye on living there. I used to holiday there with my grandparents, all terribly organised, the sort of life I've never had, and now I think it's something I'd like."

"And what about me, what is it that you want me to give?"

"Your company," he said, "at night."

"And you'll sign this place over to Sofia?"

"I will, as long as we understand each other."

Blaire had no choice. All her assets, even her jewelry in the bank had been seized and Robert was her only hope of maintaining the access to money she had grown used to.

"All right," she said, walking towards him, trying to get her head around how whiskey-soaked Robert had become. "Let's start by running a bath to freshen things up, shall we?"

"Not yet. Check into the hotel and order whatever you need."

"And the taxi outside?" she asked.

"I said I'll take care of the finances – and in the morning go and find a substantial car for yourself. I have a feeling that I will be in extravagant form by tomorrow."

Chapter 16

"Sorry about this old jeep," said George, cranking through the gears. "It spends most of its time in the airport car park, rusting between my trips home to Rousey."

Driving along up a small road, flanked by woodland which twilight crept through, they arrived at a stone archway with black wrought-iron gates.

"My mother used to say snowdrops were there to remind us that no matter how long the winter seems, the summer does come," said George, driving up a long avenue of lime trees, "and she continues to be right. Who knew May would arrive so soon, and with you beside me? You see the lights over there to the left? That's the Keeper's Cottage. Finlay and Grace live there, and have done for years, since I was a child."

"Will I meet them?" asked Anna, switching on her phone for the first time after the flight, expecting a string of texts from Gilda.

"I'll be in trouble if I don't introduce you, that's for sure," said George, parking next to a vintage-looking Bentley.

As Anna got out of the car, she saw several hydrangea bushes huddling either side of large steps leading to the front door, with stern tendrils of wisteria climbing up the building. Other than the occasional sheep *baa*, the evening was completely still.

Climbing the steps, George pushed open the heavy blue front door and carried their bags into the hall.

"Just one thing, Anna. Remember how I said my father can be quite short-tempered?"

"Yes, I remember," she said, taking off her beanie and straightening up her cardigan and scarf.

"Please try not to take it personally, okay? It's just the way he is, and apologies in advance for any insults he might throw at you."

"I'm from a pretty strong lot, as you know," said Anna, smiling. "Don't worry about me."

"I do though," said George, dropping the bags at the foot of the stairs and wrapping his arms around Anna. "It's so good to have you here with me. And I'm guessing my father must be holing up in the study for one of his racing binges."

Taking Anna's hand, he led her along a corridor lined with Spy cartoons. Walking into the study, he flicked the light switch. The newspapers, once heaped on the sideboard, had gone and pink flowering dogwood stood tall in a vase by the window which had its shutters open.

Classical music was playing from somewhere – maybe Mozart, Anna thought. Certainly it was familiar and something her father liked to listen to.

"Strange," said George, "I haven't heard music in this house for a long time," and, letting go of Anna's hand, he walked out of the room and further along the corridor. She followed.

Reaching the last door, George pushed it open.

His father was sitting in a wing chair by the fireplace, clean-shaven and looking smart in a check shirt.

"Ah," said Robert, standing up, hands on his waist. "You're here." He smiled broadly. "You must be Anna? George told me he was bringing you here this weekend." Striding across the room, he kissed her on either cheek, and then he reached out for George's hand. "George? Aren't you going to shake your old man's hand?"

Reluctantly, George did offer his hand, but with an almost blank expression on his face.

"Still not keen on touching it, are you, George?" said Robert, holding up his hand. "Tell you about this, did he, Anna?"

Anna didn't answer, seeing Robert's right hand, badly scarred.

"Some things best swept under the carpet, isn't that right, George?"

Anna quickly glanced at George. He was staring at the window.

"Well, now," said Robert, like he was on a high, "you've just caught me before I take myself up to bed."

"It's good to meet you, Mr Wyndham," said Anna, keeping one eye on George.

"Call me Robert, we're all friends here. How about a drink? Come on, George, how about a whiskey?"

Robert's voice was expensively educated.

"Anna doesn't drink whiskey. I'll make us some drinks in a moment," said George, who didn't seem to want to make eye contact with his father.

"Living in London, are you, Anna?" said Robert, picking up his glass, his hand slightly trembling as he drained the last of his whiskey. "Great town, didn't spend enough time there. Well, you two look like you have fun together – a tight unit, are you?"

"Father, what's going on?"

Robert didn't respond.

"You won't see me in the morning as I've got business to attend to in Edinburgh but it's good to see George has found a nice steady girl. I've always been a fan of the Irish. It's the Celtic blood, you see," and, turning to an ancestral-looking portrait, Robert stretched out a hand and gently brushed its rim. "How long are you staying for?"

"Until Sunday," said George flatly. "I've got some paperwork to get over to Finlay about the fishing rights and so I thought Anna and I would make a weekend of it."

Anna's phone beeped with a message from Gilda and the dogs whined in response, their big eyes staring up at George.

"They're not used to that technology," said Robert, slightly smiling. "All those damn beeps and signals. Rubbish the lot of it. No place for it here."

Anna was mortified but if she didn't call Gilda she knew there would be no peace for the rest of the night.

"Do you mind if I zip out and make a call to my boss?" she asked quietly.

"No, of course not," said Robert. "Go ahead. The passage to

144

the library is just through there," he said, pointing to double doors, lined with faux books.

Once Anna had left the room, Robert's charm bounced back to his old ways. "Make sure that you remind Finlay to fill up the log box. It's bloody freezing. And what about your gun – will you take it out?"

"I don't think so," said George quietly.

"What's that?"

"No, I won't." George checked his watch.

"All those birds going to waste," said Robert. "Nothing changes, does it?"

"No. Nothing changes."

In the library, Anna walked past two long red sofas facing each other as portraits of rather serious people glared down from the walls between rows upon rows of books. There was also a large portrait of Robert standing next to a pony, dressed for polo and holding a mallet, mounted above the fireplace. Opening a large glass door, she walked on to flagstones bordered by a granite wall and Grecian urns.

"Anna, darling, at last you've called."

"Gilda, hi."

"We've got a crisis, darling," said Gilda. "Can you come into the office now?"

"Gilda, I'm out of London." Anna could hear Kate swearing in the background.

"Kate is trying to coordinate press packs for the Master Cat Challenge and bloody Bryan has broken his finger and so Chrissy has had to take her high-maintenance husband to A&E."

"How did he break his finger?"

"Honestly, you don't want to know," said Gilda. "Trying to open a jar of marmalade. I know, don't say a word, I simply can't bear the idiocy of the man. And of course there is big drama as now he won't be able to play guitar and so his band's reunion tour is in jeopardy."

"Poor Chrissy, that doesn't sound like much fun."

"Look, darling, I need you here," said Gilda, trying to compose herself. "The girls are making an utter hames of the things."

"I can't, Gilda. I'm in Ayrshire."

"Where?"

"Scotland, Gilda, Scotand. It is the weekend, you know."

"Really, Anna, you do choose your timing, don't you?" said Gilda, put out. "All right then, when are you back? I feel I'm in crisis. I've got to go to a hideous parents' day at Orlando's prep school tomorrow and, of course, her Highness will be there."

"The Queen?" asked Anna.

"No, darling, not the Queen. I'm referring to Adrian's plastic wife Sara with her shiny Botox cheeks. And, of course, she'll be dressed in a ghastly suburban belted day coat. Honestly, Orlando is at a delicate age. Does he really need his father turning up with his crumpet? Though, to be fair, crumpet is not a word I'd use to describe Sara. I think dry toast is more appropriate, without even the tiniest smattering of butter."

"Gilda, I've got to go, sorry. I'll pick things up on Monday first thing, I promise."

"If you must, darling, but look, speaking of pick-me-ups, be a sweetie and bring back a bottle of Dior perfume from Duty Free, would you? And also the prune Chanel mascara, and make sure it's waterproof, darling – you know how I detest smudges."

Tiny streaks of light peeked through the shutters of George's bedroom the next morning and as Anna opened her eyes she looked up at the quilted rose in the canopy of the four-poster bed. Snuggling beneath the blankets her eyes ran around the ornate cornice bordering the walls above exquisite prints of birds and horses.

"Good morning, sleepyhead," said George, standing in the bathroom doorway wrapped in a white towel, his wet hair pushed back from his face. "You're looking very beautiful this morning." Walking towards her and sitting on the edge of the bed, he leant in to kiss her.

"Don't even look at my hair, it seems to have become very tangled since last night. I can't think why," said Anna, closing her eyes and yawning.

"You're perfect," he said, burying his face into her neck. "It's so good to have you here, Anna," he whispered, sending electric shocks of pure happiness down her back.

"It is?"

"Yes, and today I want to show you around the estate, so you can get to know the place," he said, getting back into bed.

"You do?" asked Anna, wiggling her toes, scrunching up her eyes, wondering if feeling so adored was possible.

"But first I need to make sure that I know my way around you. I'm not sure if I have kissed every part of your body as yet."

"Surely not?"

As he slid his hands over hers, their fingers blending into each other, Anna felt George's strength, almost weightless on top of her even though she was half his size. He felt like her protector, she was safe, she was loved and she had never felt more wanted.

"Please don't stop," sighed Anna.

"How could I?" George whispered into her ear.

"George?"

"Anna?"

"Sorry to disturb, but ..."

"What?" and slightly out of breath, George followed Anna's eyes, turning his head up to the canopy over the bed.

There was a little mouse doing an acrobatic twist before zipping down the bedpost.

"So sweet," said Anna.

"And only you, my sweet Anna, could say such a thing."

By midday, Anna was standing in the boot room watching George as he searched around.

"What's the surprise, George? I'm intrigued."

"Just one more minute. I had it delivered last week and I know Finlay put it somewhere in here. Aha!" he said, opening a trunk and lifting out a large rectangular green box with a gold ribbon around it. "I thought these might be useful for you to tackle the Scottish hills."

Untying the ribbon, and looking at George with a huge smile, Anna lifted off the lid of the box to find a pair of very smart green wellies.

"George, that is so very cool of you, thank you," and, pulling out bunches of paper from inside the boots, Anna slipped in her stocking feet. "The size is perfect."

"Good to hear it," he said. "Now, shall we take them for a test run outside?"

They went into the yard, then walked on beneath the bell tower and towards the back avenue. George pointed to the icehouse at the edge of the walled garden.

"We used to have an ice house, but it finally fell last winter. It was one of the places Mum never got around to restoring."

Anna looked over the topiary gardens, centered with a large water fountain, towards what looked like a walled garden, all with breathtaking views of the mountains and gently rolling pastures traversed by a winding river.

"You see the coach house over there? I used to spend hours in there with my soldiers. I arranged them at the door so as to defend their kingdom," he said, mimicking a soldier's march. "I don't think anyone knew I played there, not even my mother."

He stopped by a small gate by a cottage and, taking her hands, he kissed them.

"Anna, there are two very special people I'd like you to meet."

Anna felt a ripple down her spine.

The path to the Keeper's Cottage was lined with geraniums and, as they walked towards the small front door, Anna could see a lady with white hair smiling from the window. The door opened and a brown-and-white terrier raced out of the house, yapping noisily and circling George's legs.

"Hello, Pickles, you crazy dog!" said George.

Standing teary-eyed in the doorway, the old lady gave George a huge hug on her tippy-toes.

"And here she is," she said, reaching out for Anna. "George said he was bringing you home and aren't you just a beauty, my wee poppet?"

"Anna, I'd like to introduce you to Grace."

"I used to be the nanny to this wee boy, and look at him now, isn't he the handsome giant?"

"Yes, he is," said Anna, laughing.

George and Anna took off their boots and lined them up inside the door before following Grace into the sitting room.

"Now, Anna," said Grace, patting the seat of an armchair, "you sit down here and you can have a good look at the photographs on the walls. All of them Wyndhams. George's mother gave them to me, Lord preserve her." There were people on horseback and fishing on riverbanks along with numerous pictures of a young boy, who must have been George, next to ponies, fishing rods and huge trees. "I've only got a few of my own family," said Grace, taking a photograph off the small mantelpiece. "This is Gwen, my wee sister."

"She looks lovely," said Anna.

"But she died young, God rest her," said Grace. "And of course there's the photograph of myself and Finlay on our wedding day. 'Twas such a happy occasion."

"That it was," said Finlay, arriving in the door sucking a pipe. "How are you, wee lass? Looking so fine!" And taking off his cap and holding his pipe, Finlay made a bow to Anna. "Pleased to meet you, young lady. George called to tell us he was bringing you to Rousey. He did, you know – he wanted to tell us about you, Anna."

"Let's have some tea," said Grace, "or maybe you'd prefer coffee?"

"No, tea would be great. How about I come and help?" and she followed Grace into the kitchen.

Taking a batch of sausage rolls out of the oven as the old aluminium kettle on the stove started to whistle, Grace smiled at Anna.

"It's grand to have you here," she said, taking down a tea caddy from a shelf.

"It's all so beautiful, including your garden," said Anna, peering out the window.

"All thanks to Finlay," said Grace. "He's a good man. Works hard, mind, and it hasn't always been plain sailing with the family."

"As in George's family?" asked Anna, pouring boiling water into the teapot to heat it.

"Aye, and I hope I'm not speaking out of turn," said Grace, lowering her voice and watching the door to make sure no one else was listening, "but he's been through a lot in his life, you know, Anna."

"George?"

"Yes, and he has grown into the dearest man. No one finer and if you'd only known his mother, she was a real lady and what she didn't know about art, and gardens. Well, she'd take George to all the exhibitions, all the sales. God rest her, she died before her time."

"What age was she?" asked Anna.

"Too young," said Grace, her face straight as a ruler. "But Anna, he can go into himself sometimes, you know, wondering when best to return here for good. It's his father, always been difficult."

Anna stood back slightly from Grace, feeling that she was being fed possibly too much information. She'd much prefer to hear all of this from George.

"But a problem halved, you know what they say?" said Grace, tipping the sausage rolls onto a plate, and to Anna's relief she heard Finlay calling out for the tea.

"Why don't you take Pickles for a walk after tea, George?" said Grace, seeing him standing in the doorway. "You can take Anna to see your mother. Ah, you should, George. It'd do you good to have some company there for a change."

Chapter 17

Passing through a gateway into the garden, roofed with clay tiles and timber beams, Anna noticed Wyndham names inscribed on two low benches facing each other.

"My mother," said George, running his hand along a bronze plate that bore her name. "She was always known as Gussy, never seemed liked 'Augusta' really. You see the granite building over there? My mother is interred in the mausoleum, along with both my grandparents and two aunts, on the Wyndham side. She loved Rousey and so it was apparently what she would have wanted."

"Is that door bronze?"

"Yes, it is and when my mother died they couldn't actually find the key into the mausoleum, and it wasn't just a matter of going down to the high street and getting a Yale key cut."

"I can imagine more of a big, copper, *Lord of the Rings* style number."

"Exactly, so they had to fly in a locksmith from the Heritage Locksmith company in the States."

"What about her own family?" she asked.

"Her grandparents made a fortune selling copper to the Navy way back in Nelson's day. Both her parents died before I was born, and she has two brothers, my uncles, though I never see them –

both of them are living in the States." He sighed. "I remember when my father wanted to send me to prep school, the same school that he went to. I couldn't have been more than five at the time."

"Five? But that's just so little. I can imagine you at five years of age – honestly, George, who could let you go?"

"My mother thought the same. She was determined to turn her back on the haunts of titled aristocrats and sent me to a local school about five miles from here. And instead of Eton or Harrow, she wanted to send me to secondary school as a day pupil."

"And Harrow won out?"

"Yes, it did." George sat up and breathed out, like he was trying to expel any resentment he felt. "My father enrolled me into Harrow within a month of her death, and that was that."

"Can you remember your mother easily?" she asked.

"Quite well," said George. "I was eleven when she died, and it's funny, because sometimes when I really try to remember her, my mind goes blank. But then she might enter my thoughts, out of the blue, maybe when I'm tying my shoelaces or making toast, you know, something completely day to day."

Anna reached out her hand to George, their fingers intertwining.

"I guess this place was her anchor, despite my father."

"They didn't get on?"

"I don't think so … it's just hard to remember. There was definitely a feeling of tension in the house when I was growing up, but there were some funny moments, like my father's fondness for slipper fishing."

"There are slipper fish?"

"No! You see how the river runs so close to the garden? Well, the idea was that a fly could be cast from the lawn in bedroom slippers. And I know my mother couldn't stand my father casting anywhere near the house and one time she hurled a water jug from an upstairs window, belting my father on the head and knocking him out. I, of course, thought he was dead, and Grace came screaming out of the house when she saw him lying there. But my mother breezed downstairs, and put my father's head on her lap, and he woke up and they both laughed. It's a funny memory, and the closest to happiness I can remember between them."

"That is sad, George," said Anna, eyes welling up.

Then looking at Anna, George wiped his eyes and laughed. "I'm sorry, I don't mean to be gloomy."

"It's not easy though, is it?" said Anna. "Being an only child, I mean. And I imagine even less easy having only one parent alive."

"She had such plans for this place, opening the gardens to the public, putting a world-class art space into the yard and creating a bursary for artists. There's also Finlay and Grace to think of. They are both in their early seventies and more like grandparents to me than anything else, and I want to look after them. So I might have to think about bringing in some new staff, not that Finlay and Grace will like it. They're not keen on change."

"And what about you?" asked Anna.

"Change or my ambitions?"

"Both," said Anna.

"Well, as mercenary as the art world can be at times, it's been my life since I left Cambridge. Buying, selling, and sometimes buying then getting far too attached to a piece of work and holding on to it. Which is why there is hardly an inch of wall space left in my house in London."

"So you're like a sort of drop-in centre for the Masters?" Anna tried to lighten the conversation and George did smile but she could see he was going through something more frustrating than she could imagine.

"I know that Rousey is slipping away under my father's watch, but until I have direct control I can't really move things forward. There were originally five terraces cut into the steep bank above the river, and down here," he pointed to an area with statues of the Three Graces facing each other around a fountain, "the topiary and planting were immaculate."

"It must have been amazing," said Anna, thinking of how much her mother would adore this place and how Bernard would have the place licked into shape in no time.

"After my mother died, the place became overgrown – it would break her heart to see it now. Though Finlay maintains the garden around the house. As my father has no interest in maintaining the land, I decided to upscale the deer sanctuary instead, you know, something I could manage from afar, and working with Scotland's natural heritage organization. Then, I can take on restoration of the gardens when I live here one day." George turned to Anna. "Do you like the place?"

"I love it," she said, "and George, I love you."

Lifting Anna into his arms, he turned in circles. *"She loves me!"* he yelled, and collapsing into hysterics on the damp grass they lay there, wrapped in each other's arms.

After a late lunch in the village pub, Anna was looking out the window of George's bedroom overlooking the garden with a view of the river. Their walk had been incredible, and to know about his parents helped her to further understand him. She really felt she knew him now.

On the chest of drawers a large Chinese lamp sat alongside silver-framed photographs of Gussy with George on his pony, then George holding a watering can and another of him hanging upside down from a tree house. Anna couldn't help but think of ways in which she and George could transform the estate. They could renovate the yard, reroof the stables and maybe open tearooms to the public. The deer sanctuary could attract environmental groups and the coach house would make a perfect art gallery for George's clients. She felt like Lizzy looking out upon the parkland of Pemberley.

"Anna?" called George from the corridor. "Can I have you for a sec?"

"Anytime!" she said, giggling from behind the door.

"I like your thinking," said George, grinning, "but first there's something I want to show you – let's go this way."

They walked down to the ground floor and along a corridor. Next to the study George stopped by a door. "It's the reason I've been coming up here so much during the past few weeks."

"I'm intrigued," said Anna.

"I met an art historian in Milan, and he came over with an extremely experienced friend, in order to indentify ..." and, opening the door, George ushered Anna in before him.

The room was beautiful, with wallpaper that looked like original William Morris artichoke, and a grand piano by a large window.

Anna looked at George's face, which seemed to have been drained of colour.

"George? What is it?"

Over the mantelpiece there was an obvious mark on the William wallpaper, where a painting had once hung.

"George?"

"Anna, I'm sorry. I have to find my father." He kissed her. "There are some albums over there you can look at. I won't be long."

Feeling his palms sweating, George hoped that his suspicions were unfounded. Walking into the drawing room, he found his father standing by the window, with a glass of whiskey in his hand.

"I thought you were in Edinburgh," said George, closing the door firmly behind him.

"Yes, I was," said Robert, calmly. "And now I'm home again."

"Is that what you call it – home?"

"I believe so?"

"More like a fucking cash cow." George closed his eyes and, trying to stay calm, he spoke slowly and clearly. "Father, tell me you haven't taken my mother's painting from the music room."

"I cannot, George."

"You cannot what?"

"I cannot tell you that I haven't taken it."

"Where is it? It was my mother's favourite painting. You had no right to move it."

"Don't you talk to me about rights. I have every right. I have every right to do whatever I want with every stick of furniture and every painting in this house."

"You've already gambled your way through half the furniture in this house. It was my mother's favourite painting – you know what it means to me."

"Yes, it was my wife's favourite painting, and so it is legally mine."

"And where is it?" George prayed that his father hadn't done what he suspected he had.

"The Titian is now with a Chinese billionaire who bought it."

"What? You bloody well listened in, didn't you? I actually cannot believe it."

"Always assume that someone is listening, George. I once took an Italian lover, you see? I was only eighteen at the time, but she taught me enough Italian to grasp when your experts confirmed it was a Titian. How could I ignore such an opportunity?”

“You disgust me.”

“Well, at eight million I can take your disgust.”

“But it’s worth twice that! And at the very least it should have been sold to the National Gallery. It should never have left Scotland.”

“Well, it should never have left bloody Italy in the first place!”

“I’m going to buy it back. I want the dealer’s details.”

“No. That is my shortest answer for you.”

“So what now? Are you going to gamble your way through eight million? And what about the taxman – I’m sure he’ll be interested, won’t he?”

“Get out, and remember while this estate in my name it is for me to do with it what I want.”

“My mother would be disgusted.”

“Yes, I suppose she would,” said Robert, his eyes squinting. “However, I need to think about my own future.”

“I would have helped. If you had just asked, I would have bloody well bought the painting from you.”

“Liar. You’d never part with a penny of your inheritance to bail me out.”

“Mother left her fortune to me because she knew you would gamble it away. And she was right.”

“You and your mother always had your own little club of two. I wouldn’t dream of tucking into any more of her money. Came from filthy copper mines anyway. They were nouveaus, her family, your ancestors, remember? Two sides to the family tree, George, and let me tell you that you take after your mother’s side. I don’t see you as a Wyndham any more than that Titian belonged in Scotland.”

George walked to the door and turned to his father. “I bloody well wish I hadn’t missed that day,” he said.

“That’s quite a statement, George,” said Robert, holding up his hand. “And all these years I had thought you to be a rather good shot, thinking you had been aiming for my hand. But now you say you meant to blast off my head.”

“You are a bastard of a man,” said George, his eyes filling with tears. "I saw you with that woman, by the river, and Mother knew about the affair, I'm sure of it."

"And so you thought you'd shoot me for seeking pleasure elsewhere? And if I hadn't been so hung over that morning, leaving my gun unbroken by the fence while I took a leak, would you have come after me in some other way?"

"It was an accident, as you well know," said George. "I was eleven years old and curious to hold the gun, that was all."

"You may say that, but I think we both know the kind of boy you were, obsessed by your mother."

"She was dead by then, and what are you doing, waving your hand around like it is some kind of evidence in court? This is all one big joke to you, isn't?"

"On the contrary, George, and should you find yourself married to a frigid heiress one day," Robert spat, "I swear you'll change your tune about infidelity."

George left the room, slamming the door behind him and trying to control his breathing as he made his way to the music room to find Anna, but she wasn't there. His mind kept going over the moment he had pulled the trigger. His mother had been dead maybe a week, and George had been told he was to be sent away to boarding school. As an eleven-year-old, all George could think of was how his father had been with the woman by the river, cheating on his mother. Had he meant to pull the trigger when he picked up his father's gun? He remembered the weight of it, nudging it into his thin shoulder as he used all his might to point it at his father, and every time he saw the deformity of his father's hand, there was no escaping the memory of that morning in the lower field.

In the kitchen, George found Anna chatting with Grace over a mug of tea.

"Grace, hello," said George. "I'm so sorry, Anna, but we've got to leave earlier than expected."

"George, is everything all right?" asked Grace.

"Not really, but I won't explain now if you don't mind," he said, wiping his sleeve across his forehead.

Anna poured the remainder of her tea into the sink.

"Don't worry about that, Anna dear, leave it to me," said Grace, seeing the expression on George's face.

Chapter 18

As was her habit on a Monday morning, Gilda prepared to lock herself into her office for a morning of pure communications, a procedure that brought with it sound effects of hoots of laughter followed by erratic yelling, rounded off with the pop of a champagne cork before bolting her door. This morning though, Gilda was restless and called Chrissy and Anna in for a quick tête-a-tête.

"Darlings, I feel my office is lacking natural light. I've been reading about an amazing device that tracks the sun and uses a mirror to reflect whatever light there is into darker areas. Genius idea. What's more, it will be excellent for tweezing my brows, don't you think?"

Knowing what side her morning croissant was buttered on, Chrissy agreed that more light could be beneficial, despite the fact that sun was streaming through two large windows. Anna, on the other hand, feeling very down about George, could only think about the morning light peeping through the shutters when she woke up in his bedroom at Rousey, and decided to leave Gilda and Chrissy to the Charge-of-the-Light-Brigade debate, and returned to her desk to catch up on email.

When Anna arrived back to London from Scotland the night

before, she and Tilly had discussed the sudden departure from Rousey at length, the conclusion being that George writing Anna's name on the inside of her new welly boots with indelible pen was a sign of commitment, no doubt. Tilly was sure of it and those boots were to stay at Rousey. But, remembering how George was so quiet on the plane on the way back to London and saying he couldn't stay with her that night, she couldn't help but feel unnerved. Though he did hold both her hands when he kissed her goodbye and said, "I'll call soon, I promise."

Across the office, Kate, dressed in skinny jeans and heels, muddled through a box filled with packing foam to protect the electronic weighing scales from a new Japanese client.

"Anna, sorry to disturb, but any chance you could witness this?"

Throwing her empty paper coffee cup into the wastepaper bin, Anna tried to kick herself into positive PR mode.

"Okay, so what are we doing?"

"Basically, seeing if this little baby works like it's supposed to. Don't even ask about the retail price – I mean, it would almost buy you a week of watermelon smoothies in a health farm."

Bracing herself, Kate took off her long cardigan and earrings to give her weight the best possible chance.

"But, Kate, you're tiny! Light as a feather, surely?"

Standing on the scales, which looked more like a flying saucer, Kate let out a proper yelp.

"No, that's can't be right," said Anna, getting on her knees to read the digital numbers more clearly.

"I actually cannot bear it," said Kate, taking off her watch and her figure-hugging top. "This scales is claimed to be the world's most precise weight-and-BMI-measuring device in the world. Any better now, Anna, without my top?"

"I like a nice round figure, I do," said Martin, leaning against the doorway.

"*Oh Jesus!*" roared Kate, and grabbing her top she catapulted herself off the scales and into the kitchen.

"Er, Martin, were we expecting you?" asked Anna.

"Go on, Mandy, why don't you jump up onto the scales, love? I'm sure they'll weigh in your favour."

"Mandy, you're here too?" said Anna, getting to her feet and trying to remember that showing clients hospitality is fifty per cent of the game, according to Gilda.

Gilda swept out of her office. "Martin, there you are, lovely to see you, darling!" and then, dropping her smile, "And you've brought Mandy with you. Hello, Mandy."

"Gilda," said Mandy in a frosty tone.

"Well," rallied Gilda, clasping her hands together, "thank God champagne is fat-free, darlings, that's all I can say." Crossing the room, Gilda pressed her toe on the weighing scales to test it out. "Kate? Anna, where is that girl?"

"Recovering from shock, most likely," said Anna, lifting up the scales and returning it to the box, feeling short-tempered. "If you'd like an update on the Hottest Chef campaign, I'll have it ready for you after lunch."

"Good-oh, Anna. Now, why doesn't Kate take Martin and Mandy out to lunch, don't you think, darling? Kate!" then a proper roar, "*Kate!*"

"Actually," said Martin, pinging his braces, which were now necessary to keep his trousers up following the rigorous diet imposed on him by his wife, "Mandy and I have some business to attend to this afternoon – we were merely passing and thought we'd surprise you."

"Yes, well," said Gilda, losing enthusiasm for the conversation, "you know us, Martin – always at the ready."

"Good to know, Gilda," said Martin, combing back his hair. "We'll be off now – say ta-ta, Mandy."

"Ta-ta," she parroted, and out they sauntered.

"Lock the front door," said Gilda. "I cannot take another second of the Martin and Mandy Show – are they for real?"

"They seem to be," said Kate, pinging open a can of Redbull and making Gilda jump.

"My nerves. I don't know what's wrong," said Gilda.

"Why don't you sit down?" said Chrissy, puffing up a large cushion on the office sofa.

"Do you know I actually had an urge to make Shepherd's Pie last night? But, darlings? I mean, that just isn't me. That is my mother's way, not mine." Gilda was fanning her face with a copy of *Loo Reviews*. "I'm just not that kind of woman, nesting is not my thing.

Do you think it's the early menopause?" And then she sat down, very still. "Cresta is missing Adrian. I know she is, and I feel guilty as hell about it."

Anna, who still hadn't had time to properly mope about George, was longing to get out of the office and buy some mustard for her father in Fortnum and Masons. It was her long-time tradition to always bring it home.

"Are you missing Hans?"

"Not a bit," said Gilda, sparking up. "The house is blissful without him. Honestly, he was such a neat freak – now I can walk into my bedroom, fling my underwear into the air and spring onto the bed naked as a lark."

"Right," said Anna, not wanting too much more information. "Then maybe you could have a family get-together. You, Adrian, Orlando and Cresta, if you think that could help?"

"Maybe, darling, maybe, and before you go, Anna, I have an announcement!"

As she clapped her hands together, the office interns arrived back from lunch. Eager to be kept on as permanent staff, they lined up like tin soldiers standing to attention as Gilda leant against a desk and snapped a fresh rice cake in half.

"Darlings, interiors stylist Fabio Drager says you must always look to the word 'modern' as being the most important concept there is. We must stay relevant. We need to keep Winterbottom fresh and our clients impressed. Kate, are you listening?"

"Yes, Gilda," squeaked Kate from under her desk as she tried out a new batch of gel nail polish on her toes.

"I want your success as much as my own. We must all come to work as fully engaged human beings. We need our passion and expertise to sparkle in our eyes as we lead our clients towards front-page glory and social-media domination." Gilda stepped onto a chair and managed to balance herself. "And the Winterbottom mantra is?"

"*Voice to Voice*, Gilda," said an account manager, slumped at her desk, longing for a toasted cheese sandwich.

"That's the one, exactly, the '*Voice to Voice*' shall not be beaten. Your dulcet tones need to assure clients and convince journalists that we know what's what. Continue to pick up the phone and make love to that handset. Get on it, darlings! We are the tools that connect our clients to global trends. You are the storytellers and strategists of this PR generation. And remember, if the shoe fits then run on and catch that pumpkin! Now, Kate, we need to get our client list in shape. Let's start with Knicker Glories. Can I have an update, please?"

"We are awaiting a delivery of samples, Gilda, including the personalised knicker range."

"What do you mean 'personalised'? Anna – are you familiar with this aspect?"

"As far as I know you can send a photo of your choice to Knicker Glories and they will print the photo around the waistband."

"What, only the waistband?" said Gilda. "Well, that's faintly ridiculous. Let's park that for now. What about Cat's Delight? And whoever came up with that name, couldn't they have come up with something a teensy bit more interesting?"

"The Master Cat Challenge is being aired this weekend, Gilda, on the Satellite channel called The Cat's Pyjamas."

"Good, good, and who is our spokesperson?"

Kate looked rather flushed.

"Come on, Kate, out with it!"

"The Mayor of Hull," said Kate.

"The *what?*" said Gilda, scrunching up her face.

"He's big into cats," said Kate, smiling with hopeful eyes.

"How many times, how many times," asked Gilda, "do I need to express the importance of pulling-power? We need a name, a face, to pull in the punters! Now, unless I'm mistaken, this mayor is no oil painting."

"He's terribly talented though in the singing department," piped up Chrissy. "He's brings out a charity single every year. Bryan plays the bass guitar for him, says it's pretty good."

"Well, we need some pussy, I tell you. And don't look so shocked, you lot," said Gilda, looking at the interns, who were clutching their phones like they were relying on the device for body battery-power. "Sex sells – it's a cliché for a reason." Then turning to Kate, she said, "We'll need the Mayor's wife to come on board, and call Assets and get three girls into cat suits – that should hike up the ratings."

"While we're here, shall I update on Bloc It Bling?" asked Anna.

"Why not? Then I'm taking myself out for a wax followed by a glass of Chablis. Just look at the time, four o'clock already. Have none of you had lunch?"

"No, Gilda," they all said in unison.

"Well, look, Anna, hold off on the dread Bloc It Bling update, would you? And instead I'll foot the bill for you all to go to Alfredo's in Soho. Order whatever you like and tell him I'll pop in later."

Utterly relieved, the office had an exodus like Monday had never seen. And Anna, with no interest whatsoever in spending the rest of the afternoon discussing social-media accounts with the interns, blew Kate a kiss goodbye and went out to find her bike attached to the railings by St Martin's in the Fields. The Georgian church looked so beautiful as she pushed her bike towards Leicester Square. As it started to drizzle Anna stopped to put on a raincoat, which she religiously kept in the basket on the front of her bike, and by the entrance of the Tube station she looked up to find Gilda's husband standing there, swiping through an iPad in a way similar to Gilda's.

He looked up and, catching her eye, he stopped. "Anna, isn't it?" he said.

"Adrian, hello. We meet again," said Anna, wondering what on earth to say next.

"How is Gilda?"

"Oh, you know Gilda, resilient as ever."

"I understand from her mother that Hans has left."

"Yes, I think so."

"And Gilda is all right about it?"

"She seems to be." Anna could tell that he was concerned about Gilda.

"I took Orlando out from school on Sunday afternoon. Seems to be bearing up, considering how much he disliked the idea of boarding."

"I guess he's quite young still," said Anna.

"Yes, though I was sent away at the age of seven and so ten really does seem not so bad – but these days it's hard to tell, isn't it?"

A lady with a huge pack of kitchen roll under her arm grunted at Adrian to get the hell out of the way as she made her way into the Underground.

"We used to galivant around here," he said, "Gilda and I. My parents had a flat just off Pall Mall. Sold now of course, turned into a gymnasium I believe, on all three floors."

"I'd better get going before the rain really starts to pelt. Good to see you, Adrian, and safe home."

Pushing her bike into a hustle of people on the pavement, Anna wondered about Adrian and Gilda, then hearing the hunting horn sound on her phone, she pulled it out of the pouch on her bicycle basket to find a message from George.

How about dinner? XXX

Chapter 19

Standing in her dressing room, Freddie looked down at her toes and thought about painting them. No, they could wait, she decided. She felt rather stiff following a series of new poses that Dharma had taught her over the weekend. Her sleep pattern had also been continually interrupted by Harry's snoring, of which she had lately become less tolerant. Dharma explained that the stiffness was natural as she was still in the process of cleansing her aura. Rubbing her nimble fingers along the shallow lines of her forehead, she glanced at herself in the mirror and, sticking out her tongue, she had a flashback to the exercises she practised to enhance her cheekbones when she first married. "A E I O U," she said out loud, watching her cheekbones move.

It had been a brave move for Freddie to invite Dharma to stay for the summer as her yoga guru. However, she felt it was high time that Harry registered that she had interests beyond running the house and being his muse on tap. It was also no bad thing for him to know that, as a woman in her fifties, she could still have men vying for her attention. She felt a little flushed at the very thought of it.

Freddie knew how crucial she had been to Harry's success during the eighties and nineties when she was his only model and the inspiration for his successful nude portraits. But now she found his ongoing lack of appetite for painting to be rather tiring. She longed for him to return to his art binges, where he might spend three or four solid days in his studio, jazz blaring out of the stereo, the windowsills replete with barely touched tea trays, saucers overflowing with cigar ash and the distinctive aroma of whisky fumes. Those were the days in which she had enjoyed complete freedom to pose in whatever position she wished on the soft, faded green carpet of their bedroom, but Harry's interest in lifting a brush had rapidly diminished during the past year, a reaction to a lack of commissions, and instead he dithered around the house trying to fill in time before lunch or dinner.

The door opened and she looked up to see her husband arriving in clearly bouncy form, wearing mud-splattered jodhpurs having had a lengthy ride on Penthouse.

"Is that Dharma I've just seen whizzing by on the lawnmower?" asked Harry.

"Really? Where?"

"Just past the kitchen garden – he shot past me at a hundred miles an hour."

"Bernard is the limit," laughed Freddie. "He must have taught him how to use it. Dharma is so willing to help but, honestly, he is here to mentor me in my yoga not to help Bernard with the garden."

Watching his wife laugh, Harry found himself becoming unexpectedly attracted to her. Freddie caught his eye in the mirror and they held the look for a moment or two as she straightened the gold charm of the kingfisher on her pendant. And then she stepped away from the mirror, laid her yoga mat on the carpet, raised her hands over her head. As she pressed the palms of her hands together while resting her ankle impressively on one knee, her breasts looked so firm above her lean waist.

"This, my darling, is what Dharma is here for," she said with both eyes closed. "It is so that I can cope with your volatile artistic temperament." And, smiling, she opened one eye and then the other.

Overwhelmed by her beauty, Harry shook off his Musto and pulled his wife onto the bed.

"At this time of day?" asked Freddie, her long blonde hair almost golden against the white pillow beneath her head.

"Well, given that your early mornings seem to be taken up with sunrise salutations, I think this time of day is rather exquisite, actually."

"What did I do to deserve you, Harry Rose, as irksome as you can be on a daily basis?" asked Freddie, as he wriggled out of his jodhpurs.

"Well," said Harry, his face flushed and excited at the prospect of making love, "your gorgeous cleavage may have something to do with it."

Freddie closed her eyes again. Harry's attentions might not be so frequent any more but that was how their relationship worked. Short battles, followed by sporadic seduction. But, deep down, even though she knew she should be content with her lot, she couldn't but help feel a sense of regret about her life's choice.

"I am worried about Anna," she said. "She sounded so down on the phone last night."

"Hold on – we are about to make love and you want to have a deep and meaningful?" Then seeing the expression on Freddie's face he knew there was no escaping a discussion. "Who knows what's going on with his family?" he said, a little gruffly. "We had to sell a couple of paintings and a chesterfield sideboard to cover Anna's school fees. It's the way it works. Practicality has to override sentimentality at times."

"Yes, I know, but it's the underhand manner in which George's father did it. Anna said George had no idea the painting was going to be sold. She said he went white as a sheet when they walked into the room. Lord knows, it wasn't just any old painting."

"Well, my dearest, I think you can rest assured that we don't have a single painting left in this house that is of anything other than sentimental value, so there won't be any paintings disappearing to a dealer from this house anytime soon."

"Unless you start painting again and create your very own masterpiece?" said Freddie, suddenly serious.

"Tell me now, is that an invitation to paint you lying in such a seductive position, my love?"

"Seriously, Harry. You can't go on just floating from lunch to dinner with the drinks cabinet in between. We need to get your drive back."

"Actually, I have plenty of your so-called drive."

"When did you last complete a painting? Come on, Harry, you have to admit you've slipped massively in the past year – there must be an inch of dust on the easel."

"Okay," said Harry. "I will think about going to the studio this afternoon. Is that what you want to hear?"

"Yes, thank you. And I do hope Anna can make this work with George."

"Oh, I don't know," said Harry. "There must be plenty of girls are chasing after him."

"But none like Anna. She is special."

"Yes, she is, but I dare say that are many other parents with gorgeous twenty-something-year-old daughters thinking just the same of their special little treasures. As Mr Thoreau said, '*Live in each season as it passes; breathe the air, drink the drink, taste the fruit ...*"

"*... and resign yourself to the influences of each,*" she completed the sentence as he leant over and kissed both her eyelids.

"Precisely. Let's taste the fruit, my darling."

"One more thing though," said Freddie.

"Oh yes?" he sighed.

"I've really been thinking about this. What are we going to do with this huge house? We are getting older, Harry. We have to think of the future and how we're going to keep it up. We've already used up all our savings and, really, I think we might be out of touch if we think we can just live here and not make the house pay."

"I had hoped Anna might take it on one day?"

"And maybe she will, but maybe she won't want to. Who knows? It all depends on who she decides to settle down with, doesn't it?"

Both Harry and Freddie couldn't help but let their minds wander in George's direction.

"Do you think George would ever give up Scotland and take on our place instead?" asked Freddie, propping her head up on his shoulder.

"Darling, we are running away with ourselves," said Harry.

"What will be will be, remember? And in the meantime, let me hold you."

Mrs B was preparing a pheasant in the kitchen when Dharma walked in, carrying a basket filled with wild garlic leaves.

"Is that a chicken?" he asked.

"It's a pheasant, Dharma, and a lovely plump one at that. I took it out of the freezer last night and it's as soft as a berry now. Shot in December so it was."

Dharma placed the wicker basket on the table and pulled up a chair.

"You cook just like that? No salt?"

"I'm going to smother the bird in butter and herbs from the garden," she said, rinsing her hands under a tap. "I might even use some of that wild garlic you've brought in. And won't it be the most delicious roast for your supper this evening? Just you wait and see. And I know you're not a big meat-eater, Dharma, but this is a bird you've got to taste."

Mrs B was tickled to see Dharma lapping up the ways of Irish country living. When Bernard showed him how to drive the ride-on lawnmower, she told Mrs Murray in the local shop, "Well, he might as well have been driving a Formula One racing car!"

"You know, Mrs B, one of my friend in Sri Lanka killed a King Cobra in front of me."

"A what?" she asked, taking a block of butter out of the fridge and tearing off the gold wrapping.

"A cobra snake. Very big." Dharma stretched his arms as wide as they could go. "I really don't like killing. No, not at all. And it was the day we celebrate King Cobra!"

"Well, I never heard the likes of it," said Mrs B.

"And did I tell you about the big spider climbing over my bed? In my country we have huge tarantulas the size of my face, with long hairy legs."

"No! Well, I never heard the likes of it."

"They usually live in trees, but now trees are falling in Northern Sri Lanka, and they come into old houses like mine."

"And what did you do with the little beggar?" asked Mrs B, holding the hem of her apron up to her mouth.

"I jumped out of bed, picked up my brother's old cricket bat and sent the spider out the window like a – what you call it – a cannonball."

"Lord save us, we don't have any huge creepy crawlies in Ireland," said Mrs B and both she and Dharma yelped as Harry pushed open the kitchen door and walked in with speed.

"What's for supper, Mrs B?" he asked, scooping up a handful of Freddie's almonds and sunflower seeds from a large bowl on the kitchen table.

Mrs B said nothing as he took a mouthful and almost retched.

"Christ, that's dreadful stuff."

"Better than eating a cobra, that's for certain," muttered Mrs B, as she chopped the butter block into tiny pieces "And don't you go touching the apple pie. For one thing it'll burn the mouth off you, and for another it's not for you. It's for that new rector. He's due to call in, so he is, and I can feel it in my waters that it might be today."

"Well, if there is any change in your waters, could we perhaps have it this evening, with a little custard?"

Then Dharma piped up, "You know in Sri Lanka we have bats bigger than a cock chicken."

"You what?" said Harry. "Do you mean a cockerel?"

"Yes, yes," said Dharma, his beautiful brown eyes shining against the whites of his eyes.

"Now listen to me, the both of you," said Mrs B, "will you give me some room in here while I get your supper ready?"

Chapter 20

In Edinburgh, Victoria prepared to make an announcement to the press on behalf of Sofia. Arriving by helicopter onto the landing strip behind the Celtic Thistle Hotel, her skirt flared up as she climbed carefully out of the cabin. Being an LA veteran, Victoria enjoyed being in the limelight along with her clients, maximising each media opportunity to ensure the press knew exactly what they were dealing with. She hopped into a silver Range Rover, which drove her four hundred metres to the front of the hotel and then reappraised herself of the key messages. Reapplying her lipstick, she took up position on the steps of the hotel wearing a blue midi dress, where, as arranged, a gaggle of reporters were in position to hear what she had to say.

"Go on then, love!" hollered the *Sun*.

"For their own safety and with immense sadness, Blaire and Sofia Tamper have decided to distance themselves from Max Tamper, husband, father and, as it turns out, liability."

Victoria paused for affect.

"Max Tamper's actions have left both Sofia and her mother Blaire emotionally exhausted and, as you will understand, they ask for your respect at this time while they come to terms with the dishonesty of a father and a husband." Victoria slipped on her sunglasses. "And being strong and caring, Sofia and Blaire will continue to champion Sofia's chosen charity, the World Butterfly Foundation which protects butterflies from extinction."

Before the press had a chance to fire any juicy questions at her, Victoria had slipped behind two security guards and hot-stepped it into the elevator. Tomorrow would be a busy day for everyone. Victoria had lined up an exclusive interview for Sofia and Blaire with Piers Morgan, along with an exclusive for the *Sunday Express* that would document the story of a loyal daughter whose mother had fought for her independence from an overbearing husband. Between working on Sofia's new acting career and their charity work, they would try to cope with the shocking truth of Max Tamper's exploitation. A finely crafted tale, Victoria thought to herself.

Inside the luxury Celtic Thistle Hotel, Sofia paced the floor in her mother's suite, sucking on a menthol electronic cigarette. "Mom, this is so stressful. The bastard media are like bloodhounds out there. They are waiting to pounce on me, I just know it."

Blaire was lying on the bed, going through notes on her iPad.

"Sofia, sweetheart. Let me tell you it's nothing compared to seeing your husband in handcuffs."

Sofia sat down beside her mother on the edge of the bed, putting a pillow over her thin, lycra-clad legs like a security blanket. "Do you remember my first commercial, Mom?"

"I do," said Blaire, taking off her pink reading glasses. "Along with two very large tantrums."

"And that was when it all began, Mom. Did you ever think of not getting me involved in Hollywood?"

"I had no choice, Sofia. Max needed any money he could get his hands on to get his production-company up and running, and forty commercials later you landed your first lead role with ABC."

"You know, a make-up artist, quite a good one actually, said to me, 'I can't wait to see what you do next'. People always say that sort of thing to me. I just find it hard, you know, like I have to live up to people's expectations all the time."

Blaire stood up, clutching her iPad. "Yes, Sofia. And you do. Your job is to live up to expectation, like it or not."

"All right, Mom, no need to lose it with me," said Sofia, just as her phone beeped.

"No, leave it. Leave your phone down. Sofia, I've got something to tell you."

Sofia walked over to the window and saw photographers poised behind vans and bushes. It seemed that a C-list celebrity in LA can quickly become an A-lister in the UK when a good scandal appears.

"So go on then, Mom. I could tell from the moment I met you this morning that you were dying to tell me something."

"All right," said Blaire, looking as if she was about to walk the plank. "It's about Max."

"What about him? Has something happened to him in prison?"

"Just listen." Composed and in control, Blaire looked at Sofia. "He is not your biological father."

"I know," said Sofia, looking straight at her mother.

"What do you mean 'you know'? How can you know?"

Sofia lay down on the sofa. "Look, Mother. When I was about six years old, you came into my room one night and you told me that Max wasn't my daddy. That my 'real daddy', as you put it, lived in the UK."

"What?"

"You know what my memory's like? Crystal clear. I remember everything from that night, including your perfume. Why else do you think I had that obsession with the Royals growing up? Watching Prince Andrew in the tabloids, even Prince Charles, wondering if either of them might have been my father. Sounds odd, I know."

"Well, Max always called you his little princess."

"But you know what, Mom, Max gave me everything I needed. He's not such a bad guy, well, apart from the fraud."

"Why didn't you tell me you knew?"

"What was the point? We were doing all right, weren't we? We all looked good together, at all the premières and parties. We were a team."

Blaire wasn't sure where to go next with this. She had expected Sofia to fall to the floor, grieving the loss of what she thought to be her real father, making the rest of the news less important.

"So, go on," said Sofia, almost smiling.

"Go on what?" said Blaire, feeling winded.

"You haven't even told me his goddamn name, Mother."

"His name?"

"The English guy, my real father's name?"

"It's Wyndham, and he isn't English," she said quietly.

"And? Just get on with it already. Don't throw these riddles at me!"

"*I said Wyndham!*" Blaire shouted. "His name is Robert Wyndham and he lives in Scotland. In fact, he lives at a huge place there, a fairytale mansion."

Sofia's mind began to flick through her list of contacts.

"You know his son. I remember because he came to a première of your father's in London, the documentary about the big art theft. In fact, he recommended art historians to your father's team. He was very helpful and polite."

Sofia smiled a big smile, one of those smiles that a face pulls when it doesn't know what else to do. Getting on her feet, she walked over to the minibar and, rattling around a group of plastic bottles, she pulled out two mini bottles of vodka.

"Hold on," she said, twisting off the cap of one bottle and pouring the vodka into a glass. "Are you telling me," her voice was slowly building to a crescendo, "that George Wyndham is my goddamn brother? Did you not think of telling me that before I tried to sleep with him?"

"Sofia. I just don't get you. How can I keep up with your preferences?" said Blaire like she was the greatest bitch alive. And right now, she was. "George Wyndham is your half-brother and you, my darling, as firstborn child to Robert Wyndham, are going to inherit a fortune."

"I don't want his money. I can make my own," said Sofia flatly.

Blaire threw her iPad across the room, knocking over a cardboard spa menu. "*What the hell, Sofia?*" she yelled, releasing a year's worth of tension. "Robert Wyndham owes me. He owes me big time. Do you have any idea what I had to do when he discarded me and returned to his frigid little heiress of a wife?"

Sofia leant against a chair, shivering.

"With twenty pounds in my purse I ran away to London, and Max, card-shark Max, won me in a bet. He found me in a bar. A man wanted me but Max wanted me more. Can you imagine?" Blaire was now hysterical. "Max put a one-hundred-pound note on the table and said that if he got tails, I was his. And he did. He got his tails, and he took me home." Taking a deep breath and searching for composure, Blaire smoothed back her hair, rubbing mascara from beneath her lashes. "Now how about that for romantic? And Max never questioned it. I was only a few weeks pregnant. He won big the next night, and with the money we took a boat to New York, and a Greyhound to LA." Blaire took the glass of vodka from Sofia's hands and took a large sip before returning it to her daughter who looked to be in shock. "When we got to LA, Max had a plan and, you know what, it worked. He got a job with a local TV station and, as I sat at home like a beached whale, he worked his way up, and when you were born not once did he question whether you were his or not. And he loved you from the moment he saw you."

"He did?" asked Sofia, looking like a seven-year-old, and she walked to her mother and sat beside her. "I'm sorry you had to go through all that, Mom. I am sorry."

Blaire shook her head. "You have no need to be sorry, Sofia." And, after a long pause, she looked her daughter in the eye. "But don't you dare bite the hand that is trying to feed you. You will accept the inheritance that is rightfully yours. I worked damn hard by Max's side, the beautiful trophy wife, as soon as we could afford to dress me up like a chandelier. And we were soon accepted and found ourselves on the best guest lists in Hollywood."

Right on schedule, Victoria sashayed into the room, having spent the past half hour on a call with the CEO of EXR.

"Hello, ladies," said Victoria. "I'm interrupting, aren't I?" She took a bottle of tonic from the fridge and poured it into Sofia's glass, knowing instinctively that it was full of vodka, before pouring sparkling water into a glass for Blaire. She then sat behind the writing bureau, pen in hand, ready to take control.

Blaire and Sofia didn't say a word while Victoria prepared to tidy up the situation like a maid tidying up a room.

"As you both well know any false information can be broadcasted by one fan to millions of others in the blink of an eye," she said, as if she was speaking to a pair of six-year-olds. "Your reputation is riding on your next move, so we have to play this very carefully, especially at your age, Sofia."

"I'm twenty-eight for Christssakes!" said Sofia.

"Yes, exactly. Your sell-by date is just around the corner so we have got to maximise this opportunity. We do not want to blow it with *Violet Tiger*, got it? I'd like to think that a second series will be confirmed once you finish filming the first and critics have had a gawk."

"It wasn't the role I wanted. They'll have me playing a grandmother next. I want to be the action girl, not some crappy stay-at-home mom with baby-sick in her hair."

Victoria remained calm as Blaire took a deep breath and got to her feet, regaining her role as 'momanager' as the media liked to call her.

"Victoria is right, darling."

"Yes, okay," said Victoria, cutting across Blaire and standing up too. "Sofia, we need to get you to the status of a bankable actress. This is not going to happen unless we do something to steady the ship and fast. Those hacks right now are asking all kinds of questions – we are talking across New York City and LA. People talk, Sofia, they always do. Especially when there is a hundred-dollar-bill waved in front of them."

Sofia looked at Blaire, thinking of Max and his £100 note all those years ago.

"And, let me tell you, if stories of your, shall we say, party lifestyle leak then you can say goodbye to the contract with that French make-up empire that I have been busting my ass for, and not only that," Victoria was now very heated, "you are due to begin filming next month. We have got to stay focused."

Sofia got to her feet and, although Victoria was by no means short, next to Sofia she looked pint-sized.

"Let me just get something straight," said Sofia. "I bloody hate Scotland. It's freezing. It's dark, it's wet. I want to get back to London, LA, Malibu, Christ anywhere but here."

"*Don't be stupid!*" Blaire yelled.

"Hey, hey, girls, take it easy," said Victoria calmly, sitting down and snapping a pretzel in half. "Blaire has filled me in on all the latest, Sofia. And I am sorry about your father, or your non-father.

Well, you know what I mean."

Sofia glared at Victoria.

"And I know exactly how to play things," said Victoria.

Blaire threw a cushion in the air like a basketball through a hoop. "No, Victoria, this time I have the answer."

"Okay," said Victoria disparagingly. "Over to Mrs Tamper."

Blaire held up her hand like a stop sign. "I am no longer Mrs Tamper. I am divorcing Max. And, what's more, my daughter is going to do the opposite."

"What are you talking about?" said Sofia.

"You and George are going to have a mock engagement," said Blaire as if she were delivering the weather forecast. "Your father is signing over his estate to you as we speak. And George wants that estate. He has always expected to inherit it. You will ensure his cooperation by promising to sell it to him after twelve months have elapsed."

Sofia and Victoria looked at each other.

Before Victoria could stamp her foot and say "That's fucking genius," Sofia, eyes wide, shook her head at her mother.

"Okay, Mother. So you have totally lost it now."

"Just think about it, Sofia," said Victoria. "Your mother is right. No one knows about your familial connection to George. Apart from us, and of course his, well, your father, Robert Wyndham."

"And George?" asked Sofia.

"Well, now you are guaranteed to have him by your side," said Blaire.

Seeing Sofia's face, Victoria and Blaire knew they had more work to do to convince her.

"There's no way he won't do it," said Victoria. "I've read enough articles about George to know that he is obsessed with the place – the deer sanctuary, the fishing, the green element."

"And anyway, George is not your problem, Sofia," said Blaire. "You, my dear, are *his* problem. And that is why he will play ball to get you out of the picture."

Victoria checked her miniature Omega. "Okay, we've got to get moving. You ladies need to get changed. I've got wardrobe and make-up people coming up in five, and the car will be here in forty minutes."

"Just hold on. I'm not ready. Just let me think," said Sofia, trying to take it all in. "What the hell is George going to say?"

"Enough of this bullshit!" said Blaire, losing her temper. "You need to buck up and start thinking straight, my girl. It is not a case of what George is going to say to you, it's about what *you* are going to say to George. You are going lay down the law. He plays ball with you for the next twelve months, just until we get this new series in the bag. Plus he's going to bankroll you, it's your right. Anyway, Robert owes you for missing out on your childhood."

When it came down to it, Victoria was the only person who could take Sofia on this thought-path. Taking Sofia by the arm into the dressing room, she looked at her with a deadly serious expression. "Look, honey," she said, trying to find compassion, "it is not part of my remit to be your shrink. As far as I am concerned we are about to announce your engagement to one of the United Kingdom's most eligible bachelors – the media will go wild and this is key to your profile."

Sofia and Victoria looked at each other, eye to eye.

"George is handsome, famous, well respected and rich. And he is famously discreet about his girlfriends. An announcement like this is one that the media will die for. They know George isn't one to jump into hasty decision – he has their trust that he is a man of judgement – and you mark my words, once you are linked to George you will get all the respect and media-love you can lap up. And then, as soon as we have you on an even keel, second series, the modelling contract and the others in the bag, you can sell him the goddamn house of haggis. Lock, stock and corkscrew."

Sofia started to feel the possibilities and that maybe the plan wasn't so crazy after all.

"So, Sofia, to recap. Your, let's say, 'public father' is in prison, but your blood father is signing over a multimillion Scottish estate to you as I speak. You can have the life, spending George's money, and then you sell to George and you will have a solid career and a fortune in the bank. It's a no-brainer." Victoria held Sofia's chin in her hand, quite firmly. "Don't screw this up, Sofia. You know I work on commission. You owe me after all the shit I've hauled you out of, including that orgy in Vegas."

This touched a nerve and Sofia relented. "Okay, I get it. Just tell me what to do."

Chapter 21

Sitting on the bus from Dublin airport, Anna held onto the little gold bird around her neck.

She hadn't expected George to be waiting for her outside her flat when she left work early to pack for a weekend in Ireland.

"Five months already," he'd said once they were inside. "I walked up Bond Street last night and the thought struck me: five months today," and he'd pulled a Tiffany box out of his pocket.

"George," she'd said, as she opened the turquoise-blue box, "it's beautiful. It's a humming bird?"

"Yes," he said.

"Thank you," she'd whispered, and they'd kissed.

"Do we have time?"

"The plane leaves in three hours."

"What if I book you onto the next flight? My treat and I'll throw in a taxi?" he said.

"Cheeky! You think your extravagances can talk me around?"

"Absolutely."

"My treat more like," said Anna, slipping off her cardigan and unbuttoning his shirt, and she had made her flight in perfect time.

Bernard was waiting for Anna at the bus in Drummare and they drove to Farley Hall, where Anna found Freddie, wearing one of Harry's holey jumpers over stripy leggings, walking out of the walled garden with a basket filled with rhubarb.

"Darling, you're home," said Freddie, spilling the rhubarb onto the ground as she hugged Anna. "Did Bernard mention that he was going to cut the grass, I wonder?"

"He did mention it was going to rain so, knowing Bernard, it's unlikely," said Anna.

"Why are men so obsessed by the weather?" said Freddie, picking up the rhubarb with Anna. "But I'm sure George is different?"

George was perfect for Anna, in every possible way, Freddie thought. Freddie had decided she was going to focus on advice towards engagement. She even had a book called *Turning Your Engagement Into a Diamond Opportunity* that her mother had given to her when she became engaged in the 1970's.

"It reminds me of stories my mother used to tell me," she said, "about men being 'laid out for the ladies'. It sounds horrifically old-fashioned, doesn't it?"

"What, on a table?" asked Anna, doing a toe-tapping Michael Flatley impression.

"If you were invited to a dinner party, you could be sure that a man would be laid out for you. You know, invited with you in mind, so that you could avoid being a wallflower."

"Like an old-fashioned dating agency," said Anna. The thought of being hurled in the direction of someone was not her idea of romance.

"Exactly," said Freddie, as Harry came bounding across the lawn.

"Great news, girls! And hello, Anna sweetheart, welcome home!"

"Hi, Dad, how are you?" she said as they hugged.

"Bloody well excellent you'll be thrilled to hear. I've just had a call from Nadeem's assistant."

"Oh yes?"

"He has signed up to board the rocket that's going into space, would you believe?"

"I would actually," giggled Freddie. "Remember when he arrived to our fancy-dress party by plane? Jumping out dressed not as James Bond but as an Irish priest. God, everyone went wild! It was like watching a Father Ted lookalike gliding down with a lightweight parachute overhead and landing effortlessly on polished Gucci patent loafers."

"That's Nadeem alright. Not your average sheik."

"Certainly not. Anyway, it's a long time since our days of adventuring together."

"And let's keep it that way," said Freddie.

Nadeem had a love for extreme sports and with means to indulge he had taken Harry on some great adventures over the years, including mountain trekking in East Africa and stargazing in Chile's Atacama Desert. It was when Nadeem took Harry to Ferrari World in Abu Dhabi that Freddie put her foot on the brakes, when Harry suffered a minor heart attack.

"Yes, yes. Anyway, in case the rocket goes AWOL, Nadeem wants to make sure his wife has a flattering portrait of him."

"How terribly vain."

"Yes, well, my darling, when you are the son of the kingdom, you can afford to be vain. Honestly, my recent commissions, some of the budgets were so small it was barely worth my while to lift a brush, so to have something meaty, darling, that's what we need. Might even fill up the cellar now. So he'll be coming over to sit for me next month."

"Oh lord, and out with the single malt!"

"We'll be good, my darling, and now I had better go and get the studio sorted. Any chance I could borrow Dharma for a few hours to give me a hand?"

"Harry!"

"I'm sure he'd love a run-around with the hoover. You know how Mrs B complains about the mess when she goes in there, and I'm so hopeless with anything electrical, couldn't even manage the toothbrush you gave me."

"Harry, Dharma is here to guide me in mediation and yoga, not to hoover."

"Oh, all right. I'll see you girls later."

And as Harry belted into the yard to get organised, Freddie handed Anna a secateurs. "Are you happy to get stuck in, Anna, or would you like to unpack first?"

"Ready to get stuck in, Mum – honestly it's such a relief to be out of the office."

"Bravo – any buds, just whisk them off, thanks, darling."

That evening, having had a lovely hot bath after a heavenly afternoon gardening, Anna arrived into the kitchen to find Mrs B, with her hair in a sherry-coloured hairnet, making apple cake.

"That Sri Lankan fellow eats a lot for the size of him, and doesn't he thank me profusely before and after every meal, God bless him. And he won't sit down in the kitchen, he likes to stand, and when he isn't in those positions in the garden, Lord bless us, Anna, it's like having the Dalai Lama in the house. Sure isn't he talking about the bees and the harmony of the land? Bernard can't make head nor tail of him but I like his ways. He's a gentle soul, there's no doubt on that one."

"He certainly is."

"And, Lord Jesus, would you look at the clothes I've got to deal with," said Mrs B, pointing to a pair of Harry's trousers over the Aga rail. "Paint all over the cords – and those jumpers! 'Tis impossible. But sure that goes with the territory. Your mother on her head from sunrise to sunset and your father head to toe in the paint."

Anna dipped her finger into the cake mixture, like she used to do as a child and Mrs B gently slapped her wrist and they both laughed.

"You haven't done that in a while," said Anna.

"And sure look at you now, Anna. I sometimes think you're still a wee girl. I can see you now, running along after your pony, your wee curls bouncing, and then wouldn't Bernard be there with a big bucket of oats to catch the brat of a pony."

"You and Bernard arrived here around the same time, didn't you?"

"We did. And I just getting over the death of my Ned."

"And Bernard?"

"Well, you know he never married."

"Yes, I know, but what I mean is: you have both worked together for so long, Bernard in the garden, you in the house – didn't you ever consider it?"

"Well, aren't you the cheeky one!" said Mrs B. "Now, the trick with this cake is to cook it slowly so that the apples soften." The apple cake was Mrs B's signature dish. "Your mother will be complaining as usual about the amount of cream and butter I use. But, sure, a little goes a long way. It's the way we like it, isn't that right, Anna? And now here we go!" She picked up a digital timer. "I am just getting the hang of this. Wasn't that celebrity chef from Blacklion here last month, discussing his portrait with your father, and he gave me this fancy gadget to time my cakes. Lord, it's a complicated business." Adjusting her glasses and pressing the shiny silver timer three times, Mrs B sat down. "Now sorry, my pet, come and sit down. Lord, you've lost weight. Are they not feeding you over there?"

"Oh, I'm fine!" said Anna and, to change the subject, asked, "How long were you married, Mrs B? It was only a year, wasn't it?"

"Yes, only a year." She held out her hands. "You know, sometimes Ned's hands were so ragged from the mines that the skin at the joints would crack. Lord, it was the devil! I'd have to rub lanolin onto them. He was very ill in the end. He died a young man. They just didn't have the medication then. It was the mines that did his lungs in. And by the end, well, he was so miserable that he had no energy left to love me. And that was it."

"It's so sad, Mrs B."

"Yes, God rest him. Now, Anna, you need to remember that there's a lid for every pot. You'll know when it's right. But you must be wise in your choice."

That evening, Freddie and Dharma were meditating in the drawing room after dinner when Anna found Harry sitting at the kitchen table, head in his hands, sobbing as he listened to Bach's Fifth Concerto.

"Dad, what's the matter?" she asked, pulling up a chair.

"Sorry, my darling, you know how this music affects me. I just feel overwhelmed sometimes. You are my little girl and to see you with that tall, handsome fellow, well, it somehow makes everything seem like it's moving so fast. It doesn't seem all that long ago that I used to take you out riding on Penthouse. Remember how we'd cross those ditches, you sitting in front of me in the saddle, clinging on for dear life?"

"And how terrified I was?"

"But you were brave, Anna. And you knew Penthouse would never let anything happen to you. Those blissful mornings, they were so peaceful."

Anna thought of the morning rides around the land during her childhood. Crossing bogs and climbing ditches, she was like her father's good-luck mascot. Holding on tightly to the strap around Penthouse's neck, she kept her eyes firmly shut, slowly opening one eye and then the other as she and her father cantered down the back avenue and out onto the heavenly bogland.

"Remember that time when Penthouse got caught up in wire and you quoted Grandpa?"

"*The only wire on a gentleman's estate should be around a champagne cork.*"

Harry wiped his eyes and smiled. Taking a sip from his whiskey, he got up and took a small glass from the cupboard.

"A little nightcap for you, darling?"

"Go on then," said Anna. "Then I had better get my beauty sleep. Gilda's been working me like a Trojan."

"And how about that man of yours, does he work hard?"

"I think so," said Anna. "He seems to discreetly seek out art for clients, and sometimes gets involved in art preservation campaigns and things."

"Yes, I've read about him in various magazines. Seems to be respected. Doing well, considering he's still in his thirties."

Anna took a sip of whiskey, and let Guinness rest his head on her lap. "You know, I didn't think I'd meet someone like George so soon. I figured in my twenties I'd just focus on my career."

"It sounds like you're pretty serious about this George."

"It does, doesn't it?" said Anna, rubbing Guinness's ears and sitting back into the chair.

Anna and Harry sat happily in silence.

Chapter 22

As Harry buzzed into the kitchen, Mrs B was chopping up parsley and thyme with a face like thunder. "Lord Jesus, Mr Rose, sure didn't you nearly make my heart jump in my mouth."

"Sorry, old girl – you see, I'm all fired up," said Harry. "Things are on the move, Mrs B, and I'm just over the moon about it." Linking his arm into Mrs B's, he led her around the kitchen table for a quick jig. "Now, I'm going to take Penthouse out for a gallop – you know, as part of my new work routine. A quick ride in the morning then I'll settle down with my brushes."

"And ease off the whiskey, mind," said Mrs B, giving Harry a gentle elbow. "It must be Midsummer's Day that's got you all giddy."

Guinness made a break for it out the door and bounded up the stairs. Bursting into Anna's room he leapt onto her bed, snuffling her neck.

"Oh Guinness, get off, you crazy loon!" she said, laughing as he went into a barking frenzy.

Getting up and opening the shutters, she saw her father trotting down the avenue on Penthouse. Still in an afterglow of those lovely days with George, blue skies and dew twinkling on the lawn, to Anna the land couldn't have looked more beautiful. As she pulled on her jeans and a thick woolly polo-neck, she looked at her bed and thought about George and how he had lain there blowing her kisses and making her laugh.

"What a difference to the grey days we've had to put up with, don't you think, Guinness – so how about a walk?"

Running to the landing, she threw her leg over the banister and flew down the mahogany handrail to the hallway with Guinness barking beside her. Maybe she and George could live in Ireland or even Scotland. Quickly buttering a piece of brown bread in the kitchen, she set off through the yard with Guinness and into the woods. She thought of all the publicity she could secure for the gardens at Rousey. They could hire a manager to run events. George could exhibit his collections and they would have lots of big parties. It was all so hugely promising. But then she thought about George's father, and what if George wasn't the marrying kind? But he just was, Anna knew it. Hearing a blackbird trilling a love tune high in the trees, she knew it didn't matter what anyone else thought. She knew what it was like to wake up in George's arms, to hear him whisper her name as they slid beneath the blankets.

Carefully crossing the fence of barbed wire and hawthorn, Anna saw a small herd of sika deer moving across the field, with Harry and Penthouse galloping alongside them. It was a romantic sight, seeing her father and Penthouse making their way across the tufty hills. As Anna was about to take a picture with her phone, a young deer peeled off from the herd and shot off with a flared rump, thundering in a zigzag across the field. Thrilled at the sight of a lone deer, Penthouse kicked out his hind legs and raced towards the ditch. Harry managed to slow Penthouse down but he took a mighty leap over the ditch. Penthouse continued to gallop on the other side, but his saddle had slipped. Harry had come off.

Anna yelled for Penthouse but knew he would head for home and thankfully the reins appeared not to have come over his head. Anna stopped to see if she could see Harry getting up on the other side but she couldn't get a good view. As she ran downhill with wet thistles pin-pricking through her skinny jeans, her mind began to scramble. The closer she got to the ditch the more concern she felt. There were no reassuring yells or swear words coming from her father's direction. The ground was muddy and uneven, so she had to land on clumps of grass to keep her feet from sinking.

Running through a tiny gap in the hedge Anna found her father slumped on the muddy ground, the ruddy colour of his face drained to grey.

"Dad, can you hear me?"

Harry opened his eyes. "Sweetheart," he whispered, "where's Penthouse? Don't let him break his neck on the reins," and he closed his eyes. His breath was shallow and panting.

Taking off her sleeveless puffa, she eased it beneath his head. There was no coverage on her phone. "Dad, I'm going to get help. Just hold on, please, please hold on."

"Anna," Harry whispered, "get your mother."

As she ran towards the house, Anna tried to call for help but no words came out. She passed the bathtub filled with green algae in the corner of the field, taking a shortcut to the house. Seeing Penthouse ahead of her in the yard, his body heaving and covered in white foamy sweat, Bernard by his side, Anna tried to call out but could only cry.

"It's Dad," she gasped as she reached them. "We need an ambulance, quickly ... an ambulance."

Mrs B had been hanging out the washing when Penthouse came crashing into the yard. Crossing herself, she'd shouted for Bernard and stood frozen by the washing line, a tea towel and a pillowcase over her shoulder. Guinness lay down next to Penthouse, knowing there had been a terrible accident.

Freddie did the opposite of what anyone would have expected. There was no flat spin, no hysterics. She dug into her yoga mindset and calmly climbed into the back of the Land Rover, followed by Anna and Dharma. Mrs B handed them in some blankets and a hipflask. Bernard drove down the avenue, while Dharma prayed.

"Stop!" shouted Freddie as the jeep entered the field and began to swing from left to right, crossing through puddles. "I need to get out, I have to get to Harry." Opening the door, she jumped out and ran across the field. By the time Anna reached the ditch, Freddie was lying next to Harry, her hand on his cheek, not saying a word. Bernard and Dharma stood back from the Rose family, as an ambulance siren could be heard in the distance, drawing ever closer.

Chapter 23

The sky in Edinburgh was a classic grey as George walked along Exchange Crescent wearing a cream suit and dark glasses. A circle of women, gossiping around a toddler's pushchair, turned their heads as he passed them by. George was feeling uneasy having received a call from Jamie informing him about Harry's fall earlier that morning, and as Anna wasn't picking up her phone he thought he'd try the house.

"Hello?" said George.

"Farley Hall, and who's this?"

"Mrs B? Hello, it's George Wyndham."

"Ah George," said Mrs B, her voice slightly breaking. "Anna's with her poor father at the hospital, Lord save him."

"I'm so sorry." George paused. "I've tried to call Anna several times but …"

"Sure didn't she lose her phone, running through the fields to find help. The poor wee girl, white as a ghost when she arrived into the yard."

"Mrs B, please can you let Anna know that I will be over as soon as I possibly can."

"I will, George, I will."

"And that I'm thinking of you all. Please send Anna my love."

Walking into Collins & Associates law firm, he took the elevator to the fifth floor.

When the elevator doors opened, the receptionist hid her Tupperware of quinoa salad in a drawer and, not wanting to chew, tried to swallow a walnut whole but it resulted in a mortifying coughing fit. George raced across the floor and thumped her back as he looked around for a glass of water.

"I am so utterly mortified, Mr Wyndham," she said afterwards. "I must be coming down with something."

"You must be," said George kindly.

With a smile, the receptionist picked up an old-fashioned telephone handset to let her boss know that George had arrived.

"Can I make you a coffee, Mr Wyndham?"

"Nothing, no, thank you," said George, making her day by saying, "I'm glad to see you're feeling better."

In the meeting room George found himself face to face with his father. Sitting at the head of a large black oval table, Robert was dressed in a sports jacket, a polka-dot tie and a yellow checked shirt.

"Ah George, excellent, you're here," said Robert, clean-shaven with hair combed back, eyes bright and looking ten years younger. George could even smell aftershave.

"It's good to see you," said Robert.

"Is it?" asked George.

"Now, George, there's no need to make this difficult."

"Father, I need to get to the airport. Anna needs me."

"Does she?"

"Yes, she has a family crisis."

"It's a good feeling, isn't it?" said Robert. "To be needed?"

"Father, I –" George attempted to cut in.

"In fact, I feel like I've been in a coma for the past twenty-nine years and I am just waking up, and you know what, George?"

"I am sensing you are going to tell me."

"It feels bloody well fantastic."

"Good for you."

Robert felt like he had been given a second chance, even though it would sound like a cliché to any therapist. The woman he once loved, and even more so desired, had returned to him. And she had given him a daughter. After all these years, he could be with the woman he loved, and be a father to his daughter, and with a bulging bank account he felt like King Pin. Was there guilt? Maybe. But he had to let the overwhelming positives counterbalance any niggles and George was one such niggle. Since their reunion, Blaire encouraged Robert to bathe every day in a bubbling swirl of Penhaligon's Blenheim Bouquet and she had also employed a beauty therapist to trim and smooth where possible. At sixty there was life in the old dog yet, as he liked to say, and following Blaire's promises of sexual favours he was being brought back to life.

"Where is David?" asked George flatly. "You said on the phone that he has some estate papers for me to sign."

"Yes," said Robert, tapping a teaspoon against a saucer. "That's right. We have some papers for you."

George looked at his father. There was something about him. Not just his suit or his sleek hair. For the first time ever in his memory, his father actually looked happy.

"And George . . ."

"Yes?"

"Try to be civil. You must remember he is merely carrying out his duty as our family lawyer."

George was not in the mood for a lecture. He needed to get to Ireland.

"Send David in," said Robert, speaking to the receptionist via a white handset telephone. "You should take a seat, George, no point in tiring yourself out."

"I'm fine," said George.

"As you wish," said Robert. "Ah, there you are, David – you remember my son, George."

"I do, how are you, George," said David, but George looked to the floor with his hands firmly clasped together. He was in no mood for friendly handshakes.

"David, sit down, would you? There's no point in trying to get small talk out of George, is there? Now then," Robert said, clearing his throat, "the reason why I've asked you to come here, George, is ..."

"Go on," said George.

"Twenty-eight years ago, I became a father for the second time."

"You had an affair?"

"If you want to call it that, then yes."

"The woman by the river."

"Yes, George, if you must know, it was the woman by the river as you so eloquently put it." Robert paused to take a sip from his teacup, which George suspected was filled with whiskey. "And I have recently received extraordinary news."

"Such as?" George had spent years of his life trying to understand his father but now he was firmly resigned to the fact that he could never get to grips with him.

Robert, eyes shining and hands jittery, spoke quickly to get the words out. "I have a daughter. There, I've said it. I have a daughter."

"A daughter?" said George as his phone beeped with a message.

"Yes. And therefore you have a sister. Well, a half-sister. Technically," said Robert, picking up the white handset again. "Send my daughter in, would you please?"

"Father, what the hell is going on?" George's heart began to thump.

"We have all been estranged for long enough. It's time to bring things out of the dark and I want you to meet her."

George closed his eyes and stepping towards the table he pulled out a chair and sat down. "Hold on. Are you telling me that you have some kind of love child that you've been hiding away all this time?"

As the door opened, George stood up again and turned to see Sofia Tamper, smiling widely and dressed in a grey leopard-print-lined two-piece suit.

She and George stared at each other.

Then, pushing her long silky mane of hair behind her shoulders, Sofia raised her chin.

"Hello, George, or should I say *brother darling?*"

"What the hell?" George, his cheeks burning, looked from left to right, his mind reeling, as he ran his fingers through his hair.

Robert stood up. "Now this is all very straightforward," he said, presiding over them as if he were a judge directing a jury. "Isn't that right, David?"

"That's correct," said David, placing three sheaves of paper in front of him as if he was about to deal oversized cards in a casino.

"Go ahead, David," said Robert.

"The deeds of Rousey estate, six thousand acres and the house in its entirety, along with estate cottages is to be gifted to Sofia by her father, Robert Wyndham." David couldn't meet George's eyes, which were riveted on him in disbelief.

Squeezing his fists, George pulled a chair out of his way to stand in front of his father.

"What is this? Have you lost your mind?" George's eyes were red and his forehead sweating.

"Quite the opposite, George," said Robert, as if he were discussing a Christmas toy with a jealous child. "Sofia should have been with me a long time ago but," he paused, "there is no way to change the past. Isn't that right, Blaire?"

She had slipped into the office without George noticing. Blaire's dark hair with auburn highlights fell around her shoulders – the way she used to wear it when she first met Robert.

"We meet at last, George," said Blaire. "I see you have had the good fortune to inherit your father's looks."

George literally couldn't look at her. He was totally under siege.

"But she has no connection to Rousey, no love for the place," said George. "You know what Rousey means to me."

"I know what money means to you, George, and your sense of entitlement is rather unattractive," said Robert.

"You know bloody well it's not about that!"

"You have already inherited a fortune, George, thanks to your mother," said Robert calmly, "and now it's your sister's turn. Rousey is for Sofia and it is for her to decide what she wants to do with the place."

"Thank you, Daddy," said Sofia, playing her role as the angelic daughter perfectly.

"What? What evidence, I mean, what evidence can you have? You're being taken for a ride." And George turned to Sofia. "How could you do this? Did you know when I last saw you? How long have you known?"

"*That's enough!*" Robert shouted, and he began coughing,

Sofia and Blaire looked at each other, looking as if they were wondering whether he was going to keel over.

With a face of concern, genuine or otherwise, Blaire sat Robert down and began patting his back.

"I'm fine," he said calmly as he gathered himself together, taking a handkerchief from his pocket and wiping his mouth. "Now, George, you need to listen."

George, his back to the wall, was trying to control himself.

"I've always known," said Robert darkly. "The day I let Blaire walk away from me, I knew I was letting more than the love of my life go. She carried my heart with her, and as it turned out she carried my baby too." He took out his silver cigarette lighter, given to him by Gussy on the eve of their marriage and he threw it on the table. "I've no need for this any more. I've quit smoking."

"Have you even taken a paternity test?" said George.

"No, I have not."

"Seriously? Are you telling me that you haven't actually verified this claim?"

"I don't need some laboratory telling me who my own flesh and blood is," said Robert, as Blaire and Sofia positioned themselves either side of his chair. "My instinct tells me all I need to know."

"Rousey was Mum's life," said George. "She'd want me there, I know it, to raise a family there. And what about Finlay and Grace? They've been on the estate all my life. You can't just turf them out of their home."

"Well, George, if you want Rousey, you'll have to bloody well buy it from your sister. That's the only way you're going to get your hands on the place."

"Just hold on. You have to take a test, Father, you have to," said George.

"I don't *have* to do anything, George."

"Why not?" said Blaire, piping up amidst the rage with her freshly blow-dried hairdo and plum-coloured lipstick. "Let's have a paternity test. You wouldn't mind, would you, Sofia? A little cotton-wool swab in your mouth?"

"If it means calling a halt to George's accusations that we're lying, then I'm all for it," said Sofia.

"There's no need," said Robert. "I won't have scientists dictating to me who my children are. I know, I've always known. She's mine, George, Sofia is my daughter."

"Now, Robert, honey, that's all very well, but why not satisfy everyone's curiosity. Take the test. David, you can arrange for a nurse to meet with Robert and Sofia, can't you?'"

"I can certainly recommend a lab," he said.

"There then, that's settled. And now George can relax, isn't that right, George?" said Blaire, sickly sweet.

"Relax? This whole situation is a complete farce. There is no way you will get your hands on Rousey – forget it, Sofia."

"Oh, but she will, George," said Robert. "It is my gift to my daughter. And while we're at it, you may as well know that I've asked Blaire to marry me, as I should have done twenty-nine years ago."

"Just as soon as my divorce comes through," said Blaire, swelling with her accomplishment. She might as well have dusted her hands.

"There's no need to look so bitter, George," said Robert. "Your mother left you more wealth than most people could imagine. It's your sister's time now."

George stared at a light bulb, hanging from the ceiling, stuck inside a badly fitted shade.

"You know, George, apart from the country sports side of things I was never really cut out for Big House living," said Robert.

"Is that so?" said George.

"We're going to live in Geneva, Blaire and I."

"That's right," said Blaire. "Your father will go ahead of me, and then I'll join him just as soon as I get Sofia settled."

"Blaire has found a fabulous apartment in Vandoeuvres on the left bank, haven't you, darling?" he said, looking up at Blaire as if she were his saviour. "It's all set up, and I've packed very little."

"No need for filthy old cords where we're going," said Blaire.

Robert smoothed his hands down the waist of his suit. "I'm enjoying these rather luxurious fabrics, aren't I, darling?"

"All compliments of the Titian," said George coldly.

"Nothing less than I deserve. Being stuck at Rousey for so many years, living on a shoestring."

"A very long shoestring," said George, who could hardly bear to listen to any more. "I'm surprised there's even anything left to sit on in the house, so much has been auctioned to feed your filthy gambling habit."

"I am the sixteenth Wyndham to have lived in the place and you know what? *I don't give a fuck any more!*" shouted Robert, slamming his hands on the table. "That place has been the ruination of us and I want out." The apples of his cheeks were red, and spider veins crept around his nose as he spoke. "Ghastly weather and bloody nationalists, and I can't even find a fish in the river and *I – want – out*. So I'm getting out."

Before Robert got to the door George strode over to him, fist clenched ready to punch him. He pulled back his arm but he knew it wasn't in him.

"Go on then, George. Hit me. But it's not in you, is it? You always were a mummy's boy, weren't you?"

And Robert was right. George was his mother's son through and through. The car accident flashed into George's mind, and how his mother had put out her arm to shield him before the side of the car smashed into the wall. Without looking at any of them, he opened the door and walking into the lobby he got into the elevator, ignoring the receptionist's pout in his direction.

"Well done, darling," said Blaire, smoothing her hands across Robert's back. "I'm so proud of you."

"David, I'm going to leave you to it now," said Robert, who appeared not to register what he had just done to George. "You see to it that all legal documents are in place and that there are no details left undealt with. Rousey is Sofia's and George is out of the match."

Blaire straightened her suit and checked her face in her compact mirror. She wasn't far from where she needed to be now – the next step was to make sure of her own security now that Sofia had a fortune of assets, which would set her up nicely and support her while she got her career on a steady footing.

Chapter 24

Peter Lynch was widely regarded as the most handsome consultant in the hospital. This morning he stood over Harry Rose, who lay in a bed looking like he was attached to the inner workings of a ship, with wires and narrow tubes linked to several machines. With one eye on the digital monitor, Peter wrote some notes on a clipboard, which he handed to a nurse called Teresa who batted her eyelids at him. He loathed the part of his job where he had to deliver discouraging news to a patient's family, particularly when he saw Freddie and Anna leaning against the cold wall next to Harry's bed, both still in considerable shock. He would much prefer to make such beauties smile.

"The morning is a terribly common time for a heart attack," said Peter. "Larger adrenaline amounts are released at that hour. Harry was fortunate not to have broken anything when he fell from the horse."

Peter offered Freddie a chair but she declined.

"I'm afraid his condition continues to be critical."

"Please, Peter," said Freddie, "just speak plainly. Will he get better?"

"Well, our team have managed to open the blocked arteries around his heart, restoring blood flow, and as you can see by the tube in his throat we are administering oxygen to aid breathing."

Freddie and Anna winced when they looked at Harry's mouth, with a tube feeding into his lungs.

"It looks so uncomfortable," said Anna.

"Yes," said Peter, "though Harry has been heavily sedated and so he will hardly even be aware of it. The equipment can seem overwhelming, I know, but each monitor is crucial in monitoring Harry's heart, his blood pressure, and his respiratory rate."

"Can he hear us?" asked Freddie.

"I'd say so," said Peter, lowering his voice. "It is crucial that Harry has a smooth run during the next twenty-four hours. If he can do that, the outlook will improve a good deal, so let's focus on that for now, shall we?"

He wasn't sure if Freddie was registering much of what he was saying but, seeing this tightly knit family of three before him, he very much hoped that Harry could defy the likely outcome.

"Get some rest if you can," said Peter. "There's a relatives' room next door and, though it's not the most comfortable room in the world, it's somewhere for you to rest your heads tonight at least."

"Oh no, I can't leave Harry," said Freddie, shaking her head, her eyes filled with fear. "I won't leave."

"Mum, it's okay, I'm sure we can stay here," said Anna and looking at Peter asked, "If that's all right?"

"Of course. Look, I'll arrange to have an armchair brought in for your mother. As you can see space is tight, but I'm sure we can make an exception."

"Thank you, Peter," said Anna. "We'll be here."

"And the nurses will be in and out. Don't worry if they look overly serious – that's all part of their job so try not to read their expressions. That's what my dad used to tell me."

"He was a medic too?"

"Yes, a heart surgeon actually, and a rather keen fisherman. He much preferred the river to the operating theatre, but then work and play is all part of life, isn't it?"

Anna looked at her father and nodded. "Yes, similar to my father."

"I had better call Mrs B," said Freddie. "She'll be worrying about supper, and Harry." Her hands trembled as she searched her coat pockets for her phone. "She is utterly devoted to him. All those blasted pies, I told Harry to ease up, but would he listen? No, no, no ... Oh, he was so happy about the commission from Nadeem, Anna, so happy."

Freddie wiped the tears from her eyes, took a deep breath and stretched out her arms. Her gold bracelets rang like bells for evensong.

"Mum, it's okay," said Anna softly. She embraced her mother and held her.

Peter smiled kindly, bowed his head and left the room.

Once the armchair arrived, Freddie curled up like a mouse, her yoga legs folded beneath her.

Tucking a thin navy hospital blanket over her, Anna had never felt more like an only daughter. Now she had to take on a new responsibility and steer the ship for her parents as best she could.

Anna and Freddie spent the night in Harry's room. Freddie slept while Anna listened to the oxygen humming like a pump for party balloons. Dawn had broken by the time Freddie awoke.

"Anna, darling," she said, rubbing her eyes and sitting up to look at Harry. "Your father looks so very pale and weak. And you, darling, look dreadful, pale as a ghost. Go and find something for breakfast, will you? We didn't eat a thing yesterday, and we need to keep our strength up – that's the sort of thing Mrs B would say, isn't it? Please do go, Anna."

"No, you go, Mum," said Anna, peering out the window at the rain drizzling on the car park below.

"I will go once you return, I promise, Anna. Really, I want you to go first."

Feeling queasy and befuddled from her broken sleep, Anna kissed her parents and left the room in search of coffee. During the night, she had wept quietly at her father's side and longed for George.

Walking along the corridor, Anna spotted a familiar figure standing by a coffee machine, pressing a button over and over.

"Tilly!"

"Anna, you're here, thank goodness," said Tilly, giving her a huge hug.

"My goodness, how did you get here so fast? It's only 9am. That is seriously good going."

"The red-eye flight from Gatwick at six this morning," said Tilly. "Hence my looking rather bedraggled and trying to get this blasted coffee machine to work." She gave the side of the machine a whack but nothing happened. "Jamie brought me to the airport. He sends masses of love and says to tell you he's thinking of your dad, okay?"

"That's so kind. And George, does he know?"

"Yes," said Tilly, "Jamie called George this morning, just as he was going in to a meeting. George said he is going to get on the next available flight."

"Thank God," said Anna, and checking her pockets said, "Oh, I forgot! I've lost my phone." Her eyes began to well up again. "I dropped it in the field when I was running ... when I was trying to get help."

"Oh Anna, I can't imagine. Look, this coffee machine clearly has a mind of its own. Let's go and find you some breakfast. Is your mum okay without you for a while?"

"I think so, but I'd better not be too long. Oh God, Tilly, I can't believe this is happening."

"It must all be very frightening," said Tilly, spying a coffee machine in what looked like a very small waiting room. "I'm sure we can park in here for a while, can't we? And there are some muffins – let's share one, I'm sure no one will mind."

Sitting at the small table, Anna held her head in her hands.

"You're most likely still in shock. Try to eat a little of the muffin at least?"

Anna shook her head and, feeling a dreadful rush of nausea, pushed back her chair and ran out the door. Tilly followed and watched Anna plunge into a bathroom. Pushing open the door, Tilly found a cleaning lady running a mop back and forth in front of the sinks, listening to music with headphones.

"Anna?" Tilly called out, "Are you okay?"

"Hold on," called out a muffled voice from one of the cubicles.

A loo flushed, the door opened and Anna stepped out. She walked slowly to the sink with hollow eyes, barely noticing either Tilly or the cleaner. She washed her hands and splashed water over her face.

"Anna, what's going on? Did you throw up?"

"What do you expect? My father has had a massive bloody heart attack and I think he's about to die!" And then, hanging her head, she sobbed. "Tills, I'm so sorry, so sorry, I didn't mean to shout."

"No, don't apologise. But, seriously, you look so pale ... do you think you have a bug?"

"I don't know," said Anna, but the way she said it and the way she looked at Tilly, and the way they knew each other so well, meant that they were very soon thinking the exact same thing.

"No, I couldn't possibly be. Could I?"

"It depends on how careful you've been," said Tilly. "Anna?"

"Quite?" said Anna, pulling a face.

"Okay," said Tilly, taking control. "I'm going to run to the pharmacy. I saw one on my way in. It's literally by the hospital entrance. I'll be back. Five minutes."

"No, Tilly, not now. I've got to focus on Dad."

"Yes, you do. But we also have to make sure that is all you're dealing with. It's important to check, Anna."

"Yes, all right," said Anna, her shoulders sinking a little. And, walking to the door, she apologised to the cleaner for stepping on her clean floor.

"Five minutes tops," repeated Tilly. "I'll meet you back by that useless coffee machine."

"So, what does it say?" whispered Tilly, standing outside the cubicle in the ladies'. "Anna?"

Pulling back the lock of the door, Anna emerged with an uncertain smile, tears running down her face.

"And?" said Tilly.

"It's says I'm three weeks pregnant."

"Oh my God, Anna." Tilly didn't know whether to cry herself. "I can't believe it."

"I can't even think," said Anna, staring at her reflection in the mirror. "There's too much happening at once. Tilly, this has got to be put to one side for now. Not a word, okay? Especially not to Jamie."

"Of course not. Oh Anna, what do you feel?"

"It's crazy," said Anna. "I don't know how I feel, except that I am missing George so much."

"What can I do?" asked Tilly, her mind racing. Anna was only twenty-six and how long had she and George been together? Three months? Surely no longer than that?

"Did you hire a car?" asked Anna.

"Yes, a very swanky Audi, although I've no idea how to work any of the gadgets and the reverse is where my car's first gear is, so I narrowly missed flattening a poor woman pushing a trolley in the airport car park earlier."

"I know it's a bit of a hike, Tilly, but do you think you might be able to go to Farley Hall and reassure Mrs B? She must be out of her mind with worry, and Bernard too, even Dharma, who has been completely abandoned by Mum. I don't know whether he will want to stay around or fly back to Sri Lanka."

Tilly took the car keys out of her pink suede handbag and put a hand on Anna's shoulder. "I'll drive straight to Farley Hall, and I'll call my boss on the way and let him know that I'll be out of the office for a few days. I'm sure he'll be cool with it. And can you make sure to keep your mum's phone charged so we can stay in contact?"

"Yes. And Tilly, thank you for being such an amazing friend."

"It's quite a time, isn't it?" said Tilly.

Back in her father's room, Anna found Freddie fast asleep with her head on the edge of Harry's mattress, holding his hand. There they were, her parents, together, just as it had always been. With a wave of nausea, Anna counted four in the room, including the baby that was now growing inside her. Was this the circle of life that people talked about? She looked at her father, his face as still as a lake unbroken by fish or flies, his intake of breath so shallow that his chest hardly moved the blankets. Anna had an awful sense that he might not make it. Propped up by pillows, the oxygen tube in his mouth was the only indication that life still existed.

She placed her hand on his chest and watched as his eyes opened very slowly. He turned his head to one side, like a dove nestling into a breast of feathers.

"Mum," Anna whispered, "Mum, wake up."

"Anna, what is it? He isn't leaving us, is he?"

"I don't know," said Anna, afraid to even speak. She looked through the window to see if a nurse was nearby, not wanting to even press a button. The moment was so quiet, so still.

"Don't leave us, Harry?" said Freddie, choking on tears. She pulled the sleeves of her grey cashmere cardigan over her hands and she and Anna clutched each other tightly. "Don't leave us. Please don't leave us."

The door into the room opened abruptly followed by Nurse Teresa and one other nurse who began checking the machines. Nurse Teresa held Harry's pulse with one hand, and looked intently at her watch face with the other.

"That's good. Mrs Rose, I know your husband looks very weak, but he's clearly a fighter. That pulse of his is steady and it's getting stronger. I'll get one of the girls to bring you in a cuppa – that should ease you up a bit."

Beautifully bossy and confident, Nurse Teresa was just the kind of presence the Rose family needed.

Bernard was clipping a hedge on the avenue as Tilly drove up to Farley Hall. Recognising her, he laid down his shears and went to the yard to wash his boots before going into Mrs B in the kitchen for news on Mr Rose.

In the evening light, masses of swallows were swooping around the front of the house. Tilly walked around to the kitchen garden as Guinness bounded out to meet her, hoping that it might be one of the Roses. Somewhat put out to see Tilly instead, he returned to the kitchen and collapsed onto his beanbag by the Aga.

"Mrs B, I'm sorry for coming around to the kitchen, but I didn't want you to have to answer the front door."

Mrs B, seeing Tilly, who had grown into the finest friend to Anna over the years, opened her arms. Holding one of Harry's paisley handkerchiefs along with her rosary beads, she hugged her tightly.

"It must be horrid for you all, Mrs B."

But Mrs B didn't say a word until she had heaved the orange kettle on to the hob.

"It's good to see you back, Tilly."

"A long time, Mrs B," said Tilly, who put out her hand to Bernard as he walked in the back door to the kitchen.

"Hello there, Tilly, it's a sad time, a sad time," he said.

"And the word's out in the parish already," said Mrs B, taking a seat and crossing herself. "Mrs Murray says there's a rumour going around that poor Mr Rose fell from a penthouse in some fancy hotel, when shouldn't they all know by now that Penthouse is the name of that ruddy horse. I should have guessed it when I saw the rooks arriving, a big flock of them squawking and roosting high in the trees over the Reservoir Wood. Them rooks hadn't been in those trees before, or not for a long time, and I knew it was a sign. Oh, what would we do without him, Tilly? I have never been here without Mr Rose, God bless his soul."

"I'll make a pot of tea," said Tilly.

"No, no, stay where you are, Tilly," said Mrs B and she busied herself making the tea. "I don't know how many times I've boiled and reboiled that kettle! Bernard wouldn't even have his biscuits this morning, would you, Bernard?"

"I would not, that's right."

"It's not good, not good at all. I can feel it. I said that, Bernard, didn't I? Those rooks, it's a sign, I'm telling you it's a sign." Mrs B crossed herself again. "And the telephone won't stop ringing with people all asking about Mr Rose and some of them wanting to know where in the world he was when he fell from his penthouse, for goodness' sake. Lord bless us and save us, if you saw the state of Anna when she came running into the yard after she found him. The poor creature."

Dharma arrived in from the back kitchen, with a copy of *The Royal Gardening Encyclopaedia* which he was reading to increase his knowledge of European flora. Putting the book down on the table and smiling at Tilly, he held the palms of his hands together.

"My name is Dharma, I teach yoga to Mrs Rose."

"Hello, Dharma," said Tilly, shaking his hand. "I've heard lots about you."

"I meditate, and I help Mrs Rose to salute the sun."

"So I hear," said Tilly. "Well done, you."

"My words mostly come through my dictionary, but when I talk with Bernard I use his words instead – they are more powerful than the words I find in the book."

"Aye, that's right, Dharma," said Bernard, "but we'll stick to the English speaking, won't we?"

Tilly quickly understood why Freddie and Anna liked having Dharma in the house. He had a lovely way about him, undeniably peaceful, an absolute yin to Harry Rose's yang.

"I think we should hold our hands together, Mrs B, Bernard and Tilly," said Dharma. "We hold our hands together, we pray for Harry Rose."

As Guinness snoozed on his beanbag by the Aga, they all closed their eyes and prayed desperately for the Rose family.

"This standing on ceremony is not good for my joints, Dharma," Mrs B said when they had finished and the others had sat back down. "The arthritis is bothering my knees."

"I pray for your knees, Mrs B."

Nevertheless, she continued to bustle about, setting cups, saucers and side-plates on the table, together with a freshly baked fruit cake.

"And didn't Winterbottom PR send a package as big as my Uncle Ned's tea chest, full of fancy substances, jellies and vinegars and the like," said Mrs B, cutting a piece of fruit cake and passing it to Tilly on a side plate. "Not that they'll find their way into my cooking but maybe Anna will cook when she comes back and we'll keep it in the cupboard for her. I've checked the best-before date and some of them are good until 2020, Lord knows how that's possible. When I was a wee child everything was pickled."

"Admiral Nelson was pickled, no, on the way back from Trafalgar?" said Dharma with a large smile.

"Your knowledge is extensive, isn't it, Dharma?" said Mrs B.

"Extensive, yes, Mrs B," he said, "but I try not to charge my clients too much. Not too extensive and not too cheap, that's what my guru taught me in Sri Lanka."

Chapter 25

The wisteria on the front of Rousey was in full bloom as George turned his car to face the garden view. Looking at the familiar landscape rolling down towards the river, he thought how ironic it was that the place should look so magnificent, despite the lower garden having gone to seed. Grappling with the bombshells that had landed in his lap, George knew his relationship with his father was as good as over. Sofia Tamper, of all people, had somehow been converted into his half-sister and on top of that his father was now eliminating Rousey from George's future. It all felt like a very, very bad joke and he longed for a television crew to jump out of the laurel bushes and say, "Smile, you're on camera!" George tried to think if he had ever felt any sibling connection to Sofia, other than that they were both tall and dark-haired, and it was a struggle to find any similarities between Sofia and his father.

The light from the early evening sun glazed various shades of green along the edge of the woodland, with sheets of pastel dwarf phloxes propping themselves up next to mounds of yellow delphiniums and soft-blue bell-shaped flowers that had made up flower arrangements in the house when George was a boy.

Getting out of the car, he stood beneath a mulberry tree, and closing his eyes he rested his head against its trunk. It was like a gigantic nightmare and thinking of Anna made him wince – but before he could go to her, he needed to get Jamie on the case to challenge the legalities. As he was about to phone Jamie, he heard gravel crunching and looked up to see a black Range Rover with tinted windows driving up the avenue.

Blaire was determined to look the part. She had managed to fit in a blow-dry to complement her sleeveless Burberry dress, and wore lyrca underwear to suck in her waist. Her early-morning walks to Bottega Louie in LA for her daily egg-white omelette might now be a thing of the past but, once she had Sofia's future sorted out, she would carve out a fresh and stylish morning ritual for herself.

As the chauffeur-cum-bodyguard drove the Range Rover up the avenue to Rousey, Victoria briefed him as to his role, the best bodyguard being the one that nobody notices, she reminded him, and such manpower was imperative given that Sofia was about to become engaged to a man worth millions. Blaire was pleased that Victoria had made sure to take a leaf out of William and Kate's immaculate book, making sure their man of muscle was dressed in a check shirt and cords so that he could fit in with the country set. Ayrshire was no place for men with protein-shake muscles and Hugo Boss suits hugging their lean torsos.

From behind the mulberry tree, George watched as the jeep parked right next to Rousey's front steps. The passenger door opened and Sofia slid out, her long legs pristine beneath a quietly seductive cream dress. Meanwhile Blaire trotted up the steps to the front door followed by Victoria, and David clutching a brown folder to his chest. Tempted as he was to avoid this LA invasion, George's concern that Grace might be in the house meant that he had to face the situation.

Walking through the main hall, Blaire pushed open the door leading to the ante-hall and led her troupe into the drawing room. Sofia took in the ornate woodwork enhanced by velvet curtains and vast ancestral portraits, all of which made her feel uncomfortable. This place was the opposite of the streamlined modern finish she was used to and the house was cold, even though the day was warm. She instinctively felt she couldn't stay in a place like this, it just wasn't her gig, and seeing George standing in the doorway she couldn't decide if she felt shock or guilt, and instead tried to remember key messages from her mother's pep talk earlier.

"Hello, George," she said as she sat down, aware of how beautiful she must look against the backdrop of the river that flowed on the other side of the window. "The meeting this morning seems like a long time ago, doesn't it?"

"Time can play tricks, Sofia," said Blaire, "and when your father and I reunited a couple of weeks ago, it was like no time had passed at all."

"And which father would that be?" asked George, his arms folded and foot tapping.

"Well, George, since you haven't asked about Robert, I'm happy to tell you that he is about to board an evening flight to Geneva. Our new apartment comes with fabulous household staff, including an incredible chef. It's a happy-ever-after for Robert."

"Is it really," said George, smiling incredulously at Blaire.

"And to satisfy your unwavering curiosity, DNA swabs have been taken from both your father and Sofia. We went to a clinic in Edinburgh after lunch."

"Did you now," he said. "Another make-believe tale of yours?"

"If it hadn't been for me, George," said Blaire, stamping her foot like a spoilt child, "your father would still be sitting in a cigar-filled haze. He is embracing this opportunity, George, just as you should."

"Opportunity? What are you talking about? You are attempting to tear Rousey away from me."

"How about a drink? Isn't 6.30 the cocktail hour in this part of the world?" said Victoria, trying to find a way to dilute the tension.

But George didn't budge from the doorway. He looked so angry that Sofia imagined the phone he held in his hand might be some kind of explosive device.

"Okay then, scrap the drinks idea and let's just get on with it," said Victoria, flipping open the cover of her iPad. "George, we haven't met, though naturally I am more than familiar with the circumstances. Why don't you come and sit down? We have a proposition for you."

"I can hear perfectly well from here and there is actually no point in discussing anything until I speak with my real lawyer."

With the last words he threw a filthy look at David Collins, who wavered in a semi-crouch on the other side of the sofa like a gun-shy spaniel.

"It's so stuffy in here, George," said Blaire, with a look of disdain. "The dust and all that heavy fabric."

George looked at Blaire scathingly and said nothing.

"Let us progress," said Blaire. "As I said, despite your father's lack of enthusiasm about a paternity test, it was done this afternoon. David recommended the most accurate DNA testing service in the UK, and the lab sent a Scottish lab representative to the solicitor's office. The nurse took swabs from your father and Sofia, ID, paperwork, the lot."

"A certified nurse?" said George.

"Completely impartial, all certified," said David. "The laboratory's rules of ethics even stipulated that the helicopter pilot, who this afternoon flew both the nurse and samples to the laboratory in Cheshire, was impartial."

"The samples will have arrived to the lab by now, and tomorrow morning your father's and Sofia's DNA will be compared in the lab. The results will be emailed through tomorrow afternoon, and a hard copy of the report will be couriered over in the evening."

"Okay, George," said Victoria. "So, supposing the DNA samples are a match, as we suspect they are, and once you are satisfied with the evidence that Sofia is your sister –"

"Exactly, evidence," said George, "because all I see right now is a group of women pulling a fast one on my morally bankrupt father."

"How dare you speak about Sofia's father like that, you jealous brat!" snarled Blaire.

"Oh, cut it out, Blaire," snapped Victoria. "George, whatever you might think about the situation, the facts are that your father has every right to gift Rousey to whomever he chooses. Isn't that correct, David?"

"It is," he said, studiously avoiding eye contact with George.

"And your father has chosen Sofia," said Victoria, as Sofia smiled at George like the kitten with the tub of cookies and ice cream. Victoria, seeing George was about to speak, raised her finger to her mouth. "Hush, George, that is not an invitation for a question, it is a statement of fact. And yet the fact is that you are the person who truly wants Rousey."

"Correct," said George, sensing the payout was about to reveal itself.

"I'm going to lay this out for you very simply, George, okay?"

"Oh, for Christ's sakes, Victoria, would you ever come out with it?" blurted Blaire, strutting to the doorway and squaring up to George with her hands on her hips. "You, George, and Sofia are going to have a mock engagement for twelve months, after which you will be given the option to buy this place from her."

"Excuse me?" said George, astounded. "What in God's name are you saying?"

"You heard me."

"Well, firstly, Blaire, would you mind going back to where you were standing earlier, so that I can distance myself from the sheer insanity that is going on here."

"A *mock* engagement, George," said Victoria. "Mock, as in *fake*."

"I know what 'mock' means," said George. He looked at each person in the room, his eyes running from Sofia to Blaire to Victoria to David Collins. "Good God, you are actually serious, aren't you?"

"Deadly serious, George," said Victoria.

"A mock engagement with my apparent 'half-sister'?"

"You'll be at my daughter's side during her media relations-building campaign," said Blaire, pacing the room, "from celebrity events to photo shoots – I want Sofia on the cover of every magazine and social media page there is. And these articles are going to say that she is gorgeous, talented and responsible, just like you, George."

"Hold on," said George, "First, Blaire, you snare my father into making him think that he actually owes you something. Now you want me to buy back what rightfully belongs to my father, and to top it all you don't seem to think it is even remotely odd, if, and that's a large *if*, Sofia is my half-sister, we should pretend to be engaged for the sake of her public profile? Are you all out of your bloody minds?"

"Easy, tiger," said Sofia, standing up slowly. "George, we've known each other for years, right?"

"Known each other?" said George. "Who are you kidding? We've met occasionally. I've mingled at parties here and there in your company, Sofia. I wouldn't exactly call that a deep and meaningful relationship."

"Look," said Sofia, her confidence growing, "I know how hard it is for you to take all this in but you should be happy to have a sister."

"*Don't give me that!*" he shouted. "Can't you see how ludicrous this is?"

"Besides," said Sofia, ignoring his protestations, "now that I am a bona fide actress, I can fool the press into thinking we really are an item."

"We just need you to be on board for twelve months, George," said Victoria calmly. "We simply want to show the media that Sofia is steady and can hold down a relationship. You fit the bill perfectly and, even better, you are a single guy. Now I know you have a girlfriend of sorts at the moment. An Irish girl, right? So you'll have to put her on ice for this to work."

"For what to work?"

"For us to work," said Sofia. "Come on, George, in the grand scheme of things, you know that girl, Hannah, was never a fit for you. You must know that."

"Sofia, what the hell do you know about what fits me? You're all out of your minds."

And with that he walked out.

"Is that Anna girl going to cause problems?" asked Victoria, whose temper had not been improved when she snared her tights on a torn leather armchair.

"I don't know," said Sofia.

"Is it serious?" asked Victoria.

"Well, it's clearly serious enough for George to have flown to Ireland to meet her parents a few weeks ago," said Blaire.

"How do you know that?" asked Sofia, irked that her mother was better informed than she was.

"Well, he was on his way to Ireland when Robert called him about this meeting and apparently he was there a few weeks ago too. And, what's more, Robert met her here."

"Here?" said Sofia, with undisguised jealousy.

"Yes, here," said Blaire.

David Collins left the women huddled like witches over their plan. He found George in the hall, his hands pressing down upon a round table covered in coffee-table hardbacks about country houses, trees and field sports. Carefully positioning himself on the opposite side of the table, he said, "Now, George, it's not that bad. If the paternity test is positive, and we'll know tomorrow, you will simply have to attend some film industry parties and various media engagements, photo shoots, television interviews, press announcements, that sort of thing. You can keep a pretty low profile other than that though, of course, most crucially, you would have to agree to mimic the role of Sofia's fiancé."

"Mimic?" said George, laughing in disbelief. "You really expect me to agree to it?"

"You won't have to sign anything. Blaire doesn't want a paper trail."

"Of course she doesn't!" shouted George. "She's a bloody fraud! There's no way that the paternity test will come back positive." He tried to calm himself. "Look, David, is there any way around this? Can my father honestly gift Rousey to Sofia just like that?"

"Yes, George, legally he can. He believes that Sofia is his daughter, and Blaire actually offered for Sofia to have a paternity test from the word go, even before you met this morning. It was your father who declined and it took much persuading on Blaire's part. Mr Wyndham just kept saying that he always knew he had a daughter."

"But how?"

"George, your father is my client and it is not for me to question his instruction. He is dead set on transferring Rousey over to Sofia in its entirety, and the paperwork is already in motion. George, you heard Blaire say that you will be given the opportunity to buy Rousey from Sofia in twelve months' time. If the place means to you what I think it does, then you really have no option."

Would Anna understand, George thought wildly. Would she agree to such a charade? And then, with a sense of horror, he realised that he wouldn't be able to tell her. If he entered into such a deal, there would have to be absolute secrecy. He would have to weigh up Anna against Rousey, to gauge the best move, the right gamble.

He still needed to speak to Jamie, though he was sure that Jamie would tell him to do nothing until the paternity test results came back. But what if Robert really was Sofia's daughter, what the hell would happen then? He could try to battle it out with his father in court but, when it came down to it, he knew that Robert had the right to do as he pleased with Rousey.

Stepping in front of a portrait of his great-grandfather, George looked up at the old man, a war soldier in scarlet uniform with braided gold epaulettes, and wondered what he would have done in such circumstances.

Nodding at David, George took a deep breath and walked back into the drawing room and sat down in an armchair.

Sofia was the first to speak.

"George," said Sofia, who had been working out the best approach to seal the deal, "apart from Robert –"

Blaire coughed.

"I mean, my father. Apart from him, nobody outside this room knows that we are brother and sister, right? So all you have to do is play along for twelve months and then, cross my heart, I will sell this place back to you. I'll get it valued, you make a transfer and hey presto, I'm out of your hair."

"The definitive gold-digger," said George, shaking his head. "It all seems so obvious now, Sofia. Not that we've met many times though whenever we did, there you were, trying to get under my skin and steal my life."

"No, George, you're wrong," said Sofia, letting down her guard. "I only just found out about this. I'm telling you, I had no idea until a few days ago." And then, seeing her mother's scowling face, she clicked back into performance mode. "I am only carrying out my duty in accepting my father's generous gift, and we have to remember that business is business."

George said nothing as Sofia tilted her head at him.

"Just twelve months," she concluded. "That's all we're asking for."

"And I don't want your father knowing about this, George," said Blaire. "He's too old-fashioned to understand how the media works – he wouldn't understand the benefits, so I think we can all agree that it's better not to tell him."

"My father can actually read, Blaire," said George.

"Yes," said Blaire. "*The Racing Times*. And as lovely as my daughter is, I can't see them running a headline on your engagement."

"He listens to the news on TV, Blaire."

As Blaire hesitated, irritated and failing to come up with a better argument, Victoria butted in.

"Look, George, if you can just keep your head clear we can make this work for everyone. It's a win-win. We'll boost Sofia's profile, secure her long-term goals and you'll get your precious estate back, lock, stock and two smoking barrels. And I'm totally happy to work with you as your publicist because, trust me, I know what's right for you. I have it all mapped out."

"I don't need directions and I certainly do not need a publicist," said George, trying to keep his voice steady.

"You are famous for your discretion," continued Victoria. "You have the respect of so many people. I only ever hear amazing and positive things about George Wyndham. And that is why we need you by Sofia's side. We don't expect you to ram your tongue down her throat on the red carpet, but we do need you by her side, smiling and, occasionally, playing up to the cameras, okay?"

George looked at her with an expression of absolute disdain but Victoria was not to be deterred.

"So, bottom line, you put your art to one side for a while, make Sofia your number-one priority and everyone scores – you can have your precious estate back in your name, and Sofia will get to polish her own star on Hollywood Boulevard."

George ran his hands through his hair, strands flopping over his forehead, his dark eyes peering out.

"Once I see the paternity results, I'll consider the options," he said, and walked out of the drawing room for a second time.

Once again, David scuttled after him.

"One more thing, George, if I may?"

"What is it?"

"I'm actually leaving the firm. I wanted to tell you at the meeting this morning but I didn't have the opportunity."

"Opportunity?" laughed George "I don't mean to be rude, David, but I think you know all there is to know about opportunities. So, you're calling it a day, now that you have created the paperwork to put Rousey into the hands of Sofia Tamper."

"Well," said David, patting his forehead with his sleeve, "I wouldn't go quite that far. Anyway, I have a box of your mother's files which she gave to me for safe-keeping five or six years before she died, God rest her."

"And?" said George, not wanting to get caught up in sentimentality with David.

"And ... given the circumstances, I feel you should have it ... so, if you're happy, I'll have the file forwarded to your London address sometime during . . ."

George turned and walked towards the front hall while David was in mid-sentence. Checking his phone, he found five missed calls from Anna. Biting into his hand, his heart raced and sank all at the same time, and dialling into his voicemail, he deleted all voice messages without listening to them as Sofia and her entourage walked past him and out the front door.

"We'll be back with the results tomorrow," Blaire called back. "Get some sleep, George."

Chapter 26

"Good morning," said Peter, checking Harry's pulse as he admired Freddie, still so attractive despite wearing the same clothes three days running without having as much as brushed her teeth.

"Harry?" asked Freddie, waking up from her armchair.

"He's had an excellent night," said Peter. "I think we can safely say that he is out of danger."

"But that's wonderful," said Freddie, throwing the rug off her lap and leaping to her feet. "Is he conscious yet?"

"Semi-conscious, and I'm confident that by this evening there will be further improvement. We're going to remove the oxygen this morning, now that we are through the early recovery period, and along with that we will slowly withdraw sedation, which will begin wearing off this morning and I'd say by lunchtime we'll be having a conversation."

"Amazing," said Anna, appearing at the door, wiggling her incredibly stiff shoulders, having slept in the relatives' room on a plastic chair with her feet elevated on a footstool.

"This afternoon, we will transfer Harry out of ICU and into a private room in the Joyce Wing. Once Harry is conscious, I'd like to keep him in for at least a week, to monitor his heart and take blood tests – all standard procedure, nothing to be alarmed by."

"Thank you so much, Peter, for all your care," said Freddie, shaking his hand.

Feeling chivalrous, Peter couldn't resist kissing her hand and giving her his signature bow before leaving the room.

"Oh, thank God," said Freddie, bursting into hysterical tears with relief and hugging Anna. "Let's call Mrs B and spread the good news."

"No finer broadcast system, Mum, that's for sure, as she'll pass the news on to Mrs Murray in the shop who is as efficient as any radio network."

That afternoon, in the Joyce Wing, Harry was sitting on his bed dressed in sheepskin slippers and a long claret dressing gown.

"Well, that all sounds like it was quite a palaver," he said. "I haven't had that much sleep for years, not since my student days."

"And we need you to continue to rest," said Peter, from the foot of the bed.

"Is this like my back-to-school lecture, Peter?" asked Harry.

"Something like that," said Peter, "and I must underline, Harry, that we will need to make a serious commitment to lifestyle changes."

"Ease up on the rumpy-pumpy, that sort of thing?"

"Harry, really?" said Freddie, glaring at him.

Peter was amused, but then looked seriously at Harry. "We'll need you to be an exemplary patient if we are to get you into good, strong shape again, controlling excitement, physical exertion, and emotional distress which can all place strain on the heart, making it work harder. You may not be so lucky next time, Harry, if you don't play ball."

"So I'm onto a diet of lentils, am I?"

"Yes, lots of legumes such as beans, peas, and lentils in soups and salads."

"But what about Mrs B's morning fries?"

"*Passé composé*, I'm afraid, Harry," said Freddie, "and I've been reading about tea – high in the antioxidants that prevent heart attack – and cold-water fish too, high in omega-3's."

"I feel like a cold fish already," said Harry, feeling rather depressed that his life was about to turn into one large breadstick in a low-fat dip.

"The good news is that, in due course, you may drink a little red wine," said Peter, knowing that would perk Harry up. "We are talking about one glass a day though, Harry, rather than a bottle, and in due course. This is going to be a slow climb up the hill."

"But all those extra antioxidants in a fine bottle of Chateau Margot, a favourite of mine, you know?"

"Yes … and, as I say, in time and moderation," repeated Peter.

"Well, that's not so bad then," said Harry, thinking about sitting back with a stack of paperbacks and Mrs B's room service. "Time for home then?"

"Let's reassess in a week, Harry," said Peter. "And in the meantime take it easy on the nurses, won't you?"

Peter took Freddie to one side, leaving Harry to find the Racing Channel on television.

"Eh, a slightly awkward one, I'm afraid," said Peter.

"Yes?" said Freddie, looking very worried.

"Harry apparently asked one of the nurses if she'd like to pose nude for a portrait."

"Oh, I wouldn't worry about that. I'd say it's the morphine wearing off, wouldn't you? He's always been keen on nudes – in fact, it's music to my ears to hear that he is even thinking about painting again."

"Fair enough," said Peter. "It's just you know how politically correct things are these days, and the nurses, well, some might not be so keen on such suggestions."

"Leave it with me, Peter. I'll have a word."

"Thank you, Freddie," he said, again bowing as he left the room and trying to stop himself from thinking of what Freddie would look like posing nude for one of Harry's portraits.

Now that Freddie had absorbed the news that Harry was going to make a full recovery, she knew this was going to have to be a new phase for them both. When he was in a critical condition, her mind raced through the possible outcomes, of her being a widow and being alone. What bothered her most was the part of her mind that touched on the idea that, as a widow, she would be free from the erratic behaviour that living with an artist entailed and she felt guilty as hell for having had such feelings. This was also the first time in months that she had missed out on her daily yoga routine, the exercise that kept her sane. Maybe this was the reason she was having selfish, unreasonable thoughts. She had been a loyal wife for years now, more years than she had imagined their marriage might last, and it wasn't just Anna that glued them together – it was the pair-of-old-slippers analogy, scruffy and with a thinning inner lining and a worn sole, but to exchange them for a new pair had never been an option.

On the way home from the hospital Freddie was quiet as Anna played co-pilot to Tilly, who drove them home to Farley Hall. The girls' lives were so full of promise and they hadn't as yet made their choices as to whom they would share their lives with, permanently, or for a 'temporary permanency' as she had heard it described by a fellow yoga pupil during her retreat in Sri Lanka. She worried for Anna, hoping that George would keep going in the vein of enthusiasm he had shown almost consistently since they first met. Freddie knew that Harry's heart attack was going to delay any thoughts of freedom she might have had. Maybe he might never pick up a paintbrush again, preferring to sink into a lackadaisical existence of claret and memoirs that would never get written, and she would still be playing the role of supportive wife.

Arriving at Farley Hall, the aroma of garlic soup drifted up through the house from the kitchen and made Anna feel twice as sick and, to Freddie's delight and horror in equal measures, her brother Richard awaited them. Eton-educated, ex-Army and immaculately turned out, the family couldn't understand why his wife had left him. They were married for over twenty years and then out of the blue she threw her pair of Laura Ashley oven gloves at him, announcing that her wifely duties and dinner-party-placement obsession was over, and promptly walked out the door of their Hampshire rectory to live in their Shepherd's Bush flat. She declared herself to be a suppressed urbanite and at age fifty-three the time had come to please herself. Richard had handled the break-up in exemplary fashion, like a faithful army officer, resuming his bridge-club evenings and hiring a cook to fill up the freezer. "Life must go on," he told his children. While Freddie appreciated her brother's support, she was feeling utterly wiped by the hospital drama and now she just wanted to be left alone with only her yoga for company – she didn't even want Dharma's guidance.

Anna, on the other hand, feeling confident that her father was going to make a full recovery, was slowly becoming excited about her pregnancy. She tried to call George from the landline as soon as she got home, but got no answer. She was puzzled and worried. He hadn't phoned since he had called Mrs B the day of Harry's accident. Perhaps he didn't want to intrude?

After lunch, while Tilly, Dharma and Richard played Canasta in the kitchen, Anna lay back on a sunbed in the garden listening to a podcast about how by the year 2050 most people will live an urban existence. This led her to think about her own life in London, including Gilda who was going to want an update as to when she would return to work. 'Maternity leave' were two words Gilda would not be pleased to hear, not to mention her designs on Anna taking the helm of her Parisian Winterbottom starter empire. Feeling a tickle on her nose, Anna opened her eyes to see the face of a man with a long ponytail and tightly clipped beard, grinning as he held a black feather.

"Well, hello there," he said. "Doing a spot of sunbathing, are we?"

Pulling out her earphones, Anna swung her legs to one side and stood up.

"Ah, there you are, Reverend," shouted Mrs B, saluting him from the kitchen door. "I've got a lovely apple tart in the pantry, so shall I warm it up and we'll have it with a nice pot of tea?"

"That's grand, Mrs B. Sure, you're very good," he responded, and turning to Anna he put out his hand. "Marty Graham is my name, the new rector of Drummare."

"Good to meet you. I'm Anna, Freddie and Harry's daughter."

"The girl from London. I've heard all about you, so I have."

"You like the village, settling in well, are you?" she asked.

"Well, as I answered Mrs B when she enquired as to my thoughts on the afterlife . . . I pulled up my jumper . . . just like this . . ." Beneath his navy V-neck jumper he was wearing a white T-shirt with a large red question-mark. "This T-shirt says it all," he with a wink.

Anna laughed in response.

"I can tell you weren't expecting a new rector like me, just as my mother wasn't expecting me when she turned forty-six years of age

– but I can promise you that I am dedicated to this parish. Just don't ask me to any events on Saturday nights, because that's the night I have rock-band practice."

"Ah, well, that's all very good now, isn't it?" said Mrs B, arriving with a tea tray.

"Now, Mrs B, let me take the weight of the tray out of your fair hands," he said, taking the tray and putting it on the garden table, "and aren't you queer fast in making the tea, the speed of lightning!"

"I knew you would be here at some point, Marty, so I've had an apple tart ready and waiting – and I've always got a pot of tea on the go."

"And would you be a leaf or bag lady?" asked Marty.

"I beg your pardon," said Mrs B.

Peering into the teapot, Marty smiled. "Just checking for leaves," he said.

"Tea leaves," said Anna, smiling at Mrs B.

"I like a good read, so I do," he said. "My mother's an expert. No one reads the leaves like Mammy, and as I said to Mrs Murray in the pub just the other day, there's only one way to get rid of a rector from a parish."

"And how's that?" said Mrs B.

"You'll get rid of the rector by making him a bishop," said Marty, with a wink.

That evening, wearing a grey cashmere scarf around her neck, Anna found Tilly sitting by the fire in the drawing room, hugging a cushion.

"Tills, isn't it freezing? Even if it is supposed to be the summer."

"Oh, I was wondering where you were."

"I can smell Mrs B's Irish stew coming up through the dumb waiter – can you smell it? God, I feel sick. As much as I like Mrs B's cooking, I don't think I'll be able to eat more than a piece of dry toast for supper."

Tilly nodded silently, pushing the cushion away from her.

"Is that a G&T in your hand?" asked Anna.

"Yes, and a strong one," said Tilly.

"Okay, then how about a top-up?"

"No, thanks, I'm okay for now," said Tilly, taking a large sip of her drink.

Anna knelt down by the fire and reached for a log from the basket. "So, still no word from George," she said, throwing the log onto the burning embers. "I've tried to ring him but no response. He must be with his father or a client – somewhere out of reach anyway. It's just so weird. When he called Mrs B the day Dad had his fall he told her that he was coming to Ireland as soon as he could."

"But no word since then," said Tilly.

"Nothing, not a text, not an email – I wouldn't even object to a message via carrier pigeon at this stage."

"It's hard to know what's going on," said Tilly uncertainly.

"In what sense?" said Anna, catching something strange in Tilly's tone of voice. "Tilly? Do you know something? What's going on?"

"Anna …"

"I can tell by your face – what's the matter, Tilly?"

"Jamie called a few minutes ago," she said flatly.

"And?"

"Anna, there is no way to explain this," said Tilly, pulling her iPad from beneath a cushion. Pulling back the cover, she passed it to Anna.

The *Daily Mail* pictured Sophia and George getting into a blacked-out Range Rover.

'**George Wyndham, Scottish millionaire art dealer, and IT-girl-turning-actress, Sofia Tamper, raised the bar for this season's hottest couple, Sofia looking elegant in a cleavage-baring red pencil dress and nude pumps. George is said to be comforting Sofia since her father, disgraced Hollywood producer Max Tamper, was arrested in LA last month.**'

"Hottest couple? What are they talking about?" said Anna, trying to keep a strong voice. "The shaving cut …"

"The what?" said Tilly, wishing the internet connection would cut.

"There, on George's chin, can you see it? He cut his chin when he was shaving, only five days ago. The day when he gave me this necklace." Anna fumbled around her neck and held out the tiny gold bird on its golden chain. She passed the iPad back to Tilly. "What night does it say this picture was taken?"

"Last night," whispered Tilly.

"What?"

"Last night, the caption said they were at a charity drinks party in Edinburgh."

Anna pulled the scarf up to her chin, her mouth trembling so much she could not speak. In the back of her mind she had been sure George would arrive at Farley Hall, unannounced, bringing comfort, assuring her that he loved her and their darling baby in the making. Standing up, she threw another log onto the fire.

"It's not such a surprise," said Tilly, trying to reason with the situation, "that Sofia had her eye on George, but for him to leave you like this is completely out of character. Jamie doesn't understand it – he has been trying to contact George for the past three days, but can't get through. Anna, none of it makes sense."

Anna, eyes staring, nodded her head. "I agree with you that it doesn't make sense. And I cannot believe it, not yet. I know that Sofia is poison and she'd do anything to get George on side, so maybe this is her media wheel spinning. The photograph could be superimposed for all we know."

"Exactly," said Tilly, though unconvinced that there wasn't more to it. "And the baby?" She then regretted even mentioning the word.

"What about the baby?"

"You still need to let George know."

"And I will," said Anna, calmly, "just as soon as I see him. Then I'll tell him."

"Okay," said Tilly, "and in the meantime you'll tell your mum?"

"Yes, in a day or two, but first I need to speak with George and then I'll go through it all with Mum, visit the GP this week, work out timings, and so on ..." But despite Anna trying to be strong, tears started to her eyes. "George's timing is immaculate, isn't it?"

Then both she and Tilly managed to laugh, if only for a few seconds.

"Look, Anna, it may just be a bit of tabloid news. All the hype around Max Tamper's extradition to the UK – there's nothing the tabloids love more than celebrity handcuffs. There could be heaps of reasons why George is with Sofia. We need an explanation first. This could just be an editor jumping to conclusions from a photograph. Let me call Jamie again. We'll get to the bottom of it, I know we will."

"God, I feel sick," said Anna. "What if it's true?"

"Take my advice," said Tilly, taking control. "Don't take your phone to bed tonight. No social media, no research, sleep on your hands and let me see what sense I can make of things between now and breakfast time, okay?"

Chapter 27

At Winterbottom HQ, Kate and Chrissy were engrossed in an article about George and Sofia when a window by the coffee machine snapped open and a mulberry handbag dangled through from a gold chain like a rope ladder. Next came a smart white cardboard bag with pictures of cucumber slices across the front. Then alligator kitten heels attached to skinny legs clad in turquoise trousers.

Gilda landed on one leg and then the other as she adjusted her Hermes belt.

"Gilda? Are you all right?" asked Chrissy, pushing the magazine to one side while Kate went to the fridge, having learned through experience that this was the right time to pour her boss a glass of Pouilly-Fumé.

"No, Chrissy, I am far from all right, and there will be no accusations of paranoia – my therapist has already tried that. Thank you, Kate, sweetie." Gilda took a large sip of wine. "That man was following me, I'm sure of it."

"Man?" said Chrissy. "What man?"

"Roger," said Gilda and, kicking off her alligator heels, she tiptoed into her office and pulled on her gold wedge-heeled runners. "Oh, that's better. Come on in, girls – take a pew and I'll fill you in."

Kate and Chrissy sat on the leather sofa like children at story time as Gilda stood leaning against her desk.

"So, I was having lunch in Le Capro with Sebastian – you know, Kate, that good-looking Icelandic beauty therapist? Absolute heaven of a man. Anyway, we discussed his home facial app – complemented by the quality product range, it really is a no-brainer. It's called *At Home with Sebastian*, which says it all, really." Gilda dipped her hand into the white bag and threw a shiny white patent bag of samples over to Chrissy. "Are you following me, Chrissy? It's a new home Spa kit. You know, waxing, peeling, steaming, algae and silica mud masks. It's going to save the middle classes an absolute fortune."

"And?" asked Kate, who was eager to hear any story relating to Sebastian, who was certainly their most attractive client.

"And," continued Gilda, "it was all going swimmingly until I felt breathing down my neck, literally, and turning around there was that snivelling little columnist Roger, from *Camille* magazine, listening to our conversation. As I said to Sebastian, Botox in the kit may not be something I would try myself at home but, you know, it is very forward-thinking. He is to be applauded. People build wardrobes and kitchens following directions, and they aren't carpenters, are they? So why not administer a little beauty product in one's bedroom?"

"So where does *Camille* magazine come into it?" asked Kate.

"Because the little blighter Roger obviously wants to spill the beans before we launch to the media, that's why. And when I accidentally threw a glass of sparkling cranberry over my shoulder, he was not amused. His Jean Paul Gaultier shirt is a one-off apparently. Well, his face, I thought he was going to thump me."

"And so you made a run for it?" asked Kate.

"Did I hell? I called security of course and, being a regular at Le Capro, they leapt to my attention."

"And Roger?" asked Chrissy.

"He had the cheek to lambaste me whilst he was frog-marched out of the restaurant, can you believe it?"

"And you suspect he was following you?" said Chrissy, who felt it was within her remit to check security aspects of the office.

"Yes, and that is why I didn't want to risk coming through the front entrance, and so I got into Bond Girl mode and slipped back down the alley and climbed in the window."

"Ah," said Kate, "now it all makes sense."

"But enough of that, ladies," said Gilda, feeling impatient. "You are aware that we will be working late tonight, and there's a reason for that."

"There is?" said Kate and Chrissy in unison.

"Yes, because I don't want any of the interns or account execs listening in. Not to mention those useless temps, who are supposed to be pitching stories to the media although I'm sure I caught a girl – you know the rather flighty one in the cowboy boots?"

"Rhonda?" said Kate.

"That's the one, Rhonda. I found her online searching for exercise equipment, and on my time. Well, I won't have it. Chrissy, make a note for me to fire her in the morning."

"If you're sure, Gilda, but we'll still have to pay the temp agency fees?"

"I don't care. Now, back to business. The reason I asked you both to stay behind late tonight is to progress *Operation Snail*."

"*Operation Snail?*"

"*Oui*, my darlings, as you know I am absolutely seething about the George Wyndham and Sofia Tamper business, so I've decided the obvious antidote for Anna regarding the non-runner of Prince Charming is to move to Paris." Then Gilda abruptly waved her hands out in front of her. "Silence! Is that a phone ringing?"

"Sorry, Gilda, it's the handset in reception, won't be a mo," said Chrissy, launching herself off the sofa like a twanged elastic band.

"And Anna's agreed?" asked Kate, who longed for Anna to stay in the London office.

"Not as yet, but she will," said Gilda, as Chrissy returned to the office looking rather flushed.

"Sorry to disturb. but Desmond has just been on the phone – he's around the corner, coming from the National Gallery, asking to pop in for a quick chat."

"Oh bugger," said Gilda, almost in sync with the dulcet tones of Desmond, who had arrived into reception. "Around the corner indeed! He must have been standing outside the front door when he called."

"*Coo-ee!*" said Desmond, walking through reception and into the office with a roll of tweed under one arm. "Is Gilda about? Ah, Gilda, there you are, right before my eyes, didn't see you there, old girl."

"Now, Desmond, let's just get one thing straight, shall we? I'll happily be your PR girl, but I will not be your *old* PR girl, got it?"

"Quite right, Gilda, just an expression, picked it up from my father, you see – he was in the navy, you know."

"Yes, yes, Desmond, now what can we do you for and would you like a drink?"

"No, thank you, promised Jenny I'd meet her for dinner in fifteen minutes in Covent Garden, so better not dilly-dally. We are both in French mode, as in she's still keen on getting the blasted poodle, while I'm more interested in finding out where we are with launching Spicer Tweed to the French."

"Actually, Desmond, your timing might just be tickety-boo," said Gilda, having a light-bulb moment.

"Between 'cooee' and 'tickety-boo' and 'dilly-dally', I feel like we're taking part in a blooming pantomime," whispered Kate to Chrissy.

"Right, ladies, let's get *le ball* rolling. Kate, over you go to the white screen and you'll find a divine selection of Frenchmen the agency in Paris sent earlier. I need you to choose the top three whom you deem to be of most interest to the media. And make it global, darling, I want global appeal. Visualise the world atlas and find a face that may speak French but can cut it on the Mumbai fashion pages."

"Will do, Gilda, I'll try to bear it," said Kate, grinning.

"As for you," said Gilda, passing an iPad to Desmond, "I'd like you to choose your top three male models from this bank of imagery. They are between the ages of twenty and fifty-five."

"Fifty-five? That's rather ageist, don't you think, Gilda? I'll be sixty-five next month and I'd love nothing better than to accompany a fine French filly down the catwalk. I'm in good shape, you know."

"Yes, Desmond," said Gilda, trying to hold her patience.

"Would you like to see my upper thighs?"

"No, Desmond, as tempting as it sounds," said Gilda,

shuddering at the thought of him pulling down his trousers. Taking a large sip from her glass of wine, she gasped. "Okay, hold it. Chrissy sweetie, fetch me an ice cube, would you? The wine's so warm it could pass for consommé."

"Will do, Gilda," said Chrissy, racing to the fridge.

"Actually, I think I'll change my mind," said Desmond. "A glass of single malt if you would, Chrissy, and one of those cubes to loosen it up."

"Desmond, might I remind you that Chrissy isn't a barmaid, but in fact a valued member of the Winterbottom team?"

"Quite," said Desmond, enjoying the sight of Chrissy's shapely figure as she sought out a bottle from the back of the store cupboard. "You know, I get an energy, surrounding myself by young people."

"You are so right, Desmond," said Gilda, spinning on her heel, "and never has there been a more exciting time to be in PR. I'm telling you, Desmond, I am purely buzzing."

"Delighted to hear it, Gilda," said Desmond, looking like he was tempted to take her for a waltz.

"And what's more, I have never felt more positive that Anna is going to open the office in Paris for us."

"Truly?" asked Desmond, longing to get the French project underway.

"*Mais oui*," said Gilda, brightening her eyes and hoping he wouldn't twig that she was utterly unsure as to whether it would ever happen.

Chapter 28

"Royston, John Royston, ma'am," he said, with a clean-cut English accent.

He stood to attention in the library at Rousey – neatly clipped fingernails, black suit with a grey tie, short brown hair and wire-rimmed glasses – and yet he struck Blaire as looking more like a learned professor of literature than a butler.

"And tell me, Royston, why do you think you are a good fit for this position of butler at Rousey?" asked Blaire.

"I've a lot of experience in this field, Ma'am. I've worked for supermodels and A-list footballers, not to mention some rather unusual Chinese celebrities and a sheik or two."

"Can we rely on you being fast on your feet?"

"Oh yes, ma'am, I'm swift as a coursing river when required. I once had to hide three ladies of ill-repute in my own bedroom, when I was buttling aboard a yacht. My boss's wife came on board, looking in every bed, searching for pubic hairs. Of course, I had an inkling what was on the cards and so I had already ordered the maids to strip every sheet on the ship before hiding the women in my room. I knew his wife would never bring herself to go into staff quarters."

"Smart move," said Blaire, with a wry smile, "though I sincerely hope we won't need to borrow your bedroom if you were to work here. What this house needs is someone who will take charge of the day-to-day running, guiding staff, greeting guests and most importantly, setting the tone. My daughter Sofia is a little on edge at the moment and it is essential that we keep her nerves strong. I need you to attend to her every need. We must have her in an organised and supremely confident state before she begins filming a new television series at the end of the summer. How does that sound?"

"It sounds spot-on to me. I have certain standards, and I won't come down from them."

"You have housekeeping skills?" asked Blaire.

"I can get red-wine stains out of a decanter, no problem – just use denture cleaner."

"Yes, yes. That's enough detail, thank you."

"I am all about fulfilling every whim of my employer's wants, no questions asked, no excuses given."

"Okay, I like you, Royston. You're in. I'll have my solicitor draw up a legal document for you."

"Thank you, ma'am," said Royston, bowing rather grandly as he prepared to leave the room.

"You don't have any dark secrets I should know about, do you?"

"I have no tattoos or hidden jewelry on me if that's what you mean, ma'am."

"I'm delighted to hear it. Oh, and I'm not sure about calling me 'ma'am'. I prefer madam. Call me 'madam'. Don't you think? I like to keep things simple."

"Well, ma'am ... I mean, excuse me, madam, I really couldn't say."

"I wasn't looking for your opinion, Royston. Lastly, there is a tall man staying here at the moment – his name is George Wyndham."

"Yes, I know of Mr Wyndham, madam. I thought this was his father's house?"

"No, it's a little more complicated than that. Mr Wyndham is staying here temporarily but I want you to imagine he is not here at all. You answer only to me, or my daughter Sofia. Is that clear?"

"Perfectly, madam. As I'm sure you are aware, nobody talks to the butler and so I hold no information. None whatsoever. You can depend on my utmost discretion."

And, with another bow, he withdrew from the room.

George's reaction to the DNA report had appeared to be surprisingly benign. Blaire had expected him to rant and curse when she forwarded him the email with the lab results, confirming that Sofia was Robert's daughter. However, a few hours later, George telephoned her very calmly to say that he would live between Rousey and his house in London for the time being. He was going to place his commitments to both Christie's and his private clients on hold for a while, citing personal reasons. It was as simple as that.

Blaire was keen to weigh in with her matriarchal authority early on, as mother of the soon-to-be-owner of Rousey. High on her agenda was a visit to some ancient relics on the Rousey estate that had unsettled her ever since she was a child. With a light drizzle outside, she thought about carrying an umbrella but, at the risk of looking too suburban she wasn't going to chance it. Instead she slipped on her Burberry trench coat and moleskin trilby. She was the lady of the house now, or, at least, the mother of the new owner. Either way, at long last she was part of the Big House contingent and as she walked up the path to the Keeper's Cottage she thought about the day her father arrived home having been caught poaching by Finlay and took his dark mood out on her mother. This triggered further memories of how her mother was treated like a slave at home, her father threatening to belt her whenever she tried to stand up for herself. Blaire shuddered at the thought of her past and, as she knocked on the cottage door, she was comforted by the sight of expensive stitching on the sleeve of her bespoke jacket by Caroline Herrera. Who would have guessed that she would be standing there, on the doorstep of a Rousey employee, ready to call the shots? She was to be the purveyor of bad tidings, an old-fashioned payback to an estate that had shunned her family all those years ago. In a way she blamed Rousey for making her mother's life such hell.

The McCleods had been expected a visit from Blaire and so it was little surprise to see her standing on the doorstep. Peering out from behind the white lace curtain, Grace turned to Finlay who remained in his armchair, puffing on his pipe.

"I'll let her wait another bloody minute before I open the door to her," said Grace, "and God help me, but I hope the heavens open. She's like a rotten smell that won't go away until the cause is rooted out."

However, Pickles the terrier was now yapping at the door, longing to see who was on the other side. Grace conceded defeat and opened the door a crack. Peering out, she attempted to look surprised to find Blaire on the other side.

"Good afternoon, Grace."

"Mrs McCleod to you," said Grace, scowling. "I thought you'd be over."

Blaire brushed the edge of her collar as if even the air wasn't clean. "I've come to let you know that we no longer require your services at the Big House."

Grace stood to her full height, straightening the collar of her paisley blouse. "You're not telling me anything I don't already know." Her eyes, strong and steely, blazing into Blaire. "George came to see us last night."

"Did he now?"

"And before you say anything else," said Grace, "there will be no moving us. You'll not have us gone until we're good and ready to go."

"Oh really? Well, let me tell you that you –"

"We are sitting tenants. Tenants with a lease for life. It sounds grand, wouldn't you say, Mrs ... Tamper?"

Finlay arrived at the door and stood tall behind his wife.

"Aye," he said firmly, "and you can get off our property for starters."

Sitting tenants was the best response that George had been able to come up with for now. However, as if it had been rehearsed, Pickles chose this moment to jump up on Blaire's ankles, laddering her tights and scraping the toes of her expensive-looking shoes.

As Blaire tried to kick the dog off, Grace attempted to keep a straight face and said as loudly as she could, "Now, Pickles, that isn't very polite, is it, you wee monkey? Mind you, you've always been a good one at ratting."

With smoke blowing out of her ears, Blaire moved like a thundercloud down the path back towards the house, more determined than ever before to get the deeds into Sofia's name. Micro-managing her daughter's future was starting to become rather tedious. Scotland held more thistles and thorns than she could bear. Wasn't that why she had left in the first place? She resolved that once matters with Sofia were on track, she would hightail it to Geneva, divorce Max, marry Robert, put up with him six months, divorce him for the beast that he was and take half his fortune.

"Victoria?" yelled Blaire, into her phone.

"Blaire, hi, where are you? The line is terrible."

"I'm outside the goddamn house. Now listen carefully. I'm going back to the Celtic Thistle. I cannot relax here until certain things are done. So, in my absence, I want you to ensure that things run smoothly. As you know Royston has been fully briefed. Get in as much media as you can during the next few weeks – it's crucial that we maximise every moment of this opportunity. Sofia is due to arrive at Rousey tomorrow morning, okay? I'll make sure she is in top form, ready to aim and fire."

"Good to hear, Blaire, good to hear."

In the dining room, Victoria sat on a window seat with her back perfectly straight against wooden panelling. She found the light streaming through the tall windows very therapeutic. In LA she was used to light-box therapy but, considering she was in cloudy Scotland, this was not a bad alternative. She had spent the morning intricately mapping out Sofia and George's twelve-month media schedule. She was now preparing to scatter juicy and utterly fabricated details of George and Sofia's engagement like chicken feed to the hungry flocks of journalists. Then there were photo shoots – the huge paintings, velvet-covered armchairs and bookcases lined with first editions would all make great backdrops – feature interviews, gala dinners and fundraisers along with daily tweets to further fuel the tabloid interest. Pictures of George and Sofia in country-house mode, accidental selfies of Sofia clad in her favourite Victoria's Secret lingerie. And then the fun of creating all that excitement about who would design Sofia's wedding dress.

Naturally it didn't matter that she wasn't getting married but it was an excellent tool to start a bidding war for designers seeking extra limelight. And then there would be all the film screenings, pre-nomination dinners, and a big Christmas feature. Victoria knew it was going to be an intense year but it would be worth it to get everybody's career onto a more lucrative level.

"Presenting Lindsay, madam," said Royston, holding a make-up case in one hand and a large tub of hair gel in the other. "The surname is not forthcoming at present."

"Lindsay, so glad you could make it," said Victoria, welcoming the top LA stylist, who looked ghost-like in long sheer grey muslin over neon leggings.

"Like, totally," said Lindsay, with a strong LA accent. "It's all good and I'm, like, super ready for George."

"So, you know your brief. The biggest challenge is to get him out of cords, woolly jumpers and the tweed sports jacket. They all have to go."

"For sure. I'll just need a room for my merchandise and rails," Lindsay said, buffing her silver nails against her sleeve. "As big a room as you've got, please. I have, like, two stretches of hangers for George. I feel like I have the crown jewels in the people carrier out there. Man, the fuss when the designers were packing up that order – you could have sworn we were tailoring for Prince William."

"You're not as far from Prince William as you might think, young lady," Victoria reprimanded her. "As I said in my email, he may be resistant to changing his look, so you'll need to tread gently."

"I'll tread like a little fluffy Scottish lamb," said Lindsay, jumping on the spot as George walked through the door wearing a Barbour and his trademark cords.

"You must be George," said Lindsay.

"Yes," he said. "I must."

Victoria led them into the drawing room, instructing Royston to carry Lindsay's accoutrements in. Then she left them to their own devices.

Looking through the drawing-room window and out across the river, George wondered how he would get through this. He had literally gone berserk when Blair's email arrived the day before. How could Sofia be his sister? As a person she couldn't have felt more alien to him. With shaking hands he had dialled the number provided on the DNA report and spoke with a very polite young woman who assured him that all samples had been gathered officially by company representatives and that the laboratory was the securest in the country, if not the world. There was no possibility the samples had been tampered with, she assured him, gently adding that such results often "come as a shock". When she asked if she could recommend a therapist to him, George cut the call. He couldn't stand another word.

Usually a long walk around the estate was enough to clear his mind but this time it felt as if a swarm of locusts was pursuing him, crackling around his head, hoovering up all the happier memories of the past months. Anna had given George such a real insight into how their lives could run together, her upbeat and positive nature drawing him out of his reserved, aloof self. They had folded into each other so quickly, falling in love, properly, head over heels in love. And now, without even a whisper to Jamie, George had made the decision to play it alone, to abandon Anna and his old, safe life and instead to focus on the immense challenge of keeping hold of Rousey. Twelve months. That was what he kept telling himself. Twelve spins of the moon and he would have done enough to save Rousey, to rescue the MacLeods, the deer, the plantations ... and the memory of his mother. He knew she would want him to look after his own future and not to hang on to her, or to keep remembering how it felt when she had squeezed his little hand while she was dying next to him in the car that day. The memory of her grip easing from his hand, her breath blowing out like air from a hissing balloon. Her cold veins rising from her hand as a fireman told him to turn his head and close his eyes while the hydraulic cutter blades ripped through the side of the passenger door. To lose Rousey now, after all that, would slam a door on his past. He couldn't do it. He had to fight and yet everything the Tampers were firing at him seemed to be legitimate. The best response he could come up with so far was to shut himself into his bedroom at Rousey with a bottle of single malt, just as his father did when Gussy died.

George had started writing an email to Anna but he kept deleting everything he wrote. He fared no better when he tried a handwritten letter – several sheets of paper were crumpled and hurled at the bin. It was hopeless. He couldn't properly explain himself, and so couldn't defend his position. There was no defending his position unless he told Anna everything and he would be endangering the Tampers' plan if he did that. Besides, he was utterly convinced that if he did tell her she would run a mile. And rightly so. Why should she be part of this insane merry-go-round? His only option was to put his head in the sand for now, to play the Tampers' game and to try to live with himself.

"So, you and Sofia are getting hitched, huh?" said Lindsay, circling George, the bangles on her wrists clanging against her gold iWatch.

"Hitch is the word," he said, glaring at Victoria as he took off his Barbour.

"We need to define your image," said Lindsay. "That means choosing the right styles, cuts and colours to define your individuality. I'm here to give you grooming advice. You good to go?"

"God only knows," said George.

"Yes," said Lindsay, studying him scientifically. "I think we'll go for a Baptiste Giabiconi."

"A what?" asked George.

"The Undercut. Your hair. You'll see the style on most fashionable guys these days. We'll shave you short on the sides and in the back, but keep the length on top. It's gonna give us a lot of opportunities to rework your look every day."

George said nothing while Lindsay stood in front of him, putting various swatches of material against his jawline.

"You know," she continued, "I once had to give a duke a makeover. He wasn't a duke when I knew him. He was just a regular nightclub owner. He wasn't even born into royalty. He was brought up in San Francisco which is where he ran his nightclub. And then, one day, he gets a knock on the door and this dude is waving papers in front of him to say that he had a long-lost cousin and wait for it, he's a duke just like that ... I guess you never know what's going to happen next, heh??"

Lindsay took out a tape measure and, standing up on a stool, ran it across George's shoulders. "And so I had to do the opposite of what I'm doing to you. I actually had to tweed this guy up like he had been born in a castle."

Lindsay then asked George to sit in front of a tall mirror.

"I don't mean to speak out of turn, George," she said, standing behind him with a scissors, "but for someone who's engaged to a chick as hot as Sofia, you don't seem exactly over the moon."

"You know what the oldest joke in the world is?" he said.

"No, tell me?"

"It's from the Roman age. A senator sits down to get his hair cut. The barber asks how he'd like it cut. He says 'In silence'."

"Okay, I hear you," said Lindsay. "It's a pretty crummy joke but I hear you."

George picked up a copy of *The Field* and began reading.

"You have a good head shape," she said.

"Thank you, you're very kind," he said with a mild smile. He didn't want to sound continuously sarcastic but he honestly didn't know how else to react at this point in time.

"Take it from me, George, you're going to rock this look."

The next morning George stood at the top of the stairs, watching as the new butler advanced into the hallway below and grandly announced Sofia's arrival to Blaire. Sofia was dressed in a primrose-yellow, knee-length dress. She was followed by Ruby, who looked amazing in a lime-green suit.

"It's magnificent," said Ruby, twirling around with her handbag flying on her elbow. "Real life *Downton Abbey*." She stopped when she saw George looking down.

"Hello," she said.

"Hello," said George.

Sofia's head snapped back as she also looked up.

"Hello, George," she said.

"Sofia," he said evenly, slowly walking down the steps. "And I take it you are Ruby?"

"Yes," replied Ruby, feeling almost shy. "Thank you for having me to stay."

"I'm pleased to meet you," said George.

Sofia was in a mild state of shock at the sight of George in skinny jeans, a black T-shirt and navy linen jacket. For his part,

George was trying to come to terms with the itinerary that Victoria had just handed him for the "first trimester" as she put it, of the media campaign.

"Just to get things straight," said Sofia, turning crossly to Ruby. "I am the one you should be thanking. You are here as my guest and, as it happens, so are you, George – just as soon as the paperwork goes through."

George shook his head and looked up at a large portrait of a tightly bearded ancestor on the wall behind them.

"I hope you don't mind ghosts," said George. "This chap has been known to go slinking about the bedrooms at night."

"The only possible reason a ghost would slink into my bedroom would be to see me undressing," said Sofia, smiling at Ruby. "Oh, come on, George, not even a smile?"

"Sofia, for as long as I have to put up with this absurd farce, you will not get as much as a cracked smile out of me." Trying to maintain his calm, he flipped open Victoria's itinerary. "It says here that at three o'clock this afternoon we are going to stand at the gates of Rousey, and you are going to flash an engagement ring."

"I know, I read that too. Isn't it thrilling?"

"So cool," agreed Ruby, examining a collection of miniatures on a curio table.

"And so, I thought it might be worth asking you, one more time, if you would like to reconsider before this situation gets any older. I can wire you the value of Rousey to your account today. We can forget this nightmare ever happened and move on. How does that sound?"

It was like a knife through George's heart to have to pander to Sofia, but it was the only option he could think of.

Without responding, Sofia turned on her heel and walked into the library, followed by Ruby and reluctantly, George. Lifting the lid of a baby grand piano, she ran her fingers along the keys, from high pitch to low base and then closed the lid.

"In a word, George, no way."

"Two words," said Ruby, grinning uncertainly, but Sofia scowled.

"My social-media following has nearly tripled since we were photographed the other night," said Sofia. "And the way you are looking right now, there isn't a woman, or man for that matter, who wouldn't want to be in my shoes ... which is precisely the point of this twelve-month exercise."

"Fine," said George. "But you had better hope that your father isn't permitted visitors while he's banged up in prison over here."

"What the hell is that supposed to mean?" said Sofia.

"You thought I didn't know that Max has been extradited to the UK? So convenient that he's on British turf." He had been reading up on Max Tamper and knew this was one of the few ways he could get under Sofia's skin.

"And?" Sofia looked uneasy.

"Take no notice, Sofia, he's playing you," said Ruby.

"Am I? Do you think I'm playing you, Sofia? How does Max feel now that you and your mother have abandoned him when he most needs you?"

"*Get out!*" Sofia screamed.

"What? Get out of my own home? Now what would the media say to that, I wonder? I don't actually think you lot have really thought this plan through at all."

"It's straightforward, George, the deeds to this goddamn crumbling pile of rock are going to be in my name."

"Yes, a crumbling pile of rock with 17th century Italian architraves and marble cornices, not to mention some of the finest examples of stucco work in the United Kingdom."

"Like I told you, George," said Sofia, trying to sound serene, "I will sign this place back over to you as soon as this publicity campaign is complete. Now let's change the record, shall we ... brother?" Then, flicking through a copy of *Tatler*, she pulled a face. "Well, how timely," she said, laying the magazine open on the table. "According to this feature, the right dress on the right carpet can send an actress's value skywards. You see, George, appearances are everything and that is why I need you by my side. We both need to look stunning at every moment. George? Are you listening?"

"Sofia, I don't give a monkey's what you wear."

"Well, it is blatantly clear, judging by photos of you in past editions of *Bystander*, that you take absolutely no interest in how *you* look."

"Leave it, Sofia," said Ruby, sensing that George's temper was about to bubble over, but Sofia ignored her.

"I think you're still pining after that Irish girl. Isn't that what all this sulkiness is about? You know, I overheard *Anna* talking with Tilly Fairfax about you and your money."

George looked up sharply, his eyes narrowing.

Aware that she had him by the Achilles' Heel, Sofia continued, sounding as nonchalant as possible. "Yes, I gather her father is really struggling in Ireland. Hasn't sold a painting in years apparently and they're almost certainly going to have to sell their home. Sounds like she was hoping you and your millions could come along and rescue them. It's so hard when people only want you for your money, isn't it, George?"

George looked at Sofia with a face like stone. "Anna's father recently had a heart attack, and he's in recovery."

"You're still in contact with her?"

"No," he said, feeling sick to the pit of his stomach. "I am not but Jamie is. He told me, if you must know. Not that it's any of your business."

"George, look, try to be practical. If we work together we can make a huge success for both our futures. I am determined to make it big, George. I know I can and I will."

He recoiled like a ringmaster confronted with an uncontrollable lion and turned to go.

"I don't doubt what you are capable of, Sofia. Not for a moment."

Victoria had contacted virtually every media contact she had ever made in order to build up a blissful hype around the engagement.

As George and Sofia stepped out of the black Range Rover by the front gates of Rousey, the day couldn't have been more beautiful. Wrens and blackbirds darted from branch to branch as a flurry of photographers and journalists with microphones slalomed between the thick, wide-necked security guards. Wearing an iridescent three-piece suit and his sleek new hairstyle, George looked like a catwalk model. He was quite unrecognizable from his usual check-shirt look.

"Smile for the camera, won't you, darling?" murmured Sofia, between pouted lips. She was both professional and in control as she linked her arm through George's, perfectly replicating the move Kate and William had made when they announced their engagement at Buckingham Palace half a decade earlier.

"I do love my ring," she said to George, holding out her left hand for the cameras to focus upon. "An enormous diamond to show your devotion."

"I'm sure they'll soon work out it's a big fake," muttered George, "don't you think, Sofia?"

This time she decided not to retaliate. As far as the press was concerned, she was standing next to one of the world's most handsome and eligible men. George's money and his crisp clean social status was swiftly bringing them both to A-list level. Sofia felt her wings were being polished and she was ready to fly towards the limelight. Reaching for a bottle of Dom Perignon from a nearby ice bucket, she turned to George.

"Open it," she said.

'Tamper's Champers!' declared *The Daily Mail*. 'It's wedding bells a go-go as one of Hollywood's up-and-coming stars lands one Britain's most eligible bachelors. George Wyndham clearly hasn't let Sofia Tamper's father's embarrassing arrest and incarceration interfere with their plans as the couple jointly announced their engagement outside the Wyndham family home of Rousey yesterday. They look certain to become one of the most talked about couples of the year ... what should we call them? Wyndham + Tamper = Wyndper.'

That evening, utterly exhausted, George walked into the boot room to find Lindsay pulling on Anna's boots.

"What are you doing in those boots? Take them off, take them off!" he said, and like a madman he got down on his knees, grabbing her by the ankles, pulling off the boots. "Not these," he said, out of breath. "I'm sorry."

He stood up, embarrassed.

Lindsay, grasping her leather jacket, utterly mortified, thought she had pulled on the boots of a dead person. "God, I'm like, so incredibly sorry, George. I had, like, no idea. I was told just to help myself. Jeez ..."

"They belong to someone else," said George, wiping his mouth. "They are all I have left," and at that moment it really hit him, the choice he had made.

Chapter 29

In the dining room, stretched out on a large Persian rug, Freddie took the news about Anna's pregnancy surprisingly well – in fact, she almost seemed pleased to have a distraction from her own thoughts. She was still in a muddle about Harry, who was due home in a fortnight, or even less. Freddie had been wondering about how things were going to change at Farley Hall. New menus, that was for sure, and less alcohol. But, more than that, it was her relationship that might have to change. The guilt she felt about not knowing if she was still in love with her husband was driving her crazy. Meditation was helping to an extent, but trying to dig deep into her heart and ask what it was she really wanted, what it was she needed for the rest of her life was not producing an answer.

"I think your decision not to tell your father, or Mrs B, for a month or two is a wise move, Anna," said Freddie, lifting her knees and reaching around the outside of her legs before grabbing her feet until she rocked back and forth on her back. "You know Mrs B won't approve and, as for your father, well, he'll hit the roof and it goes without saying that would not be good for his heart."

"And what about you, Mum? How do you feel?" asked Anna, looking at the serving dishes stacked beneath a huge sideboard, which brought on a huge feeling of nostalgia. The lunch parties she had witnessed during her teenage years with her parents, such lively hosts in the days when Harry was motivated by his art and Freddie so keen to open Farley Hall up to as many people as possible to celebrate Harry's art in the hope of future commissions. How things had changed.

"I am training my mind not to get carried away with unproductive thoughts," said Freddie, as she rocked back and forth. "Dharma says we need to open the windows of our hearts in order for our breath to flow easily."

"I like the sound of that," said Anna, flinching as she felt a stabbing pain in her side but gathering herself together again quickly, determined to appear in control in front of her mother. "But, Mum, won't Dad notice that I'm not drinking? Do you think he'll quickly realise that I am . . ."

"Your father won't be drinking either, at least for the first while anyway, so maybe we will shock the bricks of Farley Hall and all go on the dry for a while – shock horror, don't you think! What would your grandparents say if they were alive?"

"Pass the gin bottle, I'd say," said Anna, putting all her effort into a smile in order to avoid letting out a large sigh.

"That's the first time I've seen you smile in days, Anna darling."

"I know, Mum, I'm sorry."

"You have nothing to be sorry for, Anna – it's George who is the culprit here, no one else."

"Well, please let's not talk about him again – really, Mum, I just want to move on to the next step," she said, rubbing her tummy. "Gilda sent an email earlier, didn't mention George but I'm sure she knows – oh Mum, I have got to stop mentioning his name!"

"It's early days, Anna, give yourself time."

"But he's going to be in my life, isn't he? He'll want to be part of the baby's life."

"When will you tell him?"

"I don't know, but if I saw him now I think I'd hurl one of Mrs B's baked potatoes at him right between the eyes."

"And quite right too," said Freddie, moving into a child's pose.

Leaving her mother to it, Anna walked down to the kitchen in the basement and found Tilly deeply engrossed in Bernard's stories, as he sat in his usual spot at the table for morning coffee. Dharma was standing by the Aga, stirring stock in a pot.

"Anna, have some fruit cake, it's delicious. Must get the recipe, Mrs B," said Tilly, offering her chair to Anna.

"No thanks, Tills, I'm going to snuggle into the armchair instead," said Anna, as Guinness looked up from his beanbag, only too happy to flop his ears next to Anna's Ugg boots.

"Aye, them Muslims are buried before the sun goes down," said Bernard, thickly buttering a piece of fruit cake. "I remember when Princess Diana's fella died, he was buried that same night, and my own sister was at the funeral home for five weeks before we buried her in England, God rest her. These large motorways, ah sure it was a long journey for my brother and me to get to Felixstowe from Stanstead. Were you never in England, Dharma?"

"I know Manchester United?" said Dharma.

"No, never been there," said Bernard, "but sure those big roads in England, you couldn't be doing with them."

"I see elephant on my roads in Sri Lanka. People riding into the village."

"No, I've never seen an elephant," said Bernard, taking another slice of fruit cake and standing up to pass the plate to Dharma.

Anna loved listening to Bernard's stories, which Harry was often too impatient to listen to, no matter how fond he was of the man.

While Mrs B turned the napkins drying on the Aga's hot plate, folding them into shape and wondering if they'd still need an iron, Dharma was making risotto for lunch. Anna watched him as he carefully chopped herbs and added them to the stock, stirring the pot gently. It was a therapeutic sight.

"Anna," said Mrs B, "if you won't eat my fruitcake, why don't you have a piece of toast? You hardly ate a thing at breakfast. You've got to keep your strength up now, you know that."

"Actually, Mrs B," said Anna, getting up from the armchair and stepping over Guinness, "I think I'm going to lie down for a while. I'm not feeling great, to be honest."

"Are you okay, Anna?" asked Tilly.

"I'll be fine. I just need to go to bed for an hour or two."

Following Anna out the kitchen door, Tilly knew something was up.

"Anna, are you okay, really?"

"Oh, don't worry about me. I think I'm just exhausted, you know, after everything. A few hours in bed should sort me out." She let out a huge sigh. "What time is your flight?"

"Not until this evening. Jamie is going to collect me from Gatwick."

"Oh, that's nice," said Anna, bending over.

"Anna?"

"It's nothing," and straightening up again she gave Tilly a hug. "You have been so amazing, Tills, being here all this time."

"Anna, honestly, I could just throttle George."

"I feel like such a bloody fool. Just so naïve and stupid. So bloody stupid."

"Anna, the only fool in this scenario is George, okay?"

"Okay," said Anna. "I just need to get back to work, you know, back to normal. Gilda actually called earlier and said the girls in the office made a major blunder by pressing the loudspeaker rather than the mute button during a conference call, and they were referring to the MD of Master Cat as a randy old tomcat." Anna smiled, then doubled over again.

"Anna, you're not all right, are you? Come on, let's get you into bed."

"I've been having cramps since last night," said Anna, as they started up the stairs.

"Why didn't you tell me? Or your mum? Oh Anna!"

"No, Tilly, no fuss. There's been enough fuss. I'm going to lie down. I just need to rest."

Eight days later, having miscarried the baby, Anna stopped bleeding. With every cramping pain, she had curled up into a ball beneath the sheets, while Freddie, tears pouring down her face, insisted on staying with her, allowing Tilly and Mrs B to take over to rub Anna's back and sit with her for only a few hours a day. Freddie felt utterly devastated for Anna, though, as the days passed, she realised she was crying for herself as well. She wondered what the future held for her and Harry. As she sat in Anna's bedroom, with its tall windows and soft rugs over wooden floors, they hardly spoke. Freddie just being there, helping Anna to the bathroom and making sure she drank water and opening and closing the shutters to let in and keep out the daylight, was enough. And at night, Freddie and Anna lay in the dark, both drifting in and out of sleep, thinking about their next steps.

It had just been confirmed that Harry was due to be released from hospital in three days' time, which was met by Freddie with a look of relief and horror at once. Anna knew her mother was struggling with her marriage and that as the only child she had to be strong for all of them. Taking a shower in her bathroom, she watched as the steam rose up, peeling back the old ceiling paint. The water was as hot as she could bear and even then she wished it would just burn her – anything to feel another kind of pain beyond her sadness. Mistaking the conditioner for shampoo, she rubbed a mass of saucy paste into her hair. The effort needed to rinse it out felt too much for her and splashes of ice-cold water on her face after the shower had no impact.

She found a knee-length black Jigsaw skirt in her wardrobe, but she had lost so much weight the skirt fell beneath her waist and onto her hips. Rolling up the waistband, she pulled on a burgundy cashmere V-neck. Her highlights were growing out, making her hair look streaky, and so she scraped back the mass of dull curls into a tortoiseshell clip. A shadow of her former self, she thought. Her father could never bear clichés, saying they betrayed a lack of original thought, but on this occasion she was pretty sure Harry would agree with her.

Anna thought about Tilly, and how she would have to make it up to her for all the time she took off work. She had spent a solid fortnight at Farley Hall, buoying up everyone, like the sister Anna had never had. Walking downstairs for the first time since the miscarriage, it was like walking into a different life. Anna was now all on her own, having once had the promise of George and their tiny baby. The front door seemed to demand Anna to open it, and when she walked outside onto the gravel she saw the Weeping Ash staring back at her. Anna knew that she needed to fully process what had happened, even though the chances were that her mother or Mrs B might spot her and make her go her back to bed, to rest and take it easy.

Pulling back the long branches, Anna crept beneath the old Weeping Ash, and sitting down against the trunk she sank her head into her knees. She thought about how she had almost had to say goodbye to her father, but now he was back again. But with George, there had been no goodbye and in the short time they had spent together, she had even said the words that now made her feel sick. "I think, I think I'm falling in love with you," she had whispered from her pillow, without knowing that he would declare his love – ironically beneath this tree. Anna remembered his silhouette in the darkness, waiting for his lips to say he felt the same, but instead he gave her the sweetest, deepest kiss. They blended, their contours, even the palms of their hands. She had become used to sleeping next to him, her knees melting into the back of his legs. She thought of George propping up his head on his elbow, his silky hair crisscrossed over his eyes. "Just another three minutes, then we'll get up," he'd say. Then another three minutes would pass, followed by another three. And the storm in London when they stayed in bed all day, rain pelting against her bedroom window as they made love and now, like thunder becoming more distant with every count, George had disappeared into misty skies.

Anna began to cry and she literally couldn't stop. She didn't know whom she was crying for – George or the baby? She felt like Alice in Wonderland when the door handle laughed at her for leaving the key on the table before she shrank to a miniature size. "Stupid girl, stupid girl," she said to herself through trembling lips, tears streaming down her face. "What was I thinking? I should have known, stupid, stupid Anna," she wheezed, just as Guinness pushed his way through the branches and nuzzled his head into her neck, his wet nose cold against her skin.

Freddie carried a mug of cooled chamomile tea across the lawn, contemplating the best area for her afternoon stretches. Hearing wailing coming from the Weeping Ash, she poured out the contents of the mug and ran towards the branches. Making her way beneath the tree, Freddie was almost relieved to find Anna at last letting out her utter grief.

"My darling girl," said Freddie, falling to her knees beside Anna, throwing her arms around her. "Oh, my darling, how long have you been here? You are freezing, my little one."

"I just don't get it, Mum. How could he leave me?" Anna shuddered, eyes red, nose running. "And why on earth did he come here if I was just another fling?"

Freddie winced when she felt Anna's shoulder, so thin. She must have lost at least a stone since Harry's fall.

"Breathe, my darling, you must take a breath," said Freddie, holding on tightly to her only daughter. "Think of Dharma's exercises. Breathing calms the soul, my darling."

"But everything has come crashing down," said Anna, trying to find air, trying to find anything. "How could I have read it so badly? It's all over, everything is over."

"No, my darling. It just feels like it. We'll get through it." Freddie closed her eyes and held Anna even tighter. "My poor love. You've been through so much."

And they hugged beneath the tree, until both felt like they almost had no tears left.

At last, clambering through the branches, arm in arm, they walked towards the front door of Farley Hall and thought of Harry with every step, both feeling like he was walking between them, with his hands across their backs, encouraging them on until he could return.

Chapter 30

The cool early-evening breeze came as a relief to Tilly when she walked out of Victoria Train Station. She had been in Ireland for almost a fortnight, and she had become so used to the country air. She hadn't realised how much she had missed Jamie until she got on the plane, the first chance she'd had to think properly. How Anna's father had nearly lost his life, and Anna's tiny, tiny baby having to answer nature's call to flee before it had grasped the chance of life. Feeling almost overwhelmed to know that Jamie would be waiting for her in the flat, having promised to make supper and be there for her, she walked at a fast pace towards Elizabeth Street. Checking her phone, there were no text messages, and clicking into her email she expected to find a string of emails from her boss, which there were, but at the very top Sofia Tamper's name was in the inbox. Tilly allowed herself to think about Sofia for a minute or two, wondering if maybe it was an email to explain what had happened with George, or some sort of communication stating that it had all been a horrible mistake.

Jamie was waiting for her in the flat as promised, with flowers in the kitchen and moussaka in the oven.

"Tilly, you're back!" he cried, rushing over to her, holding her head and kissing her all over her face. "God, I've missed you."

"Me too."

"Let me look at you! Gorgeous as ever. A little tired, though?"

"Exhausted," she said.

"For all the wrong reasons though," said Jamie, pulling her into his arms.

"Too right," said Tilly.

"You hungry?"

"Not yet. I want to stay wrapped in your arms for as long as possible."

"Fine by me," said Jamie. "Tell me, how is Anna?"

"Not great, and I honestly don't think I can mention your so-called friend's name. I have discussed him in depth, as you can imagine, and have looked at every possible angle of why he did it, and you know what, nothing adds up."

"And for Anna to lose the baby, oh Tilly! You know, I really want to tell him about the baby."

"I promised Anna – Jamie, you have to promise not to tell him," said Tilly, pulling out of Jamie's arms.

"How can I anyway? I can't even imagine we'll meet again after what's happened. It isn't only Anna that's lost him, you know." Jamie walked into the kitchen and checked the temperature on the electric oven.

"Oh Jamie, I know, I'm so sorry."

"George has been an amazing friend to me – honestly, Tilly, I can't tell you."

"I know what you've been through, Jamie."

"God knows where I'd be without him. And then, without any warning he literally throws himself off the top of a skyscraper and into the arms of that bloody bitch."

Tilly stood in front of Jamie, taking his hands in her hands. "My father used to say it takes three things to go wrong to make a disaster, and for Anna, she can count three things, so, Jamie, we have to count our lucky stars."

"And so Harry is going to make a full recovery?" asked Jamie, looking at Tilly, knowing how lucky he was to have her.

"Yes, amazingly, though you can tell Freddie is almost dreading his return from hospital."

"What, wondering if he will return to his old ways, drinking, smoking, eating … not a lot else?" asked Jamie.

"Exactly."

"Or, maybe he's seen the light, literally. Maybe he's had a blast of inspiration from his near-death experience and he'll pick up his paintbrushes again and really get stuck in once he's strong enough."

"Hopefully so," said Tilly. Opening the fridge, she toyed with the idea of a bottle of wine and then closed it again.

"I walked past a newsagent's yesterday," said Jamie, "and George was on the cover of a tabloid – honestly, looking like a character from *Zoolander*."

Tilly smiled a little, and looking at Jamie she couldn't help but let out a huge sigh. "Oh bugger it, let's open a bottle, shall we?"

"Good call," said Jamie. "I didn't like to suggest it, as we were in your flat and everything."

"I think we're on a level, don't you?"

"Most certainly," said Jamie.

"And speaking of George's haircut – Jamie, I think your blonde locks are turning more into surfer-dude mode than high-powered barrister."

"You're not suggesting you take the kitchen scissors to my sweet head?"

"Maybe," said Tilly, taking off her blazer.

"Well, the good news is that I trust you implicitly, and as long as your haircut makes me look amazing, I'm not fussy."

Tilly ran her fingers through his hair.

"Yes, your hair is almost long enough to plait – reminds me of plaiting my pony's tail for Pony Club."

"Actually, I'm not sure I can resist you," said Jamie, and picking her up he carried her into her bedroom.

"It's been far too long," he said, laying Tilly on the bed and pulling her black long-sleeved top over her head. Smoothing his hand over her face and seeing her eyes, he realised what a hard time she'd had comforting her best friend through the possible loss of her father's life, and then, even more so, through the loss of her best friend's baby.

As they made love, Tilly thought back to the night she and Jamie first met at Sofia's party, his openness and enthusiasm, and tonight he made love to her a similar way. He wasn't shy about telling her how beautiful she was, how much he wanted her, he told her that he loved her. It felt like the perfect homecoming.

Afterwards, lying in bed, Tilly was feeling restless. "I'm just going to run to check my phone."

"Oh come on, there's no hurry, it's been aeons since I've had you all to myself!"

"I just want to check some emails," said Tilly, wanting to see what the email from Sofia was about and whether it really was spam, which she was sure it was . . . but then again, she wasn't sure. "Did I tell you Gilda has been in contact?"

"Gilda must be utterly raging," said Jamie. "She'd have been the first to see all the coverage, with her eagle eye. I can't imagine crossing one of her most valued employees is a wise move."

"Exactly," said Tilly, "and so Gilda has set up a Google alert for any coverage about George and Sofia. She called yesterday, but I couldn't really talk, as I was with Anna, but in essence Gilda said: 'Information is power, darling, and the more we know about this George and Sofia, the sooner we'll find the link that makes this entire story so shady. I'm telling you, darling, I can smell a rat, and that rat has an LA accent.'"

"Pretty funny, if it wasn't so awful," said Jamie. "I can understand why you want to check your emails," and, jumping out of bed, he went to the table by the front door to get Tilly's phone.

"Thanks," she said, kissing him, as he handed her the phone.

She clicked into her emails as they lay back on the same pillow.

"So just look at this link that Gilda sent through." Tilly scrolled through pictures of Sofia stepping out of a stretch limo, pouting to the paparazzi. In one photo she appeared to be beckoning George to follow her. Tilly stared at that one for quite a while.

"Since when did George start wearing black V-neck shirts?" asked Jamie.

Tilly moved on to Sofia's email then sat up abruptly. Getting out of bed, she made for the bathroom.

"Tilly? What's the matter?"

Sitting on the edge of the bath, letting the shower run, Tilly shook as she tried to take in the photograph that had come through from Sofia. It was dated the night of the *Violet Tiger* when Jamie was so drunk, off his head. She tried to remember the timing. It must have been after midnight when she left the party with Anna, and Jamie had let loose. She looked at his face in the picture, sleeping with his face turned to one side, peaceful as an angel … and on top of Ruby. A bed somewhere. And they were both naked. Jamie had a reputation for being a proper womaniser before he met Tilly – at least that is what George had told Anna – and what Anna naturally had told Tilly.

"Tills, are you okay?" said Jamie, through the bathroom door.

"Just a second, I'm just getting into the shower!" Tilly's mind was racing. She took as long as possible to wash her hair, so she could think. Then she wrapped her hair in a towel and walked into the kitchen, wearing her yellow dressing gown, to find Jamie taking the moussaka out of the oven.

"Nice shower? Hopefully this will be delicious. Tilly? All okay?"

"Fine," she said, avoiding eye contact with him.

"Okay," said Jamie, "but why so serious?"

"Nothing," she said, shaking her head. "I'm fine, really," and she flicked on the kettle. "I'm just tired, that's all."

"Well, we can have some supper and then have a lovely early night, and I'll let you sleep a little, I promise – if I can resist you, that is."

He reached out but Tilly turned away.

"No, Jamie – really, I just need some space."

"What? What's happened? Is this about Gilda's email? The links she sent through about George and Sofia?"

Tilly needed to be sure as to what she was doing, and the buggering thing about it was that she utterly loved Jamie.

"Yes, it is about Gilda's email if you must know. And you can't argue George out of this one, Jamie, no matter how good you are as a barrister. What he has put Anna through, her whole family through actually – Freddie is so upset, even Mrs B and Bernard." Her voice was rising. "They are devastated for her, as if they don't have enough to deal with themselves. This is a royal fuck-up, Jamie!"

Jamie dropped the tea towel, hoping to be a little theatrical. "Well, that's got that off your chest. I don't think I've ever heard you shout before, have I? Look," he said, sitting at the kitchen table, "George runs deep, and I know that something is really not right. I know what he has done seems dreadful and it is, dreadful, and I feel for Anna, I absolutely do. But try not to judge him too harshly. There has got to be a reason why he is with Sofia."

"Like what?"

"I don't know, Tilly. But it is all completely out of character. That's all I can say right now."

"The bloody bitch, fucking Sofia! And Ruby . . ."

"Tilly, come on, let's just try to forget about all that tonight, okay? We'll have a glass of wine, we can snuggle up in front of a film. You must be exhausted after everything." He put his arm around her.

Tilly violently pushed him away. She wanted to thump his chest and grill him on every detail of the night he had got drunk but she wouldn't let herself. "I'm not hungry, Jamie. I'm sorry, I'm going to bed. It's going to be a massive week at work, having been away for two weeks, so it's going to be frantic."

"What's happened, Tilly? I don't understand. Is there something you need to tell me?"

"No," she said. "I need to sleep, that's all. I'm exhausted."

"Don't you want me to stay tonight?"

"Again, no."

"Well, okay, if that's what you want."

"It is," she said, walking towards her bedroom.

"Don't I even get a goodnight kiss?" said Jamie, trying to put on his puppy-dog eyes.

"Take the moussaka with you, Jamie," and closing her bedroom door behind her she slid down the back of the door and silently wept.

Chapter 31

"This place is heaven," said Ruby, looking stunning in a knee-length chunky sweater with leggings as she studied a landscape. "I feel I'm in a real-life house of Cluedo, with history oozing through the walls."

"Through the cracks more like," said Sofia, heaping cushions into the corner of a sofa and landing herself on top of them.

"The place needs a lot of work, but it's going to be more a case of tweaking than major renovation, apart from the basement of course, which is going to be where the magic will happen."

Ruby had covered the writing desk in the study with sketches and swatches of material. She was used to working for demanding clients and so was well able to handle Sofia and Blaire, matching their extravagant tastes with suggestions in keeping with the style of the house.

Ruby's wealthy parents had made sure to keep their children grounded and, apart from paying for their exquisite education, had left them to fend for themselves. "The family money, as people like to refer to it, is mine," her father used to say. "You lot can make your own. That's what I did, using my business head, no matter what barriers and prejudices I faced." It was sound advice which Ruby followed and, once she graduated from design school in New

York, she specialised in set design, building a reputation as one of the hottest designers in theatre circles, before focusing on residential interiors. Then she and Sofia met at a party in LA the year before, just as Sofia was rebelling against the tight belt her mother had pulled around her.

"Starting with that big room with the piano – is that the music room or something? Anyway, the light in there is magnificent, so we'll turn that into a hub for meditation and massage. I am thinking butterflies, hummingbirds, lots of floral prints – it will be so fresh, and I think we can rescue most of the wallpaper too if I bring in a top-notch restorer."

"Nice," said Sofia, loving seeing Ruby in work mode.

"We're gonna dig out the basement and put the cinema in there, along with a games room and of course a gym," said Ruby, picking up a drawing of the basement, "but we'll make sure to protect any fine plasterwork. The rooms are huge down there – a cinema will fit easily – I think a twelve-seater?"

"Sounds pretty good," said Sofia, who was trying not to worry about filming *Violet Tiger*, wondering if she was really up to the role.

"You literally won't need to step out while you're here. It's going to be a palace by the time we finish, and you should see some examples of William Morris upstairs – sensational."

"I'm up for anything if it will distract me from that script," said Sofia, wrinkling her nose at the fat envelope on the coffee table.

"I didn't know it had arrived."

"Oh yes, by courier first thing this morning, courtesy of my mother who has naturally read through the whole thing already."

"I can run some lines with you?" said Ruby, as Sofia flipped onto the floor and stretched out her long legs.

"Do you think I'm putting on weight?" asked Sofia.

"What? You're like a string bean!"

"Okay, if you say so. By the way, Mom is taking full advantage of George being overseas for the shoot."

"He was definitely not in good form when he left last night, even when I suggested that most men would be over the moon to be groomed and photographed for *Esquire*, and in Rome of all places – but he was not impressed."

"Well, that's not our problem. So, if you can run Mom through your plans, okay? Hey, aren't you thirsty? Midday already."

"Not very."

"*Royston!*" yelled Sofia.

"Yes, madam," he said, brushing the edge of an armchair as he whisked into the room.

"How do you always manage to be so nearby when I call?"

"Part of my job, madam."

"Well, I need you to turn into a bartender and bring two Bloody Marys."

"Yes, madam,"

"And Royston –"

"Yes, madam?"

"Make sure you serve the drinks in highballs this time, got it? And lots of ice."

"As you wish, madam."

As Royston left the room, Ruby scrunched up her face. "Do you have to talk like that to your butler?"

"Like what exactly?"

"Like that, exactly."

"Ruby," said Sofia, pulling at the hem of her short black skirt, "you are here to advise on interiors, not on staff etiquette, got it?"

"Yes, madam," mimicked Ruby, curtseying in front of an elk's antlers mounted on the wall.

Cursing out loud as she walked through the front door, with a steely expression on her face, Blaire was dressed in a tight-fitting salmon-pink suit.

"Royston?"

"Madam."

"Where are you in such a hurry to get to?"

"Drinks for Sofia and Ms Beecham, madam."

"What kind of drinks."

"Bloody Marys, madam."

"Well, make them Virgin Marys from now on – it is our job to keep Sofia trim and that means off the booze."

"As you wish, madam, and on that note I have taken the liberty of enlisting a top-notch catering company in Edinburgh to deliver meals for Sofia, all fat-free as you requested."

"And you've stocked the refrigerator with the list of items I sent through?"

"Fully stocked, madam, including Pinkberry's fat-free frozen yogurt, flown in from Miami," coughed Royston, but Blaire didn't bat an eyelid at such an expense.

"And staff?"

"A team of cleaners roam silently through the house at five each morning, and a florist arrives daily with vases resplendent with flowers in perfect bloom."

Checking her watch, Blaire pinched her earlobe as if the heavy-looking clip-on earring was causing her discomfort. "Good work, Royston. I want confidentiality at every point, so additional staff coming into the house while Sofia sleeps is excellent. And Royston?"

"Yes, madam?"

"It is understood that Sofia sleeps in her own bedroom so that her sleep pattern isn't interrupted?"

"Of course," said Royston.

"And her fiancé, George," said Blaire, fiddling with her pearl necklace.

"Yes, madam?"

"He is an independent young man, and he likes to keep his own bedroom also."

"Naturally, madam."

"Fine," said Blaire, who felt momentarily stupid for running George and Sofia's sleeping arrangements past the butler. Royston knew perfectly well what was going on, she was sure of it, but she also knew his considerable wage was more than enough to maintain his discretion. "When we begin ground works on the house," she continued, "we can think again as to staffing, but for now I see we are in control."

"Allow me to announce you in the study, madam."

"No need for that, Royston, I know my way."

Royston smiled as he watched Blaire swaggering along the corridor – another vain and feckless client to add to his list.

Pushing open the study door, Blaire looked at Sofia and couldn't help but feel jealous of her, so slender and effortlessly glamorous.

"Hello, Mother, I didn't expect you so soon after lunch."

"I like to surprise," said Blaire, air-kissing her daughter.

"Let me introduce you to Ruby." Stepping back, she ushered her friend forward. "As you know from Ruby's portfolio which I sent you, she is our interiors genius and has handled some of the most prominent refurbs in Hollywood."

"Yes, impressive. Hello, Ruby," said Blaire, extending her hand.

"Hello, Mrs Tamper," said Ruby, who had a pile of material swatches in her hands. "I would shake your hand but as you can see I've got a rather full load here."

"So I see," said Blaire, "and less of the Tamper please – I'm just days away from my divorce."

Ruby glanced over at Sofia to show support but she appeared oblivious to the reference to her father.

"Now, let's get down to business, shall we?" said Blaire, taking out her phone and sending a text message while she spoke. "We need to get going immediately if we are to bring Rousey to the standards of excellence we are seeking."

"I'm totally on it, Blaire," said Ruby.

"I don't recall granting permission for you to call me *Blaire*."

"Cut it out, Mother. What happens then?" asked Sofia.

"We stick to our plan, obviously, and open to the luxury hotel market. Keep up, won't you, Sofia?"

"Hotel?" asked Ruby. "But I thought ..."

"Ruby, it's okay, I'll fill you in later," said Sofia.

"And when George is here, not a word about turning this place into a hotel, understand?" said Blaire, admiring her reflection in the mirror above the mantelpiece.

"Yes," said Ruby, wondering what the hell was going on.

Sofia wandered from room to room, briefly inspecting her newly acquired ancestors. Wyndhams with pointed aquiline noses, thin lips and splendidly tailored outfits, immortalised in their oil paintings, stared down at her but Sofia couldn't look them in the eye. It was as if they knew what she and her mother were doing to George. This was the polar opposite to the Hollywood life she had been submerged in. She did feel like she was to the manor born, but the Scottish thing was confusing for her. A big old house in the middle of nowhere was not her bag. Mansion yes, but Scotland, definitely no.

The stairwell by the back kitchen was covered in photographs of more recent generations. Men stalking in tweed outfits with flat caps, and sitting on the dried bracken amid the craggy Scottish hillsides. A couple in their sixties, the man holding a rod and the lady a basket with a salmon tail popping out. And there was George himself, a chubby toddler dressed in Peter-Pan-collared shirts and corduroy shorts. Standing alongside him was a handsome woman with a very strong nose, whom Sofia guessed must have been his mother. There she was again, with George on her knee, seated on a sofa. And there was Robert, very handsome, poised by the library fireplace, his gun broken in one hand and a cigar in the other.

Sofia wondered what her mother had been in love with all those years ago. Had it been Robert Wyndham or life in the Big House that she craved? Blaire had been cast aside, young, used and pregnant, so maybe this present enterprise was nothing more than revenge. Making sure Rousey was a cash cow for her daughter. If this was the case, Sofia was ready to milk it, and as a Wyndham it was her right.

Walking into the drawing room, Sofia found Ruby sitting on a sofa in a dressing gown, flicking through a thick catalogue of antiques and looking irritated.

"So, your mom finally left?"

"Yes, and dispatched Royston to Edinburgh to pick up cocktail napkins as she walked out the door."

"She did?"

"That's my mother. When she drinks her martini, she likes to hold a napkin at the same time. Have you just taken a bath?"

Ruby stood up, flinging the catalogue to one side.

"Yes, with a miniscule amount of hot water. And speaking of unreliable systems, I'd like you to tell me what on earth is going on."

"What do you mean?"

"I thought you agreed with George that you were going to sell this place back to him."

"What's it to you?" said Sofia, shaking out her hair from a high ponytail.

"What's it to me? You asked me to come here to help you out, to give you moral support, to be with you."

"Yes ... and?"

"And you're being a bitch to George. The poor guy is totally cut up about it and who wouldn't be? His own father booted him out of the equation as soon as you rocked up."

"Exactly – which goes to show how keen my father is to make up for lost time. He owes me a whole lot of pocket money – why should I feel bad about cashing in? Anyway, George is already minted." Sofia reached out and slowly ran her hand down Ruby's arm.

"Where did you find that kilt anyway?" asked Ruby, finding Sofia's touch hard to resist. "Isn't it itchy as hell against your skin?"

"Not really," said Sofia, trailing her hand across Ruby's shoulder. "In fact, it feels pretty sexy."

Ruby slid her hand around Sofia's back, feeling her finely boned shoulders.

"I found it in a cupboard downstairs," said Sofia. "I guess it's some sort of Wyndham tartan. So you could say I'm getting back to my roots, which is funny, as the only roots I had ever thought of before now were the kind I talk about with my hairdresser."

"Hold on, you never said you were wearing lycra?" said Ruby, pulling up Sofia's kilt.

"I'm breaking it in to wear under my dress next week – it's underwear that just sucks everything in."

"But you're perfect," said Ruby, rubbing her hand down Sofia's side.

"Why don't you try the kilt?"

"That Scottish roots thing doesn't apply to me. Remember, I'm a Caribbean girl, through and through."

"Well," said Sofia, "try this on for size." Unbuckling the kilt and wrapping it around Ruby's slim waist, she let the dressing gown fall to the floor then fastened the buckle again. "And look, no panties! You're a natural Scot."

Sliding to her knees, Sofia slipped her head beneath the kilt, gently pushing Ruby back onto the sofa. As Sofia's tongue swirled and teased inwards along her thighs, Ruby made eye contact with a kind-looking man, captured in an oil painting, and she wondered what Sofia's ancestors would have thought about women adoring women within the venerable walls of Rousey.

Chapter 32

Guinness lay on his beanbag beside the Aga at Farley Hall, whining at Mrs B for leftover morning bacon.

"It's a sad day, Anna – I've got used to having you around of a morning, you know, for a long stretch instead of those short 'weekend breaks' as they say," said Mrs B, pouring hot water into a saucepan. "Ah, would you look at Guinness, slumped in his beanbag. He's missing the bacon rind from your father's fry-ups, no doubt."

"And missing the soundtrack of Vivaldi in the evenings, with Dad smoking a cigar with a whiskey nightcap."

"All change, Anna, isn't that right? And are you sure you're ready to leave? That big job of yours, doesn't it pull the living hell out of you?"

"Now that Dad is home again, Mrs B, I really think it's time for my parents to get into a new zone."

"It was a big change for him, coming home," said Mrs B.

"The big change being that he has to relax without having had a huge breakfast and several glasses of wine with lunch."

"You're right about that. And, Anna, now I don't mean to pry, Lord have mercy on me, I don't mean to, but what about you, after, well, after what happened to you?"

"You mean the break-up with George?"

"I mean losing the wee baby, Anna."

First, Anna blushed and then as the tears came she reached for a napkin from the table. Padding it against her eyes, she looked at Mrs B.

"I know Mrs Rose doesn't want me to know, Anna, and I don't mean to pry," said Mrs B, cracking an egg into the saucepan to poach. "She thinks I'd disapprove, you know, you not being married and all."

"I'm sorry, Mrs B, I should have told you – we just didn't want to upset you."

"Sure why would you worry about me? Aren't you the one we are all worrying about?" said Mrs B, putting three spoons of tealeaves into the teapot.

"I'm sorry, Mrs B."

"What your mother doesn't know is that my Ned and I, we lost a baby before we married," she said, pour boiling water into the teapot. "Only my sister knew, God rest her, and such things weren't talked about then, whether you were married or otherwise."

"Again, Mrs B, I'm really sorry for not telling you."

"Don't you worry your head – but one thing you could do for me?"

"Anything."

"Would you ever eat this lonely poached egg here, and put a bit of fat on your bones?"

"That, I can do," said Anna.

"And sure, you never know," said Mrs B, elbowing Anna, "it might have even been laid by the hen you helped rescue all those weeks ago."

Harry sat in the dining room, looking out at the view of the drumlins. The morning light was stunning, mist clearing into a pale blue sky, with cattle dotted around the top of the highest hill. He wondered if he'd have an ounce of the life he'd had before, freedom to ride Penthouse, drink whiskey late into the night until life seemed more creative, and pontificate about painting. But then he knew he was fooling himself. It had been over a year since he had painted seriously and, as a result, he could see Freddie's respect for him was waning. She was becoming increasingly distant from him, drawn instead to her yoga and so-called mindfulness. The commission to paint Nadeem had raised a spark in Freddie, and he had felt excited about it too, like it was the push he needed to get back to work, but now he wasn't sure if he was up to it. Maybe sitting in an armchair and watching the hills was all he was good for.

"Hi, Dad," said Anna, looking pale and pulling a smile across her face to please her father.

"Good morning, darling, sleep well?"

"Sort of," she said.

"I'll take that as a no then?" said Harry. "Look, sweetheart, it's going to take time for you to get this George fellow out of your system, and I think Gilda's suggestion of Paris really could be the ticket for you."

"Yes, I've begun to think so too."

"And as soon as the doc gives me the all-clear to fly, your mother and I will come to see you," he said. "It's been far too long since I've been there anyway. Anna, darling, you're crying?"

"I'm sorry, Dad."

"Well, it's been an emotional time, hasn't it? But don't you worry about me, I've promised your mother and the consultant that I'll stay on the straight and narrow. And I don't even feel like drinking, that's the worst part – I've got a metallic taste at the back of my mouth."

"It's because of the medicine," said Anna, sniffing into Harry's handkerchief, "but Peter said your sense of taste will return to normal soon enough."

"Couldn't get a laugh out of that consultant fellow, terribly serious. When I asked him if he ever watched *Carry on Doctors and Nurses*, he didn't even flinch, not a muscle, and I must say, some of those nurses were very pretty."

"Dad, you are terrible," said Anna, managing a smile.

"That's better," said Harry. "We need to see more of that smile of yours. And you know, Anna, this whole business has got me thinking. I've been given a second bite of the cherry, haven't I? Another round of the point to point, another chukka."

Anna smiled at the analogies.

"Well, I watched the sunset from my bed last night and saw the jackdaws whirling around the trees, ready to settle for the night –

all that nature out there. I really want to give life a proper shot this time."

"But you always have?" said Anna.

"Not properly though, not with your mother. If I'm being honest I've often felt she's just tagging along because she figures this is the life she signed up to when she married me."

"She loves you, Dad, you know that."

"I don't know, Anna. She feels distant, it's hard to explain."

"It's been a shock for her, Dad – we thought we were going to lose you."

"Well, look, enough about me – you need to get over this George business. You are going to get over him, aren't you?"

"Yes, Dad, I am."

"That's the spirit, my little Anna – now come and give your old man a hug."

As they hugged Freddie arrived with a yoga mat under her arm.

"Hello, you two. Just look at the light pouring through – doesn't that feel good, Harry?"

"I suppose so," he said, "except that I've only been home for three days and so far the only thing I've managed to achieve is how to work the record button on the television."

"Dad, you'll be back running on full par before long. You just have to do what you're told for a month or two."

"Do you hear that, Harry?" said Freddie, smiling.

"Well, all right, Anna, I'll try to behave, if not for my own good then for your mother's sanity. Now, aren't you going to give your banjaxed old father another hug before you leave?"

"Goodbye, Dad, see you soon, okay?"

And followed by Freddie, Anna quickly left the room before Harry could see her cry.

"Anna are you sure you want to take the bus to the airport?" said Freddie. "I'll drive you – honestly, I'd like to."

"No, Mum, Bernard's all set to drop me to the bus and, really, I'd prefer it. I just want to gaze out the window and get my head together."

Freddie held Anna tightly as they said goodbye.

"Just one thing before you go," said Freddie. "There's something I need to tell you."

"What is it?"

"It's George. He wrote a letter to me, about your father, to say how sorry he was and that he wished him a fast recovery."

"How very nice," said Anna sarcastically.

"The reason I'm telling you is because I think the main point of the letter was to tell you that he is sorry," said Freddie. "I didn't know whether or not to tell you, darling, but I just thought ..."

Anna looked at her mother, who sometimes looked so vulnerable, making Anna feel more like her big sister than daughter.

"It's okay, Mum," said Anna, hugging her again. "We all just have to forget about George. There's nothing more to say."

Anna's heart felt like a lead weight as she sat on the plane, trying to shield herself from the outside world by hiding behind sunglasses. The male flight attendant looked at her with raised eyebrows when she requested a third vodka and tonic as the drinks trolley rattled up the aisle for the final time before landing. Pouring only half the tonic into the vodka, Anna took a sip as she flicked through *Hello* and scowled at a recipe for summer pudding, which looked soggy and far too much like a trifle without the custard. Then she turned the page and froze as a photograph of George and Sofia stared back at her. Standing side by side beneath the archway at the entrance of Rousey, Sofia wore a yellow belted dress as if to announce the arrival of summer.

'The 30-year-old Sofia Tamper, engaged to one of Britain's most eligible bachelors, George Wyndham, hinted to *Hello* that her dream wedding would be a spectacular ceremony in a medieval castle. "George is a camera-shy kind of guy, so he leaves all the talking to me," she said in an exclusive interview announcing the engagement. "He is very caring. I am the luckiest girl in the world. He firmly believes in my career as an actress and he supports me 100%, so much so that he is taking the next year off from the art world so that he can be by my side."'

Drinking the remainder of her vodka tonic, Anna watched the light-footed flight attendants move up and down the aisle with white plastic bags, collecting rubbish from the passengers before landing. Turning on the camera setting of her phone to check her reflection, whatever about smudged mascara, she had a red circular dent over her eyebrow and down the side of her nose from where the sunglasses had pressed into her face. This was the rock bottom she had read about and heard about, and now it was hers first hand, every inch of the hard clay ground grating into her heart. She thought about what Dharma had said to her before she left.

"May I stand with you, Anna?" he had said, as she looked at the Weeping Ash from the kitchen garden.

"Of course," she said.

"I am sorry that you are suffering."

"Thank you, Dharma."

"I want to say to you, that if you can believe in your body's capacity to heal itself, this will surely give you strength. I pray for you, okay?"

"Do you really think I'll be okay?"

"I think so, yes, and you see that little bird around your neck?"

"I know I shouldn't be wearing it – Tilly would kill me if she knew. After everything he's done?" she said, grappling with the clasp to take it off.

"No, Anna – that golden bird, you keep."

"But he gave it to me," she whispered.

"I know, Anna. Keep the golden bird."

She couldn't decide why, but she did listen to Dharma and she kept the necklace on, even though she had every reason to tear it from her neck and throw it as far from her as she could. Maybe it was the kindness in Dharma's eyes, the sincerity in his voice. Standing next to her, he seemed to pass a sense of peace on to her.

"Your time will come again, Anna. It will come," and, watching over the hills sloping into each other for support and the trees shimmering with fresh leaves, Anna knew it was time for her to move on to new ground and that new ground was going to be Paris.

Chapter 33

Gilda hit the roof when she saw the double-page spread in *The FT Magazine* picturing Sofia, in an off-the-shoulder dress, with her jewelled wrists around George, who wore orange-tinted Havana sunglasses and a shiny, tight leather jacket.

"Christ, what's he wearing?" said Gilda, quite revolted. "He looks like a throwback to *Top Gun* and that Sofia girl is nothing but a common whore." Tuning into the impact the media charade must be having on Anna, Gilda's strategic mind began to spin.

"Kate, we need to bring Anna's move to Paris forward."

"Has she agreed to the move?"

"Not officially, but I've decided it's the only way for her to handle this George business."

"Right-oh, Gilda," said Kate.

"Try to be enthusiastic, would you, Kate? I know you don't want Anna to leave the office, but it won't be forever – it's just to get Winterbottom's stamp into the Parisian press."

"So, when are we thinking?" said Kate.

"I'm thinking this week. Call that divine man, Francois, at the estate agency in Paris and tell him I want to take possession of the keys to the apartment this week, and see if he'll throw in a cleaner, will you? The rent is extortionate although I have a feeling such an investment will be worthwhile for Winterbottom, and, in the short term it will get Anna out of this hell-hole she's been thrown into. It's going to take a crane to lift her out at this stage."

"And Gilda?" said Kate, tilting her head from one side to the other, looking so cute and innocent.

"Yes, Kate sweetie, what is it?"

"If Desmond Spicer does go for our proposal to throw the massive launch party in Paris?"

"Yes?"

"Can I be Anna's number two?" And pulling a pair of headphones out of her pocket, Kate began reciting a series of French phrases, "*Bonjour, Madame. Vous êtes très sympathique. You see Gilda, I've been brushing up on my French! Si'l vous plaît?*"

"Oh, all right, but let's score the business first – we're putting far too much mileage into Spicer Tweed already, not to mention the distraction of Desmond's tendency to drop in for single malt. I'm not sure if he doesn't think we're some sort of gentlemen's club – next thing we know he'll be requesting a massage."

"All right, love," said a man in dungarees, who looked at Chrissy as he arrived into the office holding a delivery docket as it if were a paper airplane. "Five hundred units for you, missus." Leaning against the doorway, he began rotating his hips like a Chippendale. "My muscles get awful stiff sitting in the delivery truck, know what I mean, ladies? Good to have a stretch."

"What's the delivery?" asked Chrissy.

"Bloc Bling or something like it," he said, wondering if Chrissy was single. "Bring 'em in, shall I?"

"Please," said Chrissy, in no mood for delivery-man flirtations. "You can put them in the corner."

"Right, missus – if you are a missus, that is?"

"The corner," said Chrissy, well used to that sort of chat.

Gilda was highly excited that the first lot of samples of her new client had arrived. "Bloc it Blings, darlings, all the way from Oz," she said, pulling off her ladybird clip-on earrings to put in a pair of multicoloured diamante earplugs devised to protect from noisy co-workers or tantrum-prone children. "Can't hear a word, darlings! Lord, those Australians really do know how to make quality products! I can list off some of their cracking exports, Pat Cash for one. Oh, those muscles, did I ever tell you he read my aura? Yes, angels, it was green, which of course is an excellent colour for an aura."

"Gilda, you're speaking quite loudly," said Chrissy, pointing to the Bloc-it Blings.

"*What's that?*" roared Gilda? "All this excitement is making me terribly thirsty. I'm going to pop into my office for a glass of fizz, and, sweeties, keep up the good work!" And off she tripped into her office, giving the girls the thumbs-up, utterly delighted with herself.

With Gilda out of sight, Kate pressed pink-and-white diamante-covered plugs into her own ears and put her feet up on her desk.

"Bloc it, Bling it, I like it!" she said, giggling. "What's that, my little dumplings?" she said in her best Gilda impersonation. "I can't hear a word, my sweetiekins, did you say Bolli?"

The office went into stitches just as Anna arrived, looking like hell, and they all ground to an immediate halt.

Kate jumped to her feet and quickly shuffled media clippings of George and Sofia into a drawer.

"Anna, I am so sorry," said Kate, "about everything."

"We all are," said Chrissy, following suit. "Anything we can do, Anna, anything at all."

"Thank you so much, but really I'm fine. I just want to get things back to normal." Anna's face was pale with shadows beneath her eyes. She had hardly slept the night before, feeling unsettled to be in the flat without Tilly, who sent a message to say that she was going to work from home at her parents' place in Wiltshire for a couple of weeks. All Anna wanted to do now was to lose herself in emails and any client dramas that would have inevitably occurred during her absence.

"I'll just be in reception, okay, Anna?" said Chrissy. "Anything at all, I really mean it."

Returning back to her now cold coffee, Chrissy was just about to open a magazine when the front door opened.

"All right, Chrissy," said Martin Horne, adjusting his trousers.

"Martin … and Mandy," said Chrissy, her face dropping. "What a nice surprise."

"We were just passing and thought we'd pop in for a little

update on how the campaign's shaping up for Thermidor International. You know I like to keep my London PR firm at close proximity, so as to speak the same language, like."

"Yes, Martin, very wise," said Chrissy. "I'll just see who's available to give you an update."

Excusing herself, Chrissy walked over to Anna's desk and was about to say that Martin Horne really knew how to choose his timing, when she realised he was standing right behind her.

"Anna, how do you do it?" said Martin.

"Martin? What do you mean?" said Anna.

"Keep the weight off? How do you do it?"

"Martin, how about a coffee?" said Chrissy, cutting in to the rescue.

"I wouldn't say no, would you, Mandy?"

"A tea please, no milk or sugar," she said.

"And a plate of those biscuits," said Martin. "You know, the chocolate ones you usually bring out for meetings?"

"I'll see if I can find some," said Chrissy, wishing he would leave.

"Lovely," said Martin, rubbing his hands together. "Norma's still got me on a tight leash, insists I eat granola and prunes for breakfast, to keep me regular like."

Everyone looked at Mandy and wondered why she was having an affair with such a creature. It was as if Martin had forgotten she was standing right next to him,

"Well, I think Norma's quite right," said Mandy. "Since I've incorporated prunes into my diet, my Ronan can't believe how regular I am."

"Ronan?" asked Anna.

"My fiancé."

"Congratulations," said Anna, as Kate and Chrissy both nodded in agreement.

"And when's the special day?" said Kate, cringing then to have even asked such a question.

"Oh, I don't know if we'll marry. We'll be engaged seven years in November. No, I can't see Ronan at the altar – he really isn't my type," said Mandy, fluttering her eyelashes in Martin's direction and letting out a little squeak of a laugh.

"I want to talk merchandise about this Thermidor campaign," he said.

"Go on," said Kate.

"I was on the golf course the other day and an idea struck me like a bolt of lightning."

"Which is?" asked Anna.

"A crustacean golf bag!"

"A what?" said Anna and Kate in unison.

"A red golf bag, shaped like a lobster and with a big Thermidor International logo up the side."

"I thought we were focusing on the Hottest Chef Competition, with Rocco as the judge?" said Anna.

"I think Martin means in addition to the competition?" said Chrissy.

"Exactly," he said. "And on the subject of food, have you ever tried a Seafood Doggy?"

"Sorry, seafood whatie?" said Kate.

"A Seafood Doggy. It brings the flavours from the sea and land together in one bun!"

"Sounds rather, well, rather ..." Kate was lost for words.

"Flavoursome – isn't that right, Kate?" and Anna smiled properly, feeling relief to be distracted by such random client conversations.

"Well, we must get on," said Martin.

"We spotted a lovely Italian at the top of the street," said Mandy. "We'll pop in there, won't we, Martin? An early lunch – we might even sit by the window and people-watch."

"We like that, don't we?" said Martin, gazing at Mandy, and as they left the office everyone scratched their heads.

"I thought seafood was supposed to be good for the brain," said Kate, quite baffled.

At that moment, Gilda opened the door of her office and let out a yelp of delight when she spied Anna.

"Darling Anna, you're back!" She gave her a hug before standing back to create professional distance again. "I appreciate what a time you've had, what with your father's hideous accident and that love rat."

"Thanks, Gilda,' said Anna, "but I'm absolutely fine."

"Well, my darling, we all know what FINE stands for, don't we?"

"What does fine stand for?" asked Kate.

"Don't you worry about it," said Chrissy, admiring Kate's innocence.

Guiding Anna into her office, Gilda pulled out a bottle of Bollinger from the fridge.

"Now, my darling, this may not feel like the time for champagne – however, I beg to differ. I want to help you and I think I've got the perfect recipe to mend your broken heart."

Popping the cork, which fired into the ceiling and catapulted onto the desk, Gilda charged two large goblets.

"Gilda, it's only midday. I really just need to get settled back into things," said Anna.

"Exactly. Now, let's talk Paris, and before you say anything, I've found you the sweetest pied-à-terre, I promise you will love it. Right in the seventh arrondissement, the twinkling lights of la tour Eiffel in sight, the fresh markets of rue Cler around the corner, Les Invalides just a breath away."

Anna could see Gilda was on a roll and, sitting down, she took a sip of champagne and remembered being told by a special friend of her parents, 'If you are going to be unhappy, be unhappy in Paris'. It made sense. Being surrounded by buildings of such dramatic beauty and in a city filled with such grace and passion could only make unhappiness easier to bear.

"Napoléon, darling, his coffin is there. Sorry, of course we don't want to discuss death, sorry, darling, with your poor father's close call," said Gilda, clearing her throat, "but take it from me the seventh arrondissement is stately, sophisticated and a perfect place for Winterbottom PR to seduce." She raised her glass to Anna. "Do I have our new Parisian PR director before me?"

With a deep breath, shoulders back and a big stretch, Anna stood up with her glass.

"*Santé et merci, madame, j'accepte,*" said Anna, mustering a smile.

Chapter 34

All aspects of George and Sofia's publicity were brilliantly choreographed by Victoria, from interviews and photo shoots to gallery openings and fundraisers. There was to be no mention of families, save for the happy coincidence of Sofia's Scottish ancestry through her mother. Victoria insisted that Sofia field the vast majority of the questions, with George taking on the role of the quiet but supportive fiancé. They were to present a united front and when George had to pose next to Sofia, he gave a serious, dark look that was fortunately interpreted as being smoldering and sexy by the press. However, the moment the media circus was out of sight, Sofia turned right, George turned left, and that was how they made it work. Hotel, car, event, hotel and then split. The press was in its element. George may have been silent but the paparazzi loved this new access to him. What's more, the traditionally shod bachelor was now more like an Italian catwalk model. George Wyndham looked hot and the cameras loved him. Within weeks Victoria was swamped with offers for George to feature in cover shoots, along with a string of enticing modelling contracts.

At Rousey, the celebrated photographer Diane Twigg was commissioned by Victoria to shoot photographs of the happy couple to post on Sofia's new website, *sofiatamper.com*.

However, things did not get off to quite as easy a start as Diane was used to.

"I'm afraid Miss Tamper is indisposed," said Royston, carrying a silver tray with a tub of frozen yogurt.

"What do you mean she's indisposed?" said Diane, sharply. "I've just flown in from Chicago and Victoria assured me that Miss Tamper would be camera-ready by twelve noon."

"I think you'll find it is now past twelve, madam."

"Exactly, and so she is late," she said, puffing up the back of her silver bob, and itching to get settled behind the lens.

"Madam, I will enquire as to whether Miss Tamper's manicure can be rescheduled. Follow me to the bedroom wing, please."

"Do you carry that frozen yogurt around with you all the time?" she asked.

"Miss Tamper likes a spoonful or two around this time."

"Well, why didn't I think of that?" said Diane, who was trying to find patience so that she could do her job and then get the hell out.

Walking along a corridor lined with dark-panelled windows and doors, Royston transferred Diane into Lindsay's charge. Lindsay was less than happy to be interrupted while texting her boyfriend in LA. He wanted to book tickets to the Super Bowl final, but what she had in mind was for them to spend a week in Laguna Beach, sprinkling their days with hours of sunshine, long dinners and plenty of indulgent, luxurious sex. After three weeks in Scotland, she'd had it with celibacy.

"Sorry, Diane, I'm afraid Sofia is indisposed," said Lindsay, twiddling a glittery nail file between her fingers.

"Ah, that word again. What is it with you people? Now let me get this straight. I am going to order my assistant to set up my equipment in the kitchen, okay? And in the meantime, you can tell Miss Tamper that she will damn well have to be *dis*posed."

Lindsay stood to attention and knew better than to mess with this lady. Once Diane was out of sight Lindsay scuttled downstairs to the library to find George sitting alone, with a large and very old-looking photograph album on his lap.

"Any chance I can ask for your help, please, George? I'm wary of disturbing Sofia but I've got a very serious photographer lady downstairs who has an appointment with her and she ain't happy."

George was only too happy to deliver the news to Sofia that for once she would have to dance to someone else's tune. Striding along the corridor, he knocked on her bedroom door.

"Yes," said Sofia, who wasn't having a manicure at all. "Who is it?"

"There's a photographer downstairs for you," said George, from the other side of the door.

"Come in, won't you?" said Sofia, mischief playing in her voice, and as George pushed open the door he found her sitting in front of her dressing table in a black panelled cashmere corset and red lace panties, her breasts rising above a slender ribcage and flat tummy. Looking at her reflection Sofia knew that she could click her fingers and any man, and quite a lot of women, would come running.

"Good God," said George, instantly turning around.

"Do you like my lingerie? I had it flown in from Milan, paid for by our father of course. Mom tells me he's engrossed in his new Swiss lifestyle, but I guess you haven't been in contact with him since we met with the lawyers."

"Get dressed, Sofia," said George, gripping the door handle.

"Won't you even look at me, George? Come on, you can't tell me you don't find me attractive?"

"If you want to know the truth," he said slowly, "you disgust me, Sofia, on just about every level."

As he pulled the door shut, Sofia threw a bottle of Dior Poison against the mirror but to her disappointment it just bounced back.

"Shit!" she screamed. "*I can't even smash a goddamn mirror!*"

Diane stood by the Aga, trying to visualise Sofia in domestic mode. Holding a pair of yellow Marigold rubber gloves as a possible prop, her assistant searched through cupboards looking for gadgets that could create a background to show Sofia as the 'perfect housewife', supporting the new blog Victoria had created on *sofiatamper.com*: *From Hollywood to Houseproud*.

Sofia arrived into the kitchen, followed closely by Lindsay, who waved a blusher brush at her and managed to sweep on a fresh glide of lip plump.

Sofia was wearing one of Robert's old dressing gowns.

"Oh, have I missed something?" she asked, looking around for lighting assistants and crew. "It doesn't look like you're ready?"

Stretching out her hand, Diane handed Sofia an oven glove.

"You're late, Sofia, and take off that dressing gown."

"Victoria? Where the hell is she?" asked Sofia, feeling the strict vibes emanating from Diane.

"Look here, lady, I don't tolerate divas. I've banned your staff from in here. Victoria didn't like it, but she knows I'm the best photographer there is – so you play it my way or I'm gone."

Lindsay backed out of the room and Sofia didn't say a single word.

"Geoff here is handling lighting, and you, young lady, are going to do what you are told."

Taking off the dressing gown, Sofia felt unusually shy in the corset.

"Okay," said Diane, "now put on this apron. It's Anthropology, one of my favourite kitchen brands."

Geoff, multitasking between lighting and styling, tied the apron ties twice around Sofia's waist. As the frills frisked across her bosom and just above her knees, she looked delectable. Over the next twenty minutes, Sofia whisked an old-fashioned bowl filled with egg whites, held a wooden spoon over one eye, like a patch, and lay across the kitchen table, pouting for the camera with her legs crossed.

"Nice work, Sofia," said Diane. "And remember, if your new acting career doesn't work out, there's always plenty of catalogue work. The camera quite likes you."

"*Quite?*" said Sofia.

Storming out of the kitchen, she pulled the dressing gown back on. "The nerve of the woman!" And to add chili pepper to her fury, she found Blaire pacing outside in the hall.

"There you are, Sofia. What is that vile gown you're wearing? It's so archaic. And where is that man Royston?"

"Mother, I am not the butler's keeper," snapped Sofia. "And, for your information, I have been posing with goddamn kitchen equipment."

"Not in that, I hope? Ah, for your social media campaign. Good to hear. Now, Sofia, I want to run through plans for the interiors."

"Ruby's in the library, I think, so we can speak there."

"Must she be present?"

"Mom, it's her job."

"Go upstairs and change, Sofia, I can't look at you in that tatty dressing gown."

Dressed in long white trousers and a fitted pink linen blazer, Sofia found her mother sitting in the drawing room as Ruby stared out the bay window.

"What's this? Have you both taken a vow of silence?"

"If Ruby chooses to sulk, that's her own choice," said Blaire.

"Sulk about what?" said Sofia, walking towards the window.

"No, Sofia, come and sit here," said Blaire, patting one side of the sofa. "As I have just explained to Ruby, there has been a change of plan."

"Go on," said Sofia, pulling a cushion onto her lap as she sat down.

"I've heard through the grapevine that a rather vulgar and retired Scottish player from the area, who made his fortune playing in England, is looking for an estate just like Rousey," said Blaire.

"And?" said Sofia.

"I made contact with his property agent, and as it turns out he wants to buy the whole place, the land, the cottages, the works."

"And we aren't allowed to know who it is," hissed Ruby.

"It's one of the provisos," said Blaire. "The buyer's name won't be revealed until the deal is signed and sealed."

"And since when have you ever stuck to a deal, mother? Come on, tell us."

"In fact, I'm meant to refer to him as Mr X," said Blaire.

"Mr X?" said Ruby.

"Ruby, what are you, some kind of parrot? If you'd like to join the conversation I suggest you sit with us, rather than steaming up the glass over there."

"All right then," said Ruby, sitting on a wing chair by the fireplace. "What I'd like to know is how you found this so-called *Mr X*?"

"Like I said, Ruby, the grapevine," said Blaire curtly.

"So we're not turning this place into a hotel any more?" said Sofia.

"Nope," said Blaire airily. "Mr X has confirmed that he will to pay top dollar – money is no object with him – he's planning to spend an absolute fortune on renovation to meet his wife's taste. Naturally work will only begin once Mr X signs the contract to buy Rousey."

"And what about the twelve-month thing with George?" said Ruby.

"Oh, come on, Ruby, don't be so naïve," said Blaire. "That offer was never real."

"Then why did he agree to the media stunt?"

Blaire was becoming impatient. "George is like a rabbit in headlights," she said, "and once he realised Sofia's claim was the real deal, he had little option but to take a punt."

"So it's all complete horseshit, the deal?" said Ruby.

"If you wish to describe it in such a delicate way, then, yes, Ruby, it is," said Blaire, "and now that we've all stated the obvious, shall we continue?"

"Go on, Mom – and Ruby, take a chill, okay?"

"Doesn't Robert feel even a shred of guilt about giving up his ancestral home?" said Ruby, watching Sofia to see if she would kick up at all about her mother's change of plan.

"Robert doesn't give a monkey's about this place," said Sofia, "and just as soon as I get title to Rousey, the sale can go through, and we can get back to LA."

"Sofia, must you be so disparaging about your father? I would suggest that you don't bite the hand that feeds you."

"Mom, what are you talking about? I've only met the man a couple of times."

"He's your father!"

Sofia shrugged. "So, has David Collins confirmed yet that the deeds have gone through?"

"Not yet, but we should be clear in about four weeks."

"Four weeks!"

"Now, girls, enough questions, let me show you the plans," said Blaire, opening her iPad. "Mr X has an interior consultant who sent over the new plans last night. It's one of the stipulations in Mr X's contract – as soon as we get through the legal mumbo jumbo his team will move in here like a swarm of locusts."

"And Mr X is totally in?" said Sofia, ignoring Ruby's look of disdain.

"Totally," said Blaire. "Now, ladies, are you ready for the show?"

"Ready," said Sofia, excited at the prospect of offloading Rousey in exchange for millions.

"A drone flew around the house last week, all so clever, and took images of every single room," said Blaire. "So, we take an existing image – let's start with the hall, drab and wooden as it currently is but ..." Blaire swiped onto a new image, "the computer program overrides the image with the new design – some metallic tiles, a purple deep-pile carpet and fun patterns along the walls. This is the style Mr X and his wife are going for."

"Wow!" said Sofia, oblivious to Ruby who was fuming. "That's a transformation for sure. Go to the library next."

"Sofia?" said Ruby. "Aren't you even going to –"

"Later, Ruby, I want to run through the plans first with Mom."

"So, out with the ancestors, pull out the fireplace, and voilà," said Blaire as she swiped almost violently onto an image of a room with bright orange furniture and a large sculpture of a pink swan. "This bird will centre the room and energise it. And we'll have a pewter bar over there, plus a slushy machine."

"A slushy machine? Are you serious, what age is this guy?" said Ruby.

"Oh, and over there, hold on," and Blaire, dragging a gigantic plasma television over the fireplace. "I've really got the hang of this program, don't you think? Here will be premier league football from all over the world, playing 24/7 on the screen."

"What's that?" asked Sofia, noticing an electric-blue room just behind the library.

"It's the entrance to the new spa," said Blaire, utterly engrossed. "It's so over the top, isn't it? So, it's currently the billiards room – they'll rip out the dado rails, and cover the walls in purple marble."

"Rip it out?" shrieked Ruby. "You are joking, Blaire!"

"Do I look like I'm joking?"

"But, Blaire, that's a seventeenth-century architrave. The detailing is exceedingly rare."

"Don't 'exceedingly rare' me, Ruby. I am beyond caring about such things. Now on to the ballroom."

Ruby could not believe such bad taste was possible and put her head in her hands. "Blaire," she said, "I've researched the history of this marble. It was imported from Italy, transported by ship from Carrera over two hundred years ago. You can't let them just rip it out."

Taking a large, deep breath, Blaire shook out her hair and pouted in Sofia's direction.

"How long must I put up with this, darling?"

Sofia placed her hands around her ever-decreasing waistline. "Mother, we did commission Ruby to handle the renovation – we should listen to her ideas on the project."

"Correction, Sofia. *You* employed Ruby and I gave her a chance to prove herself but all she's given us are ideas for fabric with butterflies and ivory doorknobs. In any case, her ideas are irrelevant! Don't you get it? We sell the house and it's out of our hands!"

Ruby glared at Sofia, outraged that she wasn't standing up to her mother. "Sofia, you can't let this happen to the house!"

"Mom, look, this house is in my name, right? Or at least it will be?"

"My dear Sofia, still so much to learn. You need to understand a few, appropriately named, home truths. Number one, you owe me for everything you've got. I've spent a fortune of time and money on you and your frivolous lifestyle and now, put simply, it's payback time. This place is going to be sold to my client, and that's that." Then turning to Ruby, she said, "And if you so much as utter another damned objection in my direction you will be out of here so fast your ass won't feel your legs moving."

"You'll never do it, Blaire," Ruby persisted. "The planners will be on your back."

"*Forget the planners. I won't be meeting with the planners!*" shouted Blaire, losing her cool. "Like I have said, Mr X wants to buy Rousey and by the time he does he will have his design layout complete. Planning permission, listed buildings – that is all for his architect to worry about. We will not be doing any work on the house. It is not my problem or Sofia's. No one needs to know that

Sofia once owned this pile. Publically, Sofia will have had a short engagement to an eligible bachelor and, due to work commitments and personal reasons, they chose to part."

Blaire continued with her slide show.

"But Ruby, you'll be pleased to know that the plan to install the cinema in the basement still holds – except the walls will be purple, I'm told, with diamond shapes pushed into wooden walls. Oh, and in the spa, Mr X has requested more marble than an Italian cathedral. Such an extravagant character."

"Are those Perspex toilet bowls?" gasped Ruby, quite revolted as she looked at more images of the proposed fittings and furniture in the side bar of the screen.

"They are," said Blaire, swiping onwards until another sample bedroom tipped Ruby over the edge.

"An Oval Office themed bedroom," said Blaire, "and the en suite will be entirely made of the mauve marble I mentioned before."

Sofia turned to look at Ruby, but her lover had left the room. As she stood up to go after her, Blaire grabbed her wrist.

"Careful, darling. We don't want a single scrap of sentimentality left here. And that includes having to look at any shabby bits of carpet or battered old chairs that were once owned by George's great-grandmother, or his great-aunt's clock ticking on the mantelpiece. I want it all gone. Family photographs, crockery, those tartan carpets, the whole lot. I simply cannot bear it."

"Mom, this is kind of over the top. How on earth will we do it with George in the mix?"

"As soon as the deeds go through to your name, Sofia, we'll just tell him what's happening."

"He'll spill to the press," said Sofia.

"I don't think so – he'd ruin his own reputation by exposing the media scam," said Blaire, noticing a chip in the nail varnish on her ring finger. "No, George will retreat to his London town house and lick his poor little rich boy wounds there."

"And Robert?" said Ruby.

"Robert is blissfully happy living the life in Geneva. He has no intention of ever coming back here and frankly I don't think he'd give a fiddler's if this place were razed to the ground. Did I tell you that in Geneva he has an ex-pat next-door neighbour from Herefordshire, who is an avid wine buff and loves to play backgammon? How perfect is that?"

Sofia watched her mother's eyes light up as the prospect of this new life she had sought to create was coming to fruition. It was almost as if Max Tamper had never existed and yet, as they spoke, he was sitting in prison awaiting trial for stealing money so that he could feed his family's greedy and extravagant lifestyle.

"What happens when Dad, well, you know, Max, comes out of prison?"

"I was wondering when you might ask that," said Blaire.

"And?"

"He'll have a tidy nest-egg waiting for him in a Swiss bank account. He may have been a risk-taker, but he wasn't stupid. In fact, his ability to save money is really rather impressive."

"Is it a joint account?"

"No, it's not," said Blaire, tersely. "Why else do you think we're here?"

"Because Robert is my real father?" said Sofia.

"No, Sofia, more than that. I came back to this place to fight our corner, yours and mine. The Wyndhams owe us and we are getting what is rightfully ours." Blaire took Sofia's hand. "It's all for you, darling. I want you to have every possible luxury in life – as my daughter, it's no more that you deserve."

Blaire and Ruby sat on Sofia's shoulders like the devil and an angel, and she had to juggle her desires and choices between the two, but it was becoming clear that her Ruby angel, usually so pliant and forgiving, was teetering on the brink.

Chapter 35

Anna had the softest possible landing in Paris. The apartment, aka Parisian Headquarters for Winterbottom PR, on rue St. Dominique, was as chic as she could have imagined, with high ceilings, wooden floors and oodles of light. Leaning against the copper sink in the kitchen, with white tongue-and-groove cupboards and warm grey walls, Anna was looking out over the building's courtyard.

"*Bonjour*, darling," said Gilda, sweeping around the door in an embroidered leopard-print coat. She deposited two large patterned paper bags on the table. "I've brought you delectable things from the smartest food hall in Paris, La Grande Épicerie at le Bon Marché!"

She spun around, taking in the flat.

"Yes, relaxed Parisian glamour is what the agent promised me. Don't you just love the French, darling? They know interiors. It's so instinctive for them."

"Gilda, it's wonderful. Thank you so much," said Anna, reaching for the kettle and filling it up with tap water.

"Oh no, darling, I'm not sure about the mains. Do you think you should really be drinking the water?"

"Well, surely if it's boiled?" said Anna, but Gilda turned her back and tore open the side of one of the extravagantly patterned paper bags she had brought.

"Darling, we need to use up the Seville oranges before they go overripe," said Gilda, pushing the cheese and paté to one side. "Get out the Stolichnaya, from the polka-dot bag over there, will you, sweetie?"

Anna sliced an orange in half and squeezed the juice into pair of tumblers before Gilda added a double measure of vodka, and swirled the liquids together. Then she held out a tumbler to Anna in matronly fashion, it was as if it were a spoonful of cod-liver oil. "Now drink this, sweetie, known in the seventies as a Screwdriver. And I have a little welcome-to-Paris present for you, which might be handy for a launch party or maybe even a date, imagine that? Because, my darling, you are sure to come across Mr Right in this city, you can mark my words."

Gilda went and unhooked a dress cover from the front-door latch, then returned to the kitchen and unzipped a soft grey felt cover, with an ankle-length satin red-and-cream Monique Lhullier gown beneath.

"Gilda," whispered Anna, her eyes filling with tears, so moved by Gilda's kindness. "It's beautiful."

Sniffing and propping up her mascara-constructed eyelashes, Gilda nodded her head, trying not to cry. "Oh darling, don't start, or you'll make me blub too. I've been around the block a few times, you know. I think you simply have to take a long view. One has to kiss a lot of frogs before the prince can be found and you can't take a step in this city without being surrounded by its romantic beauty. You will meet someone." Even though Gilda had no idea about Anna's miscarriage, she knew she was grieving for losing what might have been with George. "Now tell me, when is Tilly coming to stay? I thought she'd had helped you with the move? Most likely busy romancing that dishy lawyer fellow, is she?"

"Actually, I'm not sure," said Anna. "I haven't seen her since she was so amazingly supportive, and not just to me, but to Mum too, in fact the whole house. She is working from her parents' home at the moment and I figure she must be playing catch-up with her boss, having missed at least a fortnight when she was in Ireland."

"Yes, well, work does have a habit of getting in the way, doesn't it, darling," said Gilda, topping up her glass, "and on that subject it looks like Martin Horne is about to get a promotion, or so the rumour-mill tells me."

"Which means?"

"More lolly for us, darling."

"So we can continue with the Hottest Chef Campaign?"

"Oh, I think so, and I've got my mind veering towards hiring a massive yacht and sending two celebrities out to sea, and all they will be allowed to eat will be lobster."

"The challenge being?"

"How many ways can a lobster be cooked? I'm thinking of a campaign title somewhere along the lines of *Lobsterlicious* – that's what we can call the boat. Along with branding for Thermidor Interational of course – and we can paint the boat bright red."

"Well, as long as Martin doesn't arrive to the launch of the boat in his tight swimming togs, hoping for a dip in the Med."

"Exactly, darling, exactly," said Gilda, as the handle of the front door wiggled up and down. "Are we expecting someone, darling?"

Anna fortified herself with another sip of Gilda's proclaimed Screwdriver, before opening the door to find her mother, rosy-cheeked, with a yoga mat beneath one arm and a baguette under the other.

"Sorry, Anna, I lost my set of keys."

"Don't worry, Mum, and I have a surprise for you actually."

"You do?" Freddie stepped inside.

"Yes, Freddie Rose, meet Gilda Winterbottom," said Anna, feeling half exhilarated and half nervous to introduce the two strong women in her life.

"Darling, such a pleasure," said Gilda.

"Likewise," said Freddie, standing in flip-flops and stripy leggings.

"Aren't you just gorgeous," said Gilda. "What's your secret?"

"No secrets, I'm afraid," said Freddie.

"I know what you mean," said Gilda, mixing a Screwdriver for Freddie. "That's exactly what my husband said to me before we married, and little did I know he'd have a secret of his own when I was served the divorce papers."

"I'm so sorry," said Freddie, pulling out a chair. "So unpredictable, aren't they?"

"Men? You bet they are," said Gilda. "The divorce request I had expected, as I knew that woman was longing to snare Adrian, so as to secure that pert behind of hers and make sure she could swing those scrawny ankles of hers onto comfortable footstools in her dotage and tuck into beetroot crisps."

"Gilda, that's a bit strong?" said Anna.

"Not a bit, she's like that Tamper girl, eyes focused purely on the prize."

Anna's face first became flushed, then her eyes filled with tears and, battling against them, she then turned to thunder.

"No, Gilda, she is *not* like Sofia! Sofia is in a league of her own."

"Anna, darling," said Freddie, "I'm sure Gilda didn't mean it like that."

"No, Mum, I'm fine, really. Look, I'm going to leave you to it and go to bed. Gilda, I'm sure you can find a cab outside – and, Mum, try not to snore when you slide in beside me – and well done, Gilda, for arranging such a massive double bed for the apartment."

As Anna left the room, Gilda passed another Screwdriver to Freddie. "Vitamin C, darling, never mind the vodka. Now, tell me how you are after the hellish time you've had. So much to deal with, on top of worrying about that little lady of yours in there."

Freddie twisted the cluster of diamonds on her ring finger. "Anna perhaps lacks confidence at times, but like her father she can rise to a challenge."

"And your husband, is he making a good recovery?"

"Yes, thank you, he really is. In fact, he went to his studio the day before I came over here and it looks like he might be starting a new painting."

"Well, that's fabulous news, isn't it?"

Freddie thought back to when she and Harry had been so intoxicated by each other. "It's strange, but honestly? I find that I am caught between resenting him for when he was obsessed with painting, and now, for not even approaching a canvas. And this was before his heart attack. He lost interest in his work months ago."

"Men can be tricky, can't they," said Gilda.

"I used to refer to art as his mistress, but during the past year she seems to have been given the sack."

"Well, now, if that isn't a quote for a Sunday supplement

heading I don't know what is," and catching sight of Freddie's expression, Gilda quickly redeemed herself. "Naturally I wouldn't even think of the press catching wind of this story, Freddie sweetie, Mummy of darling Anna. I do apologise."

"No, it's fine," said Freddie, taking a large sip from the Screwdriver.

"But tell me, darling," said Gilda, "how is the sex?"

"Well," said Freddie, slightly taken aback by Gilda's frankness but not minding at all, "we still have the physical attraction, though Harry tends to be the one who instigates. It's just, somehow, I feel Harry understands me less, and I him."

"Couples do grow apart," said Gilda. "Hans left me a couple of months ago, and I was floored momentarily, but I knew he wasn't going to be the man I'd hang up my slippers with."

"Gilda, I can't imagine you in slippers, let alone hanging them up."

"Well, it's not all sparkles I can tell you."

"If there is one thing I've learned from my yoga practice, it is that people need to be given freedom and I greatly hope that if I leave Harry to it, he'll find the answer himself – you know, the key to his life."

"It's funny how near-death experiences make one nostalgic," said Gilda.

"Well, the last time we had to deal with anything like that was when Harry's mother died. We left Mrs Rose's ashes in a plastic tub on the kitchen table, and then Bernard, our gardener, found them and thought it was fertiliser for the tomato plants."

"He didn't?"

"He did," Freddie giggled. "Tipped the whole lot into the watering can, filled it up with water and watered the greenhouse. Oh, it's dreadful, but Harry assured me that she would have found it terribly funny."

"Naughty boy."

"Oh, he was naughty all right," said Freddie, feeling like a weight was being taken from her shoulders, talking this through with Gilda.

Opening her cigarette case, Gilda got up to open the window.

"No, Gilda, you can't possibly smoke in here," said Freddie, feeling increasingly free and easy. "Why don't we walk to the Champ de Mars? It's only nine thirty. And then we can have supper on our way home. There are some sweet places around here. Oh, come on, Gilda – I feel like letting loose."

Gilda and Freddie read the frayed menu posted in the window of the classic-looking French bistro and, peering around the door, pale yellow walls and white tablecloths were enough to seduce them inside.

"And aren't waiters beautifully dressed?" said Freddie, as a handsome waiter arrived to their table with a basket of bread and carafes of water to assuage their immediate needs.

"*Et vin, si'l vous plaît,*" said Gilda, as if she was taking part in a game of Charades, pulling a cork from an imaginary bottle. "Very dishy indeed," she added when he left, "and I'm not just talking about the menu."

Two bottles of Bordeaux were accompanied by duck confit and thinly sliced potatoes, and by the time the crème brûlée arrived, along with the bill, Gilda and Freddie were in flying form.

"Look, they've even given us complimentary sweets with the bill – do they think we're children?" cackled Gilda, thinking it was all so hilarious.

"Sugar-coated citrus candies? They may be useful in case we are breathalysed on our way home," said Freddie, whose ribs were aching having laughed so much during dinner.

"Look, the night is young. How about viewing the sparkling lights of *la tour Eiffel* up close?"

"But it's one thirty in the morning!"

"All the better," said Gilda.

Buying a bottle of champagne while settling the bill and sweet-talking a couple of paper cups from the waiter, Gilda led Freddie out on to the street.

Off they went in the direction of Champs de Mars.

Arriving at the grassy lawns and seeing the twinkling lights of the Eiffel Tower ahead of them, Freddie paused and sat on the grass. Gilda joined her.

Freddie stretched out her hands until she reached her feet, holding her legs dead straight.

"I do want to get my marriage back on track, Gilda, truly I do. Do you think it's possible?"

Gilda popped open the bubbly and filled the two cups. Then, lighting a cigarette, she lay back on the grass.

"You have loved and you haven't lost, Freddie. It's not everyone who can say that."

"And what about Adrian?"

"I'm afraid I lost my husband out of choice," said Gilda, "and it seems to be one of the worst decisions I've ever made."

Freddie, now very drunk, tried to focus on Harry's digital watch, which she had been wearing since the hospital.

"Well, that's certainly very sad," she slurred, and together they lay beneath the Eiffel Tower, in silence, thinking of the men they truly loved.

Anna woke up that morning to find an almost illegible scrawl on a piece of paper from Gilda and Freddie, saying something about them going to do morning sun salutations in the Tuileries garden.

Mum and Gilda, doing an all-nighter, said Anna to herself. That's one I would never have predicted. And, smiling, she opened the window in the kitchen and let in the morning Parisian air.

Chapter 36

In the bathroom mirror, Anna's large eyes stared back at her as she noticed new lines on her forehead and a glimpse of how she would look in old age. She could recognise parts of her father in her face – maybe she had his forehead and the shape of his eyes, and then her mother's small nose, and jawline. Anna had felt really sad saying goodbye to her mother, who had left Paris earlier that morning, still suffering from her wild night out with Gilda, even though it was two days later. Anna was now faced with a new client list to draw up for Gilda, who had given her a few days' breathing space, but now full throttle PR mode was expected to kick in and fast.

Before facing a string of emails from Winterbottom HQ, along with various demands from Martin Horne, Desmond Spicer and the new Bloc-It-Bling client, Anna decided to take a short walk to Hôtel des Invalides, built by King Louis XIV, whose giant sculpture adorned the entrance, as a hospital and home for old and sick soldiers. In the courtyard, Anna stood over a sundial facing the church with its beautiful golden dome, trying to remember what her father had taught her about Roman numerals and their significance. He might have made it up; it was one of those childhood memories that seemed so recent but now, trying to work out what her father had meant, it seemed to make little sense. Crossing the cobbled square, Anna passed a man dressed in a black collarless jacket, which reached halfway down his short legs. He rubbed his tightly clipped beard and Anna overheard him asking a ticket collector if he could recommend a romantic spot along the Seine. The man's slim girlfriend looked on as he conversed, her expression horrified, and must have been panicking that he might want to pop the question.

By the archway leading towards Napoleon's tomb, Anna came to a wide staircase and wondered if it was out of bounds until a man rushed past her and ran up the stairs three steps at a time. Following his lead, Anna climbed the stairs to find a balcony stretching around the entire circumference of the building. A single bell rang out in the courtyard, following by a celebration of ringing. Leaning over the edge of the balcony, Anna looked down on a sea of colourful hats, top hats, tails and buttonholes filled with red roses, catching sight of the bride and groom, so perfect they could have modelled as statuettes on a wedding cake. Checking emails on her phone, Anna found a stroppy message from Desmond Spicer, seeking details on the proposal to have a launch party at the Ritz. At least she had booked the ballroom, but she needed to hightail it back to the apartment to keep things smooth. Looking down at her scruffy runners, Anna realised she'd have to walk through the wedding party in order to take the exit closest to her apartment. Pulling the rim of her white trilby as far down as she could manage while still being able to see where she was going, she went back down the stairs and navigated her way through scores of guests who were waiting to cheer the newlyweds outside the church.

Dodging smart shoes, as guests spilled into each other's arms with aristocratic French kisses, Anna spied a white convertible Smart car awaiting the bride and groom in the courtyard, making the scene look like a rather smart ad for the car. The bride, pushing the pleats of her white silk dress into the passenger seat, watched as her husband lifted his top hat, saluting their guests, and the men followed suit raising their hats to salute him. It was French tradition at its best.

"*Excusez-moi, madame*," said Anna, stumbling into a lady wearing an oversized lime-green hat with an orange bow tilting over its rim, next to a group of beautiful girls posing for a photographer.

And there he was.

George.

Looking straight at her.

Panicking, Anna looked left and right, pulling her hat further over her eyes but she knew there was no escape. Damn it to hell, she thought. She wanted to scream but she was in too much shock and unprepared to challenge him.

George felt complete shock to see her and hardly knew where to look. Anna looked so small amongst the crowd of guests, and so beautiful. He wanted to reach out to her, to fall on his knees, to apologise and beg for her forgiveness. But he had to remember the long game.

"Anna, what are you doing here?"

"I was visiting Napoleon's tomb," she said, barely making eye contact with him.

"It's so good to see you," he said.

"George, I've got to go," she said strongly. "I've got to call a client urgently."

"You're working here?"

"It's a job for Gilda, maybe only temporary, I don't know."

George couldn't let the opportunity go. He had to do something. He looked around – there was no sign of Sofia.

"Anna, I know, after everything, that you can't possibly want to listen to what I have to say, but I'm asking you – please – can I take you to lunch tomorrow?"

"George, don't. Please don't," she said, squeezing her eyes together.

Taking out a silver pen, he wrote *Bistro le Chat, 1 pm* on his business card and gave it to her.

"Please, Anna, I know it sounds fatuous to invite you to lunch, after everything that's happened, but I need a chance to explain."

Feeling a tug on his sleeve, George turned to find Sofia glaring at him, peacock feathers trembling from her hat, in a teal knee-length dress.

"George, the photographer is ready, and the magazine editor wants us to meet the bride and groom," and then, scowling, she tilted her head and looked at Anna. "Oh, hello. It's Hannah, isn't it?"

"Her name is Anna," said George.

Exerting ownership, Sofia linked her left hand through George's arm to show off her engagement ring. "Oh dear, rather underdressed, aren't we? Hard to get it right, isn't it?"

Desperately wanting to take Anna's hand, George knew the only way to break free from this mess was to hold steady, which meant standing by Sofia's side as Anna walked away.

Anna held in her pain until she made it back to her apartment, but the moment she turned the key and closed the door behind her she fell to her knees, howling in despair, confusion and utter heartache. She had never been so publicly rejected. She felt like a worthless ornament thrown into a jumble sale. She just knew George had watched her as she left Les Invalides and that he must have felt such pity for her. Anna felt desperately lonely, her thoughts sweeping around each other, sinking deeper and deeper into a mass of negativity. She couldn't face having to deal with Desmond, so instead she emailed Kate in London, asking if she could soothe his demands at least until tomorrow.

After a long bath, Anna tried heating up ready-made dauphinoise potatoes but the edges had burned and so she decided to just turn off the oven and leave it there. Then deciding she was actually hungry, she opened the fridge to get some yogurt only to find that it had stopped working. It figured, she managed to laugh to herself, as she had never felt less cool. Or perhaps the fridge was trying to tell her something, like stop drinking so much white wine. Sitting on the parquet floor, her back against the fridge, Anna pulled George's card out of her back pocket. She thought about the dream she had been having for the past week, waking up in a sweat with a thumping heart. She had been in a giant birdcage with her father. Small enough to slip through the bars she had managed to escape, but her father, who tried to follow her, couldn't fit. Screaming and willing her father to fit through the bars, she saw his eyes fill with tears as he shrugged his shoulders in defeat. It was the third or fourth time she'd had this dream and each time there was just a small deviation. Sometimes Freddie joined them, trying to teach Harry yoga stretches to make him longer, thinner, more like play dough, so that he could squeeze through the bars. But no, so far, Harry was trapped in the cage. Anna remembered feeling that she could hardly bear her freedom. She wanted to return into the cage but, just as she was about to wake up, she couldn't fit back in the cage. Nothing fitted. And that was how she felt in real life. She felt lost, misplaced.

She recalled an article in *Tatler* about how to deal with a break-up – though she was dealing with loss on two different levels. Rule Number One acknowledged that getting drunk was a quick fix. But make it champagne, they warned – so much more stylish. So Anna dashed out of the apartment and bought two bottles of champagne, already chilled. *Tatler* also recommended listening to power ballads, so Anna downloaded a playlist of bands on her iPad from Aerosmith to Meatloaf and soon enough she was sitting on the parquet floor in the kitchen, drunk as a skunk and eating cold, half-burnt potato gratin from its tinfoil container, with a pot of Dijon mustard beside her.

bullshit

She knew it sounded crazy, but she felt almost afraid of looking like her father. She worried that if she looked or acted like him in any way, then she might suffer from a heart attack. When she visited the GP following the miscarriage, listening to her concerns, he asked the nurse to run an ECG on her heart to reassure her that she was healthy. And she was, perfectly healthy, but she was stressed. She could feel it. Her GP had even pointed out the way Anna sat: cross-legged, hands bound together, head tilting, eyes squinting. She was like one large knot – but how to release it, she asked herself. A bottle and a half of champagne all to herself didn't even scratch the surface of easing her tension. It was like nothing could get through. And Tilly, who hadn't returned Anna's call from five hours ago, seemed so distant, surely due to being madly in love with Jamie, which Anna felt really happy about – but, selfishly, she missed her best friend desperately.

"This is the lonely time that I've heard about, but never understood before now," she said, speaking out loud. "I'm even speaking to myself."

But then she found herself speaking to her father. She couldn't explain it even to herself, but sitting at the kitchen table she told her father about what had happened with George, that he had left her for Sofia, an American socialite.

"Always racy, those American women," she guessed her father would say.

And then, she told her father about the miscarriage.

"It was so early, Dad, I hardly had time to properly feel pregnant, but for those few weeks, when I truly thought I was going to have a baby, George's baby, I felt ..." she said, tears streaming down her face, head slumped into her elbow, "I really thought this was it, Dad." And wiping her eyes she looked up to the ceiling. "How did I get it so wrong?"

Despite the hangover the next morning, Anna felt better. Like some kind of release had taken place. She had been longing to howl over the miscarriage and perhaps like the writer's block that people talk about, she had experienced a temporary block of mourning. Maybe her body had been trying to give her some time to rebuild, before facing the grief of it all. But that morning, she knew if she was going to find closure, she needed to see George, just one more time.

Chapter 37

"Jamie, what are you doing here?"

"Well, as you seem to have vacated your flat in London and you haven't been returning my calls, I figured the only way to find you was to come here."

Standing at the front door of her parents' country house, Tilly called out for Smudge, their spaniel. As the dog scampered up beside her, Tilly strode out the door towards a long yew walk beyond the garden.

"Oh Tilly, won't you even walk next to me?"

"*I don't see why I should!*" she yelled back at him, which prompted him to run ahead of her and hold his hand out like a traffic policeman, bringing her to a halt.

"Hold up, please. Please. What have I done, Tilly? You have to tell me. I am not a mind-reader."

"No, but you're a bloody bastard for sleeping with her."

"What? Tilly, what are you talking about?"

Picking up a stick, she threw it with all her might into the woods and let out a huge scream. "*For God's sake, Jamie, I have the photo!* It is evidence as you might say in your precious bloody court. You're such a hypocrite, making all your clients swear to an oath when you are one big huge liar!"

"Stop it, Tilly. I'm telling you, I don't know what you are talking about."

"Okay, Jamie. You're a lawyer? Well, here are the facts."

"Fine."

"I received an email from Sofia, containing not a message, but a photo."

"Of?"

"*Of you in bed with Ruby!*"

"What?" Jamie's mind was racing, with flashbacks of walking up the stairs of the club in Soho with Ruby on one side and Sofia on the other. Walking into bedroom and lying onto a huge bed. He remembered the relief of lying down, but he was so drunk, that's about all he remembered. "It must have been some kind of set-up."

"No one forced you to get so twisted, Jamie. You did that all by yourself – well, apart from Anna. I'm actually still furious with her about that."

"You've got it all wrong."

"A classic denial."

"A genuine denial," said Jamie, gathering his plea. "I was off my head, that night."

"*I know!*" screamed Tilly. "You walked away, Jamie, in the club, like I was no-one."

"I had too much to drink. I knew it then and I know it now. And … before you turn away from me …"

"You were both naked in the photo, Jamie, and Ruby was grinning at the camera." Tilly crouched down to hug Smudge and as she patted his shoulder she looked up at Jamie. "Did you actually have sex with her?"

"Tilly, you saw how drunk I was. I must have passed out and Ruby lay next to me as some kind of prank. That's how girls like Sofia and Ruby operate – stupid games."

"But you were on top of Ruby."

"Well, I don't remember …"

"Of course you don't, you were too drunk to remember next morning, but it happened!"

"Tilly, you know photos can lie – they can be rigged – or doctored. You must remember that Sofia is a goddamn troublemaker."

Standing up, Tilly folded her arms. "Pathetic. I don't buy it, Jamie, and don't think you can arrive here and expect me to say it's *okay* to get off your head and then get *naked* with other women."

Jamie looked at Tilly, who looked so ravishing in jeans and the prettiest floral top.

"Okay then, if you are going to be like that. George has apparently blocked me out of his life too, so it doesn't look like I'm having a very good run of things, does it?"

"You were the one who stepped out of line, Jamie, not me."

"And I agree with you," said Jamie.

"Fine, so please leave."

And Tilly walked back towards the house with her spaniel panting next to her, hoping she might throw him another stick to fetch.

'Bad week,' wrote *Clique Week*, 'for George Wyndham and Sofia Tamper, who have enraged neighbours surrounding their Rousey estate, Ayrshire, with rumours that they will be turning their historic mansion into a building site, predicted to cause traffic mayhem around the country roads. With interior decorator, Ruby Blake, in situ, Wyndham and his Hollywood fiancé are said to have drawn up extensive refurbishment plans including a sixty-foot-long pool and a cinema. Unconfirmed reports mention that the grounds will also feature a large football pitch, floodlights and a stadium for guests. Change certainly appears to be afoot for the country set!'

"So there you are," said Victoria. "It could have been worse. Anyway, you know the press. There's always going to be a negative and it's my job to work on the upside – one of which has arisen from no less a soul than the editor of *Glamour Puss*."

"Oh yes?" said Sofia, lying on a sofa in the drawing room, having had another huge row with Ruby.

"*Glamour Puss* wants to feature you as their December cover story, something along the lines of 'Taming Tamper'. And before you say so much as boo, no, it won't involve George, so you won't have any awkward poses with him."

"*Eeeugh*, I can't stand those macho magazines," said Sofia, sitting up to take a sip from a Moscow Mule, which she had mixed herself as Royston had been ordered by Blaire not to serve her any alcohol.

"But they've changed their entire ethos these days," said Victoria, keen not to miss out on any coverage. "Tits are out of fashion. Really, the cover nudity is over. It's all very sensual and chi-chi now. I seriously think we should consider it."

"*Glamour Puss* has gone saintly?" said Sofia, disbelievingly.

"Well, they're going for a more, you know, sophisticated vibe. Camembert rather than Kraft cheese? I think they're spot on really. Porn mags are so passé. If you want porn, you can find it online in seconds, just name your fetish and off you go. So now *Glamour Puss* is homing in on elegant, sophisticated women and that's why I think it's the right fit for you, sweetie. Besides, they've already pretty much agreed to a full feature on you, when *Violet Tiger* is released."

"Sweet Christ! Victoria, we haven't even shot the goddamn series yet."

"No, but you will," said Victoria with a large smile and feeling very much in control.

Before going to Rousey, Jamie's first port of call was the Keeper's Cottage where the MacLeods gave him the usual welcome as George's closest friend. But things were clearly not good. They were exhausted from worrying so dreadfully about George, and their own future.

"He's told us we mustn't worry," Grace said to Jamie.

"And not to go near the place," added Finlay. "So that's what we're sticking to."

"And Her Ladyship up there," said Grace, wincing as she spoke, "prancing around like she's Queen Bee. And what about the poor wee doggies? Aye, they're happy enough with us for now but Mr Wyndham didn't give them a thought when he left Rousey. And now Raven and Arthur are spending every waking minute wondering if he'll ever be back for them."

"And George is up at the house?" asked Jamie.

"I'm not sure," said Finlay. "He's coming and going, we can't keep track. There's all sorts going on at the house but, like I said, George said he's going to fix things. He says that the Blaire woman and her daughter are only temporary."

"Is that all he's told you? Did he mention Anna?"

"The bonnie girl from Ireland? Not a word about her. Sure isn't he distracted with having a house full of international people?"

Jamie wasn't sure what he was going to say to George. In fact, the MacLeods weren't even sure if he was still in Scotland but, just as he had needed to see Tilly face to face in order to sort out the confusion over the photo, now he needed to do the same with George. Much of Jamie's daily mindset was based on Cabby's Law, as his favourite lecturer at law school called it: no matter who gets into your taxi, it's your job to take them to where they want to go. You are not to judge and must "remain subjective no matter how dubitable the facts appear".

Jamie knew he couldn't leave Rousey until he had got to the truth. Walking through the yard where he had played with George as boys in decades past, he found the basement door open. Passing though the boot room, he called out for George, but there was no answer. It was nearly seven o'clock, and he hadn't eaten since breakfast so it was no wonder he was starving, he reflected, as he bypassed the kitchen. On the ground floor he walked into the library and looked around at the intricately framed portraits of the Wyndham ancestors, so curiously familiar to him.

"*Hello!*" he shouted again, as he climbed the stairs. His ears pricked as he heard the sound of opera coming from the bedroom wing.

"We should get a fridge in here," said Sofia, nudging her big toe up to turn on the hot tap.

"Why?"

"Because it's such a pain to have to call Royston every time I feel thirsty."

"No, I think you're saying that just because it's so obvious that your mother has asked Royston not to serve you any alcohol whatsoever."

"Whatsoever, whatever," said Sofia. "But whatever about everything else, I think Mr X has the right idea about putting a huge Jacuzzi in here. This bathtub is far too small for the two of us."

"Well, if you'd move your pretty little feet to one side, then I could slide my legs alongside yours."

"Okay."

"Better?"

"Yes."

"Okay then," said Ruby, who was determined to get things out in the open. "I take no pleasure in arguing with you, Sofia, but can we talk about your mother's plans again?"

"Ruby, I'm just back from Paris, I'm exhausted."

"My heart bleeds for you."

"You know it was work, and deadly boring. Standing with George in the middle of strangers outside a church for a wedding, can you imagine? All because Victoria had lined us up for an interview with some swanky French magazine and they thought a shot at a traditional French event would work nicely. We even had to meet the bride and groom, like we were some A-lister couple."

"Isn't that all part of Victoria's plan, making you an A-lister?"

"Yes, but rocking up to a stranger's wedding? That's just weird. On top of all that, I found George talking to that Irish girl Hannah."

"Anna? No way. What was she doing at the wedding?"

"Oh, she wasn't at the wedding, of course. She was just, you know, on the street. She looked such a sight. Man, that girl has clearly let herself go. And not a scrap of dignity about her."

"Wow, and how did George react?"

"George? He did what he was told. We went to Paris and did the photoshoot at the wedding. End of. So, look, Ruby, I realise Mom's new plan for the interiors totally put you out."

"Yes, about as much as knowing that you are completely shafting George. You are completely going back on your agreement with him."

"Verbal agreement," said Sofia. "When he said yes, I think he was still in shock that he had a kid sister. It's such a hoot, isn't it?"

"Sofia, you know how important family is to me. Please don't joke about having a half-brother. You are dead lucky that he agreed to go along with your proposal, otherwise you and Victoria would be freewheeling without any media staircase to lift you up."

"I'd be fine without him."

"But I thought this was as much about your career as financial security?"

"Well, the career thing is my mother's vision. She's the one who wants me to be a goddess of the goddamn silver screen, or whatever the hell they call it now. Anyway, the ultimate decision about how this all pans out will rest with the owner of Rousey estate, and that, legally speaking, is me."

And, on that conclusion, she lifted a bottle of vodka from the table by the bathtub and sloshed some into a tumbler.

"Your mother is some operator, isn't she? Hey, I hope you're mixing something with that!"

"Sure, I'm mixing it with some beautiful opera and my favourite girl. Look, Ruby, I don't want the whole interior-design thing to turn into an issue between us but I'm selling up, so what does it matter?"

"It matters because Mr X has got more marble going into this place than you'd find in the Taj Mahal. Marble flooring, marble pillars, marble terraces, marble bathtubs – even the walls are marble. Sofia, come on, you must agree?"

"Ain't it marbellous?" said Sofia.

Ruby wasn't amused. "There's just one drawback," continued Ruby, as Sofia sat up in the bath. "It's glaringly obvious to anyone with an iota of taste but I guess it doesn't seem to be apparent to Mr X or his wife."

"And the drawback is?"

"That the plans are completely hideous," said Ruby. "It's what is known as the gold-taps syndrome. You know, anything that expels water?"

"I don't get why you're so surprised, Ruby. My mom is drawn to quick fixes, and if a better deal comes along, she'll take it. And she's a fighter – she boxes her way out of corners, always has, always will."

"And when George tells Robert that you shafted him?"

"They are on non-speakies. That relationship of theirs is well and truly over. Robert has a daughter now and has zero interest in listening to what George has to say. Trust me, it's game over for George. Oh, and by the way, one other thing – I may as well tell you before you read about it as planning permission tends to wheedle its way into the media."

"Planning?"

"Mom has applied for permission to empty the family

mausoleum and move the Wyndham coffins to the graveyard in the village," said Sofia. "The agent made it clear that Mr X, and particularly his wife, won't touch the place otherwise. So the deal can't be finalised until the application to exhume the bodies has been approved."

"Hold on. You're telling me that your mom is applying for permission to exhume bodies? God, that's creepy! Let's turn down the opera, it's not a good soundtrack to these kinds of conversations."

"It's just moving coffins. It's no big deal. They'll just take the coffins out of the mausoleum and discreetly rebury them."

"Including George's mother?"

"Well, yes, she's there too. She's a Wyndham after all. Just like me. *Eeeeeugh*, I guess I'll end up in the village graveyard now that I'm one of them."

"Hello, hello, what is going on in there?" said Ruby, gently tapping Sofia's forehead.

I couldn't have asked a more appropriate question myself, thought Jamie. Standing by the bathroom door, he had heard every word of the conversation. However, just as he was about to walk in he felt a tap on his shoulder.

"Peeking behind the velvet curtain, are we, sir?" said Royston.

"And you are?" asked Jamie.

"*Royston, is that you?*" yelled Sofia, running the tap again.

"Hey, that's too hot," said Ruby. "You trying to boil me?"

"I'm only ever trying to heat you up," said Sofia playfully.

"I can think of nicer ways," said Ruby.

Jamie and Royston looked at one another and raised their eyebrows.

"And let me guess – you are Sofia's butler?"

"This is my vocation, sir," said Royston proudly. "I've been poached several times of course – even by one of my ex-boss's billionaire friends. But I do love to buttle."

After long years of tedium, Royston was delighted to have a little quality scandal in the house.

Jamie quickly won him over with the same smile he had frequently used to win over both male and female members of the jury.

"Not to worry, Royston," said Jamie, striding into the bathroom as if he had been invited to a drinks party. "Sofia and I are old friends. Isn't that right, Sofia? So sorry to disturb, ladies. I hadn't realised this room was – being used, so to speak."

Increasingly tipsy on vodka, Sofia raised her leg on one side of the bathtub.

"What's the matter, Jamie? I figure you're the sort of guy who's seen two girls in a bath together before?"

"I bet you figure."

"Why don't you join us?"

"I think I'll pass," said Jamie, sitting on a large upright chair beneath a sash window. "Or maybe I can ask your friend Royston to take a photograph of the three of us and you can send it over to Tilly, eh?"

"I'm going to remain calm about this," said Sofia, quietly and with hard, cold venom, "and ask you: what the hell are you doing here?"

"The same question keeps crossing my mind."

"*Hey, hop it, Royston!*" shouted Sofia suddenly.

"Ahm, yes, if you're sure, madam?" said a voice that was clearly longing to sneak a peep around the door.

"*I'm sure!*" she yelled.

"God, you English!" chuckled Ruby. "You're famous for your etiquette but I can't believe you're just sitting there, Jamie, making small talk."

"Ah, yes, Ruby, my dear," said Jamie. "We're full to the brim with etiquette but I'm afraid we're not so polite that we don't eavesdrop."

"What's that supposed to mean?" said Sofia

"Oh, cut the baloney!" said Jamie, standing up. "I want to know what the hell is going on, you obscene bitch! And you, Ruby, what the hell made you do it?"

"Actually, Jamie, I didn't *do it*," said Ruby, "as in, we didn't *do it*. Sorry to disappoint but afraid you're not my type."

"So Tilly received the photo?" said Sofia. "I was quite pleased with the shot considering we didn't have much to work with, did we, Ruby? Not exactly steamy, as you were too busy snoring. Honestly, Jamie, I had expected you to have proper stamina. It's not as if you are short on experience of getting off your head and then landing a hot chick."

"That's enough, Sofia," Jamie said through gritted teeth.

"Hey, take it easy! She owns this place so watch your manners," said Ruby.

"No, she does not. Not yet and certainly not legally. Ipso facto, one does not become a joint owner of a spouse's property until one is married."

"Jamie, don't you know? Sofia owns this place. Her father has gifted it to her."

"He has *what*?"

"Ruby, shut it, will you!" hissed Sofia.

"Hold it, Sofia – Ruby, did I hear you correctly?"

"*Just give me some space and back out of here, okay?*" Sofia screamed.

Ruby sat uncomfortably at the other end of the bathtub, her arms clenched around her knees.

"I'm not going anywhere until you tell me what the hell is going on. What did Ruby mean about your father signing over this place, tell me. Sofia? Your father is in prison and thankfully he has nothing to do with Rousey."

"Which just goes to show that you don't know everything, Jamie Lord. Ruby is right. Robert Wyndham is my real father which makes George –"

"Your half-brother!" said Jamie. "Give me a break! Who thought up that one? And why this ludicrous engagement? I bloody well knew something was up but even I couldn't have even dreamed up this horror show."

"George is helping me out, that's all. It's a straight-up business arrangement."

Jamie shook his head. "I actually can't take this in, Sofia. You're telling me that George agreed to front the engagement with you?"

"Yes," said Sofia.

"In return for which you plan on ripping open his mother's tomb and hurling her to the wind?"

"A little brutal but I guess that's one way of putting it," smirked Sofia.

"You bloody bitch," said Jamie coldly.

"Don't speak to her like that," said Ruby, reaching out for Sofia, but Sofia shrugged away.

"This ends now, Sofia," said Jamie.

"Actually, no, Jamie, it doesn't end now. This is just the beginning. Now get out of this room, get out of this house and go sit on your moral high ground. Robert is my father. And Rousey is mine. Get out."

"Oh I'll get out all right and I'm going to expose you, Sofia, for the bitch that you are."

"What, for being Robert Wyndham's daughter? I've brought nothing but happiness to that man. He's over the moon about it. We had a paternity test, Jamie. It's proven. And it was Robert's choice to give me this place. How am I to blame that he can't stand his own son?"

Jamie slammed the door as he walked out, leaving the two girls silent in the bath.

"Ruby?" said Sofia after a while. "You know your cousin? The one who used to party with Jamie, way back?"

"Yeah, Kerina, why? What are you thinking, Sofia? You're such a minx."

"I just think those legal fuddy-duds in London might like a little reminder of how our friend Jamie Lord used to be somewhat less of an angel, know what I mean? Can you maybe ask Kerina if she might take a trip up Memory Lane and rustle up a photo or two?"

"Whoosh!" said Ruby. "Well, I guess I can ask her – for you, Sofia, but only for you."

"Just to keep Jamie in his place."

"Do you think he'll go to the press?"

"What, and make his best friend look even more ridiculous than he already does? No, despite how Jamie might seem he's just a traditional boy beneath all that testosterone. And hey, don't you think it's time you and I got out of this bath and found somewhere a little more flexible to lie down?"

Chapter 38

Riding by the market stalls on her bicycle with raised handlebars and a wicker basket, Anna breathed in a delicious aroma of blue cheese and smoked ham. Large half-barrelled baskets cradled gleaming olives and bright yellow lemons piled alongside freshly baked apricot tarts glazed with syrup. A fishmonger raised his chapeau to her as he wrestled with olive branches to decorate the surrounds of a box filled with fresh lobster and crab. Anna squinted as the sun crept through the Eiffel Tower, a monument that felt always like a friend watching over her. As she heaved her bicycle against the railings of the café, she thought about the questions she had prepared for George. She was going to demand answers, and once she'd got them, she would walk out of his life and he would feel like hell. She might also tell him about her pregnancy, but she hadn't completely decided. The main thing was to offload the baggage she had been carrying around for weeks now. It was the only way she could move on.

Closing the combination lock on the chain around her bike, Anna swept back a rebellious curl back from her face before pushing open the heavy glass door of the Bistro le Chat. She found George leaning against the bar, engrossed in conversation with a large bearded man whose smile was as imposing as his waistline.

"Anna …" said George, looking nervous and running his fingers through his hair, "It's so good to see you."

He leant forwards to kiss Anna's cheek, but she pulled away.

"Christophe, I'd like to introduce you to Anna," said George quickly.

"*Enchanté, madame*," said Christophe. "George always likes to present me with the finer things in life, don't you, George?" And with a broad grin he reached for Anna's hand.

"You're still wearing the necklace?" said George.

"Only because the clasp is stuck," she lied – Dharma's advice to continue wearing it had made superstition override her feelings.

"A glass of white?" asked George.

"Please," she said, trying to remain calm and demure.

The awkward pause between them was broken when a golden cocker spaniel galloped into the bistro, much to the joy of customers. The dog gave an almighty shake, sending water droplets flying out from his wet coat before making an unexpected beeline for Anna's ankles. As he settled himself against her feet, with his tail brushing against the flagstone floor, she reached down to smooth his long, damp ears. She thought of Guinness, who was most likely sound asleep on his beanbag in front of the Aga in Farley Hall and then, realising that Christophe was rather enjoying the view of her cleavage as he towered over the bar, she stood up again and took a large sip of wine.

She continued to shoot George icy looks but felt doubly cross with herself for still finding him so attractive.

"Your dog looks very fit," she said to Christophe, liking him despite his peeping tendency. "It's almost like he has just arrived home after a long walk in the country."

George pulled up his barstool beside her.

"You're not far off," he said, looking at Anna.

She was determined not to look him in the eye, not yet.

"He's a city dog most of the time but come the weekends he's on the game – pheasant, duck and the occasional grey partridge. He's even been known to chase the odd boar. The French love hunting, isn't that right, Christophe?"

And right on cue the spaniel sprang up on his hind legs and pawed the bar as Christophe waved a large photograph of a wild boar turning on a spit. He clicked his fingers and the spaniel went off like a bullet through a revolving door, closely followed by his master.

"Anna, your lip, it's bleeding," said George.

"God, I don't believe it. Oh bugger," she said, feeling ridiculous. "I must have bitten it."

George pulled out a handkerchief and reached forward to wipe her lip.

"No," she said sharply, taking a napkin from the bar, even though she couldn't help wondering if his hands were still as warm as they had been when he held her face and kissed her so intensely all that time ago.

"Are you hungry?" asked George.

"A little," she said, trying to maintain a hostility that just didn't come naturally to her.

"Come on," he said, "let's sit down over here."

They walked to a small circular table by the window, followed by a waiter with a bottle of Sancere.

"I went to Saint Sulpice yesterday," said George, as if they were old friends catching up after a long weekend. "Beautiful ... have you been yet?" When she didn't answer, he picked up the bottle and filled their glasses. He lifted his glass to his lips and looked at her. "You ought to go. The Delacroix murals are staggeringly good. Do you remember my telling you about it? About my efforts to persuade the French Arts Council to have it restored?"

Anna did remember. It had been at Farley Hall. She gave a slight nod, not wanting to sound interested in anything other than making him answer for what he had put her through.

A waiter arrived with two steaming hot plates of boeuf bourguignon, as the melodic voice of Jacques Brel sighed with an accordion as he sang a sad song about a seamstress from rue Rivoli, who had lost her identity after the war. Looking down at the delicious lunch, the meat resting alongside juicy mushrooms and shallots in red-wine gravy, the parsley sinking into the sauce, Anna had never felt less hungry.

George picked up his fork and then put it down again.

"Anna, can you look at me, please?"

She couldn't help it – no matter how she tried to hold it in, a tear escaped down her cheek as George reached out for her hand.

"Anna, I need to try to explain why I had to make the choice ... it tore to me pieces having to choose and I am so, so very sorry."

Pulling her hands away, Anna shook her head and coughed. "You don't have to say that, George," she whispered. "It doesn't change anything."

All of the rant she had planned to hurl at him over lunch seemed to have evaporated. She felt she didn't have the strength to take him on, and what's more, she just didn't want to go over it, how he had humiliated her, abandoned her, all while she was pregnant with his child. Seeing an elderly couple approaching, George pulled his chair closer to the table as they passed by. Anna noticed soft lines wrinkling as the couple smiled at each other, gently steering their way through the tables and chairs.

"Do you plan to stay in Paris?" asked George, just as an aged waiter arrived with two side salads and then shuffled slowly back to the bar, clasping arthritic hands behind his back.

Anna twisted the napkin on her lap, George's question still hanging in the air. And then she decided, enough of this, and cut right to it.

"Is Sofia still in Paris?"

"No," he said, as his face stiffened. "She left this morning."

Noticing violet smudges beneath his dark lashes, Anna remembered how it was always a giveaway when he wasn't sleeping properly. Outside, the day was turning bleak and overcast. She looked at her untouched beef and George tried to fork up some rocket salad, but it tumbled straight back onto the plate.

"I have to go," said Anna.

"But we need to talk!" said George. "There is so much I need to explain . . ."

Then Christophe arrived to the table before George could say any more.

"You did not like the boeuf bourguignon?" he asked, his face gravely concerned. "What can I offer you? Won't you eat something else?"

"*Non, merci, Christophe*," said Anna and, putting the napkin on the table, she stood up.

"Well, there will be no charge, George. And next time, you bring this lady back and we'll find something else on the menu that she like?"

George wanted to protest but Anna was already walking out the door, the old waiter holding it open for her and smiling broadly.

George bade Christophe a hasty farewell and hurried after her, slipping a note into the waiter's chilled hands.

Outside, he stood next to Anna's bicycle, trying to respect her wishes for him to keep his distance, though he had never felt such longing.

"Anna, please, can I see you again?" he asked, putting the end of her scarf over her shoulder. "Can I at least have your address, so I can write?"

"You have my email," she said, pushing the dial on the bike chain to click open the lock.

"I'd prefer to write," he said.

"Rue Saint Dominique," she said. "Ninety-one."

Pushing off on her bicycle, she wished the ground would swallow her up. She was furious with herself for being so weak. The purpose of the lunch was to make him feel guilty for the way he had treated her, but all she had achieved was to be landed with the conundrum of still feeling in love with him and yet feeling so angry with him at the same time. *What he did was unforgivable*

Back at her apartment, Anna was relieved to find that the landlord had fixed the fridge while she was out and, pulling out a bottle of white wine, she poured herself a glass and took it into the bathroom with her. Running the bath, she added the extravagant bath oil that her mother had brought her as a housewarming present, and tried to imagine she was in an ad where miraculous bath oil would bathe her sorrows away. Overheating in the water after only five minutes, Anna decided another glass of wine was the answer and, wrapping herself in a fluffy white towel, she walked into the kitchen, careful not to slip on the parquet floor.

Then she heard a knock at the door, along with a muffled voice calling, "Madame?"

Debating whether or not to answer, Anna decided she had better in case it was a delivery for Winterbottom PR and, opening the latch, she peered out of the door to find the building's caretaker holding out a bunch of white roses.

"*Oh ... merci, monsieur,*" said Anna, her face flushed from the bath, holding up her towel with one hand and accepting the flowers with the other.

Wondering who had sent them, she was stepping back to close the door when George appeared.

"Anna."

"George! What are you doing here?"

"I didn't think you'd want to see me, and so I asked the caretaker to make the delivery."

"You're right, I don't want to see you."

"I couldn't help myself, and so I followed him to your door because ..."

"Because?"

"Because, I need another chance to explain."

Anna didn't know what to do, the classic case of her heart wanting to say yes and her head surely saying no.

She threw the roses down on the table. "What's the idea of sending me roses? Do you think that's appropriate given the circumstances?"

"It's just a gesture, to let you know that I –"

But Anna wasn't having any of it. "You humiliated me, George. My family, my friends, even my colleagues, all feeling so sorry for me because you couldn't even telephone me to say that you were having second thoughts. No, instead you had to announce your new alliance in a national newspaper."

"Anna, I can explain –"

"What's to explain? You were with me, and next thing I know you're engaged to Sofia, all while my father was lying in bed, having nearly lost his life." Anna tightened the towel around her body. "You hurt me in every possible way, George, and now you expect me to come running back to you."

"I just need five minutes, Anna. Just five minutes," and closing the door behind him, he walked towards her.

"All right then," she said. "You can sit there, on the armchair, for five minutes and no longer."

"Okay, Anna, I'm going to try to make this as simple as possible," he said, sitting down and clasping his hands together. "It turns out that Sofia is my half-sister."

he chose a house before her

314

"*What?*"

"My father had an affair with her mother, years ago, when I was a child."

"And?" Anna shook her head and just stared at George.

"My father decided to give Rousey to Sofia. I just couldn't believe it."

"Believe what?"

"That I was going to lose Rousey." Saying it out loud, he realised how utterly selfish it sounded. "And so Sofia and her publicist and mother – don't get me started on the mother ..."

"Hold on, George, you're here looking for sympathy, because of your obsession with Rousey?"

"No, Anna, it's not about me – there's the deer sanctuary, the salmon reservoir, the MacLeods who've been at Rousey for years ... and my mother. The memory of her."

Anna shook her head, and tried to take it in. "So it's like me having to choose between you and Farley Hall?"

"Well, yes, and the future of Mrs B and Bernard? What would you do?"

Anna stood up. "I'll tell you what I'd do, George! I wouldn't get bloody well cornered by Sofia Tamper!"

"You don't understand – after nine months – less now – I get Rousey back – that's the agreement."

"And what do you expect me to do for the next nine months? Oh, I know! Why don't we have a baby and maybe this time the baby will actually survive!" and shocked at herself for saying it like that or even saying it at all, Anna put her hands over her mouth and burst into tears.

"Anna?" George stood up and moved towards her. "What do you mean, a baby?"

As she tried to catch her breath, she tried to speak but she could only cry, maybe relieved that George had explained about why he had to leave her, even if it did sound so crazy. But more so she felt relief that she had told him about the baby. In a way, she had been feeling guilty for not having told him, and now it was all out in the open.

George held out his hand to Anna. She tried to stop herself, but she reached out. *fool*

"Our hands still fit," he said, and as they kissed Anna she could feel his tears. "We were going to have a baby?" he whispered, and she could hear the shock in his voice.

"It was very early – it didn't make it past five weeks."

"It was my fault, wasn't it?" he said, holding Anna tightly in his arms.

"No, the GP said it was just one of those things, a very sad thing. There was nothing we could have done."

"And you had to go through it all by yourself, Anna. Darling Anna, I am so sorry, so very sorry."

Slowly, as the tears dried, they began to kiss, and it felt like returning to love, nothing else. Lifting Anna up into his arms, George carried her into her bedroom. They lay there, kissing passionately and expelling the emptiness they had felt without each other. Anna's towel had slipped off and he kissed her breasts, feeling the warmth of her skin, his hands smoothing over every inch of her slender body. Taking off his shirt and kicking off his shoes, he smoothed back her curls as she looked up at him, smiling faintly and reacting so generously to his touch.

Turning over, Anna climbed on top of him and was unbuttoning his trousers when he said, "Anna, hold on."

"George, what is it?"

"Are you sure you want to? I don't want you to feel uncomfortable."

"I want to," she said. "I do, want to."

"But are you okay? You know, physically, after everything?"

"Yes, I am, but let's be careful from now on, okay?"

"Do you have something?"

"I do," said Anna, reaching to the drawer in the bedside table. "All part of the must-have list when living in your own apartment, according to Gilda – who provided them of course."

"Making you an independent woman?" said George, smiling now properly for the first time in months.

"Yes," said Anna, and as she tried to tear off the corner of the foil, they laughed, just a little.

As George finally used his teeth to break through the silver wrapper and as he prepared to make love, Anna lay back and knew that she was following her heart, no matter what the complications.

Making love, they were completely in sync, both wanting to please each other. Anna had never felt herself moving so freely, letting go of any inhibitions, knowing that George had come back to her from his own choice. Feeling his heart beating as she lay against his chest, Anna felt that she was where she should have been all along, and all night they slept in each other's arms, glued to each other.

If he did it once, he'll betray her again.
he chose a lousy house ahead of her.

Chapter 39

Anna woke up to the sound of the pavement being hosed as the morning light came through a gap in the curtains, lighting up George's head on the pillow like a golden egg. As he slept so soundly, his breath hardly making a sound, Anna stared at his long lashes, lightly pressing against dark shadows beneath his eyes, and wondered what their baby might have looked like. But then she stopped herself. She had to deal with the present, and right now George was with her, and not Sofia. Feeling so wide-awake, Anna wanted to jump out of bed but at the same time she was almost afraid to move in case she disturbed what was a perfect scenario.

Slipping cautiously out of bed, feeling optimistic for the first time in weeks now that they had both levelled with each other, she pulled a long-sleeved jumper dress over her head and slipped into gold Top Shop flats. Feeling a little like Stephanie Powers in *Mistral's Daughter*, except that she wasn't naked beneath a trench coat, she clicked open the latch of the door so that she could get back inside without having to jingle a set of keys. Running down the stone steps from the apartment, she stepped onto rue Saint Dominique and saluted the Eiffel Tower. In the boulangerie next door, the lady, wearing her blue-collared baking dress, gave Anna the usual exaggerated nod followed by "*Combien, madame?*" It

318

was the same question every morning, as Anna's general order was for pains au chocolat. But this morning, she would order croissants aux amandes and a baguette in case she and George didn't feel like leaving the apartment for lunch. Anna could keep an eye on emails to keep Winterbottom happy, and together she and George could work out a strategy to sort out the huge mess with Sofia. Surely bringing Jamie into the equation could sort things out with some heavyweight legal moves?

George had woken up to find a string of missed calls on his phone and an irate voice mail from Victoria, telling him that he had missed a wardrobe fitting in preparation for a photo shoot with *Hello*.

"*One more slip-up*," said Victoria, "*and you can kiss goodbye to the chances of getting your Scottish chateau back.*"

His immediate reaction was to call Victoria to say that the deal was off, until a photograph came through to his phone from Sofia, stopping him in his tracks.

It was a photograph of Jamie, wearing a judge's wig, and snorting a fat line of cocaine with a faceless blonde kissing his neck.

'**This picture goes public this evening if you don't get your ass back for this photo shoot, George.**'

Feeling the warmth of the croissants through the brown-paper bag, Anna opened the door of her building and ran up the stone steps to her apartment, smiling, her hair feeling curly and light. Pushing open the front door, she found George by the sitting-room window, dressed except for his moleskin jacket, which he held over his arm.

She walked slowly into the kitchen, her heart thumping as she tore open the paper bag of croissants and put them onto a plate. Striking a match, she lit the gas stove for the coffee maker. She knew by the look on George's face that something was badly wrong, and she did not want to hear it. As the gas flame hissed against the aluminium, Anna stared into the courtyard where a young woman was hanging up sheets on a line.

"Anna," said George, as he walked into the kitchen, "I have to leave."

But Anna chose not to hear what he had said.

"Can you pass me the coffee, please, it's in the fridge," she said, her voice unusually high-pitched.

He found an almost empty bag of coffee and passed it to her without looking at her.

"I'm so sorry," he whispered. "I can't get out of it right now, Anna."

Changing her mind about the coffee, Anna turned off the gas.

"She's got you again, has she, George? Your so-called sister?" Picking up a wet dishcloth, she threw it him, making him look so ashamed. "What is it with me? Why is it that I am so stupid, imagining that things might just work out – that you might have had a rethink?"

"It's not as simple as that, Anna," said George sharply. "You don't understand. It's an impossible situation."

"Too bloody well right I don't understand. What the hell are you trying to do to me?"

"Anna, I –"

"No, George. I do not want to hear another single word." Her tone of voice was flat and serious. "You have torn me to pieces."

George put his hand on Anna's arm, but she slapped it away.

"I should have walked away from you while I had the chance," she said, stamping her foot on the floor. "That is exactly what I should have done," and, clearing her throat, she walked to the hallway and opened the door. "I want you to leave," she said calmly, "and I never want to see you again. Not ever."

Then, just as she was about to scream and tell him to leave again, her phone rang out with Gilda's name flashing up.

"Anna?" said Gilda, through gritted teeth. "I'm at the Crillon with Desmond Spicer, and I need your proposal pronto. You are twenty minutes late. You need to be here."

"What? I thought it was tomorrow?" said Anna, horrified.

"I emailed and texted you, Anna – now come on, *trés vite*!"

"I'm on my way, Gilda." She put the phone into her handbag, eyes narrowing at George. "And don't look at me like a whipped dog. Don't you dare feel sorry for yourself. You made the choice, George, it was your choice." And you were all I wanted, she said to herself, desperately trying not to cry.

"Anna, wait. I need to explain. It's Jamie. She is going to screw him over if I don't get back."

But Anna wasn't listening and she slammed the door behind her. This time she was the one to leave.

Unfastening the chain of her bicycle, Anna cycled up rue Saint Dominique at speed and whistled across Pont de la Concorde. By the time she had reached Place de la Concorde, a gendarme had begun beeping the horn at her from his small Fiat police car.

"*Madame, votre chapeau?*" he shouted at her, pointing to his head, and pulling up his car, he opened the door and walked towards Anna, who was standing by her bicycle.

"I am sorry," said Anna, eyes smudged and puffy, holding her hands together. "I forgot the helmet."

"*Vous êtes anglais?*"

"*Non, Irlandaise,*" said Anna, trying to smile instead of crying.

"*Ah, Guinness,*" grinned the Gendarme, "*et U2 – ils sont les rois.*"

He waved her on.

"*Merci, monsieur,*" said Anna, as she moved off.

She pushed her bicycle onto the cobbles and gave the old Egyptian obelisk on Place de la Concorde a wink, hoping it might bring her luck. With no time to lock her bicycle, she leant it against the wall by the entrance to the Hotel de Crillon and, checking her face in the mirror of a yellow motorcycle, she dabbed a little balm on her lips and pushed back her blond curls with tortoiseshell sunglasses.

Kicking her deportment into gear, Anna stepped into the hotel lobby and, walking into the drawing room, she found Gilda sandwiched between Desmond Spicer and Gerald Bate-Smith, an English freelance journalist who loved nothing better than a free lunch.

Gilda raised her eyebrows when she saw Anna arriving and, slipping her sheer gold-stocking feet into Louboutin heels, she stood up and looked at the gentlemen with as much femininity as she could muster.

"Chat amongst yourselves, won't you, darlings? Won't be a moment."

Charging towards Anna, she lifted a slender French cigarette to her lips as the barman wagged his finger, concerned that she was about to light up.

Gilda swept outside, Anna in her wake.

"Anna, where in hell's name have you been?" said Gilda, lighting up on the hotel steps. "Actually no, don't answer that. Not a word."

As Anna slipped her sunglasses over her eyes, Gilda spied her lower lip trembling.

"Darling, I would adore to sit down with you and listen to your woes, but honestly," she tapped her toe on the freshly sandblasted step, "I hadn't quite realised just how much loot Desmond Spicer had put aside for the media campaign. We are talking telephone numbers, darling, eight figures."

Slowly Anna tuned herself into Gilda's energy level and knew her only option was to pick herself up.

"Therefore," Gilda went on, "we need to be in full control and this campaign has got to be our sharpest yet." She lifted up Anna's sunglasses and peered into her eyes. "Look, darling, I know what a rotten time you've had, and I feel for you, I do. But you have got to put it to one side, no matter how shattering. We cannot afford for this to be anything other than a rip-roaring success. Okay, sweetie?"

"Got it, Gilda, I'm with you," said Anna, and she meant it.

Winterbottom PR was as steady a ship as she could find right now.

Returning to the corner of velvet sofas, pretzels and alcohol, Gilda and Ann found Desmond and Gerald deep in historical trivia.

"You do know that Marie Antoinette took piano lessons in this very drawing room when it was the private home of the Duke de Crillon?" said Gerald, raising a glass of Veuve Cliquot to his lips. "And then the poor darling lost her head just out there, on the Place de la Concorde during the Revolution. Tough times, I must say, tough times indeed."

Determined to outclass Gerald's local knowledge, Desmond sniffed the air.

"And what of Jake," he said, "in *The Sun Also Rises*? He gets stood up by Lady Ashley in this very room, so he stays and writes letters on the hotel stationary, hoping that the impressive paper will make up for the not-very-good letters."

"Yes, well, all very interesting," said Gilda, clinking her ink pen against the side of her glass. "Now, let's get back to the reason why we are all here. Anna darling, the proposal, would you like to open the floor?" Then, taking in the expression on Anna's face, Gilda changed tack. "On second thoughts, Anna, you need a stiffener."

She raised her glass in a waiter's direction, signalling for a fresh glass and another bottle.

"Right. Let us begin," she said then. "We have gathered here today to celebrate the centenary of Spicer Tweed," she said.

"Amen to that," said Desmond, sipping champagne.

Gilda pulled back her shoulders and turned her head slowly to the left and the right, about to seduce her audience with her extravagant plans.

"Spicer Tweed has come to Paris to meet with Winterbottom PR in search of a jolly good boost. A re-introduction to the media if you will." In theatrical mode now, she slipped off her shoes and raised her arms as if she were Cleopatra willing the gods to come down and join them. "From armchair slipcovers in your country house to chic wardrobe staples, Spicer Tweed ticks all the salubrious boxes. It is the luxury fabric that must be celebrated!"

"Hear, hear!" nodded Desmond, gobbling a mini quiche-puff all in one.

"And not forgetting alpaca and cashmere, all those divine interwoven knits that complement the Spicer Tweed range, Winterbottom PR has put together a media campaign that is sensitive to every aspect of your needs." Raising her hand towards Anna like a lady on a QVC shopping channel, Gilda passed the baton.

Having drained half a glass of champagne, Anna was feeling a great deal better and holding up an iPad she showed a photograph of the actress, Lavinia de Vere Parker.

"Lavina is a lifelong fan of Spicer Tweed," said Anna.

"Truly?" said Gerald, his journalist skepticism creeping in. "That's rather a coincidence, isn't it?"

"Yes, Gerald, it is, isn't it?" snapped Gilda. "Carry on, Anna."

"Look, old girl, I don't mean to be ageist but don't you think we should bring in a younger model, given that we want to bring Spicer Tweed to a younger audience?"

Gilda rose to her feet and unbuttoned her Chanel blazer.

"My dear, there is simply no point in bringing in a flat-chested twenty-something with legs up to her armpits. You will only alienate your loyal customers, and no disrespect to your twenty-something wife either, but we need someone who can carry the fabric with personality and appeal, elegance and balls."

Desmond shook his head as he and Gerald sat forward to inspect Lavinia's curves in the slide show on Anna's iPad.

"Lavinia is a key opinion leader," said Anna, back in her comfort zone now. "She has experience and people listen to her."

"Darlings, this Spicer Tweed campaign is going to be a celebration of all things Scottish, and while holding on to the country's heritage we are also going to marry the Spicer brand with sexy jewels and take the public with us on a blissful journey of opulence, humour, and heritage. We are going to be your *artisan du rêve*, 'artisan of your dreams', Desmond. We will bring Spicer Tweed to the forefront of feature editors' minds across the world."

"Yes," said Desmond, swiping through the pictures, "I do like the concept. I must say I do like it."

"That's good to hear, Desmond," said Anna, the full strength of her voice returning. "We are going to kick off the campaign with a huge launch party at the Ritz where we will have a serious guest list of A-celebs and buyers."

Gilda was watching Desmond's reaction closely. She waved a hand at Anna to go on.

"Lavinia is an inspirational speaker," said Anna, "and will touch on brand heritage, the importance of celebrating the origin of products in a world where synthetic fabrics are so common. And following that we'll go to the studio, and we'll take her on a virtual global media tour with all the top magazines along with photo shoots."

Desmond took a silk handkerchief from the breast pocket of his tweed jacket and patted his forehead. "Ladies, I'm impressed," he said and, standing up, he put out his hand to Gilda and then to Anna. "And can we bring Lavinia over to the factory in Edinburgh? It would make a terrific press opportunity in Scotland."

Just as Gilda was about to agree, Anna smoothly refilled Desmond's glass. "The only thing is," she said, "Lavinia has recently adopted the most adorable pair of miniature schnauzers."

"Schnauzers?" asked Desmond.

"Yes, you know, a little like a Scottish terrier. Lavinia is very reluctant to travel out of France, hence our being in Paris. The mountain must go to Mohammad so to speak."

Seeing Desmond's smile dissipate, Anna and Gilda looked at each other. Desmond was a man people rarely said no to, his three wives being a testament. For Desmond, the icing on the cake would have been for Lavinia to come to the Spicer Tweed factory in Ayrshire, bringing glamour from the big screen to the humble loom.

Sitting down again, Desmond adjusted the crease in his trousers and frowned.

"Oh God," said Gilda, thinking Lavina's dry-land proviso might be a deal-breaker. "This is a problem, I'm afraid."

"I knew I should have put my foot down with Jenny," Desmond said, picking up his champagne flute. "Did I tell you the poodle arrived last week? Jenny has called her Tallulah and she is besotted with the dog. I suppose Tallulah isn't the worst of breeds, but what I'm wondering is why on earth didn't I push for a schnauzer?"

Gilda and Anna both breathed huge sighs of relief.

"Arrange for Lavinia's schnauzers to spend some time with my Jenny, will you?" Desmond went on. "Hopefully, we can talk her round to getting more robust dogs in our large house."

"Consider it done," said Gilda, slapping her thigh like Doris Day in *Calamity Jane* before taking a black velvet purse out of her handbag. Opening the clasp, she pulled out a diamond thistle pendant hanging from a gold chain. "I thought I'd treat myself to some Parisian bling earlier today and I feel like this evening is a good time to take it for a test run. Would you do me the honour?" She handed the necklace to Desmond, and just like that Gilda held his attention, resulting in his signing off a gigantic budget and booking a table for dinner at Laurent, by the Elysée Palace.

"Anna darling, are you sure you won't join us?" asked Gilda, as she and Gerald stepped into Desmond's chauffeur-driven Mercedes.

"Not this time," said Anna, and waved at Gilda as the car drove away.

During the meeting, Anna had been running on autopilot without a moment to think of George but, pushing her bike across

Pont Alexander, so haunting with its lampposts and gilded sculptures, thoughts of him flooded her mind again. She felt angry and cheated of something that could have been amazing, remembering the sense of urgency, only last night, when they made love, as if a time-bomb had been ticking next to them, every touch, every moment, stolen. Rain began to fall heavily as she reached the other side and, propping her bike against the wall, she leant back and let the rain pelt against her face, and with soaking hair and mascara running, she screamed out to the river, "*George Wyndham, never, never, never again!*" With shoes soaking, she jumped up and down, feeling like a wild Irish Banshee, letting loose, breaking out of the sugar-sweet shell that people imagined her to be coated in. Well, she'd had enough. George's excuses for dropping her in mid-air did not wash. He had put bricks and mortar before her, the wrong foundations for any relationship.

Chapter 40

A copy of *Inside News Magazine* lay on the white plastic trestle table in the visitors' room as Max Tamper awaited his afternoon arrival. Reading a feature about slowing down ageing by twenty-five minutes of brisk walking each day, Max ran his hands down the back of his legs, his calf muscles feeling stiff following his morning gym session. Maybe he should switch to more gentle exercise.

He felt quite pleased with himself, having just signed a four-part tell-all story with the *Daily Express*, dishing the dirt about the divas and devils he had to work with during his film-studio years. It didn't take him long to decide on the various lucrative offers – what did he have to lose?

When Jamie arrived Max was pleasantly surprised. The English were all so well-mannered, but he had expected a much haughtier individual.

"So you're a best buddy of big-shot Wyndham, are you?" said Max.

"Not so much of a big shot actually – he's always been very discreet."

"Really, that's not what I've been reading," said Max, trying to get comfortable on the plastic chair. "Plenty of time to read in this place, and we're even allowed to go online, so I'm pretty well read in terms of social columns and cheap headlines."

"I was going to say, George had always been discreet, before he began spending time with your daughter."

"The future Mrs Wyndham?"

"Do you really believe it?" said Jamie.

"Ah," said Max. "So you're one of those smart guys, are you? You've come to me for insights, even though I'm locked up in this place."

"But you know that your wife has moved to Geneva with Robert Wyndham?"

"I had no idea," Max said, lying.

"Perhaps a Swiss bank account," asked Jamie.

"Search me," said Max. "Do you know the prison entertainments officer offered me PlayStation for 50p per week, but I resisted the offer."

And so it went on, until Max finally chilled into the conversation and began to speak plainly to Jamie.

"Blaire always followed the money. When Robert wouldn't take her, she knew I was ruthless enough to make a fortune. She could see it in my eyes, at least that's what she told me two years later as we ate dinner in Ralph Lauren on Rodeo Drive." Max patted his stomach. "You should try the chicken wings, they're sensational. But Blaire can play the victim all right and really, deep down, she's just a spoilt brat."

The prison warden tapped on the window, signalling five minutes left.

"Max, I need to ask you about Sofia," said Jamie, seriously.

"What do you need to know?"

"I'm not sure if you are aware, but it seems that Sofia . . ."

"Yes, go on, don't worry about my feelings, Jamie – I'm long past that, I can assure you."

"Are you aware that Sofia claims not to be your daughter?"

"Yes, I am aware," said Max. "You know, I actually had to take a literacy test before they admitted me, don't ask me why. Then they went through the prison rules." Max stretched out his fingers as if playing an imaginary piano. "They're playing him."

"Playing who?" asked Jamie.

"Sofia is my daughter, and Blaire knows it."

"Why should I believe you?" asked Jamie.

"You know, Sofia came to see me a few weeks ago. She was wearing a ridiculous wig. Honestly, who does she think she is? I said to her, 'Do you really think you are that important, my darling?' She was very put out, naturally."

"Go on," said Jamie.

"I was quite upfront with her actually," said Max. "'You're too flash, darling,' I said to her. 'Why are you driving around in that bloody car?' 'It's beautiful,' she said, but I said, 'What do you want this car for in London?' She said 'It's very comfortable.' Then I said, 'For Christ's sake, where are you going in it?' Do you know Sofia has got another car following her with so-called bodyguards? Nobody's going to kill her. I told her: 'If anyone wanted to kill you, which they don't, those guys that are driving in that car ain't going to help.' She got this from LA. Everyone who wants to be known there has to have a bodyguard."

"Max, get back to the question of paternity. Are you serious when you say that Sofia is your daughter?"

"As serious as I am about getting out of here," he said.

"But I gather a paternity test has already taken place, and the report was positive that Robert is Sofia's father."

"Of course the results came back positive," said Max, laughing. "It was my DNA they were testing!"

"What?"

"Blaire came to visit, you know, and had no hesitation in getting what she wanted. The moment the prison guard turned his back, hey presto, she dabbed a swap of cotton wool inside my cheek and coolly popped it into a little test tube. I told her she had found her calling as a nurse, which she didn't seem to find particularly amusing."

Jamie didn't say a word, feeling huge relief that the jigsaw pieces were beginning to fit.

"So much for this famous *impartiality* the DNA labs like to boast about," said Max. "Blaire paid off the nurse. A complete farce and the funny thing is that no one seemed to bat an eyelid, such is the faith in the laboratory system. The power of the Bunsen burner, eh?"

"So, will you agree to a paternity test and put this on the record?"

"You bet. I have to do something because it will catch up with Sofia in the end – these things always do. She is my daughter, Jamie, and it's my duty to protect her, even if it is from herself."

He ran his fingers through his greying hair and, pulling several strands from the crown of his head, he tore a corner from a page of *Inside Time Magazine*. He then folded up the sample into a triangle and passed it to Jamie as if presenting a memento to a fan.

"Getting back to Sofia's roots, eh?" said Max, with a grin.

The prison guard signalled time up.

"Just one thing, Jamie," Max said as he stood up.

"Go on," said Jamie.

"Sofia – she's not a bad girl. She and her mother, they've found themselves up so high they're afraid to look down. They can't see what they're doing. That's the truth. They've lost all sight of reality."

"Tilly?" said Anna into the phone, balancing a coffee and a bowl of muesli. "Tilly? I can't hear you, where are you?"

"I'm sorry, Anna, the reception here is terrible. I'm walking in the woods at my parents' place, trying to find some eco-therapy from the trees."

"And you're in need of therapy?" said Anna. "What's been happening?"

"I've broken up with Jamie," said Tilly, her voice slightly breaking, "no other way to explain it, I'm afraid."

"Tills, I'm so sorry, what happened?"

Following a long pause, Anna could hear Tilly blowing her nose. "You obviously had a row?"

"Yes. It was a few days ago, but I just needed to calm down before I called you."

"But what's happened?"

"He slept with Ruby."

"He what?"

"The night of the *Violet Tiger* party."

"But Tilly, I was there … and yes, I left with you, but …"

"Sofia took a photo. Sick, but she did it."

"She sent you a photo of Jamie in bed with Ruby?"

"Can you believe it?"

"Well, yes, I can actually. But more to the point, Jamie was totally off his head that night – he had been doing shots – he could barely stand by the time you and I left – and I know, Tilly, that you are still probably livid with me but I –"

"It doesn't matter," Tilly cut in. "All I know is that Jamie was in bed with Ruby – they were both naked and he was lying on top of her."

"Seriously? And Sofia took the photo. God, there's no end to her!"

"What do you mean?"

"Tilly, I understand where you're coming from more than you know. She's utterly insane – honestly, you can't believe a word," and as Anna spoke she wondered about what George had said, how Sofia had cornered him about Rousey. She didn't want to go down the road of giving George another chance but she was realising that there really must be two sides to the screw-up of it all.

"But the photo is proof!"

"Not when Sofia is taking it, Tilly, and you most likely don't want to hear it but ... look, Tilly, we badly need to thrash this out. I've only just stopped crying over George."

"Really? Why – well, not why but what brought it up again?"

"He did. We spent last night together and I am like a nervous wreck as a result. We really need to go through things, Tilly. I'm going to call Gilda and ask to work from the London office for this week, okay? I'll see if I can get on a flight first thing in the morning. I'll zip to the office and then be with you. Can you hang on till then?"

Having flown into Gatwick from Charles de Gaule, Anna jumped in a taxi for Winterbottom HQ. Feeling stronger than she had in ages, she walked into the office to find the usual mayhem, along with Desmond Spicer who had popped in to go over details for the Spicer Paris launch.

"Do you ladies know Scotland at all?" he asked, dipping into a bowl of nibbles to go with his single malt.

"I went to a twenty-first at a friend's town house, and David

Copperfield turned up to entertain us before pudding – it was awesome," said Kate, so thrilled to see Anna again, and desperately trying to impress Desmond so that she could cement her position on the team at the Ritz Paris during the launch.

"Quite," said Desmond. "Talented fellow."

"And my cousin once dated one of band members from Wet, Wet, Wet," Kate added. "Though long distance wasn't a good idea, as my cousin was living in the Maldives out of university term time."

"Fascinating," said Desmond, topping up their glasses with white wine. "What about you, Anna?"

She was looking out the window, arguing with herself about turfing George out of her mind.

"Sorry, Desmond, I was in my own world," she said.

"I was just saying – any connections to Scotland?"

"Rousey," she said automatically, then kicked herself.

"The Wyndhams' place?" asked Desmond.

"Yes," said Anna.

"Sad story. I used to know Robert of course and he was fun in the old days but never got over the car accident. The poor chap, he had to be cut out of the car and very nearly died."

"I didn't realise Robert was in the accident?' said Anna, sitting up.

"No, I mean the young chap, his son George. Poor fellow was with his mother – died beside him, you know – dreadful business for an eleven-year-old."

"I didn't realise he had been in the accident with her."

"Oh yes, but it didn't end there. His father was nearly shot soon after, poacher apparently, could have blown Robert's head off if he hadn't been such a bad shot."

"His hand?"

"What's that?" said Desmond.

"Was Robert shot in the hand?"

"You've obviously met him then," said Desmond.

"Briefly, yes," said Anna.

"Sad state of affairs at the house. She was a strong woman, Gussy."

"George's mother."

"Yes, too strict for Robert's appetite but as a mother she was first class. She loved that boy." Desmond shook his head. "Extraordinary story really, if you think how despite it all George has managed to thrive. It can't have been easy to have been left with the wrong parent."

"You're not a fan of Robert?" asked Anna.

Kate was following the ping-pong conversational match, watching Anna grow paler and paler as she listened to Desmond's account of George's parents.

"Look, his interest was gambling, you know, the horses – not parenting," Desmond went on. "Dreadful state of affairs for a boy who had grown up with every possible attention from his mother. But as I say, he's done well, and now is lined up with that actress Gilda recommended – Tamper? That's it, Tamper. Though not right for Spicer, isn't that right, Kate? Too spicy for the brand. Better with Lavinia, am I right?"

"Indeed you are, Desmond," said Kate, poised to change the subject. "Why don't we take a look at the media plan again over a cup of tea?"

By eight o'clock Anna arrived back to the flat on Elizabeth Street with two chilled bottles of Sancere, and within minutes she and Tilly were back on best-friend terms.

"Tills, I'm sure of it," said Anna. "It all adds up. Sofia is trying to sabotage you guys. I don't know why, but she clearly is."

Tilly's phone began to ring. "It's Jamie, what should I do?"

"Take it, Tilly, go on."

Tilly answered. "Jamie?"

"Tilly, don't hang up, it's me."

"Yes, I know it's you. What's the matter?"

"I need to let you know, just in case it puts any of the madness into context."

"To let me know what?" asked Tilly.

"It's too complicated to explain, but basically Sofia has been lying all along. The paternity test, it was all a lie."

"What paternity test? Hold on, Jamie, Anna is with me, I'm putting you on loudspeaker."

"Anna?"

"Hi, Jamie – go on, please, about the test."

"Anna, you know about the test?" said Tilly.

"George told me in Paris that Sofia is his sister."

"His *what?*" said Tilly. "That's too crazy!"

"Exactly," said Jamie, "but, more than crazy, it's completely untrue and I've got the report of the real test results to prove it."

Chapter 41

The moment George set foot in the Savoy Hotel he was set upon by a make-up artist, a wardrobe mistress and an artistic director, so relieved to see him. Sofia had been dressed since one o'clock and her temper was fraying rapidly. Meanwhile Victoria was on a long-haul flight from the States and had left specific instructions for Sofia and George to stay in the hotel that night so that they could go through the next phase of the strategy over breakfast.

In a hotel suite, George was transformed into what *Hello* deemed to be 'ideal birthday wear for the sophisticated gentleman,' and was then ushered in the direction of the ballroom by the hotel's executive manager, who was thrilled to tell George that he had just tweeted a picture of Sofia "looking ravishing" and how envious he was of George having "such a birthday present, wrapped up in a beautiful dress".

"And I'm guessing that it isn't actually your birthday today?" he went on.

"You guess right – eleven weeks early."

"I like to offer my good wishes all the same. Here at the Savoy, we are well used to long lead times at magazines. Last week we had a shoot here for a businessman's Christmas party, we even had Father Christmas landing on the roof, and fake snow machines blasting out tiny degradable bits of white paper outside the entrance, all in the name of publicity for his car-sales business. Any excuse, what?"

"Indeed," said George.

"Your stunning fiancé is awaiting you in the ballroom, George, and the clock is about to strike three o'clock. I do hope you have a fabulous afternoon of celebrations, sir, and perhaps time for *afternoon delight*," he said, with a wink.

Having been covered in make-up and dressed in a tight-fitting, turquoise suit, George was asked by the creative director to pose outside the ballroom door, as if he had no idea what was going to be on the other side. And in fact, the pose was correct, because he was not expecting to walk into a huge room packed with complete strangers dressed in the most glamorous outfits imaginable. An ABBA tribute band were on stage, singing 'Super Trouper' and as the blonde lookalike sang *"somewhere in the crowd there's you"* Sofia was guided in George's direction, cameras following her. Reaching out to George, she threw her arms around his neck. Dressed in a red flamenco dress, she beamed her smile at him and yelled into her hand-held microphone, *"Happy Birthday, George!"* as the crowd went wild. Gold and silver confetti fell from the ceiling, champagne corks popped from all corners of the room, waiters zipped from photo-extra to photo-extra who were in amazing form, as not only were they getting paid to attend a photo shoot, dressed up to look so amazing, but now they were being given free champagne.

At a drumroll, George was told to look at the double doors as a life-size silver Aston Martin cake with *Happy Birthday George* across the bonnet was carried in on a huge tray by six muscular waiters.

"It's time to blow out the candles," said Sofia, as she tugged George in the direction of the butter-cream-covered motor.

"Sofia, what the hell?"

"Smile, George!" roared the director of photography. *"Look this way! Now get ready to blow out the candles, and Sofia, you can help him. Blow together!"*

Except one of the extras got there first, having snaffled a bottle of champagne all to herself while they were waiting for George to arrive. Teetering towards George, she wanted to wish him a happy birthday directly to his handsome face. As she approached him with huge enthusiasm, she tripped in her outrageously high stilettos and went flying into the passenger door of the car, raising her backside over a mound of sponge as she sent a slab of heart-shaped icing flying onto Sofia's cleavage.

"*My dress! Look what you've done, you bloody woman!*" screamed Sofia.

George stepped forward and, reaching out his hand, he helped the young woman out of the car, her face blushing, with smatterings of butter-cream in her hair.

"I'm ever so sorry, George," she said, followed by letting out a large burp. "I got a little overexcited and wanted to give you a birthday kiss."

Taken with her honesty, and feeling so relieved to laugh, even a little, George kissed her hand.

"A real live gentleman," she said and, as George felt the heat of light bulbs with camera flashes around him, he turned around and walked towards the doors with EXIT flashing above them.

"*Where is he going?*" shouted Sofia. "*George, where the hell are you going?*"

But the magazine staff weren't sure where the Diva's temper was going either, and the familiar headline, **Temper Tamper**, came into real live action. As George walked out the door, brushing confetti from his shoulders and licking icing from his fingertips, the sound of Sofia's yelling at wardrobe to get her a new dress was becoming ever more distant. He'd had enough and was bowing out no matter what the cost.

George hadn't bothered to collect his clothes from the hotel suite before he left, and felt like apologising to the taxi driver for getting into his car wearing not only the much-too-tight turquoise suit, but also orange make-up from the photoshoot. Arriving back at his house on Cheyne Walk, the lion statues at the foot of the stairs seemed to look right at him and chastise him with memories of the first night he'd brought Anna back to the house. So long ago now, and yet only days ago he had held Anna in his arms with the chance to have her back and he blew it.

In the shower upstairs, George washed the silver Aston Martin icing out of his hair and watched as it merged with the orange make-up, swirling around his feet and down the plughole. It was a relief to be in his own bathroom, to walk into his own dressing room, to put on his own comfortable clothes again. No more skinny jeans and tight-fitting jackets. He observed how the place still looked fresh despite his prolonged sojourn in *Sofia Hell*. His housekeeper had continued to update magazines and art journals around the house, piling fresh copies of *The World Interiors* and *Country Life* on previous months' unread versions. The herbs in the kitchen had been freshly watered and, opening the fridge, George found fresh milk, Parma ham, cheese, French wine and Czech beer, all the bachelor essentials. Grabbing a bottle of beer, he popped the cap and took a long gulp.

The backlash of his walking out on the photoshoot would most likely result in Rousey being offloaded to a developer after all but, feeling demoralised and desperately alone, George was ready to throw in the towel. Walking into his study, he looked at a photograph of his mother as a debutante on the mantelpiece. The picture had been taken before she had met Robert, and the look of innocence and optimism on her face was heartbreaking when George thought of the future that had awaited her. Putting his beer to one side, he walked towards the filing box on his desk which David Collins had sent. It contained Gussy's papers. George's housekeeper had messaged to say that the package had been signed for. That was weeks ago, and since then he had been taking part in a ridiculous charade with Sofia. It must have been a panic reaction, he tried to reason with himself. How else could he have gone along with it?

Pulling off the masking tape from around the box and taking off the lid, George found an A4 envelope. Inside he found details of land rentals from the 1990s, along with a batch of envelopes with equally mundane details. His attention was piqued though, by the emergence of a cream envelope, with his name written in large letters upon it in his mother's handwriting, along with a photograph. They were tied together by a navy-blue ribbon. Untying the ribbon, George held up the photograph of a regal-looking lady in her seventies, seated in a chair with one hand elegantly placed over the other. *Granny (Florence Campbell), on the eve of her 75th Birthday,* Gussy had written on the reverse side of the photograph.

Propping the photograph of Florence up against a paperweight, George opened the envelope and pulled out a letter, written in blue ink.

Darling George,

I have no idea what age you will be when you open the box and hopefully find this letter. Perhaps you will never read it! Hoping that you do, however, there are some things I'd like to say, in case for some reason I don't have a chance to tell you when you are older.

I don't have a long list of advice for you, my darling, except that I hope one day you will fall in love, because I am sure it is the most wonderful thing in the world, and make sure, please make sure, that the person you find is kind and that what binds you together is real love. I say this because I want you to know the truth behind my marriage to your father, so that you can learn from it.

If it had not been for my money he would never have married me, and neither of our heads would have been turned. It was the done thing, for a man like him. His parents had raised him to think of the estate, the future of the land, but not of his heart. He is not a bad man but the traditions of his world have not become him, instead they have made him bitter and as I write this I wonder how much longer we can pretend to be man and wife. But, I do not regret my marriage, George, because otherwise I would never have been blessed with you, my darling boy. You are only eight years old as I write this letter, and this morning I stood at the foot of your favourite tree, the mulberry, at the front of Rousey, and I watched you climb all the way to the top. You looked so happy and pleased with yourself. I will remember your delightful, delighted face at the top of that tree for all my life and beyond.

Your ever-loving Mother

Holding the letter, tears welled in George's eyes as he felt overwhelming sadness for what his mother had gone through. It had all been for nothing. His father had tried to secure Rousey for generations to come but now the place was out of all their hands and George left with a feeling of complete emptiness. Pressing his sleeve against his eyes and trying not to cry out loud, he read on.

PS Beneath the papers, please find a black velvet ring box. The ring belonged to my grandmother, your great-grandmother, Florence, who told me that the colour green represents growth, patience and healing. I truly hope this ring can help you where needed, my darling.

Finding a small box submerged beneath letters and newspaper clippings, George eased open the lid to behold a gorgeous green diamond, cut as a rectangle, and set within a circle of small pink diamonds. It was breathtaking.

Putting the ring back in its box, George mourned the loss of his wonderful loving mother. She had been snatched away and he had been left with an uncaring father.

George found his memory racing back to an autumnal morning when he had ventured out for a walk with his father. It had been a week since his mother had died, and Robert had announced to George that he was to be sent away to boarding school. George remembered being convinced that his father was sending him away so that he could continue his affair with the woman by the river. George had only seen them together once, but the memory of their naked bodies on the river bank had made him despise his father. Robert, hungover and still in shock from his wife's death, had left his twelve-bore shotgun unbroken by a fence, while he took a pee. The gun weighed so much that George's legs wobbled as he lifted it up and he was still stumbling when he turned it on his father. His finger hovered over the trigger, and then the boom. The butt slammed into George's shoulder with such velocity that he dropped the gun and nearly fell over, but turning mid-fall he ran away. He didn't look back to see his father but kept running until he reached the kitchen where Grace was preparing lunch. George said nothing to her and passed off his breathlessness as being because he had run across the fields. While George ate a piece of chocolate cake, he shook inside, assuming he had killed his father. It wasn't until that evening that Robert returned to this house, with his hand heavily bandaged, announcing to Grace that a poacher had taken a shot at him but had only grazed the side of his hand. Only a scratch, he said, looking at George with unwavering dominance.

George's phone vibrated in his pocket.

"Jamie?" he said, putting the phone on loudspeaker.

"George?"

"It's been a while."

"I know what's been going on. About the engagement."

"How?"

"It doesn't matter and right now I need you to listen."

"Okay, but –"

"Sofia is flying back to Rousey this evening. I've just spoken with my new friend, Royston."

"The butler? Jamie, what's going on?"

"George, you've kept me out for long enough. It's time to put things right."

"How? Legally I haven't got a leg to stand on."

"That's why you are not in law, George. Every stone, remember? You didn't turn every one. You should have bloody well asked me for help from the start."

"I know. But when the DNA results proved that Sofia really is my sister –"

"Can you arrange a helicopter? If we leave in the next couple of hours, we can be at Rousey by ten."

"Yes, of course, but why?"

Chapter 42

In Sofia's bedroom at Rousey, Ruby squeezed half a lemon into a tall glass, threw in a sugar cube, two shots of vodka and a splash of Pellegrino. she held the glass up to the bedside lamp, watching the sugar lump slowly disintegrate before passing it to Sofia.

"Do you feel any better now that you've washed the icing out of your hair?"

"A little," mumbled Sofia, taking a large sip from the glass.

Sofia was unnerved that Victoria hadn't called to blast her out of the water for having lost her cool yet again, in front of a mass of people, including the magazine's editor, and for leaving straight for Heathrow instead of staying put as instructed. The situation was serious. If George didn't return Sofia knew she would be faced with questions from the media and if he so much as hinted that the engagement had been a sham, the backlash on her reputation would be major – the press never liked being lied to.

With only ten days to go until she had to be in Ohio for the first wave of filming for *Violet Tiger*, she had never felt less ready for anything.

"I can't wait to get back to LA, you know?" said Ruby. "And I can fly into Cleveland at the weekends."

"Sorry, what's that?" said Sofia.

"When you're in Ohio? It's only for eight weeks, though I guess the filming schedule could be extended. We can run through the script again if you like? Just to get you comfortable for the first scene."

"Remember when we found the Miner's Lettuce last summer?" said Sofia, who hadn't been listening. "And we said if we ever got stranded in the hills above LA we could eat it?"

"Are you getting sentimental on me, Miss Tamper?"

Sofia mustered a smile and, putting her drink on the side table, she pulled off her T-shirt and got into bed.

"Maybe I could ditch interiors and become a herbalist – you know, back to nature, hiking at the weekends?" said Ruby, slipping between the sheets.

"You know what? I'd love to be able to sit back and trust that everything happens for a reason," said Sofia.

"Have you been reading those self-help books again?"

"Seriously though. All the hassle about this place – I almost feel like I've got to the point where I don't want to own anything any more. Just to have the freedom, to be myself … and to be with you." Smoothing her finger over Ruby's eyebrows, Sofia gave her a tender kiss and then turned over.

"And, remind me, you're going to tell your mom about us in what century?"

"I need to wait and see how this plays out. Okay, Ruby? I can't commit to anything right now. You know that, don't you? I'm sorry, honey, but that's the way it is. And now I need to sleep."

Ruby was just reaching for her magazine when Sofia's hand stretched out and flicked off the bedside lamp.

"Sofia," whispered Ruby urgently.

"*Shhhh* – let me sleep."

"Sofia," said Ruby, sitting up and switching on the light, "I can hear footsteps."

"It's probably Royston, or one of his creepy early-morning cleaners."

"No, Sofia, I'm serious. Listen."

And as the creaking floorboards got closer, Sofia grabbed her phone. "Okay, tell me – what is the emergency number in the UK?" she said calmly.

"999 for Scotland," said Ruby, her voice genuinely scared.

As Sofia dialled the numbers, the door inched open and the girls both shrieked.

"Hello, Emergency Services?" said a voice on the phone, but Sofia cancelled the call. George stepped into the room, followed by another familiar face.

"Good evening, ladies," said Jamie. "Shall we, George?"

The two men walked over to a sofa that occupied the window of Sofia's bedroom and sat down.

"*What are you doing here?*" screamed Sofia, mascara smudged around her eyes, pulling the sheet up to her chin.

Ruby put her hand on Sofia's shoulder.

"Don't touch me!" she snarled, prompting Ruby to slide out of the bed.

George and Jamie instinctively turned away.

"So you'll break into my house in the middle of the night, but then you feel shy seeing Ruby naked?" said Sofia. "Double standards, don't you think, boys? And I thought you liked seeing lots of naked women at once, Jamie?"

Ruby pulled on her pants and a T-shirt and then looked over at the men. "You can look now, gentleman," she said, but there was no trace of humour in her voice. "Hey, Sofia, they're all yours. And, for what it's worth, I don't think I can take much more of your screwed-up family."

"Ruby, please don't leave!" said Sofia. "I mean it – I need you here with me."

Ruby hesitated then, relenting, climbed back onto the bed and folded her arms. "Well, I guess I can't really leave you here with Starsky and Hutch, now can I?"

"And what are you looking at, brother darling?" said Sofia, picking up the virtually untouched vodka next to her bed and drinking it down in one.

"The show is over, Sofia," said George calmly, rising to his feet. "Jamie has been to see your father."

"In Geneva?" she said.

"No, Sofia, not Robert," said Jamie, walking to the foot of the bed and leaning against the bedpost. "Your father who art in prison."

"*Shut up!*" Sofia yelled, looking frightened.

"Max is your father, Sofia," said George. "I've got the results of a sanctioned paternity test right here."

"Sanctioned by whom?" she spat.

"By your father," said Jamie.

"You mean Robert?"

"No, he's means Max," said George. "Your father is Max, and as soon as my father learns the truth he is going to hold on tight to this place."

"But Mom told me," she said, tears streaming down her face like a little girl. "She swore to me that Robert is my father. I don't understand what you're saying."

Jamie watched as Sofia fell to pieces and tried to work out whether she believed her own lies or maybe, he began to think, those were her mother's lies. Maybe Sofia had no idea about Blaire getting the DNA sample from Max in prison.

"Mom told me when I was little that my real father was a big country gent, a sort of lord of the manor," said Sofia, her body shaking. "He abandoned Mom because she was a *local girl*. Mom said that one day she'd get the big house, and his land, she'd get it all back for me." Sofia looked at Ruby. "I believed her. Why wouldn't I? She's my mom."

"You knew all along, didn't you?" said George, scathingly. "All the flirting and innuendo, and your hideous arrogance towards Anna. You couldn't bear to see another girl being accepted into your fake bloody high society, could you? But why did you have to try and ruin my life, and hers?"

"No, George, I swear it, I didn't know," said Sofia. "The engagement wasn't my idea. Mom and Victoria, they thought it would boost my career and they were right. It kind of has." Her eyes were alarmed as she fought her corner. "Victoria said I'd narrow my fan base if the truth got out about me and Ruby." She looked at Ruby. "I'm sorry, honey, that's what she said."

"It was a set-up," said George, standing next to Jamie. "Blaire paid off the nurse who took the DNA samples. The signatures, everything was forged. Max's sample was swapped for Robert's – that's how Blaire managed to 'prove' the paternity."

"No, you're wrong!" said Sofia. "She would never have lied to me like that."

"This ends now, Sofia," said George, regaining his composure. "You are not a Wyndham, we are not related and you are most assuredly *not* my fiancée."

Sofia crouched in the corner of the four-poster, the bed-tassels jostling as she shook. "You don't understand my mother," she cried. "What she wants for me is not what I want. Nobody knows what I want. Ruby is the only person who really gets me."

"And I totally get you," said Ruby.

Wiping her eyes, Sofia tried to pull herself together. "Let me speak to Anna. If I explain to her, she'll understand. I'll apologise."

"You will not go near Anna," said George, his voice slow and cold. "You've done enough. We have all done enough to her."

George could see the edge of Sofia's collarbone, so thin now. Her eyes had huge shadows beneath them and a cold sore was beginning to show on her lower lip.

"And don't you dare look for sympathy," he said. "You can blame your family all you want but, guess what, we can all do that. It's the easy way out. My mother dying, your father in jail. Life happens, Sofia. It punches us and twists us inside out. Now, I want you out of this house at first light, so set your alarm and book yourself a taxi."

At which point Royston appeared in the doorway, perfectly turned out, his short hair gleaming with freshly applied hair tonic.

"Can I fix anyone a drink, or a late-night mug of cocoa?"

Chapter 43

Sitting behind reception at Winterbottom PR HQ, Chrissy had spent most of the day on the phone to the Ritz Paris, trying to sort out the temperature of the ballroom with the events manager so that celebrated chocolatier Patrick Roger's eye-popping display of an edible reconstruction of a thistle wouldn't melt during the Spicer Tweed launch.

Looking at the large bowl of chocolates that Gilda insisted on keeping next to an over-the-top flower arrangement, Chrissy decided she'd had enough sweet talk for one day.

Then Gilda fell in the door with a suitcase and a bag of duty free.

"Hello, darling, so wet out, raining kittens and puppies as the children like to say!" Taking off her grey felt trilby with bright pink lining, she threw it onto the hat rack. "Not a bad throw," she said, as the hat caught safely onto a hook. "Perhaps I should consider putting myself forward for the role of M in *James Bond*?"

"Good flight?" asked Chrissy.

"Dreadful airhostess, no sense of style and terribly tight with pretzels," said Gilda. "Is Kate here? And what about Anna? I gather from Desmond they had a nice tête-à-tête the day Anna flew back."

"Gilda, it's Saturday night. I think Anna has flown to Ireland for the weekend, and Kate is on her way to the theatre, I think."

Chrissy had watched Gilda build her empire as account executives came and went and directors stayed until they could no longer manage child care and husbands' demands. She had been with Gilda for every new business preparation – late nights, early mornings, all whilst fielding calls from the press and client demands – but tonight, all she wanted to do tonight was curl up in front of the television with taramasalata on toast.

"Keep me company, won't you, darling?" said Gilda. "I'm really not in the mood for being alone."

Turning on the lights of her office, Gilda found a bag of pistachios on her desk. Tearing open the packet, she spilled them into a Thermidor International lobster-shaped Post-it-note holder.

"I must try to spend more time with the children, darling. I promised Cresta that I'd take them to the theatre when I got back from Paris. She's become very grown-up, well, for a six-year-old – she's going to simply adore the little dress I bought in Le Bon Marché."

"She'll be thrilled."

"I'm going to try to Skype Orlando in school," said Gilda, pointing a remote control towards the white screen on the wall. "Isn't this genius, Chrissy? All I have to do is press this teeny button and he should pop right up."

"Gilda, I'm not sure about that," said Chrissy, the voice of wisdom. "Won't you get Orlando in trouble? It's must be nearly time for lights out."

"Oh, all right," sulked Gilda.

"Aren't you taking Orlando out tomorrow, being a Sunday?"

"Yes, but I don't want to wait until then," said Gilda. "Mother is doing a fine job, helping me with Cresta, but I feel Orlando is missing out. I'm just not sure about boarding school at such a young age. I keep thinking of the duvet slipping off his bed in the middle of the night, and thinking I should be the one to lift it back over him, the little sweetheart."

Chrissy had watched Gilda run from meeting to drinks party and back to a meeting and then playing mother for the past few years or more, and she could see it was weighing hard.

"Chrissy darling, I've been thinking," said Gilda, trying to jazz herself up. "Do you think it might be worth my auditioning for *Strictly?*"

"Oh, I don't know, Gilda – it would be a big time commitment?"

"But think of the publicity, darling. All those potential Winterbottom PR clients, tuning in, seeing me spin across the dance floor – and I could name-drop brands during the interviews afterwards. Worth a shot, do you think?"

"Maybe?" said Chrissy, trying to sound enthusiastic but knowing it was a lame attempt.

"Well then, how about we open a bottle of Bolli?"

"Sorry, Gilda, Bryan is away and the kids are heading out so I've got to get home first to lay down the curfew law."

"All right then, I might just meditate for a moment – Anna's mother gave me some excellent tips in Paris. Won't be long. I'll just close the door to keep the meditation vibes in the room."

Closing down her computer for the night, Chrissy heard the sound of an umbrella closing and a coat being shaken out from the back entrance to the office. Her heart lightened, hoping some kind of cavalry might have arrived for Gilda.

And, peeking his head around the door into reception, there was Adrian.

"Sorry to disturb," he said, as he came in with a navy trench coat over his arm, holding a bottle of red wine and a Chinese takeaway from Gilda's favourite place in Parson's Green. "Is she in?"

"This is unexpected," said Chrissy, tucking wisps of her hair behind her ears. "She's actually just closed her office door."

"Oh, I see."

"She's trying to meditate," said Chrissy, "though I wouldn't be surprised if she doesn't pop a cork before she gets cross-legged. I'll leave you to it, shall I?"

Picking up her car keys and worn-out travel coffee mug, she switched off the light at her desk and left with her black umbrella.

Knocking on the door of Gilda's office, Adrian turned the handle and found her sitting at her desk.

"Gilda? I called to the house but you weren't there – obviously, because you're here," he said with a smile.

"I'm terribly busy," said Gilda, who had clearly been crying.

"I received a message from Orlando, I'm afraid, and Cresta got on your mother's phone."

"Naughty little noodles," said Gilda, mustering a smile.

"I read a really good feature about you last month. It sounds like the business is really booming?"

Gilda didn't react.

Walking over to the coffee table, Adrian put down the bag of Chinese and the bottle of wine.

"I'm just back from Paris," she said, trying to show strength. "Lavinia de Vere Parker would only agree to the launch party next month if we booked her into her favourite suite at the Ritz, which of course is almost always booked out, even at €16,000 per night."

"Really?" said Adrian, watching her closely.

"Luckily I had done the hotel manager a favour during the Millennium when he needed to get his hands on a bespoke set of tyres for a Rolls Royce. Remember, when I had the account for Rolls Royce?"

"I do," said Adrian.

"And a prize guest had rather publicly called it time on his relationship and his freshly axed girlfriend proceeded to take revenge by arising from the dining table and, brandishing her steak knife, striding outside like a cheetah to a white convertible Rolls Royce and proceeding to stab her steak knife through each tyre. Can you imagine? So I arranged for the warehouse to open up on a Sunday night and for the tyres to be couriered at speed to the Ritz."

"Problem equals solution, it's how you operate," he said kindly, wishing she would stop talking, if only for a moment.

"I try ... but it doesn't always work, does it?" she said, as their eyes met.

"The children say they miss me, Gilda," he said.

Gilda, not knowing what to say, reached for a Helloo Roll, pulling out sheets from a neat gold promotional pack. "I'm so sorry," she said. "I've made a mess of everything, haven't I?"

"I think we both have," said Adrian.

"Mum always talked about giving us roots and wings. You know, roots at home and wings to fly the world, and she did it. I'm afraid I'm not doing the same for our children, even though they are only small now, but they won't always be. And I'm afraid of being lonely, Adrian. I know it looks like I am around people all day, but so little of it is real."

"I was never in love with Sara, you know."

But Gilda wasn't listening and rambled on. "I've sweated blood for this place, but I'm just not sure it's worth it," she whispered, her wrists against her forehead. "I seem to have trained myself into believing everything that comes out of my mouth, but I am terrified that I am looking for the shine I had when it all began, when Winterbottom really became something, and I just can't find it, I can't get it back. That shine."

"You've still got fire in your belly, Gilda. I know it."

"Do I?"

Adrian took off his tortoiseshell glasses. "You have created all of this, don't you see? Look around you. People love you, Gilda. Your energy, your enthusiasm, your downright stubbornness that you are going to secure a client no matter what."

"Oh poppycock!" she said – a word she hadn't used in a long time, giving her a flashback to days when she used to say it, the days when she and Adrian played tennis together, when life was uncomplicated, when she wasn't so obsessed. And now, here she was, using the word again, with Adrian in her office with Chinese food, a cuisine Hans could never bear.

"Gilda, I still love you," said Adrian, quietly.

"What, what's that?"

"I'd like us to try again," he said, and walking over to her, he gave her the first proper hug that she'd had in a very long time.

Chapter 44

While the kettle boiled, Victoria took refuge behind her desk in her flat and worked on a draft statement she was preparing for the media. She had no idea whether or not George would set things straight with the press, so she had to prepare a response that would cover all bases. As her fingers lightly tapped the keys, she glanced up at Sofia and was struck by how remarkably vulnerable she looked without make-up.

Slumped on an armchair, Sofia put her head in her hands.

"I love her, Victoria," she said. "Ruby and I are made for each other. I am sure of it but how can I make Mom understand?"

"I'm not sure, honey. Not right now. But work with me and we'll find the answer. You've just got to keep a cool head. There is no point screaming at your mother because she will bite you back twice as hard, you know that."

Sofia smiled. "Tell me where the tea bags are and I'll break the habit of a lifetime and make a pot of English tea."

A couple of hours later, Blaire arrived through the door like a tornado, without so much as a hello to either her daughter or her agent.

"Victoria, do you have any alcohol?"

"I have some beer."

"Fine, pour me a glass," she said. "I can sweat it out in a sauna on Monday."

And then turning to Sofia, she began to talk in her mother-knows-best voice.

"So, now you know, Sofia."

"That you're a lying cheat? Yes, that I do know," said Sofia calmly.

"No, I mean that now you know that you will lose everything we've worked for if you go ahead with this absurdness, and don't you dare give me that look! You know perfectly well what I'm referring to. Victoria told me of your scheme to – I can hardly bring myself to say it – to come out."

"Sorry, Sofia, I had to spill," said Victoria, "I emailed your mom when I got your voicemail. If we don't keep our lines of communication open there is no way we can send out a clear message."

"Horseshit," said Sofia, standing up, while Blaire leaned against a small radiator. "This isn't about me, Mom. You just can't stand the thought of having a daughter who is gay."

"That's unfair and untrue," said Blaire, who staggered towards an armchair and sat down. "I've given you every possible shot at the American dream, Sofia, but now it appears to be fading with every passing second."

"What is it?" said Sofia, as Blaire began rubbing her temples.

Sofia and Victoria looked at each other.

"I'm fine," Blaire said. "It's a migraine, nothing more. Where's that beer?"

Victoria went over to the fridge freezer and, pulling out an icepack, she offered it to Blaire.

"Here, put this on your head while I get the beer."

"Thank you, Victoria," said Blaire, "how kind," but instead of putting the icepack on her head, she hurled it against the wall, knocking down a framed cover print of *The New Yorker*.

"Hey, watch my stuff!" shouted Victoria.

"Damn it, Sofia, why did you have to make this so complicated?" said Blaire, ignoring Victoria. "There are a million very handsome, very glamorous men who would give a year's salary just to spend a night with you. Good-looking men who will give your career just the boost it needs, even if precious George-bloody-Wyndham won't. Let me tell you, Sofia, if you carry on this nonsense with Ruby, your chances of making it big in Hollywood are dead as a doornail. Please tell me this is just some exploratory phase, honey?" Blaire's eyes looked desperate, like Goya's drowning dog, a frightful picture of helplessness and despair.

"Mom, what do I have to do to make you understand that I am totally serious about Ruby?"

"Oh God, it's worse than I thought. Can't you see that this just isn't good for you? It isn't right for you."

"Yes, it is, Mom. It's very right for me. I love her."

"I want you to think very, very carefully, Sofia. How many times have I told you that Hollywood is one of the most conservative industries in the world. Oh yes, everyone can act all liberal and open but they simply do not like their actors to go against the grain. You do so at you peril – when you go to events, someone will say, 'Just B-roll her – just let the cameras roll as she walks by', no more interviews, no more perks, Sofia. And Hollywood certainly doesn't do lesbians. How many leading ladies have come out since Ellen DeGeneres and whatshername from *Top Gun*? You can practically list them on one hand."

"Don't blame this on Hollywood, Mom!" said Sofia. "You know as well as I do that this has got nothing to do with my career. For crying out loud, I've only got a small part in a TV series!"

"Small steps, sweetie, small steps," said Blaire, trying to wriggle out of the ever-widening hole she was now sitting in.

"You are kicking up because I am your only ticket to money and success. That is your only interest, Mom. You are ruthless and you won't stop until … I don't know when you'd stop. You lied about my father. My father! Who would do that? What mother would actually do that to her child?"

"Don't be so goddamn impertinent. After everything your father and I've done for you, I've never felt so betrayed."

"Betrayed! Oh, don't be so melodramatic! Hell, Mother, I don't know whether I should be looking towards Geneva or Cell Block H when you say 'your father'."

Victoria was contemplating whether this was the moment to

introduce Sofia's draft statement, but watching the way Blaire began icily picking at her fingernails, she decided to remain quiet for a while longer.

"*Violet Tiger* is your big chance, Sofia," said Blaire. "Television is huge, it's the new focus, it's on demand, you mustn't blow it."

"Mom, you need to open your mind. We live in a world with gay prime ministers and gay pop stars. What's the difference between them and a gay actor?"

Blaire wasn't ready to throw in the towel. "The dollars, Sofia. The dollars are the bloody difference. If you want to play the game, you have to play it straight."

Victoria found herself becoming ever more supportive of Sofia. It was time she did what was best for the girl, not what her mother demanded. She passed her iPad to Sofia.

"What's that?" said Blaire.

"A draft of Sofia's statement."

"Pass it to me," ordered Blaire.

"Not this time, Blaire. This is Sofia's business. She's a big girl and she'll have to make this decision without her mommy for a change."

Buoyed by this unexpected show of support, Sofia gave Victoria a little smile and began to read aloud.

"'I've had enough with the make-believe aspects of my life,' says Sofia, from London this evening. "While my engagement to George Wyndham was a well-intentioned attempt to tame my wild side, George and I know that we both have to stay true to the people we really love, and so we have parted ways. I'd like to thank George for his friendship, understanding and willingness to help me reach this conclusion. Now it is time for me to say goodbye to Scotland and to embark upon a new life with my partner, Ruby Blake, who is a talented set designer well-known upon the boards of Broadway. I am ready to be a true actress, versatile, ambitious and always ready for the next challenge. The world has only had a small glimpse of my talents to date, but keep watching, because I'm only just warming up.'"

As Sofia finished, Victoria looked from mother to daughter and back again.

"And you will go where exactly?" said Blaire, her voice little more than a rasp.

"Well, I'm still going to give *Violet Tiger* a shot," said Sofia. "Victoria has been in touch with EXR and they are still game on, even having read my draft statement."

"In fact, one of the producers thinks it might give the film just the publicity it needs," said Victoria. "Even Disney's gone lesbian these days. And as to where Sofia will live, I gather that Ruby has a rather fine base in LA for them both."

"Yes, it's gorgeous," said Sophia. "Right up in the hills over LA. She flew out this morning. In fact, she should be arriving there any time around now."

"And what about me?" said Blaire. "You have thrown me out of the hot air balloon without so much as a bloody parachute. How am I going to explain this to Robert? He will be devastated."

The doorbell rang. Victoria got up and looked through the spyhole. She was not expecting to see two policewomen waiting the other side of the door.

"Holy shit, Sofia, what's going on?" she asked.

Sofia and Blaire looked at each other as Victoria opened the door.

Two policewomen walked in.

"Good evening, ladies," said the first policewoman. "Apologies for the lack of notice but we're seeking the whereabouts of a Mrs Blaire Tamper and we're given to understand she might be here?"

Blaire's face froze as Sofia turned to look at her.

"Mom?"

"Blaire Tamper?"

"Yes," said Blaire, visibly paling with every passing second.

"I am arresting you on suspicion of fraud. You do not have to say anything but please note that anything you do say may be given in evidence against you."

"Mom?"

"Your father's work," muttered Blaire.

"He wouldn't," said Sofia.

"Well, it looks like he bloody well has. Unless this is something to do with Robert?" Turning to the policewomen, she smiled. "I'd like to call my lawyer."

"You'll get your phone call at the station, Mrs Tamper," replied the second policewomen, taking Blaire by the arm.

"Just one thing," said Blaire, looking at Victoria. "Please don't let her release that statement. It will ruin her."

As Blaire and the policewomen walked out the door, Victoria and Sofia shook their heads in stunned silence.

"Did that just happen?" said Victoria. "Did my mom just get arrested?"

"Do you know what, Sofia? It's been a very long day. I think I'm going to make a call to the Landmark Hotel and order supper, including a bottle of Merlot."

"They do take-out?" said Sofia.

"No, not officially, but the hotel is a sometimes client of mine, and so it's one of the perks of living around the corner," said Victoria, sitting down behind her desk. "And now, we've got to issue your statement and fast – there's no telling what will follow once news breaks about Blaire."

Chapter 45

The plane from Heathrow had arrived into Dublin airport in clear blue skies and sunshine, but dark clouds were rapidly forming by the time George had picked up his hire car and started to drive north through the intense greens of the Irish countryside. Over and over again he thought about what he had put Anna through, of the nights they had spent together in London, Ayrshire, Paris and here in Ireland. Never in a million years could he have imagined dragging her into such a complex tangle of events. Logic kept telling him to let her go but, in his heart, he could not. He needed to see her again, even if it meant hearing her ask him to leave again.

"And she has every right to tell you to get lost, George," Tilly had told him the night before, when he dropped Jamie home to London. Her fury had marginally reduced since learning that Sofia had been the root cause of his atrocious decisions and having received an email from Ruby profusely apologising for the photograph stunt with Jamie, swearing that Jamie had passed out and that nothing had happened.

George had asked David Collins to fly out to Geneva and explain Blaire's fraudulence. He would make contact with Robert himself, but for now Anna had to be the priority.

Turning into the gates of Farley Hall, George's heart tightened as he saw a familiar BMW driving down the avenue towards him. As it approached he saw Freddie behind the wheel, with Harry sitting beside her, and someone else on the back seat. Was it Anna? He inhaled deeply and pulled into the verge.

The car slowed as it passed and then, as Freddie recognised him, she pulled up and buzzed down the car window.

"George Wyndham," said Freddie, with an exhausted sigh.

"Hello, Freddie ... and Harry," said George, turning off the engine. He glanced again at the back seat and his heart turned again when he realised it was not Anna but his Tamil-speaking friend Dharma. He got out of the car and walked over to the BMW, his head bowed.

"George Wyndham," Freddie repeated. She was longing to curse him but his sorrow was so evident that she couldn't restrain the tenderness she felt for him. "Thank you for your letter, George. It was good of you to write."

George bent and looked into the car. "Hello, Harry."

"George," said Harry, looking the other way, and then he suddenly got out of the car and walked around it towards him. "I may not be a big man, and I sure as hell am not a strong man at the moment, but I could wring your bloody neck for what you've put our daughter through."

"I understand," said George, holding his ground, his head still bowed.

Harry looked up at the sky and shook his head.

"However, I am a believer in second chances."

"Thank you, Harry."

"No, George, don't thank me. I said, *I* believe in second chances – that doesn't mean that Anna does."

"Presumably you're here to see her?" said Freddie, who had opened her door when her husband got out but quickly deduced that there would be no boxing match this afternoon.

"Yes," said George. "Is she here?"

"Does she know you're coming?"

"No."

"Oh. God. I don't know, George. I don't know where she is. I haven't seen her since this morning. I've been deep in yoga and Harry has been dabbling with the paintbrush, haven't you, my darling? And now we're racing to the airport to get Dharma to London to join his new client."

"I don't want to hold you up," said George. "Good afternoon, Dharma."

"Hello, George," said Dharma. "It is good to see you."

George turned back to Harry. "You're painting again?"

"The new improved me, George," replied Harry, with a flash of the friendliness that George had valued so much on his first visit to Farley.

"I am so sorry," George said. "I know I seriously messed up and I'm just so sorry for everything."

"Look, we can't speak for Anna," said Harry, "but if you mean it and if you are truly, really, prepared to make amends, then I think Freddie and I would both agree that it is worth a try." He got back into the car.

"I wholly agree," said Freddie. "In fact, I actually had it in mind to discuss you and Anna at length with Harry while he and I drove back from the airport later this evening. So you've rather preempted me on that front, young man. Mrs B is up at the house though – watch out for her, she wants you crucified. But if anyone knows where Anna is, she will. You'll find her in the kitchen, no doubt adding more dollops of butter to the batch of apple pies she's concocting. Harry has to 'lay off' the butter, of course, doctor's orders, but Mrs B has never been a great one for doctors."

"They still allow me my claret, though, George," added Harry.

George smiled and stood silently for a moment. "I don't want to keep you," he said then. "There was a lot of rain on the way up so I don't know if that will affect your journey."

"We'll be fine. Thank you, George. Goodbye – and good luck."

As he watched the BMW disappear down the drive, George got into the car and felt his heart palpitating. So Anna was here, somewhere, and now it was just going to be him and her. And Mrs B. Driving up the avenue, he tried to keep his speed down. Puffballs of grey clouds flashed across the skies above the house. With autumn on the way, the place was looking magnificent. Periwinkle and dog-rose tumbled beneath the basement windows while honeysuckle towered over an old granite trough full of fading mint near the front door.

He parked and walked towards the house, then heard a loud shout followed by what sounded like falling stones from the yard.

Running into the yard, he found Bernard up a ladder, where he was yanking ivy from a gutter running along the old coach house.

"Hello, Bernard," said George.

Bernard glared down at him and said nothing for a while.

"So. Back again, are you? Well, while you're standing there gawping you may as well make yourself useful and hold the ladder and maybe save me from breaking my neck."

George pressed his boots against both feet of the ladder, hoping he would not be kept in this position for too long. The rain began to spit again as he stood and watched Bernard roughly pulling at the tangled strands of ivy and nettles that had meshed into the gutter. Bernard flung them behind him as he worked and whether he was aware or not that the bulk of this wet, earthy debris was landing on George was unclear. It took five minutes for him to clear the gutter and, as the last clump of wet nettle roots ricocheted off George's shoulder, he looked down and grinned.

"What was it Oscar Wilde said? *We're all in the gutter, but some of us are looking at the stars.*"

"Where is Penthouse?" asked George, when Bernard was safely down. The stable was empty and he wondered if Anna was out riding.

"Up in the windmill field. Spending the summer out on grass. It's what he needs, keeps his condition up. Been there a week or more now – quiet in the yard without him though."

"And do you know where Anna is?"

"No, I do not know where Anna is, young man, and I am not sure I would be telling you even if I did. You can go into the kitchen and ask Mrs B."

George walked quickly through the kitchen yard, anticipating Anna at any moment. He carefully wiped his shoes on the mat and then inched his way around the kitchen door to find Mrs B rubbing large knobs of butter into a bowl of flour with her fingertips.

She looked up at him and, just like Bernard, she said nothing but plucked up a knife and began stirring cold water into the bowl to bind the mixture together.

"Hello, Mrs B," said George. "It's good to see you."

She moved the bowl from one part of the table to another, angrily and probably unnecessarily.

"I'm sure you must be wondering why I'm here." He was slightly out of breath, his heart thumping with nerves and a sense of urgency to find Anna. "I wonder if you can tell me where Anna is? I have something very important to say to her. Mrs Rose said I should find you and that you'd know."

"She did, did she? Well, Master Wyndham, you can sit down there a moment because I have a few *important* things to say to you."

George was longing to find Anna but he knew better than to brush off a woman of Mrs B's calibre and he dutifully pulled out a chair and sat down, feeling strangely like a schoolboy in detention.

"Now I won't lie," said Mrs B, her voice emotional. "I just won't lie. I don't know if I can even look at you straight, George, but you can just sit there and listen to me. You can't come waltzing in here with your city-slicker ways and expect everyone to run at the same pace as yourself. There's been enough of that fastness and stupidity and lies and I won't have it, I tell you. I won't stand for it." She slammed the dough onto the wooden table with a loud bang that made George jump. "That Aga is oftentimes smothered in Mr Rose's socks, you know?" she said. There were traces of flour on her cheeks. "All kinds of colourful socks – funny socks and spotty socks and big thick woolly socks and some very smart ones too."

George smiled. Mrs B was never one for staying on topic for any great length of time. He caught her eye and the unfeigned sadness behind his smile softened her a little as she worked the dough into a ball. She wanted to hurl the dough right into his face. She felt so mad with him but what riled her more than anything was that from the moment she saw him in the doorway, she knew that he and Anna were completely right for each other. The look in his dark eyes confirmed it. He had come back for Anna and that was something she was prepared to give him credit for. He was also such a good-looking boy, not an easy face to stay cross at for long.

"Pass me some of those apples, will you?"

Choosing four brambly apples from the basket, George cautiously passed them over, half expecting her to stone him with them. She set the apples down and began peeling them.

George's eyes ran over the familiar photographs blue-tacked onto the kitchen cupboards. Harry making a toast at a party, Anna hunting on a muddy Shetland pony – she couldn't have been more than five. Freddie and Harry, both beaming with happiness, standing beneath the Great Wall of China, no doubt on one of their adventures with Sheikh Nadeem.

"I was twenty-three years of age when I first came here," said Mrs B, as her thumb worked the apple-peeler. "Anna was born some years after I arrived. Through that window I watched her taking her first steps. A cold December day, and up she gets off her wee bum and starts walking towards her dad, just like that. Bonny as they come, all golden curls and dimple smiles and oh, how her daddy loved her!"

It was torturous, thought George, being here in Anna's kitchen, listening to Mrs B, seeing all these photographs of Anna looking so happy and carefree and loved. He had lost her. And yet he was now here in her heartland, with an opportunity to at least try to explain, to tell her how he felt.

"How is she?" he asked.

"Very tired, George." said Mrs B, dusting the table and rolling pin with flour before dividing the pastry dough in two. "She's tired and worn out. She ate nothing at all in France by the look of her. Mr and Mrs Rose have raised that girl to respect everyone, from all walks of people. No matter where they come from or how many or how few coins someone has jangling in their purse. Money never impressed any one of them." Carefully Mrs B rolled the pastry flat and, picking it up, she eased it into a dish. "When I think of all the people we've had in this kitchen over the years, and Anna always the heart and soul of them. Never batting an eyelid as to what letters or titles came before or after anyone's name. That was how she was raised." Mrs B looked at George sternly and, taking a long breath, she put down the knife. "You gave her a terrible knock, George, and I'd be fibbing if I thought your chances of bringing her back to you were any better than slim to none. I think you might have just gone too far. You can understand?'

"I know. Yes. I know," said George, rubbing his hands over his knees. "What I've put her through is ... unforgivable."

Mrs B didn't say a word.

"Will you tell me where she is, Mrs B?"

"Well, I can tell you she's not here, George."

George's face crumpled.

"But I can also tell you that she is not a million miles away."

"Please, Mrs B, I need to know," he whispered.

Taking off her apron, Mrs B slid open the French windows onto the kitchen garden to let in some air. "I can't mind-read but I know that at heart you're a good man. Having said that, take this as your last warning. Anna is the closest thing I'll ever have to a daughter. You've hurt her once, very badly, and I want you to promise me here and now that you won't ever do that again. And if she says that you're to leave and that she doesn't want to see you, you're to go on and leave her in peace?"

"It's a promise, Mrs B," said George.

Anna was walking through the field, with a head collar in one hand and a handful of wild grass in the other. It felt so good to be back at Farley again, even with the cold autumnal raindrops falling. Looking up at the house, she saw a figure walking down the avenue towards her. She froze on the spot, instantly knowing whom it was as the person clambered over the post and rails into the meadow and began to walk towards her. She stood motionless, unsure whether to run in the opposite direction or stand her ground and hear him out.

When he came to a halt in front of her, she couldn't look at him.

"Tilly said she called you," said George, "to let you know about the ridiculous photos Sofia sent."

Anna said nothing.

"And about the test," added George, breaking the silence.

"Yes, she called me," said Anna, looking at the ground.

"I know that leaving you in Paris that morning was unforgivable. It must have seemed so bloody weak to you. I just didn't know what Sofia was going to do next. That photo she had of Jamie and the cocaine threw me off track. I know it was out of date but Sofia might have destroyed his career. I had to do what I could to protect him."

"You could have simply told me everything, George," whispered

Anna. "I don't understand why you didn't. What was I supposed to think?"

"I know Anna, I've been over it a million times in my head. I just panicked and I thought I could go along with the Tampers' crazy scheme and somehow it would all work out quickly and smoothly."

Looking across the field, Anna tried to work out what she wanted. A large part of her wanted to slap his face and walk away, and the other half … she didn't know.

"George," she said, finally looking at him, "why are you here?"

"I've come to ask you for another chance."

"Well, it's not quite as simple as that, is it?" she said, hurling Penthouse's head collar to the ground. "You shattered my heart, George. Don't you get it? In Paris, you made me feel … I can't even begin to tell you. It was like everything was going to be okay. We talked about the baby, our baby, and about us and our future and then *slam,* you did it again."

"Anna, I know, and if I could only change things. You have no idea how much I regret it. The way I've behaved, the way I've treated you. I was blinded by Rousey, by my past, but I know now what a complete and utter fool I have been."

"You can't just turn up here and expect me to let you back in," she said, as all the hurt, and anxiety, the miscarriage, the exhaustion of the last six months, began to cascade through her body. "It doesn't work that way." Picking up the head collar, she walked towards a canopied beech, its copper leaves slowly tumbling in the drizzle. With her rain-soaked hair, she had never looked more beautiful to George.

"Anna, you were caught in the middle of something that I just didn't foresee. Sofia came out of nowhere, not to mention her appalling mother, and everything else collided together at once. I regret it so, so much and I've had to really look at my life, including my relationship with my father and, most importantly, at the truly incredible luck I had to meet you."

As George walked towards her, they both looked up to see Guinness galloping across the field towards them. He almost skidded into the beech tree before turning to bark at them, first at Anna, then at George, and then at Anna again.

"Guinness," said Anna, trying not to smile. "Shush no, I'm just here! There's no need to shout."

"Anna, I know how desperately screwed up this has been. So much has happened but I can see what's important now. I promise I can."

His voice was so steely that even Guinness seemed to register it as he ceased barking.

"I came here to tell you that I love you, Anna, I have never stopped loving you and I know what I've put you through, and I honestly can understand why you ..."

His voice trailed off as Anna finally turned to look at him.

She looked at George's gaunt face, shadows beneath his eyes, dark hair falling against his forehead as he tried to prepare himself for the rejection that was so possible.

"I want to believe you, George. A huge part of me wants to be with you but what you have put me through, the hell, the sheer hell of it, I don't think I couldn't handle it again."

She did not break her gaze and as they looked into each other's eyes George slowly leaned towards her.

"Penthouse is in the windmill field," she said, stepping back and holding the head collar against her chest. "I need to bring him in for the farrier this afternoon. Not that he's going to want to come in because there's still plenty of grass in the field."

George pulled a pack of Polo mints from his pocket.

"Might these help to lure him stable-wards?"

"Maybe," said Anna, trying to maintain her frown.

"And what about this?" he said, taking a black velvet box out of his pocket and handing it to her.

She hesitated, then opened it to find a beautiful green stone surrounded by pink diamonds.

"Anna, do you think ... is there any way you might ..."

"George?"

"Will you marry me, Anna?"

As the rain trickled down the inside of her polo neck, Anna looked at Guinness, who stared back at her as if willing her to make the right choice. This was a moment she had once longed for, when she had let herself dream of what it would be like to have George as her husband, to have a family, and dogs, and laughter, to spend the rest of her life waking up next to him. And now, the decision was hers to make. Where would they live? Could George even get Rousey back after everything that had happened? And what about Farley Hall? Weren't her parents depending on her to take the place on in the future? But whatever about the geography, Anna knew the most crucial part of the decision was to ask herself, deep, deep inside, if could she trust George. Closing her eyes, Anna could hear Penthouse whinnying in the distance and she knew her answer, clear as crystal.

"What do you think, Guinness?" she said. "Maybe if the ring comes with a guaranteed lifetime supply of Polos for Penthouse I could be persuaded?"

"What? Um, Anna?" George had prepared himself for the worst, to accept that he was too late, but now as he looked at her he saw that she was actually smiling at him, really smiling at him.

"Anna?" he said, his eyes filling with tears. "Is that a maybe?"

"No, it's not maybe. It's a yes please," she said, trying not to cry, and instead she laughed properly for the first time in so long. Stepping towards him, she felt his arm wrap around her.

"Darling Anna," he said, "I'll buy every packet of Polos in Mrs Murray's shop for starters."

He slipped the ring onto her finger and they kissed the kind of kiss that made them feel like they had really made it through some massive test and now they were exactly where they were meant to be.

As they pressed their foreheads together, they both opened their eyes at once when they heard a small shriek from afar.

Turning their heads towards the sound, they saw someone squelching through the muddy field towards them in a pair of bright pink wellie boots. A red convertible sports car was parked on the avenue, blasting out something that sounded like 'Staying Alive' by the Bee Gees at top volume, with its hazard lights blinking.

"No," said Anna, "it can't be."

The person waved at her and shouted, "*Yoo-hooo!*"

"Oh God, it is!" said Anna.

Gilda was advancing at full pelt towards them, sporting a green parka jacket and a tweed cap, waving what looked like a piece of paper over her head.

"*Anna darling!*" she yelled.

"Is that Gilda?" asked George, his face cocked to one side with almost scientific fascination.

"That is Gilda," said Anna, waving back at her.

"What in God's name does she want?"

Anna shook her head in bewilderment and turning to George she looked down at the ring on her hand. "George, are you sure you know what you're taking on? For starters, I'm not sure Gilda will even give me time to walk up the aisle, let alone head off on a honeymoon. Brace yourself!"

George grinned and kissed her gently.

Moments later, Gilda arrived beside them, breathless, sodden and with a full beaming smile.

"Now, before I tell you the news, you had better tell me who this young dish is?" said Gilda. However, she had barely finished the sentence before she recognised him. "Well, my oh my, if it isn't George Wyndham. We meet at last ..."

THE END

On Sackville Street

A. O'CONNOR

1869 – When Milandra arrives to live on Sackville Street as a young widow, she becomes the talk of Dublin. Firstly, she scandalises society by refusing to wear the mandatory widow's weeds. She then sets her sights on marrying young solicitor Nicholas Fontenoy, despite the fact he is already engaged to Bishop Staffordshire's daughter, Constance.

But is there something darker behind Milandra's professed love for Nicholas? As she attempts to lure Nicholas away from Constance, a chain of events is set off that leads to bribery, blackmail and murder.

1916 – Now in her seventies, Milandra is one of the wealthiest and most respected women in Dublin. Back in her mansion on Sackville Street, after spending Easter with family, she is astonished to be confronted by a gunman. She fears he has come to rob her, but quickly realises she has been caught up in something much bigger.

Then, as Dublin explodes with the Easter Rising, Milandra's granddaughter Amelia desperately tries to reach her grandmother who is trapped in her house at the very centre of the conflict. Meanwhile, events unfolding on Sackville Street will unravel decades-old mysteries, secrets that were to be carried to the grave.

ISBN 978-178199-8939

THE HOUSE

A. O'CONNOR

Can a house keep secrets?

1840's – When Lord Edward Armstrong builds the house for his bride, Anna, the family is at the climax of its power. But its world is threatened when no heir is born. Anna could restore their fortunes, but it would mean the ultimate betrayal. Then the Great Famine grips the country.

1910's – Clara finds life as lady of the manor is not what she expected when she married Pierce Armstrong. As the First World War rages, she finds solace in artist Johnny Seymour's decadent circle. Then the War of Independence erupts and Clara is caught between two men, deceit and revenge.

Present Day – When Kate Fallon sees the house it is love at first sight. She and her tycoon husband Tony buy it and hire the last Armstrong owner, architect Nico, to oversee its restoration.

As Kate's fascination with the house grows, she and Nico begin to uncover its history and the fates of its occupants in centuries past. But then, as her husband's business empire faces ruin, Kate realises that she is in danger of losing everything.

Betrayal, deceit, revenge, obsession – one house, one family, three generations.

ISBN 978-184223-5508

TYRINGHAM PARK

ROSEMARY MCLOUGHLIN

Tyringham Park is the Blackshaws' magnificent country house in the south of Ireland. It is a haven of wealth until its peace is shattered by a devastating event which reveals the chaos of jealousy and deceit.

Charlotte Blackshaw is only eight years old when her little sister Victoria goes missing from the estate. Charlotte is left to struggle with her loss without any support from her hostile mother and menacing nanny. It is obvious to Charlotte that both of them wish she had been the one to go missing rather than pretty little Victoria.

Charlotte finds comfort in the kindness of servants. With their help she seeks an escape from the burden of being the unattractive one left behind.

Despite her mother's opposition, she later reaches out for happiness and believes the past can no longer hurt her.

But the mystery of Victoria's disappearance continues to cast a long shadow over Tyringham Park — a mystery that may still have the power to destroy its world and the world of all those connected to it.

ISBN 978-184223-5201

If you enjoyed this book from
Poolbeg why not visit our website

www.poolbeg.com

and get another book delivered straight
to your home or to a friend's home.

All books despatched within 24 hours.

Free postage on orders over €20*

Why not join our mailing list at

www.poolbeg.com and get some

fantastic offers, competitions,

author interviews, new releases

and much more?

@PoolbegBooks

www.facebook.com/poolbeg

*Free postage over €20 applies to Ireland only